A Feeling of Home

Books by Susan Anne Mason

COURAGE TO DREAM

Irish Meadows
A Worthy Heart
Love's Faithful Promise

A Most Noble Heir

CANADIAN CROSSINGS

The Best of Intentions
The Highest of Hopes
The Brightest of Dreams

REDEMPTION'S LIGHT

A Haven for Her Heart
To Find Her Place
A Feeling of Home

A Feeling of Home

Susan Anne Mason

BETHANYHOUSE

a division of Baker Publishing Group
Minneapolis, Minnesota

© 2022 by Susan A. Mason

Published by Bethany House Publishers
11400 Hampshire Avenue South
Minneapolis, Minnesota 55438
www.bethanyhouse.com

Bethany House Publishers is a division of
Baker Publishing Group, Grand Rapids, Michigan

Printed in the United States of America

Library of Congress Cataloging-in-Publication Data
Names: Mason, Susan Anne, author.
Title: A feeling of home / Susan Anne Mason.
Description: Minneapolis, Minnesota : Bethany House Publishers, a division of
    Baker Publishing Group, [2022] | Series: Redemption's light ; 3
Identifiers: LCCN 2021057111 | ISBN 9780764235214 (paper) |
    ISBN 9780764240072 (casebound) | ISBN 9781493437238 (ebook)
Subjects: LCGFT: Romance fiction. | Christian fiction. | Novels.
Classification: LCC PR9199.4.M3725 F44 2022 | DDC 813/.6—dc23/eng/20211203
LC record available at https://lccn.loc.gov/2021057111

Scripture quotations are from THE HOLY BIBLE, NEW INTERNATIONAL VERSION®, NIV® Copyright © 1973, 1978, 1984, 2011 by Biblica, Inc.® Used by permission. All rights reserved worldwide.

This is a work of historical reconstruction; the appearances of certain historical figures are therefore inevitable. All other characters, however, are products of the author's imagination, and any resemblance to actual persons, living or dead, is coincidental.

Cover design by Create Design Publish LLC, Minneapolis, MN/Jon Godfredson

Author is represented by Natasha Kern Literary Agency.

Baker Publishing Group publications use paper produced from sustainable forestry practices and post-consumer waste whenever possible.

22   23   24   25   26   27   28   7   6   5   4   3   2   1

To my dad, Stan Moneypenny,
who passed away in 2007 before I was ever published.
As an avid reader himself, I know he'd be so proud.

Blessed is the one who perseveres under trial because, having stood the test, that person will receive the crown of life that the Lord has promised to those who love him.

JAMES 1:12

January 1944

"I need to speak to Dr. Henshaw. It's an emergency." Isabelle Wardrop stood on the front step of the Bennington Place Maternity Home, too filled with anxiety to even care about the frigid air that turned her harsh breaths into white puffs in front of her.

Pure adrenaline had driven her here, filling her with such purpose that she'd ignored the onslaught of snow that continued to swirl down at an alarming rate. If the storm didn't let up by morning, the city would be socked in.

But the weather was the least of her worries at the moment.

"I'm afraid the doctor's delivering a baby and can't be disturbed." A timid pregnant woman glanced over her shoulder to the hallway beyond, as though hoping someone would materialize and come to her aid. But the house remained shrouded in an almost unnatural silence.

Isabelle shoved her way into the foyer. If she hadn't been so desperate, she would never have acted with such uncharacteristic rudeness. "I'm sorry, but my mother's life is at stake. Surely, the midwife can manage the birth without him." Isabelle didn't know everything about Dr. Henshaw, but she did know he worked alongside a midwife at Bennington Place, a home for unwed mothers. Surely the woman was capable of handling a birth alone. Tonight would have to be one of those times.

The young woman twisted her hands together over her extended belly. "Let me get Mrs. Reed or Mrs. Bennington. They'll know more about the situation than I do."

Isabelle forced a slow breath through her nose. "Thank you. I'd appreciate that."

As soon as the girl disappeared from sight, Isabelle shot up the staircase to the second floor. She had no intention of waiting for the maternity home's matrons, who would undoubtedly try to placate her and send her away. She would find the doctor herself and make certain he understood the direness of the situation. As her mother's physician, Dr. Henshaw was well aware of Monique Wardrop's precarious health. It was his duty to come immediately and treat her.

Don't worry, Mama. I won't fail you. I promise.

Isabelle's footsteps echoed through the upper hallway as she forged on, attempting to determine which room he might be in. When she came to a standstill in the hushed area, she heard a low moaning. She followed the sound to a room at the far end of the corridor, where a door stood ajar.

"That's it, Miss O'Reilly. You're doing fine." Dr. Henshaw's voice drifted out to Isabelle.

The tension in her chest eased slightly. It sounded like a routine delivery. Once the doctor understood the seriousness of Isabelle's situation, he should have no issue leaving the laboring woman. Taking a deep breath, she pushed the door open and stepped into the room.

Right away the stench of ripe body odor assaulted her senses. She placed her gloved hand over her nose in an attempt to lessen its power and took in the scene before her.

A woman lay on the bed, a sheet covering the lower half of

her body. Dr. Henshaw and a short, plump woman stood at the foot of the bed, their heads bent together.

"It's a breech birth, Mrs. Dinglemire." The doctor's tone was tense. "I'm going to need your help to turn the child."

"Oh no." The older woman shook her gray head. "I don't think that's a good idea."

"We have no choice. We have to act now or we'll lose them both."

Isabelle's heart started to pump harder. This didn't sound promising. But she had no time for distractions. Her mother would die if the doctor didn't get there soon.

"Dr. Henshaw."

Her voice came out as not much more than a whisper, yet his head whipped up, his eyes widening in shock. "Miss Wardrop? What are you doing here?"

"You have to come at once, Doctor. My mother is dying."

A series of emotions flashed over his features. Then sympathy bloomed in his hazel eyes as he moved closer. "I'm afraid that's not possible," he said in a low voice. "I'm in the middle of a dangerous delivery, and I can't leave now. But once the baby is delivered—"

"It will be too late by then." Her flat tone hung in the air. "Can't the midwife handle it?"

"No, I'm afraid in this case she can't."

Mrs. Dinglemire came to join them. "This mother and baby are at high risk of perishing," she said. "It will take a miracle to save them."

Dr. Henshaw shifted slightly to block the midwife, his gaze never leaving Isabelle's face. "If your mother's condition is as dire as you believe, I'd suggest calling an ambulance to take her to the hospital. I'll head there as soon as I'm finished here."

"You know my mother will never allow me to do anything as crass as to call an ambulance. She trusts only you, Doctor."

Dr. Henshaw exhaled and closed his eyes briefly. For a second, Isabelle almost thought he might be . . . praying.

A loud cry from the bed drew his attention back to the woman in labor.

"I'm terribly sorry, Miss Wardrop." He shook his head. "Please call an ambulance for your mother. I have to attend to my patient." After a last regretful look, he returned to the bed.

Isabelle stood, every muscle screaming at her to do something more to change his mind. But she couldn't come up with any incentive big enough to entice the doctor, except . . .

She jerked forward. "I'll pay you one thousand dollars." She almost flinched at the desperation saturating her voice.

As his head swiveled toward her, she knew she'd made a grave miscalculation.

His postured stiffened, his expression hardening. "Your family might be used to people doing their bidding, Miss Wardrop, but I will not compromise my principles for money." He motioned to someone in the doorway behind her. "Olivia, would you please escort Miss Wardrop out?"

The laboring woman in the bed gave a terrible scream, sending goosebumps cascading down Isabelle's spine. Before she could blink, a gentle hand grasped her elbow and guided her out into the hallway.

Isabelle's footsteps faltered as a wave of resignation threatened her composure. She'd never considered when she set out tonight that she might fail to get Mama the help she desperately needed. What should she do now? She had to do something, or her mother might not see morning's light. Like it or not, she'd have to take Dr. Henshaw's advice.

Isabelle squared her shoulders and turned to the woman beside her, undoubtedly one of the home's matrons. "Would you be kind enough to call for an ambulance to 124 Chestnut Hill Road? My mother requires medical attention."

"Of course. Right away." The pretty Italian lady frowned. "Do you have a ride home, Miss Wardrop?"

"Yes, thank you. My driver is waiting outside." She clutched the handle of her handbag until her fingers ached. "I must go."

"I'll pray for your mother."

"Thank you." An unexpected rush of tears threatened to spill over Isabelle's lashes.

Prayer might be the only thing that could save her mother now.

The sun had just made an appearance in the eastern sky by the time Mark left the maternity home. A beautiful sight, but it did little to temper the frigid air. Thankfully, the snow had stopped around midnight, so the streets were at least drivable. He dragged a hand across his eyes as though he could erase his weariness with one single swipe. He'd learned that Isabelle had asked Olivia to call an ambulance to the Wardrop estate, but when Mark spoke with a nurse at the hospital, he was told that the ambulance had come back empty. As Isabelle had predicted, Mrs. Wardrop refused to leave her home.

Now, as Mark headed to the upscale Rosedale neighborhood, he prayed that Isabelle had exaggerated her mother's condition. He'd been treating the woman for stomach cancer for more than six months now and had been summoned to the house on several emergency calls. Most times, he was able to calm Mrs. Wardrop down and treat whatever symptom was plaguing her that day. However, from Isabelle's frantic demeanor last night, Mark feared that Mrs. Wardrop could be on the downward slope of the dreaded disease.

The only good news in this whole miserable evening was that Mark had been able, with Mrs. Dinglemire's assistance, to turn the baby and deliver it safely, and that despite the harrowing birth, the mother and child were in good condition.

He only prayed Mrs. Wardrop was doing as well.

Mark parked in the circular drive, made his way up the snow-covered walk to the front door of the family's mansion, and gave the brass knocker a hard rap. Soon after, the family's house-keeper opened the door.

"Good morning, Mrs. Barton. I'm here to see Mrs. Wardrop."

Instead of her usual cheery greeting, the woman's mouth remained turned down. She went to speak but clamped her lips shut, her chin wobbling in a most uncharacteristic manner for the normally staunch woman.

Mark hesitated inside the doorway, a chill of foreboding rushing through his already cold limbs.

"I'm afraid you're too late, Doctor." The woman gave a loud sniff and lifted a handkerchief to her nose. "She . . . she's gone. She passed away just after midnight."

All the air seemed to leak from his lungs. The adrenaline that had fueled him all night evaporated in an instant, leaving his legs as limp as overcooked noodles. He grasped the doorframe to steady himself. "But I saw her only two days ago. She was holding her own." A rush of guilt slapped at his senses. He'd have noticed the signs of decline if she'd been nearing her time of death, wouldn't he?

The sound of soft weeping drifted toward him, coming from the parlor to the right.

Isabelle!

His chest constricted painfully, almost as though a vise had tightened around him. She and her sister would be devastated by this loss. He had to see if there was anything he could do.

"Excuse me." He crossed the tiled floor of the foyer and entered the parlor.

Isabelle sat on the tufted sofa, one arm around her younger sister, Marissa. Wisps of fair hair hung in disarray around Isabelle's face, and her red-rimmed eyes were swollen.

Uncertainty rooted his feet to the carpet. This was a private moment of grief, one he had no right to intrude upon. Yet, after his frequent house calls to treat Mrs. Wardrop over the past six months, he'd grown closer to Isabelle, and as a friend, he felt the need to offer her comfort or, at the very least, his sincere condolences.

"Isab—Miss Wardrop. I'm so very sorry for your loss." He took a few more halting steps forward until her glare froze him to the spot.

She set Marissa away from her and rose as regal as a princess. "You have some nerve showing up here now."

Her scathing words struck him with the force of a blow. "I said I'd come as soon as I'd delivered the baby. . . ." He trailed off, realizing the futility of his words.

Her blue eyes darkened to navy. "Well, as you can see, you're too late." Despite the biting words, her lips trembled. "If you'd have come when I asked, my mother would still be alive. I hope you can live with that knowledge."

His spirits plummeted, the truth of her words convicting him. Perhaps he could have done something to stabilize Mrs. Wardrop if he'd come when summoned, but in reality, it would only have prolonged the inevitable. And if he'd left his patient at Bennington Place, she and the babe would surely have died. He scrubbed a hand over his eyes. This was the worst part of being a physician—having to make life-and-death decisions that could ultimately backfire.

Isabelle marched past him to the hallway. "Mrs. Barton, kindly show Dr. Henshaw out. And make sure he knows he's not welcome here again."

Mark tried to clear his head and think logically. "Where is your father?" Shouldn't the man be here comforting his daughters, making sure they were all right? Marissa was only seventeen, for heaven's sake.

"He's meeting with the undertaker. Not that it's any of your concern since Mama is no longer your patient."

Mark glanced past her stiff figure to Mrs. Barton standing sentinel by the front door. He realized then that he hadn't even taken time to remove his hat or overshoes. The housekeeper opened the door and gave him a pointed look.

His heavy heart sank even further. With little choice, he headed to the door, where he turned back one last time. "If you need anything at all, Miss Wardrop, please know that I am at your service."

She raised her chin to meet his gaze with a hard stare. "After last night, I doubt we'll need anything from you ever again."

2

April 1944

The scent of spring rain and newly emerging greenery drifted in through the window of the sitting room where Isabelle sat at her mother's French provincial desk. Three months after Mama's death, Isabelle was still sending out thank-you cards to her father's associates who had made donations to one of her mother's pet charities in her memory. Isabelle sighed as she laid down her pen.

Oh, Mama. I miss you so much. I'm trying to continue your work, but it isn't the same without you.

A flamboyant French Canadian, Monique Wardrop's flare for the dramatic had won the admiration of the board members of the various charities she'd chosen to champion. When Isabelle had joined her mother's work, they'd treated her with respect—mostly out of deference to Monique. But now, in her mother's absence, it was clear they considered Isabelle too young to fully grasp the responsibilities of the role. Still, she was determined to keep Mama's causes alive. No matter how long it took to be taken seriously.

"Excuse me, miss. You have a visitor." Mrs. Barton stood inside the door.

"Who is it?" Isabelle was growing weary of the constant stream of visitors who continued to drop by unannounced. Potential suitors included. Didn't they realize she was tired? That it was exhausting having to prove she was "holding up" under the weight of her grief?

"It's Mr. Noland. Shall I tell him you're indisposed?"

Isabelle glanced at the brass clock on her mother's desk. Marissa wouldn't be home from school for another hour. She could spare the time for a short visit. "No need. I'm fine." Rising from her chair, she smoothed a few wrinkles from her skirt, checked that the lines of her nylons were straight, and headed to the parlor.

Since Mama's death, her father had doubled his efforts to introduce Isabelle to as many eligible gentlemen as he could. *"Your mother's dream was to see you happily married and settled,"* he told her repeatedly. *"I must fulfill her final wish."*

The sorrow on his face tore at Isabelle every time they spoke, and she didn't have the heart to put a stop to his efforts. Instead, she took her mother's place at Daddy's side, accompanying him to the various social functions he was required to attend, even accepting the attentions of the single men her father introduced her to. Though most of them bored Isabelle to tears, Roger Noland had claimed her favor with his kindness.

"Hello, Roger." Isabelle swept into the room, her head high, determined to present a cheerful façade.

"Isabelle. It's good to see you." The tall man turned, a smile creasing his face.

Although not classically handsome, Roger did possess striking features. His long nose, regal brow, and square jaw commanded attention, and his air of confidence made heads turn whenever he entered a room.

"This is an unexpected surprise," she said, moving toward him. "What brings you by?"

He bent to brush a quick kiss to her cheek. "Do I need a reason other than to see your beautiful face?"

Warmth bled into her cheeks. Under normal circumstances, she would have replied with a flirtatious quip, but today she couldn't muster the mental energy for such an exchange. "May I offer you some refreshments?"

"Thank you, no. I can't stay long. I just wanted to stop by and invite you out to dinner tomorrow evening."

She frowned. "You couldn't have simply telephoned?"

"And give you the chance to refuse? No, ma'am. It's far easier to turn down an invitation over the phone than in person." He grinned, then feigned a pleading expression.

A smile tugged at her lips. "True enough, I suppose."

"Did it work?" His brows rose. "Will you grant me the pleasure of your company tomorrow?"

A tiny thrill started in her belly. She'd been drowning in sorrow for months now. Maybe it was permissible to snatch a few moments of enjoyment out on the town with a distinguished gentleman, one Daddy heartily approved of as a potential match.

Of all the men her parents had paraded by her in the last year, only three had stood out to Isabelle: Adam Templeton, Elias Weatherby, and Roger Noland. And of the three, Roger, a real estate broker in Daddy's firm, was the one she preferred. He had a quick wit paired with a wonderful sense of humor, and in the days following Mama's passing, he'd been the only one able to lift her spirits.

Afterward, in the weeks and months that followed, he'd kept in contact, never pushing her to go on a date but always letting her know he was available should she need him. Adam Templeton had sent his condolences along with a bouquet of flowers and had been very solicitous of her and Marissa at the funeral reception. Elias Weatherby, however, had only sent an impersonal sympathy card, and other than a brief greeting at the funeral, he hadn't contacted her since.

She lifted her face with a rare smile. "I'd be happy to go to dinner with you, Roger." Maybe her life could begin to return to some semblance of normality after all. At least this might be a start.

"Excellent." He beamed at her, his dimples on full display. "I'll make reservations at Le Beau Monde, and we'll make it a special night." With a flourish, he raised her hand to his lips. "Until tomorrow, then."

The extra gleam in his eyes caused a flutter in her chest. Le Beau Monde was a very romantic restaurant. Could he be planning to propose over dinner? Her heart began a hard thump at the thought.

If so, what would her answer be?

Mark kicked off his mud-encrusted shoes before entering the front door of the house. He hadn't planned on coming home before his shift at the hospital, but the steady rain earlier had turned the back alley of the tenements into a river of filth, and he needed to change his splattered trousers and shoes before he could think of appearing at the hospital. He shrugged off his overcoat, hung it on a hook, and was about to start up the stairs when a clanging from the kitchen caught his attention.

Mark frowned. "Josh? Is that you?" He checked his watch. His brother shouldn't be home from school yet.

"Yeah." The one-word response offered Mark no information as to why Josh wasn't currently in his science lab.

With a sigh, he headed to the back of the house.

Josh stood at the kitchen counter, pouring himself a glass of milk. Piles of dirty dishes filled the sink—dishes Josh was supposed to have washed this morning before he left.

"Why are you home so early?" Mark fought to keep his tone even, giving his brother the benefit of the doubt until he heard his story.

The lanky boy shrugged without turning around. "My lab was canceled. I came home for a snack before choir practice."

A growing irritation gnawed at Mark's stomach. "That's the second time this month your lab has supposedly been canceled. What's really going on, Josh?"

Lately Mark couldn't tell when his brother was lying to him or telling the truth, a most disconcerting turn of events. He was used to Josh's anger, which always seemed to simmer under the surface, bursting out at the oddest of times, but the boy had never resorted to lying before. Now, at this critical time in Josh's schooling, Mark couldn't allow a teenage rebellion to derail his brother's life.

"Nothing's going on." Josh whirled around, his brows scrunched together. "It's not my fault the science teacher is unreliable."

Mark pulled himself up to his full height, needing the extra six inches over his seventeen-year-old brother to appear imposing. Lately, Josh had been becoming more openly defiant of Mark's authority, and he felt his control slipping away. He couldn't allow that to happen, not until his brother's future was safely mapped out in front of him. The future his parents had wanted for both their sons. "Maybe I need to have a word with the man. Doesn't he realize there's only two months left before final exams?"

A look of unease crept over Josh's face. "It's only a lab, Mark. It's not that important."

"Of course it's important. Especially if it affects your grades. You need top scores in all your math and science courses to get into medical school."

Josh's mouth tensed, and he turned to grab his glass. "Medical school is a long way off."

"Still, top grades are crucial for getting into university. I can't understand—"

"Will you give it a rest, please?" Josh scowled, his nostrils wrinkling as he pushed by Mark. "And by the way, you smell like an outhouse. Why do you keep going to that low-life part of town?"

Mark stiffened at the disdain in Josh's tone. "Those people need medical treatment too. Just because they're poor doesn't mean they don't deserve our respect or compassion."

A philosophy their father had always preached to them. *"Poor people have the same right to medical care as rich ones, son. Never forget that.*" Thaddeus Henshaw had been the epitome of a country doctor. And even when he'd been transplanted to the city, he made everyone who entered his clinic feel important. Something Mark strived to emulate every day.

"But you're already so busy with the hospital, the maternity home, and all your private patients. Why do you need to do this as well?"

If Mark hadn't detected the flash of hurt on Josh's face, he wouldn't have realized the true source of his complaint—the fact that Mark worked grueling hours and had little time to spend with his brother.

"I've explained this to you before," he said as he followed Josh into the hallway. "For me, being a doctor isn't simply a job or a way to make money. It's a vocation, just like Dad's was. A calling to serve my fellow citizens regardless of their social status."

When he stopped by the stairs, Mark caught a whiff of the ripe scent wafting off him, reminding him why he'd come home. "I need to change and get to the hospital. There's some leftover ham in the fridge for when you get back from choir practice."

"All right."

"Oh, and Josh. We're going to talk more about how you plan to manage these last months of high school. This is not the time to lose focus."

Josh rolled his eyes before stalking out of the entryway and slamming the front door behind him.

Mark held back a sigh. Something was going on with him, something he certainly wasn't sharing with his older brother.

"Mom and Dad," he whispered, "if you're watching over us, help me figure out what's going on with Josh. And help me to keep him from making a mistake that could cost him everything."

He'd taken to praying more often lately as well as talking to his departed parents. He needed all the help he could get, because raising his brother alone these past few years had been harder than anything he'd ever done.

When their parents died in the car accident, it had taken every ounce of strength for Mark to pull himself together and finish medical school. After graduation, the plan had been to join his dad's practice and work as a father-and-son team. Thaddeus had been counting the days until that moment and had hoped that Josh would eventually come on board too.

"My two boys practicing medicine," he'd often said. *"What could be better than that?"*

Now, for the first time, Mark didn't know if he would succeed in making his father's dream come true.

He set his jaw, determination stealing through him as he trudged up the stairs. He'd just have to work harder to make sure it did, because failure was not an option.

3

"Y ou look so pretty, Belle. Where's Roger taking you?"
Marissa sat on the edge of Isabelle's four-poster bed,
watching her sister put the finishing touches on her
outfit for her date.

Isabelle glanced up from the vanity table and met her sister's
gaze in the mirror. "Le Beau Monde. He hinted it would be a
special night." Her lips curled upward, her cheeks warming.

Marissa's brown eyes went wide. "Do you think he might propose?"

At seventeen, her sister was a true romantic, already itching to
date, despite their father's forbidding it. He couldn't seem to come
to grips with the fact that his baby girl was advancing toward
womanhood and seemed determined to keep Marissa sheltered
for as long as possible.

Which was why her sister had become so fixated on Isabelle's
romantic life.

"I think he might." Isabelle slipped on her silver bracelets,
fastened her earrings, and turned to face Marissa.

"What answer will you give?"

Isabelle took a moment to think it over, and a slow smile
bloomed. "I believe I'll say yes." Her pulse quickened at the
thought of Roger declaring his undying love and his wish to

offer her a wonderful future as his wife. Having witnessed her mother navigate Daddy's world with such grace, it would be a life she was well prepared for. She only prayed she could be as good a wife as Mama.

Marissa squealed and launched herself off the bed to hug Isabelle. "I'll get to be your maid of honor and help you plan your wedding. I can't wait."

Isabelle laughed. "Don't get too far ahead of yourself. He may not propose after all."

"I'm sure he will. I've seen the way he looks at you." Marissa gave a dreamy sigh. "I hope a man will look at me like that one day."

Isabelle studied her sister. "Do you have anyone particular in mind?"

A dull red crept across Marissa's cheeks. "Not really."

"No one from the boys' school?" Isabelle raised a brow. "Or in the church choir, maybe?"

Marissa shrugged. "There might be someone I like."

"Ah, I thought so. What's his name?"

Her sister scooted off the bed and swung her honey-brown hair over one shoulder. "I'm not saying. You'll only embarrass me."

"I wouldn't do that."

Marissa crossed her arms, a look of defiance suddenly replacing the smile. "Really? You've been acting like my mother ever since—" She clamped her lips shut.

Isabelle's heart swelled on a wave of grief and regret. She *had* been a bit bossy lately, but only because Daddy hadn't been around much and Isabelle felt responsible for her sister. "I just want to keep you safe, Rissa. Promise me you'll be careful. Boys can be pushy . . . and persuasive."

"Don't be silly. There's nothing to worry about."

Isabelle laid a hand on Marissa's arm. "Good. Now, remember to finish your homework. I'll likely be back before you're asleep." She grabbed her wrap from the foot of the bed and bent to kiss her sister. "Please make sure Daddy eats a decent meal for once."

Isabelle frowned, a shade of worry creeping over her. "He hasn't seemed himself lately. And he's working too hard. See if you can get him to agree to take a vacation." If anyone could get their father to plan a trip, it was her sister.

"I'll try." Marissa followed her into the hall like a puppy. "If I'm asleep when you get home, wake me up. I want to see your ring."

"We'll see. You have school tomorrow, remember."

Marissa's disappointed frown tugged at Isabelle. She sighed. "All right. I'll wake you up if there's any news." The girl needed something happy to take her mind off missing their mother.

"Thank you. Have a good time."

"I will."

Isabelle headed downstairs to her father's study, frowning when she found the room empty. She thought for sure Daddy would be home in time to see her off on her date with Roger. He'd been so pleased to learn that she'd agreed to have dinner with him.

"Fiona?" Isabelle called.

"Yes, miss?" The redheaded maid poked her head out of the parlor.

"Has my father returned home yet?"

"No, miss. Not that I've heard." She lowered her dusting cloth. "I can ask Mrs. Barton if she knows anything."

"Please do. I'll be waiting in the parlor for Mr. Noland."

Fiona bent toward her and whispered, "Have a wonderful time." She winked at Isabelle, her green eyes sparkling.

Isabelle smiled. "Thanks. I intend to."

Only a few years older than Isabelle, Fiona had been her mother's personal maid, and after Mama's death, Isabelle made sure Daddy kept her on as one of the household staff. She and Marissa had practically grown up with Fiona. Keeping her here was like having a small piece of their mother still around.

Five minutes later, Fiona returned to the parlor. "Neither Mrs. Barton nor the cook has heard anything from Mr. Wardrop. He likely got held up at the office."

"I'm sure that's it. Thank you, Fiona."

Isabelle sat back down on the sofa, glancing at her watch. Roger must be running late as well.

Twenty-five minutes passed before Isabelle's temper began to gather into a fine steam. The nerve of Roger not even having the courtesy to call and give her some excuse why he was late.

Surely he wouldn't dare stand her up.

She marched into the hall to the telephone stand and placed what was likely a futile call to her father's office. The receptionist would have left for the day by now. Would anyone else be there to answer the phone?

"Wardrop Realty," an unfamiliar male voice answered.

"Um, yes, hello. I'm looking for Roger Noland. Is he still there by any chance?"

A tense second of silence followed. "I believe he left a little while ago."

"Oh." Isabelle's muscles relaxed. He was probably on his way here, then. "Is my father in his office?"

"Your father?"

"Yes. Mr. Wardrop." She paused, a strange sense of foreboding creeping up her spine at the prolonged silence. "Who am I speaking with, please?"

"My name is Constable Spencer."

Isabelle's knees went weak, forcing her onto the small chair next to the telephone stand. Why was there a police constable at the realty office? "Wh-where is my father? Is he all right?"

"Are you home alone, Miss Wardrop?"

"No, my younger sister is here. Why?"

"I think it's best to wait for Mr. Noland to get there."

How did he know Roger was coming to see her?

Her hands shook so badly that she dropped the receiver. It bounced off her lap and clattered onto the tiled floor. Slowly, she bent to retrieve it.

The doorbell rang. Isabelle ignored it.

"Is that the door now?" the constable asked.

"Yes."

"I'll let you go, then. Mr. Noland will explain everything."

Mrs. Barton had answered the door and let Roger in. He'd removed his hat and stood in the foyer, staring down the hall at her.

Isabelle slowly replaced the receiver. "What's going on, Roger? Why are you so late? And why is there a policeman at my father's office?"

He held out a hand to her. "Come into the parlor and sit down." The sorrow on his face matched the redness in his eyes. Something was definitely wrong.

Her muscles stiffened, and she couldn't seem to force her feet to move. He put an arm around her and guided her into the room, where she sank onto the sofa. Her heart was beating faster than a caged bird trying to escape.

Roger sat beside her and took her hand in his. "I'm afraid I have bad news." Moisture rimmed his lower lashes. "I'm so sorry, honey. Your father is dead."

Her limbs went cold, feeling like all the blood had drained from her body. "That's not true. He's just working late. He'll be home any minute."

"I wish it weren't true, believe me, but I'm afraid it is." Grief wreathed Roger's ashen face.

Isabelle clasped her shaking hands together. Her mind seemed to go blank, as though if she allowed one thought to enter, she might start screaming and never stop.

Her father was a healthy man with no hint of illness, yet perhaps the toll of his grief over Mama's death had become too much for him. It was the only explanation that made any sense.

"What happened?" she finally managed. "Did he have a heart attack?"

"No, he didn't." Actual tears appeared in Roger's eyes, and a painful-looking spasm rippled down the length of his throat. He let out a long breath. "I was about to leave the office for our date when I heard a gunshot."

She gasped, her fingers flying to her mouth.

"I ran straight into your father's office, but it was too late." Roger shook his head. "There was nothing I could do." His voice broke, and he looked away, blinking hard.

Every cell in her body seemed to recoil from his words. It couldn't be true. It couldn't. Her father would never—

"Hugh left a note on his desk, but the police took it." Roger reached into his jacket and took out an envelope. "He also left this."

She took it with shaking hands. The envelope had her name on it, written in her father's script. Apparently, he'd had enough forethought of his actions to leave her a letter. What could he possibly say to explain . . . ?

Her stomach suddenly rebelled, and she jumped up. "Excuse me." Bolting from the room, she raced to the bathroom around the corner. She made it just in time, retching over and over until the spasms stopped. Spent, she remained kneeling on the cold tiles, her mind spinning as much as her stomach, too many thoughts vying for attention.

Her father was dead. Her mother was dead. What on earth was she to do now?

"Isabelle?" Roger knocked on the door. "Are you all right?"

"Yes." She rose and turned on the tap. Cupping her hands, she scooped a handful of water over her face and rinsed out her mouth. She picked up the pristine hand towel and blotted her face, the remnants of her lipstick leaving a red smear on the fabric.

Taking a shaky breath, she opened the door and stepped out into the hallway.

Roger straightened away from the wall, his concerned gaze snapping to her face. "You've had a terrible shock. Perhaps I should call your family physician."

"No," she said sharply. "He's the last person I wish to see. And he's no longer our doctor, anyway." She moved woodenly toward the parlor. For her sister's sake, she needed to be strong, needed to hold herself together. She had to find out as much information as possible before she broke the terrible news to her.

Roger followed her back into the parlor, and she closed the French doors behind them. Walking over to the sofa, she picked up the letter she'd left there, deliberately setting it aside. She would read her father's last words to her when she had a moment alone.

Then, on a deep inhale, she turned to face Roger. "Tell me everything you know."

4

Two days later, Isabelle nursed a cup of coffee at the dining room table. A sense of unreality created a fog in her brain that refused to lift. She replayed the events of that terrible night over and over again, unable to get Roger's words out of her mind. He'd explained that her father had seemed to be struggling with depression ever since his wife's death and that he'd finally resorted to desperate measures to end his pain. Roger's recounting of the situation mirrored what her father had said in his brief letter to her and Marissa. He'd begged their forgiveness for what he was about to do but said he could see no other way out of the mess he was in. And that he missed their mother more than he could bear.

Isabelle frowned, thinking of his wording. What *mess* did he mean?

And how could she have failed to notice how deeply depressed he'd become? Should she have tried harder to get Daddy to talk? If the two of them had shared their grief, would he have handled his emotions better?

Fiona entered the room with a platter of eggs and set it down on the table, along with a jug of orange juice and a folded morning newspaper. She poured some juice for Isabelle, then pointed to the food. "May I serve you some eggs and toast, Miss Isa-belle?"

"No, thank you. I'm not very hungry." Isabelle slid the news-paper closer and flipped it to the front page. Her mouth fell open at the ugly black headline.

Real Estate Mogul Commits Suicide. Wardrop Real Estate Closes Its Doors.

Isabelle blinked hard, but the words didn't change. Almost against her will, she scanned the article underneath, which stated that the multimillion-dollar company created by Hugh Wardrop was officially bankrupt, and its doors had closed forever. As a result, the team of employees who had worked alongside her father for years had all been let go.

Isabelle's stomach threatened to heave once again at the thought of all those people being out of work, Roger among them.

How could this be possible?

Words like *overextended* and *in arrears* jumped off the page. They claimed her father had millions of dollars in loans that he couldn't repay when several banks had called them in.

Although the article didn't say so outright, it strongly implied that he'd taken the cowardly way out. It was bad enough that the few people involved knew the truth, but now everyone would know what her father had done.

Anger churned in her stomach. She set her mug down with a thud.

How could you do this to us, Daddy? How could you totally disregard the needs of your daughters? What will happen to us now?

Footsteps sounded in the hallway seconds before Mrs. Barton appeared. "Excuse me, miss. There's a gentleman here to see you."

A weary breath escaped. "Who is it now?" She was tired of the unexpected visitors once again dropping by to offer their condolences. People were trying to be nice, but she wasn't ready to face anyone yet.

However, maybe it was Roger. She hadn't seen him since he'd

come to break the news to her. He was the one person she wanted to see, the one person with whom she could let down her guard and receive comfort.

Mrs. Barton hesitated. "It's a Mr. Meade from the Bank of Commerce."

A shiver of alarm snaked through Isabelle's system. "Did he say what he wants?"

"No. He insists it's a private matter."

Overextended. Loans called in. Could it be a coincidence? Her palms began to perspire.

She squared her shoulders. "Please tell him I'm busy finalizing the details of my father's funeral. Perhaps I can see him next week sometime."

"I already tried that, miss. He says it's urgent, and he's not leaving until he sees you." The woman's nostrils flared. "Should I call the police and have him removed?"

"No. That will only make matters worse." Isabelle inhaled and let out a breath. "I'll speak with him." She pushed back her chair and rose.

"I'm coming with you." Marissa appeared in the open doorway, a stubborn expression on her face. "And don't think you're going to shield me from the truth. I want answers as much as you do."

Isabelle started to refuse but then thought better of it. There might be strength in numbers. "Very well. Let's go."

She led the way into the parlor, where a robust-looking man in his forties sat on one of the armchairs. He jumped to his feet as they entered, his gaze bouncing from Marissa to her.

"Good morning, ladies. I'm Samuel Meade, senior manager with the Bank of Commerce."

"Isabelle Wardrop. My sister, Marissa." She motioned for everyone to have a seat, then perched on the edge of the sofa. "What can I do for you, Mr. Meade?"

She prayed that perhaps this was good news, that her father

had an undisclosed sum of money stashed away somewhere that might cover his debts.

Mr. Meade loosened the button of his jacket. He sent a not-too-subtle glance at Marissa, then cleared his throat. "Perhaps we should have this conversation in private."

Isabelle looked over at Marissa, who gave an almost imperceptible shake of her head. "My sister and I don't have secrets, sir. Whatever concerns me concerns her too."

"As you wish." He reached into the leather bag at his feet and withdrew a stack of papers. "First of all, please allow me to extend my deepest condolences to you both over your recent loss."

The total lack of sincerity in his voice sent a chill down Isabelle's arms. "Thank you."

"I don't know if you're aware, but your father's company has—"

"I'm aware, thank you." Isabelle kept her tone as cool as possible. Her instincts were telling her that this man was enjoying her father's misfortune. "What does this have to do with me?"

"Recently, Mr. Wardrop took out a substantial second mortgage on this property. Given the dire financial straits of both his business and his personal finances, the bank feels they have no choice but to claim ownership of the house."

Isabelle's spine snapped into alignment, anger surging through her veins. They would not take her home away from her. Not while she had breath in her body. "How much are we talking about, Mr. Meade?"

He loosened the knot of his tie. A bead of sweat trickled down the side of his wide face as he named a figure so high that Isabelle could barely comprehend it. But she refused to let the man see that he had rattled her.

"I've yet to touch base with my father's insurance company," she said in an even voice. "Once we receive the settlement from his life insurance, I'm certain we'll be able to pay off most of the amount owed." She prayed that would be the case. Knowing her father, he must have taken out a large policy on himself.

The man shook his head. "I'm afraid that could pose a problem. Most insurance companies don't pay out in cases of suicide. I'm sorry."

She stared at the man's hard eyes, knowing he was not the least bit sorry at all. Why did people resent the success of others and delight in their downfall? Slowly, she stood, keeping her chin tilted upward. "I find this conversation extremely crass, Mr. Meade, given that my father has not even been buried. Once we've had the chance to meet with our accountant, we'll get back to the bank with our repayment plan." Isabelle willed her legs not to betray her by shaking.

Mr. Meade picked up his bag as he rose. "Forgive the intrusion, but I figured you'd want as much time as possible to pack your belongings."

"Pack? Why would we pack when this will all be resolved in the next few weeks?"

He gave her a long look. "I wish you luck with that, miss. But I'm telling you now, it will be nearly impossible to come up with the necessary funds in the next two weeks."

"Why two weeks?"

"That's how long the bank is granting you to pay back the loan in full. If you are unable to do so, the bank will be forced to repossess the house." He jammed his hat on his head and nodded. "Good day, ladies. I'll show myself out."

Mark finished scribbling down his observations on his patient's condition and looked up at the young nurse standing beside him. "Make sure Mrs. Standish has adequate pain medication. I've marked the dosage on her chart."

"Yes, Doctor." The nurse smiled as she took it from him.

He glanced at her nametag. *Megan.* He never could seem to

remember that, yet he recognized her subtle attempts at flirtation. Perhaps that was the reason he kept forgetting her name. She seemed like a perfectly nice woman and a competent caregiver, but he had no time for dating. Even if he did, it would never be with someone in the workplace.

The image of Isabelle Wardrop flashed into his mind. He set his jaw, regret clawing at his chest. His long-held hope of one day asking her out had died along with her mother.

On a sigh, he headed out into the corridor. With several more patients to see before the end of his shift, he couldn't afford to indulge in useless daydreams.

"Excuse me, Dr. Henshaw."

He turned to the woman who had called him. Nurse Peters stood by the nurses' station. "Could you sign the paperwork for Mr. Maguire's release?"

"Of course." His muscles relaxed as he approached the desk. Maisie Peters was one person he didn't mind dealing with. In her mid-forties, she was the perpetual motherly type who oozed kindness and wisdom. He'd yet to ever see her rattled or ill-tempered, no matter what type of situation she faced. Plus, she often brought him a pan of her homemade brownies. "Is Mr. Maguire's family here to pick him up?"

"Yes. His son and daughter-in-law. They're eager to get him settled in their home today."

"That's good. I'm glad his recovery is going so well." Mr. Maguire been brought into the emergency department two weeks ago with a mild heart attack and had thankfully suffered little damage to his heart.

Mark scanned the paperwork and scrawled his signature on the bottom, then handed it back to the woman with a smile. But instead of her usual cheerful disposition, a worried frown creased her brow.

"Is something wrong, Maisie?"

"Aren't you the Wardrop family's physician?"

His gut clenched. Of all the names she could have mentioned, did it have to be that one? "I used to be, until Mrs. Wardrop passed away." He studied her serious face, and alarm shuddered through him. "Why do you ask?"

She picked up a newspaper, folded it to the front page, and held it out. "You might want to read this."

The huge headline grabbed his attention. *Real Estate Mogul Commits Suicide.*

Mark's heart began to thud heavily in his chest. He snatched up the paper to read the accompanying article. His stomach sank lower with every sentence. Hugh Wardrop had killed himself in his office two days ago. According to the reporter, the man had lost his fortune, and his company had been forced into bankruptcy.

Poor Isabelle. Mark's chest ached thinking of the Wardrop sisters. They certainly didn't deserve this grief after losing their mother only a few months ago.

Three months, two weeks, and six days ago, to be exact.

"Terrible, isn't it?" Maisie's voice brought Mark's attention back to the present. "I can't imagine what his daughters are going through."

Mark could only nod, his voice having suddenly deserted him. Isabelle and her sister were now orphans. He knew only too well the type of devastation they would be feeling.

He flipped through the rest of the newspaper until he found the obituaries. At the end of the section, there was a large piece honoring Hugh Wardrop's achievements, ending with the date and time of his funeral.

Mark jotted the information down on a slip of paper. Welcome or not, he would pay his respects to the Wardrops and try to figure out some way to make amends to the family.

Who was he kidding? The main person he wanted forgiveness from was the beautiful young woman he'd had his eye on for several months now, but who'd never given him a second glance. The memory of Isabelle's last scathing words burned in his memory.

"If you'd have come when I asked, my mother would still be alive. I hope you can live with that knowledge."

Mark blew out a breath, internally vowing to find a way to offer his assistance to the girls. Maybe then some of his guilt might ease at last.

5

The church bells tolled a mournful refrain as Isabelle exited the church, her arm tightly entwined with Marissa's. For the past hour, they'd borne their sorrow in a church that was much more sparsely populated than it had been during her mother's funeral mere months ago. A slow anger burned in Isabelle's chest at the thought of her father's so-called friends and associates, who used to clamor for his presence at every social event, but who now, when faced with Daddy's undignified demise, scattered like leaves in the wind.

Squaring her shoulders, she guided Marissa down the stairs to the walkway below, where the pallbearers were loading the casket into the hearse. Once again, they would make the trek to the cemetery plot that was still freshly disturbed. There, they would lay their father to his eternal rest beside the woman he loved.

A shadow fell across the walkway. "Hello, Isabelle. Marissa," a familiar voice said. "Please accept my sincerest condolences on your loss."

Isabelle stiffened. What was *he* doing here? Hadn't she made her position perfectly clear the last time they spoke?

"Thank you, Dr. Henshaw." Marissa's voice was barely audible.

Unlike Isabelle, her sister didn't appear to hold the physician accountable for their mother's death.

Isabelle gave a stiff nod and nudged Marissa along the path toward the waiting car.

"If I can be of any help at all," he continued, "please don't hesitate to call on me."

Once again, Isabelle all but ignored him.

Marissa, however, removed her arm from Isabelle's and turned to engage him in conversation. "Thank you for your kind offer, Dr. Henshaw. You have no idea how . . . difficult this has been. Our friends have—"

"Marissa!" Isabelle hissed through clenched teeth.

Her sister lifted tear-filled eyes. "Isabelle, we can't afford to lose any allies we might have."

"We will do fine on our own. Come on, now. They're waiting for us."

Isabelle offered Dr. Henshaw a last cool nod, then managed to get her sister into the funeral car. As soon as the door closed, she sank back against the cold leather seat, resentment an icy shard in her chest.

How could you have left us in this position, Daddy? Alone with no money and about to lose our home?

She did her best to ignore the pounding in her temples and the pain radiating across her forehead. All their problems would have to wait for another day. Right now, they had to bury their father.

"Where do you want these, miss?" Fiona held up a pair of pink hurricane lamps for Isabelle's inspection.

"Put them in the box by the window. There should be room in there." Isabelle pushed some strands of hair off her face. She'd never realized how many possessions her family had accumulated over the years. Each room in the mansion contained a plethora of art pieces, knickknacks, and ornaments. Not to mention, more furniture than five families could use.

Now, sadly, most of the bigger items would be auctioned off

to pay down their father's debts. But Isabelle was determined to salvage some of her mother's treasured pieces before the bank got ahold of everything. She'd initially been resistant to the idea of starting to pack, but Fiona had made her see that waiting until the last moment for a reprieve wasn't practical. The two-week deadline was almost up, and soon someone from the bank would arrive to tell them their fate. If she wanted any control over what she kept and what the bank took, she'd better start packing her valuables now.

In the meantime, Isabelle had been trying her best to secure funding, but to no avail. None of the financial institutions she'd visited were willing to offer them any help whatsoever.

So, Isabelle and Marissa had started going through all of Mama's jewelry, keeping a few sentimental items for themselves and discreetly hiding them in with their lingerie in case collectors came to call. Any other items Isabelle thought might be worth something, she took to Mr. Jenkins, the local jeweler whom Daddy had commissioned to create the unique pieces for Mama. Mr. Jenkins had been hesitant to buy them back, but faced with Isabelle's obvious desperation, he had relented and given her one lump sum for the lot. Isabelle knew he'd paid her far less than their actual worth, but she was grateful to have something at least.

"What about this one, miss?" Fiona held up a jade green vase, a rather hideous thing Mama had brought with her from her parents' home in Montreal.

"We'll try to sell that. But I'd like to keep the other one with the roses. Pack it in with the linens."

Fiona hesitated. "Please don't be taking offense, Miss Isabelle." Her soft Irish lilt held a note of apology. "But what do you think you'll be doing with these things when you don't have any idea where you're going?"

Isabelle's hand stilled on a crystal trinket box. "I don't know. I hadn't planned that far ahead." She sat down heavily on a tufted ottoman. "I just can't let the people from the bank come in and take everything." She picked up a delicate figurine of a woman with a parasol and ran her fingers over the smooth porcelain. Her mother had loved to collect pretty things. She received a new one for every occasion.

Fiona placed the wrapped vase in a box. "There must be hundreds of trinkets throughout the house. You can't be keeping all of them."

Isabelle released a soft breath. "No, I don't suppose I can." Tears stung her eyes, but she blinked them away. She'd done enough crying. It was time to be practical.

"Where do you intend to stay if the bank forecloses on the house?" Fiona asked gently.

"I-I don't know. Maybe we can go to a hotel for a while until I can figure something out."

"Can you afford that?"

"Not really." Isabelle had hoped her good friend Candace Bingley would agree to take them in temporarily, but the girl had come up with some excuse about her parents expecting company shortly and needing their guest rooms.

Isabelle looked over at Fiona and frowned. She'd been so busy worrying about herself and Marissa, she hadn't thought to ask her friend where she would go. "What about you, Fiona? Do you have a place to stay?"

The girl had come to work for the Wardrops straight off the boat from Ireland at the tender age of sixteen and had been with them for almost ten years. The thought of not seeing Fiona's cheerful face every day made Isabelle's heart ache even more.

"My aunt has a small place across town. She's offered me her daughter's room since my cousin recently moved out."

"Oh, I'm glad. Is this the aunt you go to visit on your day off?"

"It is. She's been a widow for a while now, raising her daughter alone. Noreen finally finished school and got a job, so she's moved out. I think Aunt Rosie will be happy for the company." She hesitated, then leaned forward. "I'm sure we could make room for you and Marissa, if you wanted. I know Aunt Rosie wouldn't mind."

Isabelle smiled. "That's a very generous offer. I'll keep it in mind when the time comes." She laid another figurine on the table. "Now, to make sure Mrs. Barton and the rest of the staff are taken care of."

"It's not your responsibility, miss. Though it's kind of you to be concerned."

"You're all like family. Of course I'm concerned."

"We'll be fine. It's you and Miss Marissa we're worried about." Fiona laid a hand on her shoulder. "How are you going to live without your family's money?"

Isabelle could only imagine her mother's horrified reaction to an employee getting so personal, but Isabelle didn't mind. "I guess I'm going to have to find a job."

"Doing what, may I ask?"

"I have absolutely no idea." A nervous laugh bubbled out. "I've been trained to play the piano, sing passably well, host ladies' tea parties, and embroider. Not exactly skills employers are clamoring for."

Fiona pulled up a chair beside her. "You worked with your mother on her charities. Surely that will count for something."

Dear Fiona. So loyal and optimistic. "I hope so. I'll have to work hard to sell myself if I ever land a job interview." Her shoulders slumped. "I don't even know where to begin looking."

Fiona scanned her from head to toe. "You're a stylish dresser with a flair for fashion. You could work in the ladies' department at Eaton's or Simpson's."

Isabelle winced. The very thought of becoming a saleswoman in the stores where she and Mama used to shop was beyond humiliating. "I'd rather work somewhere I wouldn't know anyone. It's going to be difficult enough adjusting to our reduced lifestyle without . . ." She stopped, dismay filling her. "Oh, Fiona. Forgive me. I didn't mean to imply—"

Fiona shook her head. "I understand. It must be hard to fall out of your class."

The doorbell rang.

"I'll get that." The girl hopped up. "I think Mrs. Barton is out on a job interview of her own." She rushed out into the hallway, and after a moment, Isabelle heard her say, "Hello, Mr. Noland. Come in, please."

Roger? Isabelle hurriedly rose and whipped off her apron, then patted her hair into place. She peered into one of the small mirrors, appalled to find smudges of dirt on her cheek. Couldn't the man have called first?

"Hello, Isabelle. Fiona said to come in."

She whirled around. "Roger. How nice of you to drop by."

He scanned the room, frowning. "You're packing? Are you planning on moving?"

Isabelle held herself erect and, by sheer force of will, kept her smile in place. "It seems the prudent thing to do. Marissa and I don't need to keep this big house for just the two of us." Perhaps it was pride, but she didn't want him to know how destitute they'd become. She still held out the hope that Roger might propose. Yet she couldn't bear the thought that he might ask out of pity. She wanted him to propose because he sincerely desired her as his wife.

Her pulse sped at the thought. Marrying Roger could be the answer to her dilemma. At least then she and Marissa would have a place to go.

"I suppose you have a point. But don't you think you're being a bit hasty, selling the place so soon after Hugh's death?" His expression told her he thought she'd gone off the rails.

"It's . . . not for sale yet. I'm simply tidying the house to make it more appealing without all the . . . clutter." She waved an airy hand. "But you haven't said why you're here." She attempted to affect a cheery disposition, as though multiple boxes and packing paraphernalia wasn't out of the ordinary.

"Might we sit down for a bit?"

"Of course. Forgive my manners." She gestured to the thankfully empty sofa.

He took a seat beside her. For a moment, he stared straight ahead, hands on his thighs. Then, he let out a breath and turned to face her. "I've come to say good-bye, Isabelle."

The smile froze on her lips. "Wh-what do you mean, good-bye?"

He gave a rueful shrug. "I've accepted a job with another real estate firm. One located in British Columbia."

She held back a gasp. That was clear across the country. He couldn't have chosen a place any farther away. "What made you look so far afield?" she managed to ask with some semblance of normalcy.

"It wasn't intentional. A friend of the family lives out there and asked me to join their team. I figured it was a good time for a complete change."

She studied his face, suddenly realizing that her father's death had come at a great cost to Roger too. His loss was almost as deep as hers. "I'm so sorry, Roger. This has been extremely hard on you too."

He sighed. "It has. But obviously not as difficult as it has been for you and your sister."

She nodded and waited a beat before her next question. It was bold to be sure, but if she didn't ask, she'd always wonder. "What about us, Roger? I could be mistaken, but I thought you might be planning to propose the night my father died. Was I wrong?"

Regret bloomed in his eyes. "No, you're not wrong." He took her hand in his.

"Then why are you leaving? Why not try to find a job here?"

"Believe me, I've made the rounds in the city. Unfortunately, no one is willing to give me a chance. It's almost as though I've been tainted by my association with your father." He closed his eyes briefly. "I'm sorry. That was tactless."

She repressed a grimace and forced herself to go on. "Did you ever consider asking me to go with you?"

Roger hesitated, rubbing a hand over his jaw. "I did. But the sad truth is, Isabelle, that I don't have much to offer you. And I have no idea what will happen out west. To ask you to wait for me to make a life for myself there seems incredibly selfish." He caressed her palm for a second. "The kindest thing I can do is say good-bye and wish you well."

Her chin quivered, but she would not stoop to begging. With a flourish, she rose from her seat. "Then I will do the same for you. Thank you for your friendship and for your loyalty to my father. I wish you all the best in the future."

He rose as well. "Thank you, Isabelle. I truly hope you find the happiness you deserve." He bent and brushed a kiss to her forehead. "I'll write to you when I'm settled and let you know how things are going."

She wanted to tell him not to bother, that she had no idea where she'd be living, but she simply smiled and nodded. "Have a safe trip."

Then, after a last lingering look, he left the room.

Isabelle sank onto the couch and stared at the chaos surrounding her. Apparently, Roger wouldn't be her knight in shining armor after all. She pressed her lips together, determined not to succumb to panic. When everything was said and done, she had no one to rely on except herself.

Right away, an inner voice convicted her. Of course that wasn't true. They had the Lord, who would never forsake them. She drew some comfort from that thought since she would need all the help she could get to take care of her sister and make a way for them both in this world.

If only she had a clue where to start.

6

"I think it would be best if you quit the church choir for now. At least until the end of the school year, so you can devote more time to your studies." Mark glanced over his shoulder as he finished washing the last dish and attempted to ignore Josh's thunderous expression. "Anything other than your schoolwork is a distraction you can't afford."

Sprawled on one of the kitchen chairs, Josh crossed his arms. "I'm not quitting the choir."

Mark curbed the urge to yell. To demand that Josh do as he said or else. But that would be pointless. Mark owed it to Josh to delve deeper and find out what the real cause of the problem might be. He pulled the plug to let the water out of the sink. "What is it about the choir that's so special?"

Due to the fact that Mark often worked at the hospital on Sunday mornings, he was rarely able to accompany Josh to church services and hadn't seen the youth choir perform since Josh had joined last fall. Still, Mark had a pretty good idea why this choir had become such an obsession, but he wanted to hear it directly from Josh.

"You know how much I love music," he said. "How important it is to me."

Mark quirked a brow. "The constant strumming of the guitar

coming from your room makes that pretty apparent." Ever since Josh had found their dad's old Gibson in the back of the closet two years ago, he'd lost interest in the piano and become obsessed with the new instrument, plucking strings until he somehow managed to teach himself how to play. For Mark, who didn't have a musical bone in his body, it was a pretty impressive feat. If only his brother would put as much time and energy into his studies.

Mark waited a beat to see if Josh would add anything further, but he stubbornly remained silent. "There are other ways for you to have music in your life. Why do you need this choir?"

Josh's scowl deepened, but he only shrugged.

Mark wiped the countertop, sweeping the crumbs into the trash can. "Is there maybe a girl you're interested in?" He kept his voice as nonthreatening as possible, while his heart thumped uncomfortably fast in his chest. He knew from personal experience how distracting a romance could be to a student. Especially if that romance turned sour.

Josh's nostrils flared, but he didn't answer.

"I'll take that as a yes." Mark dried his hands on a towel, recognizing the need to tread carefully. He remembered all too well how powerful a young man's emotions could be. The toxic effect of his first relationship had almost gotten him kicked out of university. "Are you . . . dating this girl?"

Josh huffed out a breath. "No, we're just friends."

"But you're hoping for more."

"That's none of your business."

"If it affects your future, it is." Mark paused to count to ten and rein in his frustration. "Don't let a girl ruin your plans. She's a distraction you don't need right now."

"You don't understand." Josh pushed his chair back. "She's going through a really rough time right now and needs her friends. I won't abandon her."

Mark held back a sigh. It made perfect sense that Josh could relate to a person going through a crisis. He was only thirteen when their parents died—a terrible time for an adolescent to have the foundation of his life ripped away, leaving him with an older brother who was immersed in medical school. "I understand why you'd want to help this girl, but—"

"She's lost both her parents. Just like . . ." Josh trailed off, a nerve twitching in his jaw.

"Just like you, four and a half years ago." Mark closed his eyes briefly against the sudden wave of grief. How could he deny his brother the opportunity to help someone facing a similar tragedy, or deny this girl a friend who could offer her comfort? "All right, Josh. I'll make you a deal. If you do your best to bring up your grades in this last semester, you can continue with the choir."

The lines in Josh's forehead eased. "Really?"

"Yes. But the minute I see bad marks coming in, all extracurricular activities will be pulled. Are we clear?"

Relief seemed to ooze from his brother's pores. "Clear."

"And that means no more skipping your science labs."

Josh hung his head. "Okay."

Mark started for the door but then stopped, an uncomfortable sensation churning in his gut. "Do I need to talk to you about the proper way to treat a girl?"

A rare shade of crimson stained Josh's cheeks. "No, you do not."

"Good. I trust that if you care about this girl, you'll behave like a gentleman."

Josh rolled his eyes.

Realizing it was the best he could expect right now, Mark cut his losses and left the room.

Isabelle set her suitcase beside the trunk at the front door and paused to take a deep breath. So far, she'd managed to prevent the crushing grief and fear from overwhelming her by keeping herself in constant motion.

She pressed a hand against her abdomen, where a hard knot

of anxiety had taken up residence. Today, they were leaving their home, the only place she and Marissa had ever lived. Despite Isabelle's best efforts, she hadn't been able to come up with a way to pay back the loan. Tomorrow, the bank would repossess their house, and they would no longer be welcome here.

She swallowed hard. Marissa was finishing her last-minute packing upstairs, likely wanting a few minutes on her own. Isabelle understood that. Understood the need to spend these last few minutes saying good-bye in their own way. As painful as it might be, Isabelle needed to walk through the rooms on the main floor one last time.

The ornate living room and dining room, where her parents had entertained their guests, were beyond beautiful, but it was her mother's cozy sitting room that caused a rush of grief to sting her eyes. She could still picture Mama sitting at her desk, penning invitations or other correspondence for one of her many projects. Isabelle ran her hand over the desk, lingering over the tiny scratches and dents. "Forgive me, Mama. I wish we could bring this with us, but we just can't." She took a last look around, inhaling the familiar scent of the room, then, with a sigh, continued her tour.

She made her way to the kitchen, a reluctant smile twitching at the memories of learning to bake bread and cookies with her nanny when she was young—a talent that might come in handy now that she and Marissa would be without a cook for the first time. Leaving the room, she headed down the back hall to her father's study. The lingering burn of anger over the way he'd taken his own life constricted the air in her chest. How could he choose to leave them alone, knowing they'd be destitute?

Isabelle had gone over every inch of this room in the hopes of finding some documentation that might save them. Some secret bank account her father might have in a different city. Some wad of bills in his safe. And though she did find a tidy sum of cash her father had kept as emergency money, it was nowhere near enough to do anything about the mountain of debt he'd incurred.

She inhaled the fading scent of Daddy's pipe tobacco, and then swallowing back her regret and pain, she closed his door for the last time. Out in the foyer, she ran her hand over the newel post, her gaze traveling up the impressive split staircase. Memories of her and Marissa sliding down the banister brought the wisp of a smile to her lips. The thrill had been worth the tongue-lashing they'd received later, yet they'd never dared to repeat the escapade.

A hand lightly touched her shoulder. "Are you ready, Miss Isabelle?" Fiona asked gently. "Tom's bringing the car around now."

Isabelle blinked to clear the mist from her eyes, then turned to face the woman, who, though she'd been a servant, was more of a friend than anyone else in her life. "As ready as I'll ever be, I suppose."

Footsteps sounded on the stairs and a somber-looking Marissa appeared, her cheeks blotchy from weeping. She dragged the last of her bags with her and came to a halt at the foot of the stairs.

"I'll take that, Miss Marissa." Fiona gently grasped the handle of the largest bag. "We'll be waiting out front. Take your time." She gave Isabelle a sympathetic look, one that said she understood how hard this moment was for both the girls.

"Thank you, Fiona." Isabelle turned and pulled Marissa into a hug. "Do you need more time to say good-bye?"

Marissa shook her head. "I've already been through this floor. It was my room that was hardest to leave."

"I know." Isabelle ran her hand over her sister's honey-colored hair. "You never really appreciate what you have until you lose it." She swallowed. "But we're going to be all right. Eventually. I need you to bear with me until I can figure it all out."

Marissa's eyes welled again, and she nodded. "I'm so thankful I have you, Belle. I don't know what I'd do without you."

"Well, you'll never have to find out, because we're in this together." She squeezed her sister's hand.

They walked out the front door to find Tom, their chauffeur, standing in full uniform beside the black sedan.

"You didn't have to dress like that, Tom. We aren't going to a fancy part of town."

"Doesn't matter, miss. I'm doing this out of respect for Mr. Hugh. He'd want his daughters to go out in style." Tom tipped his hat. "I'll get the last trunk, and we'll be on our way."

Isabelle nodded, then crossed to the circular driveway, where she viewed the outside of their home for the last time. The impressive front porch and portico, the majestic windows that now seemed to stare out blankly over the boulevard, and the manicured landscaping that softened the brick and mortar.

Wiping away a tear, she headed to the car that would take them away from the only life they'd ever known and drop them into an uncertain future.

Dear Lord, please be with us on this journey and help us to find our way.

7

Tom slowed the car to a crawl as they entered what could only be called a slum. Isabelle tried to keep the horror from her face at the sights that met her unblinking gaze. Dilapidated shelters, garbage littering the streets, laundry flapping on makeshift lines tied between the buildings, and children running among wild chickens.

What kind of world was this? If Isabelle didn't know better, she'd think Tom had whisked them away to some impoverished foreign country. The tightening of Marissa's fingers on hers told her that her sister was just as appalled.

Where on earth did Fiona's aunt live? She knew Rosemary existed on a limited budget, which was why Isabelle often gave Fiona whatever extra food they could spare from the cook's pantry to take to her aunt when she went to visit. But Isabelle had never experienced this type of poverty before.

"Aunt Rosie lives on the outskirts of this area," Fiona said over her shoulder, a note of apology in her tone. "Her place isn't quite as . . . run-down as this."

Isabelle didn't know what to say, so she remained silent. And prayed that she and Marissa would be able to adapt to wherever they might find themselves.

There seemed to be a family sitting on every doorstep, with

babies on their laps and toddlers hanging on their mother's skirts. All stared at the sedan cruising by as though they'd never seen a car before. Isabelle slunk a little lower in her seat. She hated being under such scrutiny and certainly didn't want to seem to be flaunting a wealth she no longer possessed.

Finally, Fiona pointed to a rather ramshackle building with peeling paint and shutters hanging at odd angles. "That's it there, Tom. Thank you."

The car slowed. Tom turned off the engine and went around the back to retrieve their bags. Fiona got out and held the door open for Isabelle and Marissa.

Isabelle's hands shook as she watched Tom set their trunks by the rickety wooden steps.

He removed his cap and came to stand in front of them. The wind blew his gray hair across his forehead. "Well, I guess this is it, Miss Isabelle." Tears glistened in his eyes. "I hate to be leaving you here, but I trust Fiona will look after you."

Isabelle stepped forward and held out her hand. "Thank you for everything, Tom. I wish you and your family all the best."

He took her hand and nodded. "And you as well. God bless you both." He gave them a brief smile, then walked back to the car. He would leave the vehicle at the house, where the bank would claim it as part of the estate.

It comforted Isabelle somewhat to know that, like Mrs. Barton, Tom had found another position, so he and his wife would be fine.

If only she could say the same about her and Marissa.

Isabelle stood beside her sister and watched as the car disappeared around a corner, willing herself not to cry. Other than Fiona, Tom was the last link to their former life. Her chin quivered, and a film of moisture blurred her vision. The knot in her stomach grew into an ache, and she folded one arm over her waist, suddenly realizing how an orphan must feel when dropped off at a strange new place.

As she drew in a shaky breath, she could almost hear her

mother's final words. *"You are stronger than you think,* chérie. *You will get through this . . . in time."*

I hope you're right, Mama.

Squaring her shoulders, Isabelle turned to take a better look at their temporary quarters, determined to count their blessings and not their losses. Aunt Rosie hadn't hesitated to invite them to share her humble abode until they could find their footing. Though in need of repairs, the residence at least seemed cleaner than most. The windowpanes were clear of grime, the stoop well swept. From the outside, the building appeared to be a triplex, with an apartment above Aunt Rosie's and a basement apartment below.

"Come on in," Fiona called from just inside the door.

Isabelle linked her arm through Marissa's, and they climbed the few steps to the front door that stood open in welcome. Pasting on a smile, she stepped inside the main room, which consisted of a small kitchen and sitting room. A black potbelly stove took up one corner, near a counter with a sink. Did they have running water or an indoor lavatory? Surely they wouldn't have to use an outhouse. She held back a shudder at the thought.

"Welcome, girls," a cheerful voice said. "Please make yourself at home." A woman appeared from what must be a bedroom. Her graying hair was pinned up into a bun. She wore a plain brown dress and sturdy shoes. "I'm Rosemary, but most people call me Rosie or Aunt Rosie." Her face beamed as she came toward them.

"I'm Isabelle, and this is my sister, Marissa." Isabelle's manners kicked in, and she attempted a smile. "Thank you so much for inviting us to share your home until we find somewhere else to go."

"I'm happy to be able to repay your kindness to us over the years."

Isabelle started to protest, but Rosie held up a hand. "I know you were the one who always sent Fiona back with leftovers on her days off. They were very much appreciated." She took a kettle and set it on top of the stove. "I'll get the tea started. I'm sure everyone could use some."

"Please don't trouble yourself."

Fiona laughed. "It's no trouble, believe me. We have tea for every occasion here." She motioned for them to follow her. "We'll put your trunks in my cousin's room. I'll share with Auntie, and you two can have Noreen's old room."

Almost in a dream state, Isabelle crossed the living space to one of the three doors down a tiny hall. Inside the plain room, she found two twin beds, separated by a small nightstand and lamp. Faded floral wallpaper peeled down from the ceiling, and the wood trim around the single window was rotting in places. But the beds looked inviting and clean.

After seeing some of the filthy areas they'd passed on their way here, Isabelle could only raise heartfelt prayers of gratitude that they had somewhere decent to lay their heads tonight.

"There's a bathroom at the end of the hall," Fiona said. "It's nothing fancy, but it's better than an outhouse." The girl gave an apologetic shrug. "I'm sorry it's so far from what you're used to."

"Please don't apologize," Isabelle said. "This will be more than adequate for us. Thank you."

A few minutes later, they all sat around the kitchen table with their tea in front of them. A window over the sink was open, allowing a slight breeze to blow the curtains.

"I was ever so sorry to hear about your parents," Aunt Rosie said after she'd poured the four cups. "I can't imagine what you've been through."

"Thank you." Isabelle cupped her hands around the chipped mug. "It has been . . . difficult."

"Well, I'll do whatever I can to help. After all, your family has been so good to Fiona all these years." She passed a plate of biscuits around.

Marissa raised her head. "Fiona's been like another sister to us. I don't know what we'd do without her." Her lips trembled.

Aunt Rosie reached over to squeeze Marissa's arm. "Just know you're not alone. The good Lord is watching over you. He'll be helping you through this." The woman's Irish lilt softened her voice.

Isabelle attempted a cheerful tone. "Tomorrow Fiona and I are going to look for work. If we're lucky, we'll find something soon."

Aunt Rosie set her cup down. "What type of work are you thinking of, Miss Isabelle?"

"Please, it's just Isabelle." She took a biscuit as she considered her answer. "I'm not sure exactly. I'm good with figures, so perhaps I could work in a bank."

"That sounds like an excellent place to start. And what about you, Fiona darlin'?"

Fiona shrugged one shoulder, looking somewhat sheepish.

"What is it?" Aunt Rosie demanded. "Do you already have a new job?"

"Just an interview."

"Really? That's great." Isabelle's gaze snapped to her friend, a surge of hope lessening the weight of despair in her chest. "With whom?"

"I hope you don't mind. . . ." A blush stained Fiona's cheeks. "One of Mr. Wardrop's acquaintances stopped by last week when you were out. When I told him you weren't home and he saw some of the boxes, he asked if I might be looking for work. Apparently, he needs a new maid at his house."

A pinch of annoyance crept up Isabelle's spine. Which of her father's friends would approach Fiona without consulting her first? "Who was it?"

"Mr. Templeton."

Adam? That didn't sound like something he'd do, but maybe it had been a spur of the moment conversation. "You didn't tell me he came by."

"I didn't?" Fiona blinked. "I'm sorry. In all the confusion, I must have forgot. He asked if you were moving. When I said yes, he wanted to know if I was going with you." She paused. "I thought it was nice of him to think of me at all."

Isabelle glanced at her friend's bright green eyes and red hair and had no trouble imagining why Adam had noticed her. But from what Isabelle knew of him, he seemed to be a decent man. She believed Fiona would be safe enough in his employ.

"You don't mind, do you?" Fiona's worried voice brought Isabelle out of her musings.

"No, of course not. Though he should really have spoken to me first."

"You're sure?"

"Positive." Isabelle forced a smile.

A flash of relief lightened Fiona's features. "I'm glad. I wouldn't wish to cause you any more grief." Her cheeks grew even redder.

Isabelle squeezed the girl's arm. "You don't have to worry about me. You and your aunt are doing so much for us already. Taking us in. Giving us a roof over our head and food to eat."

"Well, you're more than my employer. As Marissa said, you're like sisters to me." Fiona leaned over to hug Isabelle.

Aunt Rosie nodded. "I'll say some prayers for both of you and ask the Lord to guide your steps and keep you safe."

A new determination rose in Isabelle's chest. Despite the obstacles in her path, she would make sure that she and her sister not only survived this tragedy but thrived in spite of it.

No matter what it took to make that happen.

Mark parked his car in the Wardrops' driveway and got out. Something seemed different about the house today. The residence appeared almost vacant, as though the life had gone out of it along with its owner.

He shrugged off the macabre thought and braced himself for Isabelle's reaction to his presence here. He'd tried to stay away, but a niggling sense of worry about the two young women on their own wouldn't let him rest. He needed to make sure they would be all right, and that despite their father's business going under, they had enough resources to keep up with all the expenses that running a household entailed.

One thought gave Mark comfort. Hugh Wardrop certainly would've had the foresight to provide for his family in the event of his death. Surely he had a hefty life insurance policy that would keep the girls afloat until they both found suitable husbands.

His chest constricted at the idea of Isabelle marrying. However, the hope he'd once held that she might see him in a romantic light had long since shattered. No, if Isabelle found a decent man with good prospects who could make her happy, then she deserved the stability of a fine marriage.

Even if it wasn't with him.

Mark climbed the stairs to the double front doors. Before he could knock, a piece of paper caught his eye. In bold red letters, it read, *Notice of Foreclosure. Bank-Owned Property.*

Mark blinked and stared. He knew the Wardrop Realty business had gone under, but he never imagined that the girls could be in jeopardy of losing their home.

He banged loudly on the door several times, but no one answered. Were the servants gone too? Mark blew out a frustrated breath and turned around in time to see the Wardrops' chauffeur drive past Mark's car, heading to the garage in the rear. Perhaps Tom would have some answers.

Mark ran down the stairs and along the wide driveway toward the garage.

Tom had just gotten out of the car when he spotted Mark. "Dr. Henshaw. What brings you here?"

"I came by to check on the girls and make sure they're doing all right. But no one's answering the door, and there's a notice of foreclosure posted."

Tom took off his cap and scratched his head. "Aye. It's such a shame. I worked for Mr. Wardrop for almost twenty years. I can't believe it's come to this."

Mark walked closer. "How can the bank take the house? Surely Mr. Wardrop kept his business finances separate from his personal ones."

Tom opened the double garage doors, one at a time, then turned to Mark. "Apparently, there was another hefty mortgage taken out on the house. When the girls couldn't repay it, the bank foreclosed."

Mark's muscles tightened. "What a rotten thing to do. Couldn't they have given them more time?"

"You know how impersonal banks are. It's all about the money."

"What are they going to do now?"

Tom shrugged, not quite meeting his gaze. "They've gone to stay with a friend until Miss Isabelle can find work and they can get a place of their own."

Mark couldn't imagine Isabelle having to get a job. To his knowledge, she'd never worked a day in her life. Granted, she helped her mother with many charitable projects, but that was a far cry from working for a demanding employer, one who wouldn't tolerate a pampered young woman's high-strung temperament. Isabelle, as Mark well knew, could sometimes be hotheaded and stubborn. Yet she possessed a kind heart and above-average intelligence. If someone would give her a chance, she would make an excellent employee, he was sure.

"Is there an address where I might reach them?" he asked Tom. "I'd like to offer any assistance I can give."

Tom gave a slow shake of his head. "I'm afraid Miss Isabelle asked that I keep her whereabouts to myself for now. I'm sorry, Dr. Henshaw. I know you only have her best interest at heart."

"I see." His spirits sagged at the thought that he might never see her again. But his hands were tied, and there was nothing else he could do. "Well, if you hear from her, please tell her if she ever needs anything, she can find me at the hospital."

"I will do that."

Mark stuck out his hand. "Best of luck to you, Tom."

"Thank you. And you too, sir."

As Mark drove away from the beautiful home, he reflected on how fast a person's whole life could change, something he and Josh had learned the hard way themselves. Now Isabelle and Marissa were facing a similar hardship, and he was powerless to help them.

The best thing he could do was add them to his nightly prayers and ask the Lord to watch over them and keep them safe.

8

Sitting at the breakfast table with Fiona and Marissa four days later, Isabelle's vow to thrive in spite of their tragedy came back to mock her. After trudging up and down almost every street in the city, Isabelle was no closer to finding a job. Three banks, two department stores, two ladies' boutiques, and four offices had outright rejected her requests for employment. The fact that she'd never had a paying job before weighed heavily against her, and no amount of volunteer work with her mother's charities seemed to make a difference.

Thankfully, Fiona had been more fortunate. Her interview with Adam Templeton had gone well, and she'd accepted the position as a maid in his household. His estate, she told Isabelle, was nicely decorated and seemed well run. The other servants had nothing but good things to say about their employer, and Fiona was certain she'd be happy there.

The one bone of contention had been Fiona's living arrangements. Adam had wanted her to live in the house, but Fiona insisted on living away from the mansion for the first few weeks until she was sure the job would suit her.

"Once I feel more comfortable, I'll consider living there," she'd told Isabelle. "But for now, I prefer it this way."

Isabelle couldn't be more relieved to have Fiona with her for a while longer.

Aunt Rosie bustled over to the table with a plate of toast. "I heard from a friend of mine yesterday that the hospital is hiring." One brow rose as she picked up the teapot.

"For what type of position?" Isabelle took a slice and placed it on a chipped plate.

"A laundry room worker." Rosie gave an apologetic shrug. "I told Mildred you wouldn't be interested. That you wanted something more . . . clerical."

Isabelle let out a long sigh. "True. But at this point I might not have the luxury of being so picky."

Marissa's face contorted into a grimace of near horror. "Oh, no, Belle. You shouldn't have to do something so menial."

"It would only be until I find something more suitable."

"But it's not fair."

"Life isn't fair, honey. You should know that by now." Isabelle smiled against a sting of tears. "Now, hurry up and get your books or you'll miss the streetcar and be late for school."

"All right." In typical adolescent fashion, Marissa wore an air of tragedy as she picked up her schoolbag, kissed Isabelle's cheek, and left the house.

Isabelle watched her go, a thread of worry winding through her. If she didn't know better, she'd think some new problem was weighing on her sister. Gone was her usual sunny disposition, her optimistic outlook on life. Maybe it was a result of all the upheaval in her life lately, but something told Isabelle there might be more to Marissa's sullenness.

Isabelle drained her cup, then looked over at Rosie. "Which hospital is hiring?"

"Toronto General. Are you thinking of applying?"

"I might as well. I'm not having much luck anywhere else."

Fiona rose from her chair. "Well, I'd better be going too. I'm training with the Templetons' housekeeper today." She paused to squeeze Isabelle's shoulder. "I don't know whether to wish you luck or not. In any case, have a good day."

Isabelle very much doubted that would be the case.

Mark rushed up the sidewalk toward the hospital entrance. *Late again.*

It was happening more often lately, mostly due to Josh and his tendency to oversleep. A fact that irritated Mark to no end and made him even more annoyed with his brother. If that were possible.

Mark pushed through the door and barreled across the lobby in the direction of the elevators until he smacked right into someone in the middle of the bustling area. The woman's chin struck his chest with the force of a ball-peen hammer, and his briefcase crashed to the ground, spilling its contents over the tiled floor.

"I beg your pardon, ma'am," he sputtered, while doing his best to hold back a rare curse. Now he'd be even later to start his rounds. "Are you all right?"

"I-I think so." The woman pulled back, her head bent, brushing a hand over her dress. "But you really should watch where you're going."

Mark's mouth sagged open at the familiar voice. "Isabelle?" He swallowed a groan. Of all the people he could crash into, why did it have to be her?

She looked incredibly beautiful in a blue polka-dot dress, her blond hair pinned in place under a pert hat with netting over her forehead. His heart banged hard against his ribs, and his mouth went dry as he gazed down at her.

Her eyes widened in recognition, then her nostrils pinched as tight as the lines around her mouth. "Dr. Henshaw. Why am I not surprised? Only a boor would run down a lady like that."

Heat scorched his neck. "It wasn't on purpose, I assure you.

I'm late for my shift." To avoid the outrage on her face, he started gathering the papers that had fallen out of his case. "What brings you to the hospital?"

"Just business." She straightened the cuff of her sleeve.

"One of your mother's charities, I suppose." He almost winced as soon as the words were out. The last thing he wanted to do was remind Isabelle about his role in her mother's death.

"No, it's nothing to do with that." She bit her bottom lip. "I was applying for a job."

A job here in the hospital? Where Mark might see her more often? The very thought lifted his spirits. "That's great. How did it go?"

She raised her head, and the directness of her gaze caused his throat to constrict.

"Well enough. I start on Monday."

"That's wonderful. Which floor will you be working on?" He assumed she'd be doing a clerical job of some sort. Perhaps she'd even be stationed in the ER, near him.

Her cheeks grew red. "I'll be in the basement."

He stared at her, his mind clicking through the departments on the lower level that might be hiring. His eyes widened. "Not the laundry room?"

She lifted her chin. "That's right."

He couldn't imagine Isabelle in the bowels of the hospital, toiling over hot vats of boiling water, stirring soiled bed linens. "That's incredibly physical work. Couldn't you find something more suited to your skills?"

The hint of defiance left her, and her shoulders drooped. "I've tried, believe me. It turns out I'm not qualified for, well, pretty much anything." She blinked rapidly.

"I can't believe that's true. You're very accomplished."

Her eyes narrowed as though she didn't believe he was being sincere.

"I saw how hard you worked alongside your mother, raising

money for her causes. And I saw how tirelessly you cared for her during her illness."

She shook her head. "Unfortunately, none of that matters when it comes to finding a job. I've tried everywhere I can think of—banks, stores, offices. No one will give me a chance."

He took a step toward her and, with one finger, tilted her hat back up where it belonged. "I have quite a few contacts in the city. I could ask around and see if anyone's hiring for a position that might suit you better."

For an instant, the old animosity flared in her eyes, only to fade, replaced by an air of resignation. "I suppose I can't afford to turn down any help. Thank you."

Mark nodded, trying not to take umbrage at the stiffness of her acceptance.

"Dr. Henshaw, please report to the fifth floor." A voice over the loudspeaker echoed across the lobby.

"I have to go. Where can I reach you if I have any news?" Did she hear the note of desperation in his voice?

She bit her lip, seeming to hesitate. Then she released a breath. "I'm staying with Rosemary O'Grady on Gerrard Street. She doesn't have a telephone, but you can leave a message with Mr. Sweeny at Sweeny's Drug Store."

"Got it. Well, take care of yourself, Isabelle."

"You too."

Despite his tardiness, Mark watched her until she exited the building. Then, as he waited for the elevator, he frowned. Sweeny's Drug Store was in a rather rough area of town, just outside the tenements where he treated many destitute patients.

What on earth was Isabelle doing there?

Of all the humiliating experiences, running into Dr. Henshaw like that. Clearly, it had been his fault. He hadn't been paying attention to where he was going. Though to be honest, she hadn't either. Eager to escape the degrading act of practically begging for a position in the laundry room, she'd been rushing through the hospital lobby as though a pack of wild dogs were hounding her.

"Where can I reach you if I have any news?"

Isabelle stiffened in her seat on the streetcar as realization set in. Dr. Henshaw must know she wasn't living on Chestnut Hill Road anymore. Had the news of their downfall spread through the whole city? She shuddered at the thought, imagining the things her former friends would be saying and the mean-spirited gossip that must be circulating. She knew only too well how cruel the upper crust could be.

Isabelle got off the streetcar and walked five blocks to Rosie's house, fighting the pull of despair with every step. Though she should be happy to have finally landed a job, Mark's reaction to the news only reinforced her distaste at working in the dungeon-like setting, filled with steam from the huge tubs of boiling water, the air saturated with the stench of bleach and harsh laundry soap. It would be backbreaking work for sure.

When she reached the house, she slowly climbed the stairs and headed inside, eager for a rest before dinner. At the sight of her sister sitting at the kitchen table, however, Isabelle's heart began to gallop. "Marissa, what are you doing home so early? Are you ill?"

Marissa looked up from her textbook. "No. The headmistress sent me home."

Isabelle set her purse on the table. "Why? Did you break one of the rules?"

"No." Marissa twisted a lock of hair around one finger. Then, with a resigned sigh, she pulled an envelope out of one of her textbooks and handed it to Isabelle. "She asked me to give you this. I don't think it's good news."

Isabelle sat down and opened the letter. She scanned the typed page, then closed her eyes against a pounding in her temples. Apparently, her father hadn't paid Marissa's tuition last semester. If Isabelle didn't settle up what they owed by the end of the week, they would require Marissa to withdraw from the school. How unfair was that? To deny her sister the last few weeks with her class before graduation?

"It's about my tuition, isn't it?"

Isabelle nodded and stuffed the letter back in the envelope. "It's just a little mix-up," she said briskly. "I'll take care of it."

"How? We don't have any money."

"Let me worry about that. For now, just concentrate on passing your courses." Isabelle rose and placed a kiss on the top of Marissa's head.

Then she went into their shared bedroom and closed the door. Her legs shook as she breathed deeply, trying to regain a sense of calm. Somehow she needed to find a way to pay that tuition. Even with her new job, she likely wouldn't get her first paycheck for a couple of weeks, which would be too late. Her stomach sank. It looked like she would have to use the money she'd found in Daddy's safe to save Marissa's school year.

Anxiety clawed its way up her throat. She'd hoped that money would last until she'd found a decent job and a new place to live. Losing the last of their savings would take away her security blanket and leave her feeling even more vulnerable.

But what other choice did she have?

Before she could change her mind, she reached under her mattress, where she'd hidden an envelope with the funds, and pulled it out. Glancing at the door to make sure it was still closed, she counted out the bills. Just enough to cover the tuition with a few dollars left over.

Grimly, she deposited the envelope in her purse and snapped the clasp closed.

Tomorrow she would accompany Marissa to school and pay

off their debt. At least Marissa's immediate future would be secure for the time being.

Once Isabelle started working in the laundry room, she could begin to save her money again to one day get a place of their own. This was just another minor setback. One she couldn't allow to derail her from her purpose.

9

Mark exited the flat of one of his patients and removed the handkerchief from his nose. He thought he was used to the smells in these buildings, but the odor surrounding Mrs. Shea in that sickroom was almost more than Mark could stomach. He jogged down the filthy staircase and burst out into the open, gulping the fresh air into his lungs.

Unless he was wrong, Mrs. Shea was not long for this world, yet she refused to allow him to call an ambulance. Why did so many people, especially those in disadvantaged circumstances, have such a fear of hospitals? It seemed he was the only person they trusted, and that was largely because he came to see them and didn't force them into a clinical setting. Time and time again, Mark had to fight to get them to accept treatment.

He turned the corner and headed in the direction of Sweeny's Drug Store, his thoughts turning to Isabelle and the good news he had for her. At least he hoped she'd consider it good news. Now, he just needed to find her and ease his mind that she was all right.

Four blocks later, he crossed the street to enter the store. He'd used this pharmacy a few times when he desperately needed some medicine for a patient. It was a quaint store that reminded Mark what an old-fashioned apothecary might look like. The smell of herbs and tobacco made him expect to see a mortar and pestle on the counter filled with plants to be ground. The wooden floors squeaked as he crossed the room, walking down the aisle to the rear of the store. Mr. Sweeny, the owner, was a sweet, older gentleman with dark skin and frizzled gray hair, who always tried his best to accommodate Mark's requests.

"Dr. Henshaw. It's good to see you. It's been quite a while." The owner beamed at him from behind the counter.

"It has, Mr. Sweeny. How have things been with you?"

"Very well, thank you. Business is steady, and that's a blessing."

"Indeed."

"What can I do for you, Doctor? You need something for a patient?" He pushed his eyeglasses up on top of his head.

"Not today. Actually, I'm looking for a young woman who's staying with Mrs. Rosemary O'Grady. On Gerrard Street, I believe."

"Oh yes. Rosie's taken in two new boarders as well as her niece. Lovely girls, all three of them. And I must say Miss Isabelle is a real beauty."

Mark cleared his throat, attempting to keep the heat from rising in his cheeks. "Yes, well, I have an important message I need to get to her."

He waited to see what approach Mr. Sweeny would take. Would he offer to deliver the message himself or give Mark the address? Mark had gotten the impression Isabelle might not want him to see where she was living.

The man stroked his mustache, an expression of curiosity creasing his brow. "You know Miss Isabelle and Miss Marissa?"

"Yes, sir. I was their family physician until their mother passed away a few months ago."

Until Isabelle couldn't bear the sight of me anymore.

"Then I suppose she wouldn't mind me giving you the address." The pharmacist came out from behind the counter and pointed out the front window. "The quickest way is right up Bay Street to Gerrard. Number 22. Rosie lives on the first floor."

"Thank you, Mr. Sweeny. I appreciate your help."

"Give the women my regards."

"I certainly will."

Mark's heart beat a little faster as he headed in the direction Mr. Sweeny had pointed. Would Isabelle be there? Would she possibly be happy to see him—a familiar face in her new environment? Or would she resent his intrusion?

His steps slowed as he approached the building on Gerrard Street. Although these units weren't nearly as run-down as some of the tenements he visited on his rounds, they'd definitely seen better days. Rickety stairs led to the peeling front door at number twenty-two. Yet the plain windows appeared clean enough. Mark gingerly climbed the stairs and knocked on the door. Seconds later, an older woman in a faded dress appeared.

She regarded him in some surprise before asking, "May I help you?"

"I hope so. My name is Dr. Henshaw. I'm looking for Isabelle Wardrop."

Her features brightened. "Dr. Henshaw. It's lovely to meet you. I've heard many good things about you."

Mark frowned, studying her face for any trace of familiarity. "I'm afraid you have me at a loss, ma'am."

"Oh, forgive my manners. I'm Rosemary O'Grady. Please come in." She ushered him into the front room of the apartment, which was tidy and rather homey-looking, with a sofa and several arm-chairs surrounding a braided rug.

"How is it that you know me, ma'am?" He hoped he hadn't treated one of her family members and simply forgotten. Usually, he was quite good with the names and faces of his patients.

"I only know you by reputation. You treated the son of a dear friend of mine for the measles. She said you were wonderful with her boy and that he recovered quickly due to the medicine you provided for him."

"Ah, that must be Mrs. Simpson and her son Liam." The woman and her three children lived several blocks to the west in terrible conditions.

"Yes. Alice has become a good friend. My daughter, Noreen, used to babysit for her when she needed to go to an appointment." She smiled. "But you didn't come here to chat about the neighbors. You said you were looking for Isabelle?"

"That's right." Her intrigued expression sent the heat to his cheeks. "I have some information about a possible job for her."

"Why don't you sit and have a cup of tea? Isabelle should be back any moment. She went to meet Marissa at the bus stop."

"That's kind of you. Thank you." He removed his hat and took a seat at the small kitchen table.

Mrs. O'Grady used a dishcloth to lift an enormous teapot off the stove and pour two cups of tea. He'd just taken his first few sips when the front door opened.

Mark's heart seized at the sight of Isabelle, laughing with her sister. He got unsteadily to his feet, but the moment she spotted him, her smile faded.

"Hello, Isabelle. Marissa."

"Dr. Henshaw!" Far from the stiff-lipped reaction of her sister, Marissa rushed forward and engulfed him in a hug. "How wonderful to see you again."

He rubbed an awkward hand over her shoulder. "Nice to see you too."

"Why are you here? Is someone ill?"

He gave her a gentle smile. "No. Everything's fine. I have a possible job opportunity for your sister." He raised his head to meet Isabelle's gaze. "Something that might suit her better than doing laundry."

Isabelle's features relaxed, and she took a step toward him. "You do?"

He nodded. Then, becoming painfully aware of the undisguised curiosity of the other two women, he cleared his throat. "Might we speak in private?"

"Yes, of course. We can talk outside." She opened the door and walked out.

Mark grabbed his hat. "Thank you for the tea, Mrs. O'Grady."

"You're very welcome, Doctor." She winked at him. "Come by any time."

Outside, Mark took in a deep breath of fresh air. Isabelle stood with her back to him and, despite the relative warmth of the day, she rubbed her hands up and down her arms.

"Are you all right?" He kept his voice low, nonthreatening.

"As well as I can be, given our circumstances." Her shoulders sagged as she turned to face him. "I take it you've heard about what happened with the house."

"Yes, and I'm so sorry, Isabelle. You don't deserve this."

"Does anyone ever deserve their misfortune?" She shrugged. "Anyway, you said you had news for me?"

"Oh, right." He reached into his pocket and pulled out a piece of paper. "I spoke with a friend of mine, Mr. Johnson. He's the manager at the Royal York Hotel. I asked if he might have any job openings, and he said they are currently looking for new maids as well as a switchboard operator. I gave him your name and said to expect you." He held out the paper. "This is his phone number. I put mine on there too, in case you ever need it."

She moved closer to take the paper from him. "Thank you, Doctor. That's very kind of you."

"Please, it's Mark."

She looked up and blinked. "What?"

"My name. It's Mark."

A slow smile lit her features. "It's a very nice name." She held his gaze for several seconds. Caught in the blueness of her eyes,

Mark thought his chest might explode from lack of oxygen. Then she folded the paper and put in in her pocket. "Thank you again. I appreciate your help."

"Don't thank me yet. Not until you get a job."

A laugh tinkled out. "All right. And if I do, I'll buy you a cup of coffee as thanks."

A grin twitched at the corners of his mouth. "I intend to hold you to that, Miss Wardrop." He set his hat on his head and nodded. "Good luck. Let me know how you make out."

"I will. Good-bye, Mark."

"Good-bye."

He smiled to himself as he walked away. The sound of his name on her lips felt most promising indeed.

"Thank you very much, Mr. Johnson." Isabelle shook the hotel manager's hand. "I really appreciate you giving me this chance."

"Well, Dr. Henshaw doesn't offer recommendations lightly, and he spoke about you in the most glowing of terms."

Heat rushed into her cheeks. "I won't let you down. I promise."

"I hope you're right. And again, I'm sorry I couldn't offer you a post on the switchboard, but with the lengthy training involved for those positions, I need to be certain you'd be up to the task. As I said, if you prove yourself working as a housemaid, then I'd be open to consider you for the switchboard at a later date."

Isabelle nodded. She'd imagined it would be a lot easier to answer telephone calls than to clean rooms all day, but after seeing the massive switchboard room with over a dozen workers and hearing that it took almost a year to be fully trained, she realized she'd grossly underestimated the skill involved. "I understand, sir. I'm just happy to have a job."

"Very well, Miss Wardrop. You may report tomorrow morning at seven to begin training. The head housekeeper, Mrs. Herbert, will be expecting you."

"I'll be there. Thank you again, Mr. Johnson."

Isabelle almost floated across the hotel's elegant lobby. She'd landed a job. Something better than doing the hospital's laundry. Granted, it still wasn't the type of work she'd ever envisioned doing, but she could learn. Hopefully it would be a temporary measure until she could find a position in an office or a bank. Maybe she'd take some night courses to help her qualify for such a job. Perhaps she could learn to type. Become an executive secretary. Something eminently respectable. Something Marissa could be proud of.

And if she saved hard enough, maybe she could afford to send Marissa to college—if not this fall, then next fall for sure. Marissa would get a good education and become whatever she chose to be. It would take hard work, but they could do it. They would make a bright future for themselves, despite their father's mistakes.

Isabelle hummed to herself as she walked toward the bus stop. She'd pop into Mr. Sweeny's on the way home and telephone the hospital to let them know she'd found other employment.

She gave a start, suddenly realizing that she now owed Mark Henshaw a coffee. Surprisingly, the thought didn't disturb her as much as it would have several weeks ago. After all, he'd followed through on his promise and helped her find a job that was infinitely preferable over the grueling work of the laundry room. Without his recommendation, another door would have slammed shut in her face.

"*. . . he spoke about you in the most glowing of terms.*"

Mr. Johnson's words replayed in her mind, causing her footsteps to slow as she approached the bus stop. What exactly had Mark said about her? He really didn't know her well, and to be honest, the majority of the times she'd encountered him, she'd treated him rather abominably. Still, despite everything, he'd always been gracious to her. More gracious than she deserved. And now his reference had helped her secure this job.

A shiver of doubt raced through her. What if she couldn't do it? What if she got fired after her first few days on the job?

Recalling the kindness in his eyes and how he'd gone out of his way for her, she squared her shoulders.

She would do her very best to live up to his assessment and prove that his faith in her hadn't been misplaced.

10

The next morning, Isabelle arrived at the hotel a full twenty minutes before she was due. She'd taken an earlier bus, wanting to make sure she wouldn't be late on her first day. Now, as she walked across the plush carpet in the lobby, she took a moment to fully appreciate its grandeur. She'd dined here in the Royal York's Imperial Room—a popular restaurant for the rich and famous—several times over the years with her family, and Isabelle was now ashamed to admit that she'd ignored the beauty of the hotel, even complained to her parents that it was too stuffy and boring. Had she really been so arrogant, taking her privileged lifestyle for granted?

An ironic laugh bubbled up inside her. Here she was, no longer one of society's elite members being served in the dining room, but a maid set to clean the rooms that the wealthy patrons would be occupying. She shook herself from any hint of self-pity and reminded herself how lucky she was simply to have a place to lay her head at night as well as the opportunity to earn an honest living.

She approached the check-in counter, where a man in a black suit and tie smiled at her. "Welcome, miss. Checking in?"

"No. I'm starting a new job in the hotel. I'm supposed to report to Mrs. Herbert."

His smile instantly evaporated. "She's likely in her office in the basement. One level down."

"Oh, I see." Isabelle bit her lip, hesitating to ask where the stairs might be.

"In the future, you will come in through the employees' entrance in the rear and use the servants' elevator. We do not allow staff, other than the bellhops, to walk through the lobby or use the main elevator, which is reserved for guests. Today, you may use the stairs. Around the corner on the right."

"Thank you," she said, biting back her indignation. The man was only reciting the rules.

She took her time walking away, savoring the beauty of the furnishings, the potted palms, and the ornate clock that dominated the grand curving staircase. It seemed this would be the last time she'd be allowed to enjoy the lobby's splendor.

Isabelle located the stairs and walked down to the next level. She found herself in a long, damp corridor, which she followed until the murmur of voices could be heard. A group of uniformed women stood in an open area near a table. A time clock hung on the wall, and an uneven stack of what were likely timecards teetered on the table beneath it. The women stopped talking to gawk at Isabelle as she approached.

"Hello. I'm looking for Mrs. Herbert," she said in a halting voice.

One woman blew out a stream of cigarette smoke and gestured with her head. "Down that hall. The name's on the door."

"Thank you." Isabelle lifted her chin as she walked past the group. Her nerves jumbled in her stomach as she neared the office. Taking a deep breath, she knocked on the door.

"Come in." The harsh voice only increased Isabelle's anxiety.

She entered the cramped space to find a rather large woman seated behind a metal desk.

"Good morning. I'm Isabelle Wardrop, the new housemaid."

The woman stared at her over her bifocals, then slowly removed them. She glanced up at a clock on the wall. "You're on time. That's a good start. However, in future, you must arrive at least fifteen minutes before your shift starts. You'll need time to change into your uniform, make sure your cart is fully stocked, and get up to the floor you're assigned to for the day."

"Y-yes, ma'am."

The woman rose from her chair, a large ring of keys rattling at her waist. "I'll take you to your locker and introduce you to Miss Eggerton, who will be training you. You will shadow her for the first week, and next week you'll be on your own."

Isabelle nodded and quietly followed her back down the corridor. The group of women stopped talking, and the one smoking stubbed out her cigarette in an ashtray on the table.

"What are the lot of you doing standing around?" Mrs. Herbert barked. "Get your carts and get to work."

"Right away, ma'am." Immediately, they scurried off down the hall.

Mrs. Herbert entered a door directly across from the time clock. Rows of metal lockers flanked both walls, with a long bench running the length of the room. Mrs. Herbert took out a key and fitted it into one of the upper lockers. "This will be yours. Once you've changed into your uniform, store all your belongings in here. And don't lose the key. You'll have to pay for a new one if you do."

"Yes, ma'am."

A toilet flushed from somewhere in the room. Then footsteps sounded, followed by running water.

"Miss Eggerton, is that you?" Mrs. Herbert called.

"Yes, ma'am." A young woman not much older than Isabelle came around the corner of lockers. She was dressed in a black maid's uniform with a white apron over top and a white cap covering her dark hair.

"This is the new hire, Miss Wardrop. She will shadow you for the week. I trust you'll train her properly."

"I'll do my best, Mrs. Herbert."

Isabelle studied the younger woman's face, attempting to discern any hint of animosity for having been assigned this task, but to her relief, she found none.

"Miss Eggerton will give you a fresh uniform, and once you've changed, you'll begin your shift. Due to the late start, you will subtract fifteen minutes off your lunch break." The woman paused, scanning Isabelle's attire and hair. "From now on, you needn't fix your hair in that fancy do. A plain bun is all that's necessary under your maid's cap."

Isabelle could only nod as Mrs. Herbert gave her a final look and bustled out of the locker room. Once the door closed, Isabelle let out a breath and turned to Miss Eggerton.

"Hello. My name is Isabelle."

"I'm Mary." Miss Eggerton smiled. "Come on. I'll find you a uniform and we can get started."

On Wednesday, Mark visited the expectant mothers at Bennington Place, but he couldn't seem to get his mind off the argument he'd had with Josh that morning. No matter what he said to his brother lately, or how congenial he tried to be, Josh seemed to want to fight with him. The only time the boy seemed the least bit happy—though happy was a relative term when it came to Josh—was when he was heading out to choir practice, making Mark more certain than ever that a girl was involved. Short of reneging on their agreement and forbidding him to attend the practices, Mark had no idea what to do about the situation.

A feminine throat cleared rather loudly. "Dr. Henshaw?"

With a blink, Mark snapped out of his stupor and did his best to give his full attention to the young woman he was examining. He straightened from her belly and draped his stethoscope around his neck, forcing his lips into a semblance of a smile. "Your baby seems to be doing very well, Miss Southby. I estimate you have about four more weeks until he or she makes an appearance."

"That's a little sooner than I thought." She smoothed her dress down while giving him a hopeful look. "You will be there during the delivery, won't you?"

Mark moved a few steps away. "The midwife takes care of most of the births. Unless a problem arises, which I don't anticipate, you'll be in good hands with Mrs. Dinglemire. She's had years of experience."

Mark and Mrs. Dinglemire took turns doing the women's checkups, so that no matter who ended up delivering the baby, they'd both have a solid familiarity with the woman's medical history.

Miss Southby pouted and batted her lashes at him. "But I'd feel so much better if *you* were taking care of me."

Heat flashed up his neck at her blatant flirtation. He quickly turned away to repack his medical bag. The problem in dealing with the maternity home residents was that the majority didn't have husbands, and some seemed to think Mark would make an excellent candidate. He always had to be careful to tread a delicate line between being kind and keeping a professional distance. "You'll be fine, Miss Southby. I'll see you for your next checkup."

Before she could say another word, he exited the room and headed downstairs to the maternity home's main level.

Olivia Reed, one of the home's matrons, was coming down the hall as he reached the first floor. She greeted him with a wide smile. "I'm glad I caught you before you left, Mark. There's fresh coffee if you'd like a cup."

Though he did have other patients to see this afternoon, he couldn't resist the lure of a conversation with his friend. "I'd love that. Thank you."

He'd known Olivia for several years now. After helping her recover from an illness that almost took her life, they'd developed a close friendship. Mark greatly admired her for the way she'd overcome adversity in her life and devoted herself to helping unwed mothers, and he'd been more than happy to assist Olivia and Ruth Bennington with their mission.

They brought their cups from the kitchen into Olivia's office, where they could have a bit of privacy.

"How are you?" Olivia asked once she was seated beside him in one of the guest chairs, angling it so she had a better view of him. "It seems we haven't had a chance to talk in ages."

"I'm fine. And you?" The automatic words flew off his tongue.

She tilted her head, staring at him over the rim of her mug. "You don't seem fine. You look tired and distracted. Are you getting enough time off?"

Olivia always chided him about working too hard, between the hospital, the maternity home, his private patients, and his volunteer work in the tenements. But he could never choose which one he would want to give up.

"It's not just the workload," he said. "It's Josh." If anyone, Olivia would understand. She knew all about his dedication to his brother. If it hadn't been for his commitment to Josh, Mark might have been tempted to marry Olivia a few years back, when she needed a husband in order to adopt an orphaned baby. But in the end, things had worked out for the best when she met and married the love of her life, Darius Reed, and she and her new husband had managed to adopt little Abigail after all. Now, in addition to Darius's daughter, Sofia, they had a beautiful baby boy as well. He'd never seen Olivia look happier.

Her slim brows rose. "What's happening with Josh?"

Mark quickly filled her in about his brother skipping his science labs and his fixation with the youth choir. "I'm positive he has a crush on one of the girls. I recognize all the signs. And I'm worried his obsession will derail his career."

Olivia's brown eyes filled with compassion. "That must be hard for you. I know you want only the best for him."

Mark nodded. "Right now, I don't know what to do. Everything I say to him turns into a fight."

"May I offer a word of advice?" she asked gently.

"Certainly. I'd welcome it." Even though Olivia was younger than he was, he knew her to be wise beyond her years.

"Josh is a young man, possibly in love for the first time. It's a big event in his life. Trying to ignore it or minimize its importance isn't fair to him, and it won't make his feelings for this girl disappear."

"What do you suggest I do, then? I can't let him ruin his future over some teenage crush." He ran a hand over his beard. "Maybe I should consider taking a job somewhere else. Move him far away from temptation."

Olivia's brows rose. "That's a bit drastic, don't you think?"

He shrugged.

"I doubt moving would improve the situation," Olivia said. "If anything, it might make it worse." She laid a hand on his sleeve. "Be patient with him. Don't do anything to risk alienating him altogether. Forcing him to choose between you and a girl could cause irreparable harm to your relationship. Believe me, I know from firsthand experience that a family rift causes immeasurable pain." She leaned toward him, her expression pleading. "Try talking to him and really listen to what he's feeling. Maybe he's scared about going to university. Maybe he wants something different for his future, but he's afraid to disappoint you."

Tension raced up Mark's spine, propelling him to his feet. Afraid to disappoint him? Josh was doing a great job of that lately without even trying.

She came over to his side as he stared unseeing out the window. "You're a wonderful man, Mark, but you remind me of my father in a way. Your standards seem a little hard to live up to."

He stiffened. Was she right? Did Josh resent Mark's expectations for him?

"Have an honest conversation with him and try to see his point of view." Olivia patted his arm. "It couldn't hurt, could it?"

Mark's lungs deflated on a rush of air. "I guess not."

"Good." She leaned up and pressed a kiss to his cheek. "For the record, I hope you never move away. Bennington Place would lose a valuable team member, and I would lose a very dear friend."

By the time Isabelle got off the bus that night, every muscle in her body ached, and she could barely force her feet to walk the few blocks to Aunt Rosie's house.

When she entered the kitchen and sank onto one of the chairs, Aunt Rosie took one look at her and clucked. "Oh, you poor dear. You look exhausted. Let me draw you a hot bath with Epsom salts."

"That sounds heavenly."

Seconds later, Isabelle heard the creaky bathroom taps open as Aunt Rosie began to fill the iron clawfoot tub. Then she came out to put on the kettle. "In case the hot water runs out, we'll add some from the kettle."

"Belle, is that you?" Marissa emerged from their bedroom.

Isabelle mustered a smile. "It is."

"How was your first day?"

"Exhausting."

Her sister's face fell. "Oh, Belle, I feel terrible. I go to school all day and sit at a desk while you're doing hard labor."

"Don't worry. I'll get used to it." Isabelle patted her hand.

Marissa pushed her hair over one shoulder. "As soon as school's finished, I'll get a job too and help out."

"Let's not worry about that right now. We can talk about the summer later." Isabelle's stomach grumbled loudly, and she realized how hungry she was, having had no time to eat lunch. Tomorrow, she'd remember to bring a sandwich or something to eat to keep her fueled for the afternoon.

"You go soak for a while," Rosie said, "and I'll heat up some stew for you."

"Thank you, Aunt Rosie. You're an angel."

The woman laughed. "That's the first time anyone's called me that. Go on now before the water cools."

"Is Fiona not home yet?" Marissa asked.

"I imagine she's working late at the Templetons'." Rosie sighed. "What I wouldn't give for a telephone in here."

Isabelle paused at the bathroom door. "After I eat, I need to make a call myself. If I go down to Mr. Sweeny's store, would you like me to telephone the Templeton residence?" Isabelle knew Aunt Rosie worried about her niece coming home alone on the streetcar late at night. "Maybe I could meet Fiona and walk home with her."

"That would be most kind, luv."

The thought of going out again was less than appealing, especially as she passed her cozy bed. What she wouldn't give to curl up beneath the quilt and sleep for twelve hours straight. But she owed Mark Henshaw a telephone call to thank him, and if she could do something to ease Aunt Rosie's mind, she would gladly do it.

No matter how tired her feet were.

11

"You really didn't have to do this." Mark gave Isabelle an amused glance over the rim of his coffee cup. They'd met in a small diner several blocks from the hospital after his shift. He felt a little funny accepting her invitation, given her obvious financial straits, yet the urge to see her again proved too strong to ignore.

"It's the least I could do after you helped me get a job at the hotel." When she smiled at him, her features softened with a warm glow. "Without your recommendation I doubt Mr. Johnson would have hired me."

Today, she wore her fair hair pinned up under a pert black hat that matched the collar on her green dress. She looked so pretty and sophisticated. He couldn't imagine her in a maid's uniform, cleaning hotel bathrooms. Yet he had to admire the fact that she hadn't quit after her first week. "I'm glad he was able to offer you a position. How are you finding the work?"

She wrinkled her nose. "To be honest, it's a lot harder than I imagined. But I'm slowly getting used to it."

"I'm proud of you, Isabelle. It takes real courage to go through everything you have and come out on the other side."

"It's not as though I had any choice in the matter," she said with quiet dignity. "I'm determined to do whatever I can to secure my sister's future."

He paused, his cup in mid-air. "And your own, of course."

She shrugged. "I'll be fine. It's Marissa I'm worried about. I want her to be able to go to college and make something of herself."

"I know what you mean." Mark set his mug down. "I feel the same way about my brother." He met the question in her eyes. "I've been raising him since our parents died almost five years ago in a car accident."

"Oh, Mark. I'm so sorry. How terrible."

"Thank you." He lowered his head. "It was a huge shock at the time. I was almost finished with medical school, and I started my internship soon afterward. But with my long hours at the hospital on top of my private patients, making time for Josh is a real challenge."

"I can imagine. Did you start at the hospital right out of university?"

"I did." Mark set his cup down. "I was supposed to join my father's practice, but everything changed after the accident."

She nodded, studying him. "You really do understand what I'm going through, don't you?"

"I do. Although we were luckier in one regard. We weren't forced to move."

"You're still living in your parents' home?"

"Yes. I figured since my brother was only thirteen, he needed the stability of staying in the same house. . . ." He grimaced. "Forgive me, Isabelle. That was completely insensitive."

"No. It's all right." She shook her head, yet tears stood out in her eyes. "We probably would have sold the house anyway. It was far too big for just the two of us."

He reached out and placed his hand over hers. "If you ever want to talk to someone who knows what it's like to lose your parents, I'm always here."

She lifted her head, a look of gratitude on her face. "Thank you."

Their gazes held for another few seconds, then she shook her head, breaking their connection.

"I owe you a huge apology," she said quietly, staring down at her mug. "I treated you terribly after my mother died. I had no right to be so cruel." She raised her gaze back to his. "Can you forgive me?"

The sincerity in her voice loosened the tension in his muscles. He'd never seen her so unguarded, so truly herself.

He gave her a gentle smile. "There's nothing to forgive. You needed an outlet for your anger and pain, and I was an easy target."

Relief flooded her features. "Thank you. That means a lot."

"Believe me, you're not the first family member of a patient to do that. And you probably won't be the last." Mark could no more hold a grudge against Isabelle than he could against his brother for his reaction to their parents' deaths. "Grief is a strange thing. It makes people behave in ways they normally wouldn't. I've had some less-than-stellar moments myself as I tried to navigate my loss while being a new doctor and a guardian to a teenage boy."

"That's good to know. I've had a few of those myself."

"And there will be more. Just allow yourself a little grace. And offer the same to Marissa as well. If she's anything like my brother, she'll have moments of anger and rebellion. Try not to take it personally." He gave a short laugh. "I'm still trying to master that particular piece of advice."

"I know what you mean. Marissa hasn't been herself at all since . . . well, since all of this happened. Yet I can't help feeling that something more is going on with her. She's been secretive and overly quiet, which isn't like her. She usually shares her troubles with me." A trace of hurt sounded in her voice.

"Perhaps she feels you have enough to worry about and doesn't wish to add to your burden." Watching Isabelle's troubled face, he wished he could be her confidant, her protector, the man who solved all her problems for her. "Give it some time. I'm sure she'll come around."

She gave him a brief smile. "Did it take long for your brother to recover?"

He swallowed the last of his coffee, then returned his cup to the saucer. He didn't want to give her false hope, nor did he wish to discourage her any more than she already was. "It's an ongoing process. There are good days and bad. But overall, he's improved greatly."

"I'm glad. What's your brother doing now?" A genuine flicker of interest shone in her eyes.

"He's about to graduate high school. Then it will be on to university with the hopes of getting into med school."

"Oh, he wants to follow in your footsteps, does he?"

"That's the plan. Eventually I hope to open our own practice so we can work together. It's what my father would have wanted." He paused. "Although right now my brother seems more interested in playing his guitar than studying."

She gave a light laugh. "He sounds like Marissa. She's distracted by daydreams of romance. One of the drawbacks of attending a private girls' school, I suppose."

Mark didn't add that Josh might be having the same romantic daydreams himself. He studied her, suddenly curious about her love life. "Were you as preoccupied with boys as Marissa is?"

She let out a genuine laugh. "I had my moments, but no. I was more focused on pleasing my parents and joining my mother in her charity work after graduation."

Mark's throat tightened. And now she had to put her own life on hold to provide for her sister. Isabelle's courage and selflessness made him respect her even more.

"You mean you've never had a serious boyfriend?" He couldn't believe it. A girl as beautiful as Isabelle? Why she wasn't married yet was a mystery to him. Not that he minded. It fueled his hope that someday she might see him differently.

"There was one." A sad expression stole over her face. "Roger worked for my father and was about to propose when . . ." She paused, a frown drifting over her brow. She cleared her throat. "Anyway, after Daddy's company was dissolved, Roger was out of work. He ended up taking a job in British Columbia."

Mark frowned. "He didn't ask you to go with him?"

She shrugged, playing with the handle of her cup. "He said he had nothing to offer me, and it wasn't fair to ask me to wait."

"I'm sorry, Isabelle. That must have been hard." One more disappointment she'd had to deal with on top of all the rest.

"If I'm honest, it was probably for the best." She raised her head. "I'd planned to accept his proposal, but I realized afterward that I couldn't have really loved him or his leaving would have been far more devastating than it was."

As he gazed into the blueness of her eyes, his heart swelled in his chest. She'd been through so much hardship in such a short space of time, yet she never wavered. Never gave in to self-pity or tears, at least not that he could tell. "Well, if it had been me," he said huskily, "I never would have left you behind."

Her pink lips parted, but no sound came out. Then her lashes swept down to cover her confusion. "That's sweet of you to say. Especially after you've seen me at my worst." A rosy color bloomed in her cheeks.

A blush for him? His pulse picked up speed. Could her feelings toward him be changing? But even if it were true, he couldn't rush things. He was simply grateful that she didn't seem to loathe him any longer.

Mark glanced at his watch. Though he'd love to stay and talk, he had other obligations. Besides, he didn't want to overstay his visit. Now that he'd finally broken through Isabelle's wall of anger and distrust, he wouldn't risk spoiling that for anything. "I really should get going. Thank you for the coffee and for the company."

"You're welcome."

"I'll be praying everything continues to go well for you and Marissa from now on. And please don't hesitate to call if you need anything."

"I will. Thank you."

Mark carried the vision of her soft smile with him for the rest of the day.

Isabelle paid the bill at the diner and checked the time. Marissa would be getting out of school soon, and since the diner wasn't far from the girls' academy, Isabelle decided to surprise her and accompany her home.

This was Isabelle's first day off work from the hotel, and she'd been happy that Dr. Henshaw—or Mark, as he'd insisted she call him—had been able to meet her for coffee. Truth be told, she was happy to set aside her animosity toward him. Now that she'd apologized, perhaps they could have a more cordial relationship. It helped knowing she had another person on her side. Someone who knew everything she'd been through and still seemed to value her friendship.

She was coming to learn that the true measure of a person's worth was how they treated a person when circumstances brought them to their lowest point. The people who offered assistance or a kind word were invaluable. Those who had turned their backs on her had never been true friends in the first place.

And Mark Henshaw was proving that he truly cared about others. He seemed genuinely remorseful for having let her mother down. In hindsight, she could admit that even if he had come that night, he likely wouldn't have been able to stop the inevitable outcome of her mother's death.

Isabelle made an effort to set all negative thoughts aside, determined to enjoy her walk. It was a beautiful spring day, and the temperature was perfect for a stroll. In the distance, a school bell rang, and shortly after, the sound of voices met her ears. She increased her pace slightly, realizing that she might miss Marissa before she caught her bus.

As she neared the school, a sea of uniformed girls came rushing down the main driveway to the sidewalk. Isabelle strained to catch a glimpse of Marissa but found it nearly impossible to tell one girl from another in their similar attire.

She stood on the sidewalk near the brick wall and waited until the crowds thinned, scanning the girls as they passed by. When only a handful of students remained, Isabelle feared she'd missed her sister. Or perhaps she was still inside, talking to one of her teachers. Isabelle decided to go in and see if she could spot her.

Just as she was about to head up the driveway, she noticed two people standing close together on the sidewalk, somewhat hidden by the brick wall. Isabelle walked closer, her steps becoming slower. Her heart sped up as she recognized her sister. Who was the young man with her, and what was he doing outside an all-girls school?

They seemed involved in a rather animated discussion. Marissa gestured with her hands, her features contorted with apparent frustration. Isabelle hesitated, not wanting to intrude right away. Perhaps if she observed them a little longer, she might get a clue as to what was troubling her sister. If only she could hear what they were saying.

Marissa's shoulders seemed to sag, and she hung her head. The boy pulled her against his chest in a hug.

Isabelle's muscles seized. What was going on here? Was this boy the reason for her sister's depressed mood lately? Fighting with herself, Isabelle stayed back to watch the scene play out.

The boy handed Marissa a handkerchief, and she straightened away from him. She dabbed the cloth to her eyes, appearing to listen to whatever he was saying. Then she nodded and handed him back the handkerchief. The boy took it, leaned toward Marissa, and kissed her cheek, then started off down the sidewalk in the opposite direction from where Isabelle was standing.

Isabelle hurried toward her sister, but all she could see when she got there was the back of the young man's jacket.

"Marissa! Who was that?"

Her sister sprang away from the wall, her eyes widened with a hint of panic. "Isabelle. I . . . what are you doing here?"

"I was in the area and thought I'd travel home with you. Who was that?" she repeated.

"Um . . . no one. Just a friend from the church choir." Marissa's cheeks flared red.

Isabelle frowned. "Does this friend have a name?"

Marissa glanced down the sidewalk. "It's . . . Josh. He stopped by to ask when the next practice is . . . because he missed the last one."

Isabelle saw through the fib right away. The choir met the same time every Tuesday night. "Your conversation looked more serious than that. And why are your eyes red? Were you crying?"

Marissa huffed and started walking. "I'm fine."

Isabelle fell into step beside her. "Are boys even allowed on school property? I imagine the headmistress wouldn't approve."

Marissa's head whipped up. "He wasn't technically on the property, Belle. Stop acting like I committed a crime." Her face was set in a thunderous expression, her amber eyes darkened to the color of Daddy's fine whiskey.

Isabelle inhaled and attempted to rein in her indignation. They walked in strained silence for a few moments before she spoke again. "You only have a few weeks left of school," she said quietly. "Don't do anything to jeopardize your graduation."

Marissa came to a sudden halt. "Haven't you ever liked someone?" she demanded. "And hoped that maybe he liked you too?"

Ah, so she did like this boy. At least she'd admitted it.

Isabelle paused to consider her reply. "I thought I felt that way about Roger, but if he truly loved me, he wouldn't have moved clear across the country." She stared ahead down the sidewalk, her stomach twisting with an uncomfortable emotion. "I've learned you can't base your life decisions on the whims of a man."

Marissa touched her arm. "You can't give up on love just because Roger was an idiot," she said. "Don't you want to get married someday?"

A lump rose in Isabelle's throat, and she gave a humorless laugh. "What man would want to marry a woman who scrubs toilets for a living?"

"You're beautiful and intelligent, Belle. Someone is bound to realize that sooner or later."

Isabelle shook her head. "Never mind about me. It's you I'm concerned about. I want to make sure you have every opportunity in life. I won't let you throw away your future. Especially over a boy."

Marissa looked like she might argue, but instead her eyes filled with tears, and she drew Isabelle into a hug. "All I want is to make you proud," she whispered.

"You will. I have no doubt about it." Isabelle's heart swelled as she hugged her back, and a tiny flicker of hope lit within her.

Maybe she'd gotten through to her sister after all.

12

Mark swallowed the last bite of roast beef and patted a napkin to his mouth. It wasn't often he made it home to eat dinner with Josh, and lately guilt had been plaguing him over how little time they spent together. He'd thought he was doing the right thing, working hard to provide for Josh, but had Mark's dedication to his patients caused him to neglect his brother? Maybe Josh's lack of focus on his studies was a passive form of rebellion, a cry for attention.

Olivia's words had been playing around in his mind for days now, and Mark was ready to give her advice a try. Maybe if he spent more quality time with his brother, instead of trying to control his every move, he'd have a better chance of understanding him. And that would start tonight.

Josh stood up and took his plate to the sink. "Thanks for dinner. I've got to get ready for choir now."

Mark pushed back from the table. "I thought I'd go with you."

Josh turned around, a stunned expression on his face. "Why would you do that?"

"I have the night off, so I figured I'd come and see this choir you love so much." Mark turned on the tap to rinse his plate, then set it on the counter.

Instead of seeming happy, Josh scowled. "You just want to spy on me because you think some girl's trying to trap me."

Josh's words hit a little too close to home, but Mark kept his expression neutral as he dried his hands. "I never get to see you play on Sundays because I'm working, but tonight I'm free. I thought we could spend the evening together. What's so terrible about that?"

He eyed him skeptically. "You're only coming this once?"

"Probably. I don't have many nights off, as you know." Mark didn't mention the hoops he'd had to jump through to switch tonight's shift with a colleague.

Josh shoved his hands into his pockets. "Well, as long as you promise not to embarrass me, I guess you can come."

"Gee, thanks." Mark thumped Josh's shoulder, attempting to lighten the mood. "Don't worry, I'll sit quietly in the background. I won't speak to anyone unless you give me permission."

A hint of a smile twitched on Josh's lips. "All right. I need to go change."

"I'll be waiting."

Half an hour later, Mark pulled up to the curb near St. Philip's Community Church and turned off the engine. Josh jumped out, retrieved his guitar case from the back seat, and waved as he jogged over to the church.

Mark shook his head as he got out of the car, making his way over at a more leisurely pace. Even though Josh didn't use the guitar for the church music, he always took it with him. Sometimes, Josh had told him, they stayed after the practice for a while, and he played for them. If he wanted to do that tonight, Mark would gladly wait. Anything to get back to some semblance of the sibling relationship they once had before Mark had become a parent figure.

He followed Josh in through the side door and down the stairs to the church hall. A rambunctious group of teenagers had gathered near the stage, laughing and talking. A man—presumably

Mr. Henchley, the music director—stood by an upright piano, thumbing through the sheet music.

Mark scanned the group that consisted of a surprisingly equal number of boys and girls. With all of them clustered in groups, it was hard to determine who Josh might have a crush on. Perhaps Mark shouldn't have told him he was coming. That way he might have been able to catch a glimpse of him interacting with his friends in an unguarded fashion. Now Josh would probably stay far away from the girl he liked, just so Mark wouldn't know who she was or try to talk to her.

Mark found a folding chair and took a seat near the back of the room. Seconds later, the music director called everyone to order. The students quickly got into their choir formation, while Josh took his place at the piano.

Soon they were singing a familiar hymn, a lilting tune that reminded Mark of his mother. In his mind, he could still hear her clear voice singing proudly. He swallowed back his emotion and focused on the choir. Scanning the faces of the female singers, he tried to determine which one had captured the interest of his brother. His gaze stopped on one brown-haired girl.

His stomach dropped to his shoes. *Marissa Wardrop?* Surely she wasn't the one Josh was fixated on. Mark could only imagine what Isabelle's reaction to such a liaison would be. He had just started to re-earn her trust. This could ruin everything.

The rear door squeaked as it opened. Mark automatically turned to see who had entered. His heart jolted in his chest when Isabelle herself appeared. She stood watching the choir for a moment before she glanced his way. Her eyes widened, her brows winging upward.

He gave a brief wave, his pulse quickening as she made her way over to him.

"Mark, what are you doing here?" she said in a low voice.

"My brother's in the choir. I thought I'd come and watch since I had a rare free night."

"I had the same idea."

Mark jumped up. "Here, take my seat. I'll grab another."

"Thank you." She smiled as she smoothed her skirt beneath her.

Mark found another chair and set it down beside her.

Isabelle leaned toward him and whispered, "They're quite good, aren't they?"

"Surprisingly, yes."

They listened in silence for several minutes, until the choir paused at the end of a hymn and chatter broke out.

"Which one is your brother?" she asked.

"The one playing the piano." Mark couldn't help the swell of pride that rose in his chest.

A frown creased her brow as she leaned forward to look at the boy behind the piano. "What's his name?"

"Josh. Why?"

She closed her eyes briefly. "Oh no."

"What's wrong?"

"We need to talk. But not in here." She glanced around, then reached over to grab his hand. "Come with me."

The feeling of her delicate hand in his sent his mind into such a turmoil, he couldn't even formulate a response. Instead, he blindly followed her out into the empty corridor.

She turned to face him. "I think my sister and your brother are . . ." She bit her lip.

"Are what?" Dread pooled in his chest.

"Well, I'm not sure exactly, but the other day, when I dropped by Marissa's school, I found her talking with a boy. When I asked who he was, she said he was Josh from the choir. I had no idea he was your brother." She looked fairly horrified.

"Is it possible they're simply friends?" Yet as he said it aloud, he remembered Josh saying that the girl he liked had gone through a terrible time, that she'd lost both her parents. Why hadn't he put this together at the time?

"Josh hugged her and kissed her on the cheek," Isabelle said. "If they hadn't been in such a public place, who knows what would have happened?"

His stomach sank. It was worse than he feared if Josh had sought Marissa out at her school.

"What are we going to do? We can't let this continue." Isabelle bit her lip as she paced the corridor. "Marissa needs the best marks possible to earn a scholarship into college. Heaven knows that's the only way she'll be able to go."

Mark nodded. "Josh doesn't need the distraction either."

She stopped pacing to look over at him. "So, we're agreed? We'll do whatever we can to keep this . . . relationship from developing?"

"I'll do what I can on my end." He didn't want to commit to anything too outlandish. After all, he'd just begun to try to repair his relationship with Josh. Any outright interference could push him away altogether. "It's probably best not to forbid them from seeing each other. I've learned that giving Josh ultimatums only makes him do the opposite."

"You're right. Marissa can be equally as stubborn."

"I've told him that as long as he keeps his marks up, he can continue with the choir. But if he starts skipping classes or getting bad grades, he'll have to quit."

Isabelle nodded. "That sounds reasonable. For the time being, I'll come to as many of these practices as I can to keep an eye on things."

"Good." That way he didn't have to be the bad guy. He'd have Isabelle's eyes and ears covering the situation. He smiled and held out a hand. "Partners?"

Her lips quirked upward as she slipped her hand in his. "Partners."

His heart quivered with a new hope. Perhaps once Isabelle got used to her new situation in life, they could meet each other as equals. And with no disapproving parents around to dissuade her, he might even have a shot at dating her.

But first, they needed to focus on their respective siblings and make sure they graduated high school.

The swell of the choir voices drifted out into the hallway.

"Shall we go back inside?" he said.

She nodded and gave him a relieved smile, her eyes bright with what looked like admiration. His chest warmed under this new sensation.

And as he escorted her back into the auditorium, he reveled in the satisfaction of not only being on good terms with her again but also working with her toward a common goal.

Things were indeed looking up.

From the rear of the church hall, Isabelle watched her sister, paying close attention to how often she glanced over at Josh. Of all the boys in town, why did Marissa have to form an attachment to Mark Henshaw's brother? Isabelle's relationship with the doctor was already tentative at best. The last thing she needed was another layer of conflict.

From what she could determine, either her sister was purposely avoiding eye contact with the piano player, or she wasn't nearly as smitten with him as Isabelle thought. Maybe she wasn't lying when she said they were just friends.

But Isabelle knew the signs of infatuation, and she was sure her sister was romantically interested in someone. Yet no matter how closely Isabelle watched, she couldn't discern any real interest on Marissa's part in one particular person. Her attention remained focused on the instruction of the choirmaster.

As soon as the practice ended, however, Josh rose from the piano bench and went over to talk to Marissa. Isabelle frowned. Maybe the feelings were more on the boy's part rather than her sister's.

Still, this matter warranted her attention, and she and Mark would have to keep them both under surveillance as much as possible. After all, with Mama and Daddy gone, it was up to

Isabelle to protect her sister's reputation and set her on the right path for her future. Once Marissa was safely off to college, she would be able to breathe easier and focus on her own life.

"I'd offer you ladies a ride home, but I fear it would only encourage Josh if I did." Mark's low voice broke Isabelle from her thoughts.

"That's kind of you, but we'll be fine taking the bus."

"I'd feel better if you took a cab." The concern in his voice was endearing, but she had no money to waste on cab fare.

She shook her head. At moments like this, she dearly missed Tom and the car that used to be available to them. "We'll be all right together."

"Very well." Mark rose from his chair. "It was nice seeing you again, Isabelle."

"You too."

He hesitated. "If there's anything to report about my brother or Marissa, will you let me know?" The soft lighting in the hall muted the color of his hazel eyes. Tonight, they seemed like brown velvet with golden flecks.

"Of course."

"Thank you." He smiled at her. "Well, good night, then." He seemed reluctant to leave, but it was likely his chivalrous instincts holding him back.

"Good night." She lowered her head to hide the beginning of a blush and started walking toward the stage.

With their new alliance forged tonight, Isabelle felt a sudden kinship with Mark that she never had before. After her mother's death, she thought she'd never speak to him again. Now, he seemed more like a friend and peer. It turned out they had a lot more in common than she ever would have imagined. Both had lost their parents at an early age, and both were acting as guardians for their younger siblings. It was a rather odd start to a friendship, but she supposed there had been less auspicious alliances forged over time.

God willing, they could keep Josh and Marissa on the right path and, by doing so, safeguard their futures.

On the way home during the silent car ride, Mark debated what to say to Josh. Confronting him about his ill-advised feelings for Marissa would do no good. As he said to Isabelle, it would only succeed in making his brother even more determined to do the exact opposite.

No, Mark needed to be smart about the way he handled this. Instead of dwelling on the negative, perhaps he should focus on the positive.

"I really enjoyed the choir," he said finally. "I'd forgotten how well you play the piano."

"Thanks." Josh threw him a wary glance as though he didn't quite trust the compliment.

"Do you think they'll ever let you use your guitar for any of the songs?"

Josh snorted. "I doubt it. Mr. Henchley is pretty old-fashioned."

"That's too bad. I think it would be nice for a change."

Olivia's advice swirled in his mind. *"Try talking to him and really listen to what he's feeling. Maybe he's scared about going to university. Maybe he wants something different for his future, but he's afraid to disappoint you."*

Mark waited a couple of minutes before speaking again. "Josh, I want to talk to you about going to university in the fall. I hope I haven't given you the wrong impression that it's nothing but years of stress and drudgery."

"You haven't."

"Oh. That's good." He shot a glance at his brother. At least it seemed like Josh still planned to go on with his education. "I also wanted to make sure that you're still on board with the idea of us opening our own practice one day." He slowed at a stoplight, the car motor making a soft knocking noise. "I've been

103

getting the sense lately that you might have had a . . . change of heart."

Josh pressed his lips into a tight line. For several seconds, he remained silent, then he exhaled and shook his head. "Nothing's changed. I've sent in my acceptance to the university."

"You have?" A wave of relief crashed through Mark's system. "Why didn't you say anything?"

Josh just raised a brow.

"All right. I get it. You don't need your brother overseeing everything you do."

"Exactly."

Mark turned the car onto their street. "I'm sorry if I've been a bit . . . overbearing lately. It's just that I've been worried about you." He pulled up in front of the house and turned off the engine. "From now on, I promise to do my best to give you some space and respect your independence."

Josh turned to look at him fully for the first time. "You mean it?"

"I'm going to try my best." Inwardly, Mark cringed a little. It was harder than he thought to relinquish control. How did parents do this? "But if you ever have a problem or need help with anything, you only have to ask."

A half smirk played on Josh's lips. "Now that you mention it, I'll need you to pay the first portion of my tuition soon."

Mark laughed out loud, easing the tension in his chest. "I knew I was good for something."

As they headed into the house, he gave a silent prayer of gratitude. Maybe—just maybe—he and Josh had turned a corner in their relationship tonight. And that could mean all the difference in keeping Josh on track for his future.

13

Isabelle backed out of the hotel room she was cleaning and tugged the Hoover vacuum with her. The wheels hooked onto the lip of the entryway and refused to budge. Giving it a sharp yank, she pulled until the wheels suddenly gave way and rolled over the bump into the corridor. Fighting to keep her balance, she backed into her supply cart, jostling it hard. In one desperate movement, she reached out to grab a bottle of bleach that almost fell off the side.

Disaster averted.

She took a moment to catch her breath, then set the bottle back in its spot. Mrs. Herbert would have her head if she ruined any of the items and would likely deduct the cost from her pay. Isabelle had been working on her own without Mary Eggerton's supervision for a few days now, and she needed everything to go smoothly. She moved the cart closer to the wall and wiped her sleeve across her forehead. Thankfully, all the supplies appeared intact.

"Isabelle? Is that you?" An incredulous male voice came from farther down the hall.

She looked up to see Elias Weatherby staring at her, his mouth agape.

Humiliation burned Isabelle's cheeks as she smoothed down

her apron and suppressed a groan. Of all the people to run into, a former suitor.

She pulled herself up tall. "Hello, Elias. What are you doing here?" He lived in the city, so he'd have no need for a room, unless he was having a secret rendezvous with a woman. Her palms began to sweat on the cart handle.

"I was about to call on a client who's visiting from out of town. We're to have lunch together." His eyes narrowed as he scanned her from the top of her maid's cap to her sensible rubber-soled shoes. "Don't tell me you're working here?" His voice notched up in disbelief, matching the rise of his fair brows.

"Very well. I won't tell you." She gave the cart a shove toward the next room on her list.

"I heard about your father's company, but I had no idea things had gotten so dire." His horrified expression did nothing to ease her discomfort.

"Yes, well, extreme circumstances call for extreme measures. This is only a temporary step until I find a more suitable position."

He followed her down the corridor. "What happened to Roger Noland? I heard you two were serious and that he was about to propose. That's why I stopped pursuing you myself."

Isabelle was fairly certain Roger wasn't the only reason, but she was too polite to challenge him. She fumbled with her ring of keys. "Roger got a job out west in British Columbia."

"And he didn't take you with him?"

"No." She fit the key into the next room's door. "If you'll excuse me, I have a schedule to keep."

"Isabelle . . ." His eyes swam with sympathy.

Sympathy she didn't want or need.

"It was nice to see you, Elias. Please give my regards to your family." She slipped inside the room and closed the door firmly behind her. With her back to the hard surface, she squeezed her eyes shut and waited for her heart rate to slow. After several seconds, she heard muffled footsteps retreating down the hall.

She let out a long breath. She supposed it was to be expected that she would run across former friends and would have to bear the discomfort of their pity. The Wardrop debutante now relegated to working as a mere hotel maid. She imagined Elias would waste no time relating her fate to all who used to know her.

Think of Marissa. You can endure anything for her sake.

Isabelle took another deep breath, cracked the door open, and looked out into the corridor. Satisfied that no one was around, she went out to retrieve the vacuum and then continued with her work, determined to put the encounter with Elias behind her.

As she pushed the Hoover over the plush carpet, her thoughts inevitably returned to her sister. Despite the conversation they'd had while walking to the bus the other day, Isabelle still wasn't convinced that Marissa would abandon her relationship with that boy. She obviously had a crush on him, which could impede her common sense. Isabelle needed to do whatever she could to discourage the budding romance so it didn't end up distracting Marissa from getting a college education.

Isabelle wielded the vacuum with extra vigor. As she'd told Mark, she planned to accompany Marissa to the choir practices from now on, as long as her schedule permitted. That would give her a much better idea of exactly what she was dealing with. And with Isabelle as a chaperone, Marissa would be far less inclined to do anything reckless.

Isabelle pushed the vacuum into the hall, then returned to the room, leaving the door slightly ajar. She pulled back the blankets and began to strip the bedsheets and pillow slips. Wrapping them all into a large ball, she took them out to the hallway, grabbed the clean linens, and returned inside. She was leaning over the mattress, smoothing the fresh sheets into place, when a man walked into the room.

"Well, hello there," he drawled. "Who do we have here?" His large shoulders spanned the width of the doorframe.

Isabelle jumped upright, her heart slamming into her throat. "I-I'm sorry, sir. I can come back later when it's more convenient."

He closed the door behind him. "That won't be necessary. I just came back to change my jacket. The clumsy waitress spilled coffee all over it." He began to unbutton his jacket, his eyes never leaving Isabelle. The lustful look he gave her made her skin crawl.

She edged her way toward the end of the bed, eying the path to the door. "Excuse me, I need to get something from my cart." Head down, she rushed toward the door.

But he moved quickly to bar her way. "It can wait for a few minutes."

"No, it can't. I have a tight schedule to keep. In fact, my supervisor should be here any minute to check my work." She gripped her hands together to hide their trembling, praying he believed her fib. She lifted her chin and forced herself to look him in the eye. "Let me pass, *sir*."

He stepped closer, a menacing sneer on his face. "Be careful, missy. You wouldn't want me to complain about your work to the hotel manager, would you?"

"Go ahead." Her insides quaked, but she held her ground. *Heaven help me.* Would anyone hear her if she screamed?

He gripped her upper arm. "I don't think you understand your place. Or exactly who you're dealing with."

"And I don't think you know who you're dealing with." Isabelle stomped down on his foot with all her might and shoved him in the chest.

He teetered backward, howling his rage.

Taking advantage of his imbalanced state, she raced for the door, yanked it open, and dashed out into the hallway. Up ahead, two men emerged from one of the rooms.

She rushed toward them, praying they possessed some shred of decency.

One of the men turned, and relief made Isabelle's knees threaten to sag. "Elias. Thank heavens you're still here."

His fair eyebrows winged upward. "Isabelle? What's wrong?"

She paused to catch her breath.

"You're white as these walls." Elias's features radiated concern. "Tell me what's happened."

"I . . . I . . ."

Footsteps sounded behind her. "Grab that girl. Don't let her get away."

She stiffened her spine and straightened, pressing her lips together.

Elias moved forward to intercept the man. "Is there a problem, sir?"

"There most certainly is. This little chit has stolen money from my room." The man's mustache quivered with his feigned outrage.

Isabelle's lungs seemed to seize, but she forced herself to take a breath. "You're lying. I did no such thing."

Elias moved between them. "There must be some mistake. I'm sure we can sort this out." He reached into his pants pocket and removed his wallet. "How much is missing?"

The man's mouth opened and closed. "The amount doesn't matter. Theft is theft. I want this woman prosecuted."

Elias turned back to his companion. "Mr. Sellner, would you take Miss Wardrop down the hall, please?"

Mr. Sellner appeared completely baffled, but he nodded.

Elias leaned toward her. "Please go with my friend. I'll handle this."

She longed to stay, to argue her innocence, but the glowering hotel guest stole her bravado. He held the power to get her fired from this job. A job she desperately needed. As Mrs. Herbert constantly reminded them, the guests were right ninety-nine percent of the time, and the other one percent didn't matter. Isabelle gave Elias a nod and walked over to Mr. Sellner's side.

"What will it take to make this . . . situation disappear?" Elias's curt words followed her down the hall.

"I take it you and Mr. Weatherby know each other?" Mr. Sellner asked as he escorted her to the far end of the long corridor. He was a middle-aged man with salt-and-pepper hair and kind eyes.

"Yes. In another life." She resisted the urge to peer over her shoulder to see if Elias was having any luck with the man who could ruin her.

"I see." Mr. Sellner glanced over at her. "What really happened back there?"

Isabelle twisted her hands together. "That man came in when I was changing the bed. He . . . he cornered me, but I managed to get away."

"The cad. And he has the nerve to accuse you of theft?"

"He threatened to lodge a complaint before I got away. Trying to coerce me into submitting to him. But I would never do that." She raised her eyes to his. "You believe me, don't you?"

"I do. I've seen enough men like him in my day, trust me." They reached an alcove at the end of the corridor. "Let's wait here."

She sank onto a bench, her legs too shaky to hold her up. Mr. Sellner stood in the corridor, almost like a guard, providing her some comfort.

A few minutes later, Elias appeared.

Isabelle jumped to her feet. "What happened? Is he going to tell the manager?"

Elias took her hand. "It's all right. You won't have to worry about him anymore."

"Why not?"

"I won't bother you with the sordid details. Just promise me you'll avoid his room until he's gone."

She covered his hand with hers. "I don't know how to thank you."

Elias smiled. "No thanks needed. I'm only glad I was here. Will you be all right?"

"Yes, I think so."

"Very well. Take care, Isabelle. I hope to see you again."

Mr. Sellner gave her a bow, and they headed toward the elevators.

Thank you, Lord, for Elias Weatherby. Without him I most assuredly would have been fired . . . or worse.

Isabelle took a deep breath before heading back to her cart and pushing it to another room much farther down the hall. From now on, she would put on the inside lock while she cleaned. It would at least buy her time to react if anyone ever walked in on her again.

14

In the unnatural silence of the emergency room cubicle, Mark's labored breathing was the only sound that broke the stillness. Even the other background noises seemed muted, as though time had come to a standstill.

Sweat poured from Mark's brow and drenched his clothing.

"I'm afraid he's gone, Doctor," one of the nurses finally said.

Reluctantly, he stepped back from the body on the gurney. Defeat saturated his muscles and spread through his torso. All his efforts to get the young man breathing again had failed. He checked the clock on the wall. "Time of death is fourteen twenty-three." He peeled the blood-soaked gloves from his hands and threw them into a nearby trash can. Turning his back to the others in the room, he closed his eyes and pinched the bridge of his nose.

The man had been just been brought in, apparently hit by a car while crossing the street. Immediate surgery to stop the internal bleeding was needed, which meant that his vital signs had to be stabilized. But the damage had been too great, and all their efforts to save him had been in vain.

Mark sensed someone come up behind him.

"Dr. Henshaw, the family is waiting for word," one of the nurses said.

He squared his shoulders, made sure his professional mask was in place, and turned. "I'll go and inform them now. Will you and Nurse Hart please clean the area and prepare the body? The family members will want to view their son."

"Yes, Doctor."

He pulled off his facial mask and stripped off the soiled gown. Thankfully, his clothing underneath remained clean, although somewhat soggy from perspiration. With dread building in his chest, he walked out to the waiting area.

Immediately, two people shot to their feet. A man and woman clutched each other, their expressions a mixture of hope and terror.

Mark's stomach sank the closer he came to them. "Mr. and Mrs. Brower?"

"Yes, that's us. How's our son, Doctor?"

He hesitated, delaying the moment before these people's lives would change forever. At last, Mark couldn't put off the inevitable any longer. "I'm terribly sorry, but I'm afraid he didn't make it."

A wail escaped from the woman, who crumpled against her husband. Mr. Brower bore the news stoically, though his eyes radiated his unspoken pain.

"I'm sorry," Mark said again. "I did everything I could. The damage from the accident was simply too extensive."

The couple clung together, grief etched in the lines on their faces.

"Can we see him?" the gentleman asked.

"Yes, of course. If you'll follow me, I'll take you to him."

The woman's heart-wrenching sobs over her son's body stayed with Mark for the rest of the day, haunting him. Later that night, as he made his way home, he couldn't get the patient off his mind. The young man was barely twenty-one years old, and his life had been snuffed out by a random motorist's wrong turn. All Mark could think about was Josh. It could be him lying on that steel table. His body the one the coroner was taking to the morgue. He shuddered at the thought and vowed to try even harder to work on their relationship.

Life was too short to take anything for granted.

❖

Isabelle clocked out of the hotel at three o'clock on the dot. It was a rarity to finish her shift right on time. Usually, one of the guests would waylay her with a demand for more towels or an extra pillow and she'd have to make the long trek to the supply cupboard to fulfill their request.

After quickly changing out of her uniform, she grabbed her purse and ran up the stairs to the main level, then out the side door to the street. If she hurried, she might even catch the three-thirty bus and make it home in time to help Rosie prepare supper.

The warm afternoon sun shone on her face as she walked briskly down the sidewalk. She breathed deeply, attempting to rid herself of the frustrations of the day. The work itself was more than challenging, but it was the crass treatment by the hotel guests that rankled the most. Today, a woman had stopped her in the hallway and demanded that Isabelle crawl underneath her bed to retrieve an earring she'd dropped. Isabelle had had to bite her lip to keep from telling her to find her own earring. But Mrs. Herbert's warnings about the guests always being right rang in her head, and so she'd begrudgingly complied.

Isabelle came to a halt along with the other pedestrians at a red light. She tapped her toe and strained to see down the street for any sign of the bus arriving.

"Isabelle!" a male voice called. "Isabelle, wait up."

She turned to see Elias Weatherby rushing toward her, one hand holding his hat in place.

"I thought I'd missed you," he puffed as he reached her.

She pushed down a thread of annoyance. Not that she didn't appreciate his rescue last week, but it didn't mean she wanted him to keep showing up in her life. Still, her manners kicked in, and she managed a brief smile. "Elias, hello. Is there something you need?"

He paused to catch his breath. "I was hoping we could maybe get a coffee and . . . talk."

Her mouth went slack. What on earth could they have to talk about? "I-I have to catch a bus right now. Perhaps another time?"

"If you can spare me a few minutes, I'll drive you home myself. I'm sure it will be quicker than the bus."

Dismay wound through her system. She did not want her former suitor to see where she and her sister were living now. Immediate shame engulfed her, imagining how hurt Rosie would be to know Isabelle's thoughts.

"Please, Isabelle. It's important."

He seemed so earnest that she hesitated. After all, she owed him one since he'd helped her out of a bad situation. She supposed it wouldn't hurt to at least see what he wanted. "Very well."

"Thank you." Relief spread across his features. "There's a coffee shop on the next block." He put a hand to her back and guided her in the direction he indicated.

A strained silence fell between them as they walked, with only the sound of passing traffic to ease the discomfort. Elias ushered her inside the diner and chose a table by the window. The smell of frying bacon and strong coffee permeated the air. A waitress arrived almost immediately to take their order of two coffees and a slice of apple pie for Elias.

Once the girl left, Isabelle leaned forward. "So, Elias, what do you wish to discuss? Does this have something to do with the incident at the hotel?"

"Not directly, no." His fair brows bunched together as he opened a napkin and draped it across his lap. "The truth is that ever since I ran into you, I haven't been able to get you off my mind. I feel terrible for what you've been through, losing your parents and your home. I can't imagine how distressing this has been for you."

She held his gaze, biting back the remark that sprang to mind. If he felt so terrible, why had he ignored her since Daddy died? "It has indeed been a trying time. But Marissa and I will land on our feet again."

A dull shade of red crept into his cheeks. "I owe you an apology for not being more . . . solicitous after the death of your father."

Ah, perhaps now he'd confess his reason for avoiding her.

"I did come to see you in the days that followed. Twice, in fact. Both times Roger Noland was there. When I saw his car parked almost permanently in your drive, I surmised that he must have proposed and was there as your future husband. Not wishing to intrude, I opted to simply send a card. A poor substitute, I know."

She remained silent for a moment, taking in his confession as the waitress delivered the coffee and pie. Once she'd left, Isabelle said, "Thank you for telling me this. I assumed you were ignoring us, like so many others, out of embarrassment or disdain for the way my father died."

"Not at all. Unfortunately, my motives were more selfishly motivated, trying to save myself additional heartache."

Heartache? Was it possible he cared for her that much?

Elias reached across the table and covered her hand. "I hate seeing you like this, Isabelle. In such a lowly position, cleaning people's rooms, being subjected to vile men like the one who tried to accost you." He shook his head. "You were born for better than that."

Isabelle stiffened. Though being a maid wasn't ideal, it bothered her to hear him describe it in such a demeaning manner. "It may not be pretty, but it's good, honest work, Elias." She almost winced at the statement, realizing that a year ago she never would have uttered such a thing.

"I'm sorry. I meant no disrespect." When his gaze met hers, a host of emotion swirled in his gray eyes. Concern, admiration, and maybe a hint of nervousness?

Isabelle couldn't begin to fathom what he was thinking.

"What would you say if I asked permission to court you again?"

Her heart began a loud thump in her chest, and she wrapped her hands around her coffee mug. What did he mean, insulting her job in one breath and asking to court her in another? "I-I don't know."

A film of light perspiration appeared on his forehead. "I hold you in the highest regard, Isabelle. I always have. Even when you seemed to prefer Roger over me, I only wanted your happiness, which is why I backed away. But now that I know the true state of affairs, I'd like to try again, if you're willing."

She hesitated, her mind swirling with possibilities. Elias was a man of high standing in the community, a man of comfortable means, seemingly honest and of good character. She'd always found him amiable in an unexciting but pleasant sort of way. What could it hurt to go on a few outings with him and see where it led?

"I suppose that would be acceptable," she said slowly.

"Wonderful." The tension eased from his rigid frame as a smile slowly creased his face. "Will you have dinner with me tomorrow?"

Thoughts raced in her head. "I suppose so. I could meet you around five o'clock. Or is that too early?"

"Five is fine." He frowned. "But I intend to pick you up, as a proper date should. Where are you staying now?"

She bit her lip, loath to have him see how low she had fallen. "My sister and I are staying with friends. I'd prefer that Marissa not know we're seeing each other yet. Until things are more settled one way or another."

"I understand." His brow furrowed. "Is Grange Park anywhere nearby? I thought perhaps a picnic might be nice if the weather cooperates."

Relief surged through her. "That sounds lovely. Grange Park isn't far at all." If things progressed with their courtship, Elias would have to eventually know where she lived, but for now she wanted to present the best possible picture for him.

"All right. I'll meet you at the entrance on Beverley Street at five o'clock tomorrow."

"Agreed." She managed a genuine smile.

He lifted her hand to his lips. "You've made me very happy, Isabelle. Until tomorrow."

15

What now?

Mark paced the hall outside the office of the head of the emergency department. Dr. Shriver had sent a message, asking Mark to come to see him as soon as he had a free moment. A highly unusual invitation.

Nerves roiled in his stomach, making him wish he hadn't downed that second cup of coffee. Was this to chastise him over losing a patient? Had the boy's parents demanded an investigation into their son's death? He'd done everything in his power to save the boy's life, yet a feeling of guilt persisted, nagging him that he could possibly have done more.

High heels sounded on the tiled floor as the doctor's receptionist appeared. "Dr. Shriver is ready for you now, Dr. Henshaw."

"Thank you." As he headed inside, Mark said a silent prayer for the wisdom to deal with whatever situation lay ahead.

Dr. Shriver looked up as he entered. He was a fit, middle-aged man, known for being blunt, which wouldn't win him any awards for congeniality.

"You wanted to see me, sir?"

"Yes. Sit down, please." He motioned to the guest chair.

As he took a seat, Mark tried to gauge the man's mood. From

his expression, he didn't appear upset. Maybe he wasn't going to get a reprimand after all.

"I'll get right to the point." Dr. Shriver's features didn't change, save for a subtle tic in his jaw. "There have been several concerns brought to my attention, and I've been asked to address them with you."

That didn't sound good. Mark shifted his weight. "What type of concerns?"

Dr. Shriver kept his gaze steady. "First off, there's long been talk about your association with a local home for unwed mothers. The hospital board thinks this makes it look like we condone the lifestyles and poor judgment of the women who make use of this establishment."

Mark's jaw locked, trapping his outrage inside him as he struggled for an appropriate reply.

"Second," Dr. Shriver continued, "your visits to the tenement buildings have raised concerns that you might be inadvertently bringing unwanted disease into the hospital. I'm sure you're aware of the recent cases of polio and rheumatic fever that have been reported there."

"I'm very aware, sir. Which is precisely why I go to treat the people who wouldn't otherwise seek any type of medical help."

"A noble intention. However, you must see the risk involved in exposing other staff and patients to these maladies."

"I'm always extremely careful not to bring any sort of contamination with me. Just as I am inside these hospital walls. As for my patients at the maternity home, I neither condone nor condemn their actions. They are simply expectant mothers who need medical help. The women—and more importantly, the babies—deserve the same level of care that any other mother and child receives." He took in a slow breath and released it. "If I were to withhold treatment of any patient based on how I view their actions, the list of people I treat would be woefully small."

Dr. Shriver tapped his fingers together as he studied Mark.

Finally, he leaned forward. "Your passion for the less fortunate members of society is admirable, Dr. Henshaw. I am simply passing on observations from the hospital board of directors and concerns from various staff members. I'm not attempting to tell you what to do. I am merely offering you insight as to what might prove detrimental to your career going forward. Trust me, this is not the type of attention you wish to attract."

Mark clenched his hands into fists on his lap and used all his willpower to remain calm.

"There is another important item of concern that may be loosely tied to the first two issues." The other man tilted his head. "Some of your colleagues mentioned that lately you appear over-tired and somewhat distracted while on duty. I can only assume this is due to your burning the candle at both ends."

Mark pressed his lips together to keep from blurting out something he couldn't take back. However, the truth was that Dr. Shriver had a point. He had been working many more hours than usual and not getting enough sleep.

"One of the nurses noticed you weren't at your best yesterday when the Brower boy was brought in." A hint of accusation laced the man's tone.

Mark's head snapped up. "Is she insinuating I contributed to his death?"

"Not directly, no. Just that you weren't performing at your best."

Mark gripped the armrest, fighting a rising sense of betrayal. Was everyone conspiring against him?

"The hospital can't dictate what you do on your off time, except when it impacts your performance within these walls." Dr. Shriver paused, a frown creasing his brow. "I'm afraid I must insist that, at the very least, you quit working at the maternity home."

Mark struggled to keep control of his emotions. "Other doctors have practices outside the hospital. Do you give them these types of ultimatums?"

"If their work is unsatisfactory, then yes. But most of the doctors who have privileges in this hospital manage to balance their practice with their hospital duties. Forgive me for being blunt, but it appears to me that your life has become woefully out of balance."

Dr. Shriver gave him a frank stare. "The reality remains that if you work for a hospital, there are rules that must be followed. We need you performing at your best."

Mark took in the unwavering set to the man's jaw and realized that arguing with him would be futile. "I understand."

"I've decided to give you a week's leave to make the necessary changes. Or you can take it as vacation time. Your choice. I trust this will be sufficient leeway to get your . . . priorities in order." Dr. Shriver picked up his pen, a signal that the conversation was over. He didn't need to add the implied "or else."

Mark rose and nodded. "Understood."

Forcing back his agitation, Mark exited the office and made his way to the staircase. The reprimand poked at Mark's deepest doubts concerning his career and where he wanted it to go. He'd sensed for some time that his work on the side wasn't approved of by the hospital, and Mark chafed at their dictating his life outside this institution.

Like his work with the maternity home.

Mark grunted as he pushed through the staircase door. How was he going to break the news to Olivia and Ruth? And to all the people he took care of in the tenement buildings? People who counted on him to help the children and the elderly?

His dream of opening his own medical practice, where he could see the patients he chose without any outside interference or judgment, remained murky at best—somewhere in the distant future, once Josh was close to finishing his degree.

Besides, Mark had no money to pour into a business right now, not when he had years ahead of helping Josh with his tuition.

No, there really was no other option at the moment. He'd have to set his own desires aside for the time being and follow Dr. Shriver's directive.

After work on Monday, Isabelle studied her wardrobe in the small closet. What did one wear for a picnic in May? Nothing too fancy, since they would likely be sitting on the ground. Perhaps a simple dress with ample material to cover her legs while seated on a blanket. She selected a blue dress with tiny yellow flowers and a matching cardigan, in case it got cool.

Bracing herself for the barrage of questions, Isabelle stepped out into the living area.

Marissa glanced up from her schoolbook. "You look nice, Belle. Are you going somewhere?"

"I'm meeting a friend from the hotel for dinner." The practiced words rolled smoothly off her tongue. It wasn't a direct lie, since Elias was a friend and she had run into him at the hotel.

"That's nice," Aunt Rosie said, turning from her spot at the stove. "You deserve to have some fun. Where are you going?"

"It's such a beautiful day. We might have a picnic in the park." She busied herself tidying her purse, avoiding their eyes. Fastening the clasp shut, she smiled. "Well, I'd best be off."

"Have fun." Aunt Rosie waved her off with a cheery salute of her wooden spoon.

Isabelle went out the door, glad Fiona was hardly ever home this early. Her friend would surely have seen through her ruse in a second.

The ten-minute walk to the park dispelled the rest of her tension, and by the time Isabelle spotted Elias on the sidewalk, she was in a much more relaxed mood. He wore gray slacks and a white shirt. In one hand, he carried a picnic basket, with a blanket draped over his other arm.

"You look lovely." He greeted her with a smile.

"Thank you. It seems you came prepared."

"I hope so. It certainly is a beautiful day for a picnic."

They turned onto the path leading into the park. When they reached a somewhat secluded area beneath a large oak tree, he set the basket on the grass. "Does this spot suit you?"

"It's perfect." Private enough for a conversation, but still within view of the people out for a stroll.

He unfolded the blanket and spread it over the grass. Then he took her hand and helped her sit down.

"I picked up the food at Schmidt's Deli." He laughed. "I didn't want to subject you to my culinary skills just yet."

"I'm sure it will be delicious."

He removed several wrapped sandwiches, two bottles of lemonade, and some linen napkins.

She opened a napkin on her lap and took the sandwich he offered. "Smoked ham and cheese. One of my favorites."

"Mine as well."

They ate in congenial silence for a while, then Elias began telling her how his investment business had been slow of late but that he had hopes of it picking up soon.

"And how is your family faring?" Isabelle asked as they topped off their meal with homemade apple tarts. She remembered that he lived with his widowed mother and sister in their family home.

"Very well, thank you for asking. Mother keeps busy with her church group and her charity work. And Christine has recently become engaged. She hopes to be married by Christmas."

"How nice," Isabelle murmured politely. She'd only met his mother and sister a few times at various church and holiday functions. They seemed pleasant enough, though a bit standoffish.

"Which brings me to a topic I wish to discuss."

The intensity in his expression made nerves jump in her stomach. "Oh?"

"I'd hoped to take more time with this, but with Christine already planning a wedding in the near future, time doesn't allow me to dally." He reached over to take her hand and looked her in the eye. "I have admired you for several years now, Isabelle. I believe our personalities suit each other and that we could make a most congenial match." He took a breath. "I hope you don't think this terribly improper, but I would be honored if you would consider marrying me."

"Marrying you?" She blinked, certain she must have heard wrong.

"That's right." He leaned closer, his expression earnest. "I can offer you and your sister the type of lifestyle you were used to. You wouldn't have to work or worry about where you're going to live. And Marissa would have the security of a good family name behind her. Your futures would be set."

Isabelle's heart began an unsteady rhythm as she allowed herself to imagine her life as Elias's wife. She would be married to an investment broker, a man well respected in the city. Their lifestyle would be similar to the one her parents had shared. Elias would be the breadwinner and Isabelle would play hostess for his various parties and social functions. In addition, she could fulfill her promise to her mother and continue to support her charities.

But best of all, Marissa would have every advantage. She wouldn't have to depend on a scholarship to go to college. She could do whatever her heart desired. And it was within Isabelle's power to give her that. How could she refuse such an opportunity?

She glanced up into Elias's expectant face. He wasn't a handsome man, but his features exuded kindness. Even though he was a fair bit older than her, Daddy had thought they'd make a good match. She'd gone out with him a few times, and though he seemed nice enough, she simply hadn't felt any romantic spark. Not like she had for Roger. Still, she was fond of Elias, which was a good foundation for a marriage, or so she'd been told. Fondness could grow into something more, couldn't it?

"I-I don't know what to say, Elias. You've certainly caught me off guard."

"You don't have to decide right this minute. But promise me you'll think about it." When he lifted her hand to his lips, a hopeful expression lit his face.

"I doubt I'll be able to think about much else."

He sat back and studied her. "Would a couple of days be enough time?"

"That should be fine." Isabelle picked up her purse and rose from the blanket.

He rushed to his feet. "Please allow me to drive you home."

"Actually, I'd prefer to walk, if you don't mind. You've given me a lot to think about."

"Of course. I understand." He gave a slight bow, ever the gentleman. "I'll wait for you to contact me, then. But don't leave me in suspense too long." His smile belied the uncertainty in his gaze.

"I won't. Thank you for the lovely picnic." She flashed him a brief smile before heading down the path out of the park.

Once out of his sight, she clasped her trembling hands together, her thoughts churning more than the acidic lemonade in her system.

If she married Elias, she'd never have to clean another toilet or take orders from another surly hotel patron again. Something to keep in mind as she weighed the pros and cons of his proposal.

16

Grimly, Mark climbed the stairs to the Bennington Place front entrance, feeling as though he was approaching the gallows. He'd purposely waited until after dinner to meet with Ruth and Olivia, hoping that most of the women would be settled in for the evening. Josh had already left for choir practice, and with no other excuses to delay this meeting, he'd telephoned and asked the two women if he could speak with them.

He had barely been able to eat a bite of dinner, knowing what he was about to do. He dreaded giving them the news, dreaded letting them down this way. Ruth Bennington had been one of his first private patients. Her standing in the community had opened many doors for him. Now, he was about to leave her and Olivia in the lurch. Would any other doctor be willing to take his place at the maternity home?

He recalled the way the two women had been forced to fight the neighbors and other businesses in the area to stay open. It had been a hard-won battle with the city council to obtain that right, which proved how many people still held on to old prejudices and judgments.

Ruth greeted him at the door. "Hello, Mark. Please come in."

The tension around her eyes told him she knew this meeting was out of the ordinary.

"Thank you for seeing me on such short notice."

"It's no problem for me since I live here. Luckily, Olivia's husband didn't mind looking after the children this evening." Ruth gestured down the hall. "I thought we'd sit in the sunroom. It's a little more spacious than my office."

"Fine." He'd never seen Ruth act so . . . formally around him.

Olivia was already seated on the wicker sofa in the glass-enclosed sunroom. The beginning of an orange sunset cast a warm glow around the space.

"Hello, Mark." Olivia's smile was tentative.

He nodded to her, his throat too tight at the moment to speak. He took a seat across from her while Ruth joined Olivia on the sofa.

"We won't waste time with pleasantries," the older woman said. "I sense something serious is afoot for you to have requested this meeting."

Mark looked from her regal face to Olivia's worried one. "Unfortunately, you're correct." In terse terms, he told them about the hospital's ultimatum.

"Oh, Mark. I'm so sorry." Olivia's brow furrowed with concern. "I often worried that your association with us might prove detrimental to you in some way, and now it has."

"What about your private patients?" Ruth asked. "Do you have to give them up too?"

"Dr. Shriver didn't say so outright. Most doctors have their own practices and see other patients. But he did mention that some of the staff aren't thrilled about my work in the tenements."

Olivia frowned. "I know how much it means to you being able to help the less fortunate. What are you going to do?"

"I'm not sure." He rose and shoved his hands into his pockets while he paced to the wall of windows. "If I didn't need the security of my job at the hospital, I'd start my own practice now, instead of waiting until Josh graduates from medical school. But with his tuition to pay for the next several years, I'll need that steady paycheck."

"Where were you thinking of basing this practice?"

The change in Ruth's tone had Mark turning to face her.

"I'd hoped to find something fairly close to the tenements so the residents would feel comfortable coming in."

"Wouldn't that make it difficult for other people who might not want to venture into that area?" Olivia asked.

"The best-case scenario would be something on the outskirts, a location accessible to both the poor and the middle-class residents. For my more affluent patients, I could drive to their homes and see them privately."

"I think what you're proposing would be a godsend for those people." Ruth's brow furrowed, indicating she was deep in thought. "What would you say if I could find an investor willing to help fund such a clinic?"

Mark's eyes widened. "I'd never even considered that. Do you have someone in mind?"

"I don't wish to say just yet. Let me make some phone calls tomorrow and see what I can do." She leveled a pointed look at him. "In the meantime, I suggest you start looking for an appropriate office space."

Mark's mind whirled with possibilities. Could this really be happening?

"And if you need to appease your supervisor at the hospital until we see what happens, I will accept your *temporary* resignation." Ruth winked at him.

He shook his head. "I don't know what to say. This is all a little overwhelming."

Olivia clapped her hands together and rose from the sofa. "I know it's always been your dream to open a clinic. This might be the perfect way to accomplish it."

"Maybe so." Mark smiled. What had only been a vague dream

for the future now shimmered within his reach. "I'll let you know if I find a suitable space, Ruth. And I look forward to hearing from you about a possible investor." He paused, emotion tightening his chest. "Thank you both. I'd been dreading this conversation, but you've managed to turn this into something positive."

"My pleasure." Ruth gave him another wink. "I always enjoy getting my peers to part with their money."

Mark left the maternity home in a state of excited bewilderment. The meeting had certainly not gone the way he'd expected. Instead of coming out in defeat, he felt filled with new purpose.

He could hardly wait to get home and tell Josh about it.

As he got into his car, he checked his watch. His brother should be home from choir practice by now. Hopefully he would be as excited as Mark was about this potential change in plans.

But the house sat in an unnatural stillness as Mark let himself in. Odd that no lights were on in the kitchen. His brother was notorious for leaving them on, claiming he didn't like being alone in a dark house.

Mark flipped on the kitchen light and looked around. The room appeared unusually clean. No dirty dishes on the counter or bread left out. Normally the first thing Josh did when he got home was make himself a snack.

Mark's gut began to churn with a sense of unease as he walked upstairs to the bedrooms. Josh's door was closed. Mark knocked on it twice. "Josh, you in there?"

When there was no response, Mark opened the door and turned on the light.

The bedroom was as empty as the kitchen. Mark's gaze snagged on the black case in the corner, and his heart jumped into his throat.

Josh's guitar. He never went to practice without it.

Something wasn't right.

All thoughts of his good news instantly fled. Without taking time to think, Mark raced back out to his car and headed directly over to the church. If he was lucky, perhaps he'd find Josh there, chatting with some of the choir members. Maybe there would be a perfectly innocent explanation for him not being home.

The door to the church basement was unlocked. Mark breathed in a sigh of relief at the sound of voices coming from below. They were still here. Everything was all right.

He rushed down the stairs and into the auditorium. The choir director was there, talking to a few students. But none of them was Josh.

Mr. Henchley turned at the sound of Mark's footsteps. "Oh, Dr. Henshaw. I'm glad you're here. I tried telephoning you several times earlier this evening but there was no answer. Is everything all right with Josh?"

The air thinned in Mark's lungs. "What do you mean? Isn't he here?"

"No, he didn't show up tonight. That's why I was calling. But when there was no answer, I hoped there was a simple explanation."

"You mean you haven't seen or heard from him?"

"No, I haven't."

The vision of his patient lying lifeless on the steel gurney flashed through Mark's mind. He put a hand to the wall to steady himself. Where on earth could Josh be?

Mr. Henchley brought over a chair. "Here, have a seat. I'm sorry to give you such a shock."

"When Josh wasn't at home, I assumed he got held up here. I have no idea where he could be." Mark leaned over his knees and inhaled deeply.

"I wouldn't worry too much. Young men sometimes need to blow off a little steam."

What did he mean by that? In Mark's whole life, he'd never blown off any steam. He ran a hand through his hair. So much for giving Josh some space. The first bit of freedom and this is what he does?

"Maybe he and Marissa ran off together," one of the girls said with a laugh.

The boy only snorted. "Yeah, in his dreams."

"Well, it's no secret he has a huge crush on her."

Another girl gave a high-pitched giggle in response.

Mark's ears burned. Not only was Josh missing but . . . "Did Marissa not show up either?"

"No, she didn't." Mr. Henchley's face was grim. "And since she's recently moved, I had no way to contact her family."

Mark held back a groan. Isabelle must be out of her mind with worry. Unless Marissa was at home and had decided not to attend choir practice tonight. Either way, Mark needed to find out. If the girl was home, she might be able to shed some light on Josh's whereabouts.

"Thank you for your time, Mr. Henchley. I'm sorry for the trouble."

"Good luck."

The words rang in Mark's ears. *Please, God, help me to know where to look and keep them both safe until I find them.*

17

Isabelle sat up and rubbed her eyes, trying to get her bearings. The pounding in her temples from her headache earlier had thankfully subsided, but something had awoken her from a deep sleep. The murmur of voices drifted in from the outer rooms. Was Marissa home from her choir practice already?

At dinner, Isabelle had been preoccupied to say the least. With Elias's proposal uppermost on her mind, her headache had only gotten worse. So much so that Marissa had insisted she stay home and rest.

Begrudgingly, Isabelle had agreed, fulling intending on making it to the church in time to accompany her sister home. She jerked to her feet, realizing it was pitch dark. Was she too late?

A low male voice sounded from the other room, sending a prickle of unease up her spine. Who would be here at this time of night?

She turned on the bedside lamp and took in a deep breath. Then smoothed down her hair, straightened her clothing, and went out to the kitchen.

Mark Henshaw stood just inside the front door. Beneath a sweep of brown hair, his brow was furrowed. Aunt Rosie hovered beside him, a grim expression on her face.

"What's wrong?" Isabelle's stomach tightened, and she pressed a hand against it, as if to shield herself from what was to come. She couldn't take one more bit of bad news.

"Marissa isn't home yet." Aunt Rosie's quiet statement had the hairs on Isabelle's neck rising.

"And Josh is missing too," Mark said.

"W-what time is it?"

"A little after nine."

"Oh." Isabelle's legs grew weak, and she sank onto the arm of one of the living room chairs. Where could Marissa be? Had she gone somewhere after choir?

Mark came over and stood beside her. "Marissa never showed up at the church. Neither did Josh. I can only assume they're together."

"Never showed up? But she left hours ago." The blood in Isabelle's veins seemed to run cold amidst the panic rising in her chest. "Could they be at your house?"

Mark shook his head. "I got home about eight-thirty, and there was no sign of them."

Her worst fears were coming true. This relationship seemed to be gaining momentum by the day. Where would a young couple go to be alone? She took a deep breath. "Do you have your car here?"

"Yes. It's right outside."

She rose on shaky legs. "We have to look for them. Let me get a sweater."

"I'll go." Mark moved to the door. "Why don't you stay here in case she comes back?"

She stiffened, resolve infusing her with strength. "Marissa is my responsibility. I'm coming with you."

Guilt churned in Isabelle's stomach as Mark pulled the car away from the house. Judging by the way he held the steering wheel in an iron grip, he was feeling the same sense of anger and worry. What could Marissa be thinking, running off like this without telling anyone?

A terrible thought crossed her mind. What if she and Josh had eloped?

Right away, she dismissed the idea as ridiculous. They were both too young to be married without an adult's consent. Thank goodness for that.

"I thought you said you were going to attend all the practices from now on." Mark's tone sounded faintly accusatory, and she couldn't really blame him. If she'd kept her part of the bargain, they likely wouldn't be in this mess right now.

"I'm sorry. I intended to go, but I had a bad headache and went to lie down for a while. I must have fallen asleep." Her voice trembled. "I can't believe this is happening."

"Can you think of anywhere they might have gone? What about her school? That's where Josh met her before."

"We could try there." Isabelle tapped a finger on her purse. Where else could they be? "Marissa also loves to go to parks or take walks down by the water."

"Good. We'll try the school first and then check any nearby parks."

"The academy is on Lonsdale Road, near Spadina."

"All right." He made a quick left-hand turn at the next inter-section. "What about restaurants or coffee shops? Anywhere she likes to go with her friends?"

Isabelle bit her lip. "None I can think of."

"I don't really know anywhere Josh hangs out either." He frowned. "I guess I should have been paying more attention. Maybe then I'd have some idea where he might have gone."

"Me too." Isabelle always thought she and Marissa were close. That her sister told her everything. Now she realized how little she really knew about Marissa's life, like who her friends were and where they liked to go for fun.

"There's the school up ahead on the right." Isabelle pointed to the tall brick building.

Mark slowed the car, drove into the circular driveway, and shut off the engine. The darkened school windows didn't look promising.

"Maybe we should check around the back," Isabelle said as she opened the car door.

Rifling through the glove box, Mark pulled out a metal flashlight. "We may need this."

He caught up with her on the sidewalk, and they made their way to the rear of the building. With no light save for one wire-caged bulb over a rear door, the school yard was indeed imposing in the dark, and Isabelle was grateful for the narrow beam of Mark's flashlight. After a scan of the yard and the empty benches, it quickly became apparent that Josh and Marissa weren't there.

They returned to the car, and Mark restarted the engine. "Is there a park close by or maybe one in your old neighborhood she might go to?"

"There's one near our house. . . ." Isabelle sucked in a breath, a sudden idea dawning. "Wait. Do you think she could have gone back to the old house?" Maybe Marissa was feeling homesick. That might explain the change in her mood lately.

"Of course. We should have thought of that first." Mark made a sharp turn and steered the car in the opposite direction.

Isabelle pulled a handkerchief from her purse, twisting it between her fingers. "I don't know what's going on with my sister lately. I feel like I'm losing her."

Mark reached over and covered her hand with his, the warmth from his palm oddly reassuring. "Don't worry. We'll find them. I promise."

Somehow, she believed him. Soaking in his steadying presence beside her, it felt good to have someone to share her burden, and for the first time in a long while, she didn't feel quite so alone.

She grasped his hand, gratitude welling in her chest. "Thank you, Mark. I don't know what I would have done if you hadn't shown up." She couldn't imagine where she'd have begun looking for her sister without Mark to drive her.

His hazel eyes darkened. He gave her a quick nod before turning his focus back to the road.

"Do you think they would come this far on foot?" Isabelle squinted ahead.

"Possibly. Or they could have taken a bus."

Isabelle checked her watch. It was now past ten o'clock. Marissa had been gone for over four hours. Isabelle's stomach churned, anxiety and guilt eating at her.

"How did I let this happen?" she said. "I was too distracted at dinner. Too wrapped up in my own dilemma. I should have noticed something was wrong."

"What dilemma?" Mark turned narrowed eyes on her.

She hesitated, then gave a sheepish shrug. "I was trying to decide what to do about the marriage proposal I received yesterday."

18

Shock reverberated down Mark's spine. "Marriage proposal?" he choked out.

She nodded, and for a moment he thought she wasn't going to say anything more. But then she let out a soft sigh. "Last week at the hotel, I ran into someone I'd dated a few times. Elias saved me from a rather difficult situation with a hotel guest." Her delicate brows scrunched together. "When he asked me out for dinner, I couldn't very well refuse after he'd been such a help."

Mark stiffened. What did she mean by a difficult situation? "Go on."

"After we'd eaten, he told me he thought we made a good match and asked if I would marry him. I was shocked, to say the least."

The air inside the car seemed overly warm. Mark rolled down the window an inch, then waited a beat before asking, "Did you give him an answer?"

"Not yet. I asked him for time to consider the idea."

Somewhat relieved, he slowed the car's speed to a more acceptable level. That was something, anyway, although he'd have preferred it if she'd refused outright.

"Aren't you going to offer me any advice?" She gave him a sidelong look.

"Since I don't know the man in question, nor your feelings

toward him, I'm not exactly qualified to offer advice on the subject."

"Fair enough." She gave another small sigh. "Marrying Elias would certainly solve a lot of our problems."

"Hardly the best reason to rush into marriage." He bit his tongue as soon as the words escaped.

"People have married for far less practical reasons." She tilted her chin up. "Elias could offer Marissa the stability she desperately needs right now."

"That's fine for your sister. But what about you?" He clenched the wheel harder. "You shouldn't have to sacrifice yourself in order to make Marissa's life easier." The irony of his words struck a chord. Hadn't he been doing just that for Josh's sake?

"I can't afford to be selfish, Mark," she said quietly. "I have to do what's best for her future."

As much as he'd like to, he couldn't offer any further argument, because if he were in her position, wouldn't he do anything he could to ensure his brother had a smooth road ahead?

"Promise me you won't do anything hasty, Isabelle. Think carefully before you make your decision. Give the matter over to God and ask for guidance."

"I will. Believe me, I've never prayed so hard in my life lately."

The familiar Wardrop mansion came into view, and he turned up the long driveway. A *For Sale* sign sat prominently on the front lawn.

Isabelle gave a soft gasp.

How gut-wrenching must it be for her to return to her childhood home and see that sign hanging there? He shut off the engine and got out, rounding the vehicle to open the door for her.

She took his extended hand, her fingers trembling in his. But she pulled herself up tall and took a step forward. Only one exterior light glowed near the front door, while the rest of the house remained shrouded in darkness.

"Let's go around back," Isabelle said. "She'll likely be there if anywhere."

"Lead the way." He handed her the flashlight since he'd never been to the rear of the house before. Whenever he'd come to treat Mrs. Wardrop, she'd been upstairs in her suite.

They entered the backyard through an iron gate. A walkway wound around to a large covered patio that overlooked what must be a magnificent garden when in full bloom. Farther back, an in-ground swimming pool was still covered from the winter.

Mark could see no evidence of Josh or Marissa.

Isabelle marched across the flagstones, aiming the flashlight at the back porch, then out toward the pool. Suddenly, she stilled.

He followed her gaze to what looked like an oversized shed on the other side of the pool. A sliver of light shone from under the door.

Surely, she didn't think . . .

Before he could utter a word, Isabelle took off across the lawn like a military general on a manhunt. He jogged to catch up with her.

When she reached the structure, she didn't hesitate for a second before flinging open the door and barging inside.

"Isabelle, wait!" What if some drifter had taken refuge inside?

She gave a loud gasp, and he rushed in after her.

Josh and Marissa were curled up together on a lounge chair, their eyes closed, seemingly asleep.

"Marissa Wardrop, get up this instant." Isabelle shook her sister's shoulder, the ferocity of her words matching her jerky body language.

Marissa's eyes flew open, and she stared at her sister in apparent shock.

Josh sprang to his feet, running a hand over his unruly hair. "Mark! What are you doing here?"

Heat streaked up Mark's neck. "What am *I* doing here? I think the more fitting question is what are the two of you doing here?"

He glanced at Marissa. Her hair was disheveled, her skin blotchy. Had she been crying?

His mind whirled, trying to make sense of what he was seeing. Trying to piece together the story. But all he could come up with was the glaring fact that his brother had put Marissa in a compromising position—the exact thing he'd sworn to Mark he'd never do. Mark could only be thankful they were both fully dressed.

"Outside. Right now," he ground out.

Josh looked at Marissa, a tortured expression on his face.

"Now!" Mark shouted.

Josh pushed by him, out the door. He stalked across the lawn several feet, then stood with his arms folded over his chest.

Outrage flowed through Mark's veins. He drew in several deep breaths, willing his system to settle before he said something he couldn't take back. Reaching for some sense of calm, he came up behind his brother. "I'd like an explanation of what exactly happened here tonight."

The look Josh gave him was pure venom. "Why should I bother? You've already tried and convicted me. I doubt anything I say will change your mind."

Isabelle shook with a mixture of relief and fury. Relief that Marissa was safe, but outrage that she was alone in the poolhouse with Josh, twined together like a pretzel. Her sister's hair was a mess, her clothing rumpled. Isabelle could only imagine the worst.

"What's gotten into you, Marissa? Didn't you know I'd be worried sick, wondering where you were? And then to find you here, alone with a boy?" She threw up her hands. "What were you thinking?"

Marissa got to her feet and ran a hand down her wrinkled skirt. "Josh was trying to help me with a problem I was having, and we fell asleep."

"Oh, I can see how he helped you." Isabelle pointed to the rumpled cushions on the lounge. "Have you lost all sense of self-respect? Or do you no longer care about your reputation?"

Two red patches appeared in Marissa's cheeks. "It's not what you think. Josh is the kindest, most wonderful—"

"I don't want to hear how wonderful he is. If he had any sense of decency, he would have brought you home." Heat flashed up her neck to match her rising temper. "Let's go."

Marissa seemed ready to argue further, but she clamped her lips together and marched out of the poolhouse.

Isabelle made a quick scan of the room to see if anything else was amiss. Other than the lounge chair they'd dragged inside, the changing rooms and the storage area appeared the same as they'd left them the day they moved out. She turned off the light and headed outside.

Overhead, the clouds parted, and the glow of the nearly full moon bathed the yard in soft light. Marissa was already halfway across the lawn, striding past Mark and Josh, who stood glaring at each other. Isabelle could only imagine the heated things Mark must have said to his brother.

She snapped off the flashlight, no longer requiring its assistance. "Mark, would you please take us home?" she asked quietly.

He gave a curt nod, then pointed toward the driveway. Without a word, Josh headed in that direction.

Mark raked a hand across his bearded jaw as they walked. "I'm so sorry, Isabelle. I never imagined Josh would behave this way."

The fact that he was so outraged by his brother's behavior spoke to his decency. She knew Mark was a principled man, one who valued honesty and integrity. It must be killing him to have found his brother in this situation.

"They're both at fault," she said. "At least it appears we found them before anything worse happened."

"I hope so." A nerve ticked in his jaw. "In any case, I won't let Josh off the hook about this. Putting themselves in such a tempting position is only asking for trouble. He needs to understand it can never happen again."

She nodded. "I intend to deal with Marissa sternly as well." Just knowing that Mark was on her side eased the tension sheathing her spine.

As they drove home in silence, Isabelle decided to wait until tomorrow to question her sister further, given the lateness of the hour and the fact that everyone's emotions were running high.

Maybe after a good night's sleep, they'd all feel better in the morning.

19

Isabelle couldn't have been more wrong.

The next morning, Marissa seemed surlier than ever and not the least bit remorseful for having caused Isabelle such worry.

"I don't want to talk about it" was all she'd say every time Isabelle tried to bring up the subject.

"Like it or not, you're going to have to." Isabelle fastened the button on her skirt as she finished getting dressed. "I have a right to know what's going on. As your guardian, I'm responsible for you."

"Only until I'm eighteen, and that won't be much longer," Marissa shot back as she weaved the strands of her hair into a braid. Anger rolled off her in waves, and she wouldn't even look at Isabelle.

What had she done to deserve such an attitude? Isabelle was the one in the right here. So why did Marissa make her feel like *she* was the one who'd committed a crime?

"If that's how you're going to be, you leave me no choice. From now on, you're not to leave this house except to go to school. No seeing your friends and no more choir."

Marissa whirled away from the warped mirror above the dresser. "You can't do that."

"I most certainly can." Isabelle inhaled and slowly released the breath in a futile attempt to rein in her temper. "This is for your own good, Marissa. You only have a few weeks of school left before you graduate. I won't let you throw your future away over a boy."

Moisture sprang to her sister's amber eyes, then almost immediately her expression turned mutinous again. "I never thought my own sister would turn into a dictator." She grabbed her schoolbag and stomped out of the bedroom.

Isabelle's heart pinched with regret. She hadn't handled that in the most diplomatic way, but sometimes desperation caused one to act rashly.

She sank back onto her mattress with a weary sigh. Thank goodness she had the day off work. She doubted she could concentrate with everything weighing on her mind.

Elias would be expecting an answer to his proposal soon. At the very least, the situation with Marissa had given Isabelle a sense of clarity in that regard and had solidified her decision. With her sister's well-being at stake, Isabelle couldn't afford to think about herself right now. She had the power to affect her sister's life in a positive way, and she'd be a fool to turn it down.

On Wednesday afternoon, Isabelle waited at the entrance to the diner for Elias to arrive. Nerves twisted her stomach into knots, and her lungs seemed determined not to allow any air in.

She was doing the right thing, wasn't she?

"Isabelle, my dear. I hope I didn't keep you waiting." Elias appeared with a sweep of his hat.

"Not at all. I only got here moments ago."

"Wonderful." He ushered her to the same table they'd sat at several days ago. A waitress appeared almost immediately. "Coffee, Isabelle? Or would you prefer tea?"

"Just a glass of water, please."

Elias ordered coffee, and the woman left them alone.

Without any preamble, he pinned her with a studied look. "Do you have an answer for me? Or do you still need more time?"

Isabelle took a deep breath, then looked him in the eye. She'd made her decision and she would declare it boldly, with confidence. "I don't need any more time."

"Well, please don't keep me in suspense." His hopeful expression only made her more nervous.

The waitress chose that moment to return with their drinks.

Elias thanked her and turned his focus back to Isabelle. His fair brows rose in a question.

Isabelle took a quick sip of water, then cleared her throat and smiled. "After a great deal of consideration, I have decided to accept your offer of marriage."

Joyful surprise burst across his features. "That's wonderful." He grasped her hand across the table. "I hadn't dared hope for such an outcome, but I must say I'm delighted."

She kept smiling until her cheeks ached.

"When would you like to marry?" Elias rubbed his thumb over her hand. "I'm happy to leave the details up to you."

Isabelle had given the matter equal consideration. "My sister graduates at the end of June. I'd like to wait until after that. Maybe sometime in early July?"

"That sounds perfect." He beamed at her. "I'm certain my mother would love to help you with the plans in any way she can."

Ah, Mrs. Weatherby. A rather intimidating widow in her late fifties. Isabelle had met her a few times at holiday parties, as well as at some church functions. What would she think of her son marrying Isabelle now? "Do you think she'll approve of our union after the scandal involving my father?"

"Of course she will. She doesn't blame you for your father's mistakes." He took a hasty slurp of his coffee, not quite meeting her eyes.

Perhaps Mrs. Weatherby wasn't as accepting as he claimed. No matter. They'd work it out . . . in time.

"I'd be happy to include your mother in our plans," she replied. Best to start this relationship off on the right foot. Winning over her future mother-in-law would be a good place to begin.

But all Isabelle really cared about now was keeping Marissa on the right path, and if marrying Elias would ensure that outcome, then she would do whatever was necessary to smooth the way.

On Wednesday night, Mark knocked on the door to Rosie's apartment, trepidation beating in his chest. How would Isabelle react to him now? Would she view him as her enemy again after Josh and Marissa's latest escapade?

"Good evening, Dr. Henshaw," Mrs. O'Grady greeted him. "Won't you come in?"

"Thank you, ma'am."

"Now, now. I told you to call me Rosie." She wagged a finger at him as she ushered him into the sitting room. "I imagine you're here to see Isabelle."

"Yes, please, if she's home."

A door opened down the hall, and Isabelle appeared. "Mark. This is a surprise."

She looked as beautiful as always, wearing a pink blouse and blue skirt. Her fair hair was swept off her forehead, with the rest sitting in waves about her shoulders.

Isabelle smoothed her skirt over her legs. "Aunt Rosie, could we have some tea, if it's not too much trouble?"

"When has tea ever been too much trouble?" Rosie chuckled.

Once she was busy at the stove, Isabelle motioned to the living room, and they both went in and took a seat.

"I came to apologize again for my brother." He lowered his voice in case Marissa was in the other room. "And to see how you and your sister are doing. I hope Josh hasn't caused her any undue distress." He still had no idea why the girl had been crying and prayed it wasn't because of something his brother had done.

Isabelle gave him a sympathetic look. "First of all, you have no need to apologize. You're not responsible for your brother's actions."

"As his guardian, I feel I am. Just as I'm sure you feel a measure of guilt over your sister."

She gave him a wry look. "I can't argue there."

He lowered his voice again. "Have you been able to get any more information about what happened last night?"

Isabelle glanced toward the hall leading to the bedrooms, then bent her head closer. "Not a word. She won't talk to me. She's sullen and irritable, and I can't figure out what's going on with her."

"I'm having the same problem with Josh." Mark frowned. "I hoped Marissa would be more forthcoming."

"Unfortunately, no." Isabelle gave a sigh. "I'm afraid I lost my temper with her. I've forbidden her from seeing her friends and from going to choir practice. The only thing she's allowed to do is go to school."

Mark nodded. "I guess if they can't see each other at choir, that solves one problem. But I wouldn't put it past Josh to try to approach Marissa at her school again." He shook his head. "All we can do is try to keep one step ahead of them."

Rosie came over with a tea tray and set it on the table in front of them. "Did you tell the doctor your news?" The sharp look she gave Isabelle made Mark's pulse start to hammer.

A flush crept into Isabelle's cheeks. "I was just about to." She kept her gaze trained on Rosie pouring the tea, then finally lifted her head. "Today, I accepted Elias Weatherby's marriage proposal. We're to be married right after Marissa's graduation."

Married? The floor seemed to fall away from beneath him, leaving him floundering for balance. This couldn't be happening. Not when he'd made such strides in his relationship with her.

"Until then, Elias has offered us the use of his driver," she continued, seemingly oblivious to his distress. "Marissa will be well supervised both going to and coming from school."

Mark swallowed in a futile attempt to pull himself together and pretend that his world hadn't come crashing down around him. "I see." Politeness dictated that he should offer his congratulations, but he simply couldn't make himself utter such a falsehood. Not with the weight of disappointment crushing his chest. "Did you tell Elias about the incident at the poolhouse?"

"No. I just said my sister might be heading down an undesirable path, and that I'd appreciate his help until she's finished her schooling."

Mark nodded, his throat too tight to offer a reply. He should be relieved that temptation would be removed from Josh, but this seemed the worst possible way for it to come about. He took a long drink from his cup, then set it back on the tray. "Well, I'd better get going. Thank you for the tea."

Isabelle walked him to the door. "Thanks for coming, Mark. I hope we can now get our siblings back on track." She hesitated, and for a moment, regret flashed over her face. "I want you to know that I appreciate everything you've done for us, and I wish you and Josh all the best in the future."

The note of finality in her voice slammed the truth into him. With the tie of their siblings severed, this might be the last time he ever saw her. He studied her face in an attempt to commit her features to memory. The vivid blueness of her eyes, the rosy hue of her skin, the delicate slope of her cheeks.

"I wish the same for you, Isabelle. You deserve every happiness." He tried to smile but couldn't force his lips to cooperate. "I hope Elias realizes how lucky he is."

She pressed her lips together, as though trying to contain her emotions. "Take care of yourself."

"You too. And my offer still stands. If you ever need me for anything, I'm only a phone call away."

20

For the next few days, Mark threw himself into scouting potential locations for a medical clinic with relentless zeal, meeting with a local realtor to tell him the neighborhood he preferred and the type of building he wanted. He also saw more private patients than usual, barely allowing himself time to do anything but fall into bed, exhausted, at the end of the day. Anything to distract himself from the reality that he'd lost Isabelle for good.

Despite his efforts, he was having no luck so far with finding a suitable space. However, this afternoon Mr. Remington had a few more sites to show him. Since Mark's week off was nearly over, he hoped that today would be successful. He also hoped to hear from Ruth soon, because he could never sign a lease without some assurance of financial backing.

"Are you sure you want to stay in this area of town? I can find you a much nicer location in the downtown core." The realtor looked at Mark, clearly exasperated. Nelson Remington was a middle-aged man with a slight paunch that protruded over his belt. His gray hair was thinning on top, and he wore it swept over to one side.

They'd looked at three different buildings so far, but they'd all been too run-down for Mark to even consider. The amount of money needed to refurbish the space into something presentable would be way beyond his means.

"I'm sure. This is where I'm needed." He scanned the street. "But we could go a few more blocks to the east. As long as it's not too far from the tenements."

"All right." Mr. Remington sighed. "I have another two rentals to show you. Follow me."

The next place they came to was located above a butcher shop in the Jewish market area. The rooms themselves were decent, but the steep staircase to access it would prove problematic to many of the patients.

"Something on the ground level is preferable," he told the realtor.

"Perhaps you'll find the next one acceptable." Barely disguised sarcasm dripped from his voice.

Mark bit the retort that sprang to his lips. Shouldn't realtors be nicer? More accommodating to their clients' needs?

They walked about four more blocks until Mr. Remington stopped in front of what appeared to be a former delicatessen.

"You'll have to use your imagination," Mr. Remington said as he fit the key in the door. "But I think this place has a lot of potential."

Mark was beginning to hate that word.

However, once he stepped inside, the first stirring of excitement rumbled to life within him. Despite the lingering odor of cured meats, the space seemed in good shape. A large wooden counter ran down one side of the room and the other housed several tables and chairs. Down a small hallway, Mark found two other rooms that would do well for examining patients, plus another he could use as an office. After a bit of paint and a good scrub, this place might do.

Mark continued back to what used to be the kitchen. With its large sink, refrigerator, and steel table, this room could work for storing medication, and even serve as an area for minor surgical procedures.

"Well, what do you think?" Back in the front area, Mr. Remington patted the wooden countertop. "This could be your reception area. You could put chairs against the far wall. Get some newspapers and magazines, maybe a plant or two, and you'd be all set."

Mark nodded. The location was good. Near enough to the tenements to make it accessible, yet located in a respectable business area of town. It could be ideal as long as the rent was affordable.

The situation suddenly became very real as he scanned the room. How would he make all this work out? He'd need a receptionist, and probably a nurse as well. How would he afford to pay them?

He took in a deep breath. One step at a time. "Can you find out more about the rent and what conditions would be involved in signing a lease?"

"Certainly."

"In the meantime, I'll speak with my potential business partner."

The man beamed. "Wonderful. I'll be in touch as soon as I can."

Mark ran a hand over the wooden countertop and took one last look around before heading out the door.

His mind was still preoccupied when he returned home. He set his keys down, then headed back to the kitchen. He'd just pulled a pitcher of lemonade out of the fridge when the telephone rang. He set the pitcher down to answer it.

"Dr. Henshaw? It's Rosie O'Grady." An unusual tension laced her voice. "I hate to bother you, but could you come by my apartment? Marissa isn't feeling well, and it would ease my mind if she were seen by a doctor."

Mark's heart began to hammer. He'd been doing his best to avoid thinking about Isabelle, but Rosie's call brought all the pain rushing back. For his own self-preservation, he should suggest that she find another doctor for Marissa, but that would mean putting his personal discomfort ahead of his patient, something he could never in good conscience do.

"I'll be right over."

———✦———

Isabelle's feet ached. Walking home from the bus stop had become a subtle form of torture at the end of a busy shift. How much longer would she have to keep working? Several weeks, at least, until she married Elias and could take on the duties of being his wife.

Her thoughts turned to Marissa, and she frowned. If anything, her sister had become even moodier since learning of Isabelle's engagement. She resented having Elias's personal driver take her to school, saying it hindered her freedom. Even the prospect of moving onto the Weatherbys' beautiful estate seemed to hold little appeal for her. Isabelle had imagined Marissa would be eager to reclaim the type of lifestyle she was used to, to be able to have her friends over, and to enjoy the summer break. Yet she seemed more depressed than ever.

Was Isabelle doing the right thing?

Lord, I seem to be making a lot of wrong turns lately. Please help me to do what's best for my sister. And please release Marissa from whatever burdens she carries. Allow her to trust me enough to share her problems with me, so I can help her find a solution.

Despite her tired feet, the walk home each day was becoming Isabelle's favorite time to pray. To open her heart to God and confess all her troubles to Him. She needed to stay strong and trust that God had a plan for both her and her sister. Yet lately that had seemed more difficult than ever before.

As she turned onto Gerrard Street, a familiar car parked near the apartment caught her attention. Immediately her pulse sped up and nerves fluttered in her stomach. She hadn't heard from Mark since she'd told him of her decision to marry Elias, but he was here now. What did that mean?

She quickened her pace, unable to deny her eagerness to see him again. Perhaps he had learned something from his brother about what really happened at the poolhouse. Maybe he could shed some light on Marissa's newfound misery.

Isabelle opened the door and let herself in with an expectant smile. However, when she saw the grim expression on Aunt Rosie's face, she froze. "Rosie, what's wrong?"

Mark's jacket and hat hung on the coatrack, but there was no sign of him.

Rosie let out a sigh. "Marissa came home from school feeling ill. I was worried, so I went up to Sweeny's and called Dr. Henshaw to come and take a look at her."

"Is it the flu? Does she have a fever?"

"I don't know. She felt very lightheaded, like she might faint. She threw up at school and says her stomach's been upset for a few days. It could be a virus."

"I'm sure Mark will figure it out." Despite her unease, warmth spread through Isabelle's chest, knowing she had complete confidence in Mark's abilities—a far cry from the time right after Mama's death when she never wanted to see him again. The unfairness of her censure still continued to prick at her conscience, yet Mark had forgiven her without a second's hesitation.

Isabelle walked toward their bedroom. The door was open a few inches.

"Are you sure, Dr. Henshaw?" Marissa sounded terribly young, reminding Isabelle how she used to cry for their mother when she felt under the weather.

Mark cleared his throat. "Fairly sure. It's not likely the flu since you don't have a fever or body aches or any other worrisome symptoms."

A noise like a stifled sob sounded.

"Take it easy for a few days," Mark continued in a soothing tone. "Try some toast and tea until your stomach settles. And take your time getting up from a sitting position. Your blood pressure is a bit low."

Was that the problem troubling Marissa lately? Was she unwell and hadn't wanted to say anything? Isabelle peered inside the room. Mark was placing his stethoscope in his leather bag.

"I'll come back and check on you in a couple of days. If you start to feel worse, please have Isabelle or Rosie call me." He leaned over to pat Marissa's shoulder. "You've had a traumatic time these last few months. This could be your body's way of telling you to rest."

"Thank you, Doctor."

"You're welcome."

Isabelle backed a few steps down the hall and waited for Mark to exit the room. From what she could gather, the ailment didn't appear serious, but until she heard the reassurance from him directly, she wouldn't rest easy.

His brows rose when he saw her. "Isabelle. Hello." Immediate color flooded his cheeks.

She gestured for him to follow her.

Once they were in the sitting room, she turned to him, anxiety fluttering through her system. "How is she?"

He took his time setting his bag on a side table before answering. "She'll be fine."

"It's nothing serious, then?" Isabelle bit her lip. If anything happened to her sister, she didn't know how she'd go on. Marissa was all she had left of their once close-knit family.

Mark's usually smiling eyes were shadowed, his expression grim.

Alarm bolted through her system. She gripped his arm. "Mark, please. If there's something wrong, you have to tell me."

Mark's stomach sank as he stared into Isabelle's eyes. Anxiety dulled their usual vibrant color, and the way her fingers dug into his arm gave further evidence of her concern.

If only he could brush off her question, give her some trite answer to satisfy her for the time being. But that wouldn't be fair and would betray her trust in him. He owed her the truth of what might be happening with her sister.

"Walk me to my car?"

She nodded.

He draped his suit jacket over his arm. It was a warm enough day that he didn't need the extra layer.

When they reached his car, he set his bag and jacket on the seat. Dread saturated his muscles. How could he tell Isabelle what he suspected? If he had any way to avoid it, he would. With a sigh, he turned to face her.

"Please tell me, Mark. I need to know if my sister is all right." Her fearful expression tore at his tightly held composure.

He'd do anything to spare her from this latest catastrophe, but there was no way to soften the news. No way to shield her from another terrible blow.

"If my suspicions are correct," he said slowly, "I believe Marissa may be . . . pregnant."

"What?" The color drained from Isabelle's face. "No. That's impossible."

"Believe me, I wish I was wrong, but judging from her symptoms and from her physical appearance, I'm fairly certain my diagnosis is correct."

Isabelle paced the area in front of the stairs, her brow furrowed in tiny ridges. She stopped in front of him. "But we only just caught her and Josh in the poolhouse. You couldn't possibly tell that quickly, could you?"

"No. That wouldn't be enough time." Mark did his best to put on a professional air. There was no way to sugarcoat this. "However, in this case, I estimate her to be about four months along."

Isabelle's lips parted, and her eyes went wide. "That would be right after Mama died. Before Daddy . . ." She swallowed, and her frame seemed to crumple in on itself. "No," she whispered. "It can't be."

He couldn't bear her distress any longer. Expelling a breath, he pulled her gently against his chest and wrapped his arms around her. "I'm so sorry, Isabelle. You didn't need this on top of every-thing else." After all the pain she'd been through over the last sev-eral months, he hated to add one more burden to her shoulders. He wanted to ease her troubles, not compound them.

Her whole body trembled, and warm tears seeped through his shirt.

"It will be all right. We'll figure this out together." He clenched his jaw, just imagining what he would say to his brother. How could Josh have sunk so low as to take advantage of a grieving girl that way?

Isabelle sniffed and pulled away. He took a handkerchief from his pocket and handed it to her.

"Did you tell Marissa?" she asked.

"Yes. It turns out she suspected the same thing herself."

"No wonder she's been acting so strange lately." Isabelle stared up at him, and the sadness shadowing her features broke his heart. "This relationship must have been going on for some time, then," she said. "How did we miss it?"

"I don't know." He stared across the street where three chil-dren played hopscotch in the dirt. "I blame myself for being too wrapped up in my work."

"And I was consumed with grief over my mother's death. Still, I thought I was doing a good job of looking out for her."

"I suppose if they wanted to keep their relationship from us, there's not much we could have done." He reached out and took her hand. Gratitude spread through his chest as her fingers curled around his. "I promise to make sure Josh takes responsibility for his actions."

She nodded. "I know you will. You're an honorable person, a man of your word."

"Thank you, Isabelle. That means a lot coming from you."

Her lashes fluttered down. "I still regret the terrible things I said to you after Mama died. Since then, you've shown us nothing but loyalty and support when most others have shunned us or delighted in our downfall." A swirl of different emotions shone in her eyes. Sorrow, regret, and—dare he hope—affection?

His chest constricted with longing. With one finger, he wiped a trace of wetness from her cheek. "I've admired you longer than you know, Isabelle. And your courage in the face of adversity has only increased my esteem."

Her pink lips parted as he moved imperceptibly closer to her. Then her eyes went wide, and she pressed a hand to his chest. "I almost forgot I'm getting married soon."

A pang of regret shot through him with more sharpness than an arrow. Did he have no more self-control than his teenaged brother?

When she stepped away from him, the few inches between them might as well have been a chasm.

"Forgive me for nearly forgetting myself," he said gruffly.

She shook her head. "No harm done. It was an understandable gesture of comfort."

He straightened his shoulders. "I'll be in touch to see where we go from here. In the meantime, try not to worry."

Forcing his mouth into a smile, he gave her a slight nod before getting into the driver's seat. As he drove away, he set his jaw and forced his mind to the grim task ahead. His biggest fear for his brother had become a reality. Josh had gotten tangled up with a girl, so much so that their lives would be forever linked. How would Josh react to this news? And how on earth would a seventeen-year-old kid support a baby?

Suddenly, Mark felt far, far older than his twenty-eight years.

21

When Isabelle reentered the apartment, she avoided Rosie's questioning gaze and went to sit on the sofa. Her legs shook and blood thundered in her ears. Before she went to talk to Marissa, she needed a minute to catch her breath and prepare what she wanted to say.

Her instinct was to rant and rail at her. How could she be so irresponsible? How could she throw away her life like this? But hurling recriminations would only make the situation worse. Marissa would need her support and understanding to help her through this difficult period.

"You look like the stuffing's been knocked out of you." Rosie's quiet voice startled Isabelle from her thoughts. "What did Dr. Henshaw say?"

She bit her lip. It wasn't her place to tell Rosie or Fiona what was going on with her sister. If the diagnosis was confirmed, telling their housemates about the pregnancy would have to come from Marissa.

"He's not entirely sure. He said she should take it easy for a couple of days, and if her symptoms get worse, to call him again."

"Well, I suppose if it's a stomach bug, we'll all have to be careful not to catch it."

Isabelle had the insane urge to laugh. No need to worry about catching a pregnancy. She met the woman's worried gaze. "Thank you for calling Dr. Henshaw. I feel better knowing Marissa is in good hands."

"I'm glad I could help."

On impulse, Isabelle rose and gave the dear woman a hug. "You've been so kind to us. I don't know where we'd be if not for you."

Aunt Rosie squeezed her back. "It's been equally beneficial for me. Instead of missing my Noreen, I've made two wonderful new friends."

Isabelle blinked back tears. "I'd better go check on Marissa. Then I'll come back and help you make dinner." She paused in the hallway. "Oh, and the doctor recommended nothing but toast and tea for Marissa until her stomach settles."

"I've already got the kettle on."

Isabelle gave a half-hearted smile. How she wished Marissa's symptoms could be resolved with such ease. But unless Mark was mistaken, Marissa's condition would go on for the next five months.

Silently, Isabelle opened the bedroom door and slipped inside. Marissa lay on her side, facing the far wall.

"Rissa? How are you feeling?" Isabelle asked quietly.

Her sister shifted on the bed. "A little better, I guess." Her voice sounded muffled, garbled almost.

Isabelle hesitated. How did she approach this delicate situation? Marissa must be so scared. It was up to Isabelle to make sure she knew she wasn't alone. She let out a long breath, then sat on the foot of the bed. "Dr. Henshaw told me what he suspects," she said. "I want you to know that I'm here for you, no matter the outcome."

Slowly, Marissa rolled over. Her eyes were puffy from crying. "You don't hate me?"

"Oh, honey. I could never hate you." She rubbed a hand over Marissa's arm. "I do feel like I failed you, though."

"How can you say that? I'm the one who failed you." Tears dripped down her cheeks. "I'm so ashamed."

"You made a mistake. A rather large one, granted. But we'll figure out a way to get through this together."

"Oh, Belle. What would I do without you?" Marissa threw her arms around Isabelle's neck and hung on tight.

Despite the terrible circumstances, Isabelle relished her sister's show of affection and the return of the closeness they once shared. At last, there were no longer any secrets between them.

A few minutes later, Marissa pulled away with a loud sniff. "I'm scared, Belle. I'm not ready to be a mother."

"Mark told me he's going to make sure Josh takes responsibility for his actions, so you won't have to face this alone."

Marissa blinked. She opened her mouth, then closed it again.

"Is that what you and Josh were doing at the poolhouse? Were you telling him you might be pregnant?"

Marissa bit her lip and nodded.

Isabelle remembered how she'd found the pair, curled up together on the lounge in the cabana. Josh must have taken it fairly well. He hadn't abandoned her sister, which gave Isabelle hope that perhaps Josh might turn out to be as honorable as his older brother. Would he offer to marry Marissa and raise the baby together? Did Isabelle even want that for her sister?

She was sure Mark would never have chosen this path for his brother. He had high hopes for Josh, just as she did for Marissa. Dreams for the future that would now be impossible.

What a colossal mess. The course of two lives forever altered for what? Fleeting teenage love?

Isabelle stroked her sister's arm, knowing there was little she could do to ease her pain. This certainly wasn't what she or Mark had envisioned for their younger siblings, yet it appeared the young couple had no choice but to face the life-altering consequences of their actions.

Anger simmered under the surface of Mark's skin as he entered the house. He'd taken the long way home to try to gain control of his emotions. Instead, the magnitude of the situation had sunk in and begun to fester. How could Josh have been so reckless? Having a crush on a girl was one thing, but getting her pregnant? That was beyond irresponsible. Especially at his age.

Mark slammed the door and threw his keys onto the hall table. Hands on his hips, he paced the narrow hall, trying to calm down before confronting his brother. The urge to wring his neck was almost too strong to contain.

Footsteps sounded down the stairs.

"Hey, Mark." Josh stopped short when he saw his face, his expression turning wary.

"We need to talk." Mark strode into the living room and across to the fireplace, keeping his back to the door. When he finally felt he could talk in a normal tone, he turned to face his brother.

Josh stood with his hands shoved into his pockets. "What's wrong now?"

"Is there anything more you'd like to tell me about your relationship with Marissa Wardrop?"

His brother's brown eyes darkened to ebony. "Not this again. I thought we'd gotten past this topic."

"Apparently not." Mark crossed his arms and waited for Josh to say more.

"I've already told you we're good friends. I was helping her after she'd had a bad day. End of story."

"I wish that *was* the end of the story."

Josh's brows swooped down. "What does that mean?"

"I was called over to treat Marissa earlier today."

Alarm leapt into his brother's eyes. "Is she all right?"

Mark stared at him. "No, Josh. She's not."

His brother's face went white. "Is she . . ." He swallowed. "Is it serious?"

"You could say that." Mark's chest tightened with growing irritation. "It appears that Marissa is expecting a baby."

Josh remained silent, though a dull red blotch appeared in each cheek.

"This news doesn't seem to surprise you." Mark studied Josh, waiting for a crack in his armor, but the boy stubbornly held his ground. "That's why you two skipped choir practice that night, isn't it? Because Marissa was telling you what she suspected."

Josh seemed to fold in on himself as his shoulders slumped forward. He let out a long breath. "Yes."

Mark raked a hand through his hair. "I can't believe this. After everything I've done to prevent something like this from happening." He clenched his hands at his side, mentally counting to ten before continuing. "What do you intend to do about it?"

Josh's hair stood up in unruly tufts. "That's between Marissa and me," he said quietly.

"I disagree. As your guardian, I should have some say in the matter." Mark could hardly get the words out. How was Josh going to support a child when he was barely more than a child himself?

Josh took a breath and squared his shoulders. "This is my problem, Mark. I'll figure it out." He turned and left the room.

Mark's first instinct was to charge after him and shake some sense into him. But that type of heavy-handed reaction would solve nothing and would only increase Josh's animosity toward him.

Olivia's words suddenly rushed back to him. *Have an honest conversation with him and try to see his point of view.*

Mark rubbed his weary eyes and sank onto the sofa. She wouldn't be at all impressed with the way he'd handled this one. For everyone's sake, it was better that they both had time to cool down before he attempted to talk to his brother again. Maybe next time, Mark would be able to put Olivia's advice into practice.

22

A few days later, Isabelle worked longer than usual at the hotel, partly to make up for being late again that morning, partly as an avoidance tactic to delay going home. She dreaded returning to the heavy atmosphere that had permeated the apartment ever since Marissa had come home sick.

After spending two more days in bed, her sister had finally gone back to school. She stuck to the story that it had been a stomach virus, yet Isabelle suspected Aunt Rosie wasn't fooled, given that Marissa had shown no evidence of a fever and hadn't thrown up again.

Rosie and Fiona had been giving Isabelle questioning looks, adding to her guilt of keeping Marissa's secret. She just didn't know how to encourage Marissa to tell them. Besides, deep down she still hoped Mark's diagnosis was wrong and that Marissa would soon laugh with relief and pronounce it a close call. And she would learn her lesson and swear off boys forever.

Or at least until she was forty.

But with every day that passed, her hope deflated a little more.

When Isabelle finally made it home, the apartment sat hushed in silence. She found a note on the table from Rosie, saying she'd gone to help a friend and that she'd left some chicken stew for dinner.

Isabelle headed for the bedroom to see if Marissa had eaten yet and if she wanted to share the meal. To her surprise, the room was empty, although the rumpled quilt and the textbook on Marissa's pillow told Isabelle that her sister had been there recently.

Telling herself not to worry, that she had likely gone for a walk, Isabelle sat on her bed and pulled off her shoes and stockings. After rubbing her tired feet for a few seconds, she slid them into her slippers. The warm air drifting in through the window, along with the calm solitude of the house, lulled her senses. Her heavy eyes longed to close. She lay back on the bed and allowed her lids to drift shut, relishing the peace and quiet. For a few moments, as she hovered in the elusive realm between waking and sleeping, she could almost pretend her problems didn't exist.

"Are you sure, Josh?" Marissa's tense voice came from somewhere nearby. "What about university?"

Isabelle's eyes flew open. Her sister must be close by if she could hear her.

"I never really cared about that." Josh's response allowed Isabelle to pinpoint that the voices were coming through the open window. "Medical school was Mark's dream, not mine. Anyway, that's not important now. I've heard the logging camps up north are hiring. They pay better than average wages. I'll work there all summer and save money for when the baby arrives."

Isabelle scrambled to her knees on the bed and moved the curtain aside so she could see out. Marissa and Josh stood not far away, near the ramshackle shed in Rosie's small backyard. Thankfully, they were so engrossed in their conversation they didn't look her way.

Frowning, Marissa seemed to be studying the dirt at her feet. "I hate leaving you for so long, but at least I know Mark and your sister will be around to watch out for you." He took one of Marissa's hands in his. "You know how much I care about you. I promise we'll get through this and be all the stronger for it. And maybe once I get back, you'll change your mind about marrying me."

Isabelle almost fell off the bed. *Josh had asked Marissa to marry him?*

"I don't deserve you, Josh." Marissa shook her head. "I feel like I'm ruining your life."

Isabelle could tell by the tremor in her voice that she was close to tears.

"You're not ruining anything." He stared down at Marissa with such tenderness that Isabelle held her breath. "I love you, Marissa. Nothing will change that."

Then, slowly, he leaned down and kissed her.

Marissa's arms wrapped around him, and she kissed him back, clinging to him like a life raft in a storm.

Isabelle sank back on the bed, vaguely ashamed for spying on such an intimate moment. Yet, for the first time, she realized just how much Joshua Henshaw cared about her sister, and an unexpected stab of envy hit her hard. What would it be like to have a man feel so strongly about her? A man who would be willing to sacrifice his future for her sake and do whatever it took to ensure she was safe and cared for?

Her thoughts turned to Elias. True, he seemed to care for her, but his marriage proposal hadn't exactly exuded passion or undying love. Could she trust that he would stand by her through thick and thin, when no one in her life had ever done so before?

Mark has always been there for you.

The unbidden thought popped into her head, convicting her. She took a moment to examine its validity, though deep in her heart she knew it was true. Even when she'd been hateful to him, he'd never stopped caring about her welfare.

Why had she never thought of Mark in a romantic light? He

was handsome, kind, and loyal, and he embodied every quality she found admirable in a man. There was no doubt in her mind that he would make an excellent husband and father one day.

Too bad she hadn't realized it sooner.

With a huff, Isabelle pushed her frivolous reflections aside and went out to the kitchen to wait for her sister. A few minutes later, Marissa entered the apartment, seeming very subdued. Isabelle waited for her to notice her seated at the table.

"Isabelle. When did you get home?"

"Not long ago. Was that Josh I saw with you?"

Marissa nodded.

"Is everything all right? You look upset."

Marissa hesitated, biting her lip, looking toward the bedroom as though she'd like to flee.

"Talk to me, honey," she said softly. "I want to help. What's going on between you two?"

Finally, Marissa let out a sigh and took a seat at the table. She clasped her hands together on the tabletop. "Josh is leaving soon to take a job up north for the summer."

"Really? Why not get a job here in the city?"

"He says the pay is much better, and he can earn a lot more for me and the baby."

"What about finishing his school year?"

"The principal at his school is going to let him write his final exams early. But he'll miss graduation." An expression of such sadness crept over her features that Isabelle winced. Likely Marissa was thinking of her own graduation, which she'd have to miss as well, since her condition would be evident by then.

Isabelle sat in silence, letting the news settle while praying for the right words to say. "How do you feel about him going away?"

"Horribly guilty." Marissa's throat muscles worked. "Like I'm ruining his life."

"Honey, both your lives have been forever changed by this pregnancy. I'm glad he's taking responsibility. Aren't you?"

She shrugged.

"Josh seems to care about you very much." Isabelle paused. "I'm surprised he didn't offer to marry you."

Marissa glanced away, furrows forming between her brows. "Actually, he did. But I turned him down."

Too many things weren't adding up. Yet what did Isabelle know about a girl in Marissa's situation? She reached over to clasp her hand. "Explain that to me. If you care about him enough to be carrying his child, why would you refuse to marry him?"

Marissa removed her hand and placed it over her abdomen as if to protect the child within. "I do care for Josh. Very much. But I won't force him into a marriage I know he doesn't really want. I won't let him sacrifice his future for me."

"What about your future?" Despite her best efforts, a hint of exasperation bled into her tone. "Why should you be the only one who pays for your mistake? You didn't get into this mess alone."

Marissa stuck out her chin in a defiant way that reminded Isabelle of how she'd looked as a child. "I don't want someone to marry me out of obligation. If I married Josh this way, I'd never be certain of the real reason." A tear slowly trickled from the corner of one eye.

Once again, Marissa's romantic side peeked out, the part that dreamed of handsome princes and fairy tales. Unfortunately, real life rarely lived up to those unrealistic expectations, especially not when a girl was seventeen, unmarried, and pregnant.

"Having a baby changes things," Isabelle said gently. "But it doesn't mean that there can't still be love between you."

Marissa didn't respond, crumpling a tissue between her fingers.

Alarm bells went off in Isabelle's head. "Marissa, look at me." She waited until her sister lifted her sorrowful gaze to hers.

"I want to know how you feel about the baby. Do you want to keep it, or are you considering giving it up for adoption?"

"I don't know, Belle. I'm so confused." Marissa pressed the tissue to her lips to contain the sob that erupted.

Isabelle went over to put her arms around her. "It's all right. You have time to figure it out. I'll help you make that decision when you're ready." She stroked a hand down her sister's golden hair. "Maybe it's good that Josh is going away for a while. It will give you time on your own to come to terms with your situation and see how you feel before he comes back."

Marissa lifted her head, looking slightly relieved. "I never thought about it that way."

"They say absence makes the heart grow fonder. I guess we'll see how true that is."

She gave a small smile. "I guess so."

"In the meantime, we're going to have to tell Aunt Rosie. It's only fair since we are living under her roof."

Marissa grimaced. "Will you tell her, please? I don't think I can face her yet."

"All right. I'll speak to her and Fiona when they get home."

Because it was a warm spring night, Isabelle decided to sit outside on the front stoop after she tidied the dishes. Marissa had eaten very little and had returned to their room right afterward, probably because she knew Isabelle was going to tell their house-mates the unfortunate news as soon as they got home.

As Isabelle waited, she prayed for the courage to drop this bombshell on them and for the grace to accept whatever their reaction might be.

Finally, she saw the two women walking up the street.

"Look who I ran into on my way home," Rosie called.

Fiona, still clad in her uniform, minus the cap and apron, walked with her arm looped through Rosie's.

"Have you eaten yet?" Isabelle asked as they approached. She didn't want to delay them if they were ravenous.

"I had dinner with the other staff," Fiona said.

Rosie stopped at the foot of the stairs. "And I had some stew earlier."

Isabelle looked from one woman to the other. "Could you two

join me for a few minutes, then? I have something I need to tell you."

"That sounds ominous." Fiona plopped down beside her, while Rosie took her time settling onto the top step.

With the soft breeze teasing her hair from its pins, Isabelle searched for a way to start the conversation. Across the street, another family sat on their front steps, watching their children play ball in the street. "I know you're both aware of some tension in the house lately," she began.

"We'd have to be blind not to notice," Fiona said wryly.

Now that Isabelle was about to tell them, the magnitude of the situation seemed to hit her like a blow to the midsection. She pressed her lips together.

"Whatever it is, I'm sure there's a solution." Aunt Rosie's voice was as soothing as ever, but it couldn't calm Isabelle this time.

"There's no easy way to say this." The words seemed to stick in her throat. She swallowed. "Marissa is expecting a baby."

Fiona gasped.

Aunt Rosie crossed herself. "Saints preserve us. She's only a child herself."

"I know." Isabelle stared across the street at a young mother in a worn housedress, rocking a baby in her arms, a barefoot toddler tugging on her skirt. That could easily be Marissa's fate one day. Living in tenement housing with little or no money, tending to her babies as best she could.

Tears blurred Isabelle's vision, but she stubbornly blinked them away.

"How . . . I mean, when did this happen?" Fiona seemed as baffled as Isabelle.

"The doctor suspects she's about four months along, which means it happened sometime right after Mama died." Isabelle leaned over her knees. "I don't know how I missed it. I must have been too caught up in my own grief to notice."

"This is not your fault," Rosie said firmly. "You couldn't be aware of your sister's every move."

"I thought it was good for her to be in the church choir. I imagined she'd be safe. Who knows how many times she skipped practice and went off with that boy?" She blew a lock of hair off her forehead. "The ironic part is that he's Dr. Henshaw's younger brother."

"Oh dear." Aunt Rosie clucked her tongue. "They're both so young. What are they going to do?"

"I'm not sure. I think Marissa needs time to process the whole thing before making any major decisions."

"Of course. This must have come as a terrible shock." Fiona squeezed Isabelle's hand. "Well, we'll be praying for you both."

"Thank you." Isabelle attempted a smile.

The three of them sat in sorrowful silence for a few minutes, then Fiona cleared her throat. "I have a wee bit of news myself. Nothing so dramatic, mind you, but I thought you should know."

"What is it?" Isabelle was almost afraid to ask, unable to imagine one more piece of bad news.

"Mr. Templeton and his family are getting ready to move to their summer home for the next few months. They usually go in July, but with rumors about a polio outbreak, Adam—Mr. Templeton—is worried for his younger sister. She's rather a frail thing, and he wants her out of the city just to be safe." She shot a glance at Isabelle. "And they're bringing most of the staff with them."

Aunt Rosie leaned forward. "Does that include you, Fiona?"

"Yes, it does." Her green eyes fairly danced. "I've seen pictures, and the house looks grand. Not as big as the one in the city, but it overlooks Lake Muskoka. There's apparently water and trees as far as you can see."

"It sounds wonderful." Isabelle rubbed a hand over her eyes. Daddy had always talked about buying a summer home one day but had never gotten around to it. Now that she knew the truth about his finances, she understood why.

"You'll be gone for the whole summer, then?" Aunt Rosie asked.

"It looks that way. I feel bad leaving you, especially with Marissa in such a state."

"Don't be silly." Isabelle leaned over to hug her friend, forcing cheer into her voice. "We're happy you're having this opportunity. Right, Aunt Rosie?"

"Aye. And we expect you to enjoy every moment you can. That good northern air will do wonders for you." Rosie pulled herself up from the stoop. "Now, who wants a glass of lemonade? I'm feeling a bit parched."

Isabelle gave a half-hearted reply, her mind still spinning with all the changes that were happening. Fiona and Josh were both leaving town for the summer. And Marissa was going to become a mother.

Her mind suddenly flew to Elias and their upcoming wedding. Her stomach clenched with a new dread. As her fiancé, he would be affected by this news as well. She needed to talk to him soon and let him know how things stood.

That was another conversation she would not be looking forward to.

23

Mark heard Josh come in the front door and waited in the kitchen for him to appear. He almost always raided the fridge when he got home. However, the distant clunk of footsteps indicated that Josh had gone right up to his room. Mark turned off the stove and wiped his hands on a rag. No point in putting off the talk they needed to have any longer.

With a sigh, he started up the stairs. Josh's door was closed, but a strip of light shone beneath it. Before he knocked, Mark took a moment to center his emotions and to ask the Lord for guidance. Then he rapped sharply on the door.

"Yeah."

Mark opened the door and poked his head inside. "Can we talk for a minute?"

Josh sat at his desk, staring at an open textbook. "I guess so. As long as it's not another lecture."

Mark leaned against the doorframe. "No lectures, I promise." He tried not to grimace at the clothes that lay scattered over the bed and floor, the guitar shoved in the corner, and the piles of books on the ground. "First, I want to apologize for reacting badly the other day. I guess I was just angry and disappointed with the whole situation." He drew in a breath. "But I'm over that now, and I want to help you come up with a plan."

A nerve ticked in Josh's jaw. "I had a plan, but Marissa wouldn't go for it."

"What was that?" He had a sneaking suspicion what his brother was about to say.

"I asked her to marry me. But she turned me down."

Mark schooled his features to hide his dismay. "Did she say why?"

Josh stared at the wall and shrugged. "Something about not wanting to ruin my life." The pinch of his lips highlighted the misery dogging his features.

Mark held back a grunt. *A little late for that now.* But as he took in his brother's dejected stance, sitting with his head in his hands, the truth hit Mark hard. Josh had real feelings for this girl, and he was suffering because of her rejection.

Olivia's words came back to him again. *"Josh is a young man, possibly in love for the first time. . . . Trying to ignore it or minimize its importance isn't fair to him."* If what his brother felt for Marissa was anything close to what Mark felt for Isabelle, then he deserved Mark's compassion.

"I'm sorry, Josh. I know you must care about her very much."

Josh looked at him fully for the first time, a hint of relief on his face. "I do."

"What are you going to do now? You'll have to find a way to support her and the baby." Mark's chest grew tight with disappointment. "I hate to admit it, but university might not be in the cards for you. The best thing you can do is focus on graduating high school and then getting a job."

"I know. I've already been looking . . . and I found something I want to do." He got up and walked over to the bed, where he picked up a newspaper. "I've decided to take a job up north for the summer at the lumber camps." He handed Mark the paper.

Mark looked down at the circled ad and frowned. "Why go all that way? You could get a job around here just as easily."

"Yeah, but the pay is almost double what I'd make in the city. It would go a long way to help with the baby." He shrugged. "I want to prove to Marissa how committed I am to our future, and hopefully when I come back, she'll have had a change of heart and agree to marry me."

Mark inhaled and slowly let out his breath. His brother had obviously given it a lot of thought. "When would you leave?"

"Next week. And before you say anything, I've already made arrangements to take my final exams early." He gestured to the books on the desk.

Mark ran a hand over his jaw. What could he really say? Josh was making mature decisions, trying to do what was best to accommodate this unexpected change to his life. He tried to put himself in his brother's shoes and see how scary this must be for him. Digging deep for words of wisdom, he moved closer to Josh. "I know these problems seem insurmountable right now, but everything will work out in time. I promise."

"I wish I could believe that."

Mark laid a hand on his shoulder. "I hope you know I'm here for you, no matter what. We'll get through this together."

Josh's eyes widened, yet a hint of disbelief lingered. "You really mean that?"

"I do."

Josh swallowed hard, and moisture appeared in his eyes. "Then while we're at it, there's something else I need to tell you."

Mark's muscles tensed, and he forced himself to slow his breathing so he wouldn't react with anger. "What's that?"

Josh walked over to look out the window. "I don't want to be a doctor, Mark. I know how much you wanted us to work together, but I can't become a doctor just to please you. I have to live my own life, whatever that turns out to be."

The air seeped out of Mark's lungs. Hadn't Olivia tried to warn him about that in one of their conversations? But he'd been too stubborn to listen, too set on his idea of what Josh's future should look like.

"I don't even like science," Josh was saying. "I hate chemistry and doing labs. And I almost pass out at the sight of blood."

Mark ran a hand over his eyes. How could he have been so blind? "I'm sorry, Josh. I was so busy trying to make sure you'd get into med school, I didn't even ask what you wanted."

"I should have told you sooner, and definitely when you asked a few weeks ago. It's just . . ." Josh trailed off, darting a hesitant glance at Mark.

"You were afraid to disappoint me."

"Yeah."

Mark blew out a breath. "That's my fault. I assumed you were happy to follow in my footsteps." He grimaced. "Pretty arrogant of me."

"You just wanted what's best. I get that." Josh came over to lean against the desk. "You've given up so much for me. I didn't know how to tell you."

Mark studied his brother's serious features, the brown eyes, the shock of unruly hair over his forehead. Like it or not, he wasn't a kid anymore. He was going to be a father soon. "So, before this situation with Marissa happened, what did you want to do?"

"I was thinking of becoming a music teacher." He shrugged. "Guess that will have to wait now."

Mark nodded. "Well, the good thing about dreams is that there's no time limit on them. You can always make them happen later, if you really want to."

But now it was time for Mark to step back and let his brother go. "I'm proud of you, Josh." His throat tightened, making his voice hoarse. "You made a mistake, but you're doing your best to take responsibility."

"Thanks, Mark." Josh shoved his hands in his pockets and hunched his shoulders. "It . . . it means a lot to have you on my side."

"I'll always be on your side." He moved closer and pulled his brother into an awkward hug. The boy's frame remained rigid for a second or two, then he finally relaxed and hugged Mark back.

For the first time in a very long while, Mark felt his parents would be proud of his efforts, despite the less-than-desirable circumstances. For now, he had to trust that God would guide Josh's steps and turn this unexpected roadblock into something good.

24

June was fast approaching, which meant there wasn't much time before the end of the school year. Isabelle had pictured Marissa's graduation day a thousand times in her mind. Her sister, dressed in her cap and gown, walking across the stage to accept her diploma, with Isabelle in the audience bursting with pride. Yet if Mark's prediction was accurate, by the end of June, Marissa would be about five months along. She could never parade her swollen shape in front of all the other students and teachers, which meant she'd have to forgo the ceremony.

And that wasn't the only event that would be ruined. Isabelle had wanted Marissa to be her maid of honor in her wedding to Elias, but that would be impossible too.

Isabelle swallowed a sigh as she entered the employee locker room and started to take off her apron. She hadn't had a chance to meet with Elias yet, but she was going to have to tell him about her sister's condition very soon.

She had no idea how he would react, but if he wanted Isabelle as his wife, Marissa was part of the deal. And that would soon include another mouth to feed. Even if Joshua took responsibility for the baby, he still had little means to support a wife and child. It would be Isabelle and Elias who would have to take care of them initially, until Marissa figured out what to do. She only prayed that this wouldn't be too much for her new fiancé to handle.

Almost as though Elias had been privy to her thoughts, she found him waiting for her when she emerged from the hotel after clocking out.

"You are one hard lady to reach, Miss Wardrop," he said, pushing away from the brick wall. "I've been relegated to stalking hotel exits to find you."

"I'm sorry to cause you such inconvenience, sir." Isabelle managed a teasing tone. "Now that you've found me, what can I do for you?"

His gray eyes lit at her banter. "I thought that since we're engaged, it was time to go on another date. Are you busy tomorrow?"

"I do have to work."

"What about after your shift ends? I have a place I'd like to take you."

"That sounds intriguing." The prospect of doing something for pleasure seemed a foreign concept. But this could be the opportunity she'd been waiting for to tell Elias about her sister without fear of being overheard or interrupted.

"Is that a yes, then?"

She smiled. "I'd love to."

"Wonderful. Where can I pick you up?" He studied her. "Or do I have to meet you somewhere again?"

Isabelle hesitated. Since they were already engaged, she supposed she could allow him to see where she was living. "You can pick me up." She gave him Rosie's address, noting the slight frown as he registered the neighborhood.

But he was quick to smile at her. "I look forward to seeing you tomorrow."

Isabelle would have felt the same, if only having to tell him about Marissa wasn't weighing her down with dread.

The next afternoon, when Isabelle returned home from work to get ready for her date, she was surprised to see Rosie sitting on the sofa, staring at a telephone on the coffee table.

"Aunt Rosie, I didn't know you planned to install a phone."

"I didn't." The woman raised her brows at Isabelle. "I thought you might know something about this."

"Me? Why would you think that?"

"The man from the Bell Telephone company said the order had been placed by a Mr. Weatherby."

Isabelle dropped her purse on the kitchen table with a thud. "Oh, goodness. I had no idea." She glanced at Rosie. "Are you upset?"

"I was a little put out at first, but when the installer assured me that the monthly cost was being handled by the same person who placed the order, I could see no point in objecting." The older woman grinned, a twinkle of mischief in her eyes.

"That is certainly generous of Elias. I'll be sure to thank him when I see him later."

Wanting to appear her best for the occasion, she hurriedly changed into one of her prettiest dresses, lilac with white stripes, and a matching hat, paired with small white gloves. But even her favorite outfit couldn't quell the nerves invading her belly.

Isabelle waited on the front step, gratified that Elias arrived right on time. When he stepped out of the car to greet her, Rosie opened the door.

"Are you the person responsible for my new telephone?"

"I am." Elias stood tall, neither arrogant nor repentant.

"Then allow me to thank you. I've never had the luxury of a phone before."

"You're welcome. Although I'm afraid it was mostly a selfish action on my part." He shrugged. "I wanted to be able to contact my fiancée if I needed to."

Isabelle's brows rose in surprise. She'd never expected him to admit such a thing.

Rosie laughed. "Selfish or not, I'm grateful. Now, off you go, the pair of you, and have a lovely evening."

It was a beautiful afternoon for a car ride. Forty minutes later, however, Isabelle had to wonder just where Elias was taking her. They'd driven a fair distance outside the city, and she wasn't even sure where they were anymore.

At last, he turned into a parking lot. She squinted at the sign on the low building in front of them. *Welcome to the Royal Botanical Gardens.*

"I thought we could take a walk inside and eat in the restaurant here," Elias said. "Most of the flowers will be in bloom by now, and I've heard they have some beautiful water plants as well."

"That sounds lovely." Had he remembered her love of flowers when he planned this outing?

Elias ushered her through the entrance, paid the fee for them both, and led her out into the most glorious gardens Isabelle had ever seen. Acres of blooms stretched out before them.

"It's amazing," she breathed.

"Nothing quite like it in the city, is there?" He headed toward a stone path that wandered through the greenery.

"Not like this." She inhaled the heavenly scent of water, freshly cut grass, and perfumed flowers.

They wandered in companionable silence. Now and then, he pointed out a particularly gorgeous array. The sun was out in full force, sparkling off the ponds that were scattered along the route. Elias must have been warm in his suit and fedora, but he didn't give any indication of discomfort.

After a few minutes, they came to a scenic bridge that spanned a lily pond. As they crossed, she looked over the rail to watch the fish nibbling at the surface. A frog jumped from a lily pad into the water with a quiet splash.

"There's a spot over there where I thought we could sit for a minute." Elias pointed to a bench in a covered area, where they would be out of the direct sun.

"Perfect." She could still hear the water gurgling, and the raised platform gave them a nice view. She took a seat in the shade, and Elias sat beside her.

For a few moments, she simply breathed in the fragrant air and attempted to calm her nerves. But the conversation could not be put off.

"I'm glad we're here, Elias. There's something important I need to discuss with you."

His expression instantly changed, becoming guarded. "You haven't changed your mind about marrying me, have you?"

"No, I haven't." She hesitated. "But you might change yours after you hear what I have to say."

He reached for her hand. "That sounds serious."

"I'm afraid so."

"Whatever it is, I'm sure we can handle it together." His expression was so earnest, Isabelle dared to hope he would react better than she feared he would.

"Ever since my parents died," she began, "my sister has been struggling. I didn't realize just how traumatized she was until recently."

"That's only normal, I'm sure. Losing your parents has been a huge blow for the both of you."

"Unfortunately, Marissa handled her grief in a more detrimental manner." Isabelle looked down at her lap. There was no easy way to say this or to prepare Elias for her announcement. "I've recently learned that she is several months pregnant."

Elias's hand jerked on hers. "What?"

"I know. I'm as shocked as you are." She glanced at his profile. His throat worked up and down, and he stared straight ahead.

He remained quiet for several long seconds, then at last he turned to her. "Have you . . . has she decided what she's going to do?"

"Not yet."

Elias took out a handkerchief and mopped his face. His brows scrunched together, creating vertical creases between his eyes.

"I realize this will have a bearing on our wedding," she went on quickly. "But I'm certain we can find a way to work around it."

Elias inhaled, seeming to make an effort to compose himself. Then he stood and walked away from the bench. His agitated movements bore witness to his unsettled thoughts. People strolled by them on the paths with not a care in the world. A distinct contrast to the tense drama playing out between them.

When he turned back to face her, shadows from the leaves above him played over his grim features. "You must realize that our wedding will be one of the biggest events in Toronto society. My mother is preparing the guest list and other details as we speak. All the most important people will be in attendance. I could never embarrass my family by including your unmarried pregnant sister at our nuptials in St. Bartholomew's Church."

So many of the things he said struck a jarring chord within her, but she needed to keep focused. She squeezed her fingers together in her lap and attempted to remain calm. "We could delay the wedding until after the baby is born. A few more months shouldn't matter in the long run, and we could still be married before Christmas." Not the most ideal situation since she and Marissa would have to stay with Rosie for the next several months or more, and it would be extremely cramped in their bedroom with the addition of an infant.

Disappointment radiated from his face, mirrored by his slumped shoulders as he sat back down beside her. "Is there a possibility that Marissa might marry the father?" he said at last.

"That seems unlikely." No need to tell him that Marissa had turned Josh down.

"Will she put the child up for adoption, then?" A flare of hope lit his eyes.

"I-I don't know. She hasn't made any decisions yet." Perhaps Isabelle should have waited until she had more answers before she broached this conversation with him. If she had a clear path forward with Marissa, she wouldn't sound so . . . pathetic.

"If marrying the father is out of the question, I assume she'd have no other option but to give the child up."

She took a breath and met his gaze. "Does my sister truly have no other option, Elias?"

The quiet question hung in the perfumed air between them.

When his gaze slid away, she pressed on. "If we go ahead with our plans to wed, Marissa could keep her baby. She'd have a home and a family to help her." Isabelle prayed the film of perspiration on her brow didn't give away her nerves. "I promise she wouldn't be a burden. As soon as she's able, she'll find work to support herself. All she needs is some time to get back on her feet."

In the seconds that followed, the discordant beating of her heart drowned out all other sounds around them.

Elias stared at a mother and her little girl as they walked by, his brows pulled together in a frown. At last, he turned to face her. "Please believe me, Isabelle, I wish the circumstances were different. However, for me to take an unwed mother into my home . . ." He closed his eyes. "This may sound selfish, but it could bring disaster to my family's reputation and possible ruin to my investment business." He shook his head. "I was having a hard enough time convincing my mother and sister that our union would be a good one. This news would make that impossible."

Her throat tightened, making a response momentarily impossible. She squeezed her eyes shut and attempted to calm her erratic breathing.

"If your sister were to go away somewhere to have the baby and give the child up, we might be able to continue with our plans. But without that guarantee . . ." Elias slowly shook his head. "Despite my esteem for you, Isabelle, I don't think this union will work out—for either of us."

All her muscles went suddenly lax. Yes, she was disappointed, but she couldn't really blame him for his reaction. She knew only too well how fickle the elite members of Toronto society were with their favor. Elias needed to stay in their good graces if he wanted his business to thrive. "I'm sorry, Elias. I truly am."

He reached over to touch her hand. "I am too. If the situation changes, please let me know. If not . . ." He let out a long breath. "I hope there are no hard feelings between us. I wish you nothing but the best, Isabelle. I really do. I hope you can find it in your heart to do the same."

"Of course." Her innate breeding took over, and she rose from the bench with as much dignity as she could muster. "I suppose we should be getting back then."

"I think that would be best." He got up as well, and they slowly retraced their steps to the main entrance of the gardens.

This time, the beauty of the scenery was lost on Isabelle. She kept her posture stiff as she walked, making sure she didn't inadvertently bump into him. So much for her marriage to Elias being the answer to their problems. She would have to come up with another solution—and soon.

But as much as she hated to admit it, mixed with her disappointment at Elias's decision was a very real sense of relief that she would not have to become Mrs. Elias Weatherby after all.

25

A knock on the front door woke Mark from a light sleep. He jerked upright on the living room sofa, blinked, and rubbed his face, then glanced at the clock on the mantel. Eight o'clock. He must have fallen asleep after dinner.

He ran a hand through his hair, fastened the top button on his shirt, and went to open the door.

Isabelle stood there, looking so beautiful he couldn't quite catch his breath. She wore her hair down in golden swirls over her shoulders. Her blue eyes seemed extra wide as she smiled at him. "Hello, Mark. I hope I'm not disturbing you."

He blinked and reminded himself to breathe. "Not at all. Come in."

He ushered her into the living room and quickly crossed to the sofa where he'd been sleeping to rearrange the throw pillows. "Have a seat."

"Thank you." She sat down, setting her purse on her lap. The fitted skirt of her dress showcased shapely legs crossed at the ankle. "You have a very nice place," she said, scanning the room with undisguised curiosity.

"Thank you, although it could use a few renovations if I ever get the time." He chose the armchair nearest to her and attempted to appear relaxed, even though his heart was racing in his chest. "How did you know where I lived?"

Her cheeks grew red. "There was a telephone booth near the bus stop, so I looked up your address in the phone book." She gave a slight shrug. "I hope you don't mind."

"No. I'm glad you came." More glad than he should be. "Can I get you something to drink?"

She hesitated. "I'd love a glass of water if it's not too much trouble."

"Not at all. Are you sure you wouldn't like some coffee or tea?"

Her stomach made a loud noise that echoed in the quiet room. She pressed a hand against her midsection and grimaced. "Sorry. I guess I'm hungrier than I thought."

"Didn't you have dinner?"

She shook her head, her eyes darkening with apparent distress.

He leaned closer. "Isabelle, what's wrong?" His muscles were poised, awaiting her response. Whatever the problem was, he would do his best to fix it for her.

Under the soft light from the floor lamp, her lashes cast delicate shadows on her cheeks. "I was supposed to have dinner with Elias."

He stiffened at the mention of her fiancé. "What happened?"

"Before we ate, I told him about Marissa, and he . . ." She inhaled deeply, then released it. "He broke off our engagement and brought me home." She shook her head. "I couldn't go into Rosie's and face everyone, so I came here instead. I didn't know where else to go."

His heart jackhammered in his chest as he struggled to make sense of her words. Had she just said her engagement was off? He inhaled slowly to temper his reaction, aware she must be distressed at this turn of events. "I'm glad you thought of me. Why don't you come back to the kitchen, and I'll make you something to eat?"

"Oh no. I didn't intend for you to feed me."

186

"It's no trouble. I have leftovers from dinner. For once, Josh didn't polish off the whole meatloaf."

A hint of a smile emerged as she stood. "You mean I'll get to sample your cooking?"

"You will." He led her down the hall and into the kitchen. "I don't claim to be a gourmet chef, but my food is usually edible—if Josh is any judge, that is." He chuckled as he pulled out a chair for her at the table. "But then again, teenage boys will eat anything."

She looked around the room. "This kitchen is cozy."

He scanned the counter and sink, glad that he'd cleaned up before flopping on the couch after dinner. As he pulled the leftovers out of the refrigerator, he tried to gauge her mood. "How are you feeling about Elias's decision?"

"It's hard to put into words." She looked down at her folded hands on the table. "I'm disappointed as well as a bit hurt. If he truly cared about me, shouldn't he want to help my sister?"

Tiny pricks of jealousy heated Mark's skin. She must have really wanted this marriage if she was hurt by his reaction. "You would think so," he said carefully.

"He was more concerned about tarnishing his family's reputation, though I guess that was to be expected." She let out a long sigh. "He thought Marissa should go away somewhere to have her baby and give it up for adoption. It seemed the only way he might consider going ahead with the wedding."

Mark paused as he buttered the sliced bread. "I'm not overly surprised. It's a common reaction, I'm afraid." He shook his head. "It's hard to believe that people have so little compassion for women who find themselves in trouble. They don't get into those situations alone, yet it's always the woman who pays the price."

Isabelle tilted her head, a look of gratitude softening her features. "You're the first man I've ever known with such a modern opinion. How did you come to be so understanding?"

He shrugged one shoulder. "Working with the women at Bennington Place has given me a great deal of compassion for their situations. I try to treat them with the same kindness I would any other expectant mother. And I suppose it's also due to my upbringing. My parents set a good example for us, one that's served me well in my profession. As a doctor, I can't afford to judge people. Sometimes my patients' illnesses or accidents are the result of their own foolish behavior. Over time, I've learned to become very tolerant."

"You're more than tolerant, Mark. You're sympathetic and understanding. You've never once judged me or my family for anything that's happened. It's a refreshing change from the people I've been surrounded by my whole life."

The admiring look in her eyes made his neck heat. He busied himself cutting some pieces of cheese and adding them to the meatloaf on the bread. "I try to put myself in other people's shoes and see things from their perspective." He sliced the sandwich in two and set it in front of her.

Isabelle's lips curved upward. "How is it that some lucky woman hasn't snapped you up by now, Dr. Henshaw?"

His heart began an unsteady gallop as her blue eyes held his, and another rush of warmth bled into his cheeks at her teasing tone. "I guess I've been too busy to think about a relationship. Josh has been my priority for the last several years. I didn't think it fair to divide my time and attention even further." He turned back to the counter, where he poured them each a glass of milk, then he joined her at the table.

"I understand that. Being responsible for a sibling is a daunting prospect." She picked up the sandwich and took a large bite.

"How is Marissa feeling these days?"

She finished chewing and swallowed. "Physically, she seems better now that her stomach is more settled. Emotionally, however, she's not handling this well."

"Josh is struggling too. Although he does seem to have a plan for a summer job."

"Marissa told me." She patted a napkin to her mouth and

frowned. "I thought by my marrying Elias, Marissa would have a safe haven until she had her baby. But now I don't have any idea what to do."

His heart went out to her. She'd been doing her best to handle everything on her own. She deserved someone to share her troubles with. Elias should have been that person, but he'd made a different choice. Mark waited until she finished the sandwich before saying, "I do have an idea I'd like to share with you. Why don't we go and sit in the living room?"

"Okay." She rose and carried her plate to the sink, and then they made their way back to the living room.

He took a seat beside her on the sofa. "First," he said, "tell me what's worrying you the most about Marissa's situation." He wanted to make her feel that she was in charge, not that he was trying to tell her what to do.

"I suppose the most immediate issue is her finishing school." Lines formed between her brows. "But now, even if she passes her exams, she won't be going to her graduation ceremony."

He nodded. Likely she'd be showing quite a bit by then.

"And then there's where we're living. It won't be fair to Rosie to bring an infant into that small place. The walls are paper thin, and the baby's cries are sure to disturb her. But I don't think I can afford a place of our own yet."

She seemed so dejected that he couldn't help but reach out and take her hand in his. "I have a solution that might help in that regard. If you'll allow me, I could talk to my friend Olivia, one of the matrons at the maternity home. I'm sure they'd welcome Marissa there."

Isabelle stared at him. "I can't send my sister away like that. It would seem like I'm trying to get rid of her. Or punishing her somehow."

"Trust me, Bennington Place isn't like that." He purposely kept his voice soothing, like he often did with his fearful patients. "Ruth and Olivia opened the center specifically to help women in such situations avoid judgment. The mothers-to-be are treated with kindness and respect."

She shifted slightly on the sofa, gently pulling her hand free of his. "I hate the thought of us being separated. She's all the family I have left." Moisture magnified the blueness of her eyes.

Mark fought the strong desire to take her in his arms. "It would only be for a few months, until the baby is born. It would give you both time to determine a plan for the future." He paused for a minute. "Why don't you think it over? At least keep it in mind as an option."

"How . . . how much would it cost?"

"There's no charge. Some of the residents pay a small fee if they're able, but Olivia would never turn someone away because of money."

A few seconds of silence ensued. "All right. I'll think about it." She clasped her hands together. "I hate feeling so helpless. So out of control. Not knowing how to help Marissa or what the future holds." Pushing to her feet, she strode over to the window.

Mark closed his eyes. Her suffering was almost tangible. He could feel it vibrating in the air around her. He got up as well and walked toward her. "I know it seems overwhelming," he said. "But I have to trust that God hasn't forsaken us. That He's by our side during these difficult times." He laid a gentle hand on her shoulder, dismayed to feel a shudder ripple through her.

"I'm finding it hard to believe that when one disaster after another keeps happening." A small sob escaped, and when she turned to look at him with an expression of such hopelessness, an overwhelming need rose within him. The need to ease her burdens. To offer her comfort. To make her feel cherished and safe.

He pulled her gently against his chest and wrapped his arms around her, offering her shelter from the storms of life. Her floral scent intoxicated him, filling his senses until nothing existed outside this moment, this room, this woman.

She leaned back to look up into his eyes.

He raised a hand to caress her cheek, then, without thinking, he lowered his lips to hers.

Isabelle's heart thudded against her ribs. She could barely comprehend what was happening as Mark's mouth moved gently over hers. When he pulled her even closer, tingles of electricity shot through her, igniting every cell in her body.

Before she realized it, she'd wrapped her arms around him and was kissing him back. The soft bristles of his beard brushed her skin, and the scent of clean soap and coffee filled her senses.

Home. The word drifted through her mind as she reached up to cup his jaw. Warmth filled her chest. She'd never felt so connected to anyone before, as though their very souls had come together. She'd certainly never experienced a kiss like this before.

When they finally drew apart, he rested his forehead against hers. "I've dreamed of doing that for a long time."

"You have?" She blinked. For someone normally poised in all situations, she now found herself completely out of her depth, her mind racing with too many thoughts to process. "Why didn't you ever say anything?"

"The truth is, your father intimidated me."

My father? Mark had been attracted to her for that long? "How so?"

He gave a rueful shrug. "He would never have considered me good enough for you. I'd hoped in time he'd come to see me as an honorable man, one worthy to court his daughter. But in the end, it didn't matter. Everything changed the night your mother passed away."

She swallowed. Humiliation burned deep as dreaded memories surfaced. Oh, how she must have hurt him with her callous words. Her heart continued to beat too fast as she waited for him to say something more.

He ran a finger down her cheek, an apologetic expression on his face. "As much as I enjoyed kissing you, it probably wasn't the smartest thing to do. The timing doesn't seem right for us to . . . get involved."

Looking into his hazel eyes, she gave a sad smile. "I know. We have to focus on Josh and Marissa right now and do whatever we can to help them."

Yet a wave of disappointment rushed through her. She should definitely *not* be thinking about kissing him again, which would only serve to confuse matters even more. As he said, the timing simply wasn't right.

"I agree. They have to be our priority now." A determined light glowed in his eyes. "Hopefully, between the four of us, we can come up with a solution that will work for everyone."

She nodded. "Thank you, Mark. I feel better knowing we're in this together."

He laid a tentative hand on her shoulder. "Are we all right, Isabelle? I don't want there to be any awkwardness between us." His anxious eyes searched hers.

Warmth spread across her chest. He was always so kind, so solicitous of her feelings. She managed a smile. "We're fine."

The lines in his forehead visibly relaxed. "I'm glad. If you need me for anything—"

"I know. I have your telephone number." She laughed.

"Have I said that too often?"

"Not at all. I don't mind hearing it." In fact, knowing he was only a phone call away was a huge reassurance in her life. He'd been the first person she wanted to see after her disastrous date with Elias. "Speaking of phones, Elias put one in for Aunt Rosie." She frowned. "I hope he doesn't take it out now that we're no longer getting married."

"If so, let me know. I'll do what I can to help. I feel better knowing you have a way to reach me if you need to."

She laid a hand on his arm. "You'll never know how much it means to have your support."

Oh, how she wanted to say so much more. Especially with him looking at her with such emotion glowing in his eyes. Had any man ever looked at her that way?

He smiled. "My pleasure. Come on. I'd better drive you home."

26

The next day, Isabelle got off the streetcar and began the five-block walk toward Aunt Rosie's place. Fatigue and melancholy pressed down on her like a heavy blanket, making her joints ache. She'd been called into Mrs. Herbert's office at the end of her shift and given a stern reprimand over being late again last week and for not being accommodating enough with one of the hotel guests. After showing enough remorse to satisfy the supervisor, Isabelle had left with another black mark on her record.

Today, the reality had set in that she would have to continue working as a maid for the foreseeable future, and she realized how much she'd been counting on being able to quit once she and Elias had wed.

But that option no longer existed, and she had yet to come up with a better plan—or any kind of alternative, really. She and Melissa would have to figure out a solution on their own before the baby came.

The humid air clung to Isabelle, fusing her damp blouse to her back. Overhead, gray clouds scuttled across the sky, portending the rain to come.

When she arrived home, Fiona's suitcase stood in the middle of the sitting room. It hit Isabelle then how much she'd miss her friend. Between both of their work schedules, they hadn't had a lot of time together, but it was comforting to know that she was always nearby if Isabelle needed her.

Fiona came out of her bedroom and looked up. "Isabelle. I'm glad you made it home in time for me to say good-bye." She looked lovely in a trim blue dress that highlighted her reddish locks. Her face fairly glowed with excitement.

"You're leaving tonight?" Isabelle couldn't keep the wistful tone from her voice.

"First thing in the morning. But I decided to sleep at the house tonight with the other girls to save time tomorrow."

"That makes sense." Isabelle blinked to hold back her rising emotions.

In the kitchen area, Rosie set her wooden spoon down and came over, wiping her hands on her apron. "Make sure you watch out for bears and snakes up there. Those woods are likely filled with all sorts of dangerous creatures."

"Oh, Aunt Rosie." Fiona laughed. "I'm not going into the wilderness. The house is just as modern as the one here. I won't even have an outdoor privy to contend with." She pulled her aunt into a hug.

"I'm going to miss you, luv. Take good care of yourself."

"You too, Auntie." Fiona kissed her cheek. "I'm grateful you'll have Isabelle and Marissa to keep you company."

"We'll watch out for her, so don't you worry." Isabelle put on a brave smile. "Promise me you'll have a wonderful summer filled with adventures and fun."

"Aye. I intend to. And I'll write you and Aunt Rosie as often as I can." Fiona threw her arms around Isabelle and squeezed. "I'll be praying everything works out for you and Marissa."

"Thank you." Isabelle swallowed hard.

A car horn tooted. "That must be my ride." Fiona dashed over to grab her suitcase. "Tell Marissa I said good-bye. And God bless you all until we meet again."

"Amen to that." Aunt Rosie wiped her eyes and turned back to finish her kitchen duties.

Isabelle walked to the window and watched until the car pulled away, pushing back an unfamiliar stab of envy. How was it that her former maid had found such happiness working in another household and was now off to spend the summer on Lake Muskoka?

Resolutely, she pushed down all bitterness and went to help Rosie with her chores.

Someday, God willing, Isabelle might find a similar happiness and peace with her situation. If only she could determine when that might be.

Mark parked his car in front of Rosie O'Grady's apartment, attempting to shake off his grim mood. After another two people in a nearby building had fallen ill with polio, there was no getting around the fact that they were dealing with a possible epidemic. Between Josh leaving for his job up north and his dealing with these polio cases, Mark had had no time to do anything more about the clinic or even to talk to Ruth about any news on a potential backer. He hoped to do that soon, but first he needed to warn Isabelle and Marissa about the seriousness of this outbreak. He got out of the car and went up to knock on Rosie's door.

Isabelle answered. "Mark, this is a surprise. What brings you by?"

"I was in the neighborhood seeing some patients." He peered over her shoulder. "Could we talk out here?" He didn't want to upset Marissa with talk of epidemics if she was around.

"Sure." Isabelle followed him down the wooden stairs to the sidewalk below. "What is it? You look worried."

"Unfortunately, I have some unsettling news." He steered her farther down the walkway, away from the few neighbors chatting outside. "There's been an outbreak of polio in a tenement building two blocks away. From the way it seems to be spreading, I fear it could easily become an epidemic."

"That's the second time now I've heard about a polio outbreak. Fiona mentioned something about it before she left." She reached up to finger the necklace at her throat. "That's a disease that can cause paralysis, right?"

"Yes. It attacks the nervous system and the muscles and can cause the lungs to cease working." He pressed his lips together before continuing. "It infects children and young people more than others. For pregnant women, the virus is even more serious. It can cause a miscarriage, or the baby could be born with the illness. I don't say this lightly, but for Marissa's sake as well as yours, I think it would be prudent to find somewhere else to live for the next while."

Her brows winged up. "You want us to move? That seems rather drastic."

"In this type of housing, where the shared sewage system is fairly crude, the virus is difficult to avoid. And believe me, if you ever saw a patient living in an iron lung, you'd know I'm not exaggerating the danger."

"But where would we go?"

He hated having to add one more worry to her growing list of burdens, but their safety was his number-one concern.

"Perhaps it's time to seriously consider Marissa going to Bennington Place." He paused. "Why don't you come and meet the owners? You can make up your mind from there. We'd still have to find somewhere for you to go, but right now Marissa is the one in greatest jeopardy."

"You're really worried for her?" She stared up at him with such trust that his chest constricted.

"I wouldn't be here if I wasn't."

Isabelle was quiet for several seconds, then finally she nodded. "Let me talk to her and see if she's agreeable."

"Thank you." He reached for her hand and gave a gentle squeeze. "But please don't wait too long. I fear this epidemic might spread faster than we think."

27

Two days later, Isabelle finally convinced Marissa to see Bennington Place. At first, her sister had been dead set against the idea, but when several cases of polio occurred at her school, she'd finally agreed to go for the baby's sake. When Isabelle called Mark to let him know, he had been more than willing to come and get them.

Now, as Isabelle got out of the car, she paused to study the beautiful ivy-covered house before her. The residence was nothing like she remembered from the dark, snowy night she'd come here in January, desperate to save her mother. Instead, its homelike quality and peaceful atmosphere served to ease some of Isabelle's trepidation about the upcoming meeting. Marissa opted to leave her bags in Mark's car until she determined whether or not she would stay.

Mark entered Bennington Place with an ease born of familiarity. A pretty, dark-haired woman came forward, a smile lighting her features. "Mark, it's so good to see you."

Isabelle realized then that this was the same woman who had called an ambulance for her mother and had offered to pray for her.

Mark leaned over and kissed the woman's cheek. "Thank you for seeing us on such short notice."

Her brown eyes radiated warmth. "I'm always happy to help, and knowing these two are friends of yours, well, of course I dropped everything." She winked and moved past him to extend her hand. "Welcome to Bennington Place. I'm Olivia Reed."

She was young, in her late twenties, Isabelle surmised. She wore her dark hair in a tidy roll at the nape of her neck. Her flawless skin and full lips added to her natural beauty. What was such a lovely woman doing running a maternity home?

Isabelle shook her hand. "I'm Isabelle Wardrop, and this is my sister, Marissa. I think we met briefly back in January."

"Ah yes. I remember." Olivia turned to Marissa. "Please come in and make yourself comfortable. I have refreshments waiting." She took the girl by the arm and escorted her into the parlor.

Isabelle hung back in the foyer, grappling with everything she'd seen so far. It was apparent Mark and Olivia shared a connection, but what exactly that was, she didn't know.

"Is something wrong?" Mark stared down at her.

"No. I'm just surprised. Olivia is so young . . . and beautiful. I expected someone more mature—"

"Someone like me, perhaps?" A tall, gray-haired woman appeared in the hallway. She chuckled as she came toward them.

"Ruth. So good to see you again." Mark stepped forward to embrace her.

"You as well." Ruth raised a brow. "And who is this lovely young woman?"

"This is a friend of mine, Isabelle Wardrop. She's here with her sister to see if the home might be a good fit for Marissa. Isabelle, this is Ruth Bennington."

"Nice to meet you." Isabelle smiled at the woman, whose impressive height and elegant carriage made her think she came from royalty.

"Likewise, my dear. Shall we join the others?" Ruth gestured to the doorway on the right.

Mark took Isabelle's elbow. "Don't worry so much," he whispered. "Everything's going to be fine."

Inside the parlor, Isabelle was immediately struck by its hominess. Olivia was seated beside Marissa on the sofa, engaged in conversation. It appeared Olivia was doing her best to put Marissa at ease.

Introductions were made, and Isabelle took a seat in one of the cozy armchairs by the fireplace. Mark and Ruth chose chairs on the other side of the coffee table.

"I was just about to explain a bit about our home to Marissa," Olivia said. "We can accommodate up to sixteen women and their babies, though most of the time we're not at full capacity. And the mothers give birth at different times, so the nursery is more than able to handle the infants."

"Do the women give birth here or in the hospital?" Isabelle asked.

"Most of the time, they have the babies here. We have a wonderful midwife, Mrs. Dinglemire, who assists with the births. If there's ever an instance where something goes wrong, the ambulance can be here in mere minutes to take the mother to the hospital. So far, that's only happened twice since we've been open."

"What happens after the baby is born?" Marissa gripped her hands together in her lap.

Isabelle could practically feel her tension.

"That depends on the mother." Olivia gave her a gentle smile. "Those who wish to keep their baby usually stay on until they've found a part-time job and affordable accommodations. We do our best to support each woman's decision, whether it's to keep her baby or to give the child up for adoption. We work with a wonderful lady from the Children's Aid Society who helps our mothers make the decision that's right for them. And, to be clear, we don't pressure them one way or the other. We only offer practical advice and aid."

Isabelle's tense muscles eased. She hadn't realized just how much the responsibility for her sister's pregnancy had been weighing on her. Perhaps she and Marissa weren't alone in this after all.

"Would you like to see our rooms and meet some of the girls in residence?" Olivia asked.

Marissa nodded. "If they wouldn't mind."

"Not at all. You'll find everyone here is friendly. At least they are once they settle in. Most of the woman are a little guarded at first, understandably so. Some have experienced terrible things, hardships we can't even fathom." A shadow crossed Olivia's features. "But it's our policy to allow our guests to share as much or as little as they're comfortable with. Once they realize this is a safe place, they usually relax and open up." Olivia rose and turned to Isabelle. "Would you care to join us?"

Isabelle glanced at Marissa, who gave a subtle shake of her head. "I think I'll let you and Marissa have some time to talk. I'll wait here, if that's all right."

"Certainly." Ruth stood and crossed to a side table where a silver tea service sat. "We'll have some tea while we wait. Mark, would you prefer coffee?"

"Tea is fine. Thank you."

Ruth poured the three cups and passed around a plate of tiny cakes. Isabelle chose one to be polite, though she doubted she could eat with her stomach so unsettled.

"Is something wrong, my dear?" Ruth placed a hand on Isabelle's shoulder as she passed by her chair.

Isabelle glanced up, astounded that the woman was almost able to read her mind. "It has nothing to do with your home. This sounds like the ideal place for my sister."

"Then what's bothering you?" Mark gave her a sympathetic look.

Isabelle hesitated. She hated to talk about such personal feelings in front of this woman who was a stranger, no matter how nice she seemed. However, with both Mark and Ruth waiting for a response, she set her plate aside. "I know Marissa will be in good hands here, but . . ." She swallowed and stared down at the floral carpet before looking up. "She's my baby sister."

"You don't want to leave her here alone." The kindness in Ruth's eyes matched her voice.

Isabelle's throat thickened, and all she could do was nod. The thought of being separated from her was too painful to bear. They'd stuck together through every hardship. It seemed wrong to be parted now when Marissa would need her the most.

"The girls have recently lost both their parents," Mark explained.

"And now it feels like I'm abandoning her somehow." Isabelle blinked back moisture from her eyes. "I know that sounds silly."

"Not at all." Ruth leaned toward her. "Let me assure you that you're welcome to visit your sister as often as you wish. The residents are free to come and go to whatever degree they feel comfortable with. They're not confined or restricted in any way."

Isabelle nodded. "That's good to know. Though I'll be here so often I fear I may make a nuisance of myself."

"Nonsense. The more support an expectant mother has, the better."

Isabelle's respect for the woman grew with each of her statements. "Thank you, Ruth. Your attitude is certainly refreshing."

"Olivia and I understand exactly what these girls are going through and have made it our mission to help them experience better outcomes than we had ourselves."

Isabelle's mouth fell open before she quickly recovered herself. "That's most admirable."

Ruth eyed her. "I believe we can help one another, Isabelle. I hope your sister will see it the same way." The kindness and sincerity in her eyes gave Isabelle comfort.

Isabelle sent Mark a grateful look. "I do too."

When he smiled back at her, the admiration on his face sent warmth surging through her whole body.

Thank you, Lord, for bringing Mark into our lives. I don't know where we'd be without him.

"How are you doing with all of this, Mark?" Olivia asked a while later. "You must have been terribly disappointed for your brother."

Mark looked down at his hands, grateful for this time to speak with Olivia and Ruth alone while Isabelle helped her sister move into her new room. After one of the residents had taken them upstairs, Olivia had come to sit beside him on the sofa, and he'd confided Josh's role in the situation. If anyone would understand how hard this was for him, it was these two women.

"I'm struggling with it, as you might expect." He gave Olivia a brief smile. "But I've been trying to put your advice to good use and really talk to Josh about it—and listen to him too."

"Good," Ruth said. "He'll need your support now more than ever."

"He also finally admitted that he has no desire to become a doctor. He just didn't know how to tell me."

"I'm sorry, Mark." Olivia put a hand on his arm. "I suspected as much, but it's better to know now before spending all that money on tuition."

"You're right. I won't have to worry about that for a while. Josh has taken a job up north where the pay is good so he can support Marissa and the baby."

"That's very responsible of him." Ruth's expression remained serious. "Marissa not only has her sister's support, but yours and Josh's as well. She's one of the luckier ones."

"I realize that. I've told Josh we'll figure out a way to make this work for everyone involved."

Ruth studied him as she sipped her tea. "Has your brother's decision changed your mind about starting your own practice?"

Needing to move, Mark got up and walked over to the fireplace.

"I was up late last night thinking about that very thing. I decided that even if Josh won't be joining me, I'd still like to go out on my own, if possible."

Ruth tilted her head. "I've talked to some potential investors, two of whom have shown interest in your endeavor. Have you had a chance to look at any potential sites?"

"I have, though it was a while back. There's one I think might be perfect. However, it does need some renovations."

"I'd like to see this location, if you don't mind. That way I can get back to the investors with more detailed information."

"By all means. I'll call my realtor and set up an appointment as soon as I can."

"Wonderful." Ruth beamed at him. "Then we'll be one step closer to becoming a reality."

Isabelle stood in the middle of one of the Bennington Place bedrooms and took in the homey simplicity of the space. A country manor couldn't have been more charming. Twin beds flanked each side of the room, with a nightstand and lamp between them. Lovely handmade quilts adorned the beds, and pale blue curtains accented the floral wallpaper. Two high-top dressers and a rocking chair rounded out the furniture. Ruth and Olivia had obviously gone to great lengths to make the rooms cozy and inviting.

Marissa set her suitcase on the floor. "It's nice, isn't it?"

"Very." Yet no matter how wonderful the setting, Isabelle couldn't force any cheer into her demeanor. The idea of leaving her sister alone here sat like a cold lump in her belly. "Are you sure this is what you want, Rissa?"

"It's best for everyone." Marissa's eyes filled with tears. "You will come and see me, though, won't you?"

"I'll be here so often they'll think I live here." She pulled her sister into a tight hug, her throat burning as they clung together.

If only their mother was here to guide them. What advice would she give at a moment like this?

"Remember what Mama always said," Isabelle whispered. "God is with us in our times of trouble. He'll help us through this. Hold onto that thought, and it will bring you comfort."

"I'll try." Marissa's lips trembled as she stepped back from Isabelle. "I miss Mama so much. I hate to think how disappointed she'd be with me."

Isabelle shook her head. "She would have loved and supported you no matter what. Just as I do." She ran a hand over her sister's soft hair. "Use this time wisely," she said. "Take advantage of the advice these women have to offer in order to make the decision that's right for you and for your baby."

"I will."

"And remember, if you change your mind about staying here, we can always find another solution."

"I'll be fine." Marissa seemed to pull herself together. "At least the other girls here understand what I'm going through."

Isabelle sniffed and did her best to smile.

"What about you, Belle?" Marissa smoothed a hand over her expanding midsection. "Where will you go?"

"I'm not sure yet. I want to talk to Rosie before I make up my mind."

"Don't take too long. I don't want you to risk being exposed to that disease."

According to Mark, the Bennington Place neighborhood so far had no reported cases of anyone with polio. Isabelle was grateful that her sister would be safe here. "You don't need to worry. Besides, I doubt Mark will stop hounding me until I'm somewhere he deems acceptable."

They both laughed.

Isabelle motioned to Marissa's suitcase. "Shall I stay and help you unpack?"

"No thanks. It won't take me long."

A light footfall sounded as someone entered the room. "Oh, hello. You must be my new roommate." A dark-haired girl stepped inside the doorway. From the look of her fresh face, she couldn't be much older than Marissa, which made her large belly all the more shocking.

The girl gave a wide smile. "My name is Laura. What's yours?"

"I'm Marissa and this is my sister, Isabelle."

"Nice to meet you." Laura's cherry-apple cheeks beamed. "I'm so excited to have someone to share my room."

"How long have you been here, Laura?" Isabelle asked.

"About four months now. I had another roommate for a while, but she had her baby and left." The girl drifted over to her side of the room and plopped down on the bed. "You'll like it here, Marissa. Ruth and Olivia are wonderful. They make us feel like we're one big family."

Isabelle pushed back a spurt of resentment. *She* was Marissa's family. She was all her sister should need. But just as quickly, an inner voice convicted her. These people could give Marissa something she could not, and she had no right to begrudge her these new relationships.

"I'm glad to hear that." Isabelle slid an arm around Marissa's shoulders. "I want to make sure my sister is in good hands."

"Oh, the best. Believe me."

Suddenly, Isabelle felt in the way. Though she hated to go, Marissa needed to take this next step of her journey on her own. It was a small comfort that she'd have a roommate so she wouldn't feel totally alone.

"Well, I suppose I should take my leave, then." Isabelle blinked hard, determined she would not break down until she was far away from Bennington Place. "Take good care, Rissa, and call me often." Isabelle was more grateful than ever for the new telephone in Rosie's apartment, one that Elias had graciously continued to pay for, perhaps to ease his guilt for breaking their engagement.

"I will. I promise." Marissa hugged her again, clinging for just a moment too long. Tears stood out in her eyes as they parted.

Then, with a last watery smile, Isabelle left the room and made her way down the stairs to the front hall where Mark would be waiting to take her home.

28

Seated on the bus the next morning, Isabelle checked her watch, and a sinking feeling spread through her. Of all the times for the vehicle to break down. Even if she got out and ran the rest of the way to the hotel, she'd be late for her shift. Another black mark on her record would not bode well, but maybe, if luck was on her side, Mrs. Herbert would be busy elsewhere in the hotel and not realize that Isabelle was missing.

By the time Isabelle reached her locker and changed into her uniform, she was more than forty-five minutes late. She'd just picked up her timecard when a door opened down the corridor, and a frowning Mrs. Herbert appeared.

Isabelle's stomach dropped at the woman's hard stare. "I'm so sorry I'm late. The bus broke down on the way to work and I had to catch another one."

"No explanation is required, Miss Wardrop." The surprisingly calm voice didn't match her frosty expression. "Effective immediately, your employment is terminated."

"W-what?"

"You will turn in your uniform, your locker key, and your ID badge and leave the premises immediately."

The timecard slipped from Isabelle's fingers and fluttered to the floor. "Mrs. Herbert, please. Give me one more chance. I promise it won't happen again."

"You said that the last two times you were late. I'm afraid you're out of second chances. Good day, Miss Wardrop."

Slowly, Isabelle picked up the card and stood, staring at the tabletop. Her legs began to quiver, and she grabbed the wall to steady herself.

She'd lost her job. Her only source of income.

What on earth would she do now?

Woodenly, she changed out of her uniform, cleared out her locker, and returned the required items to Mrs. Herbert's office. "I'm very sorry." Isabelle felt compelled to apologize again.

The woman only nodded. "I wish you the best in your next position, wherever that may be. However, I won't be able to provide you with a reference, should you require one."

"I understand." Isabelle couldn't really fault the woman. The rules were the rules, after all. Too bad Isabelle had such a hard time following them.

Once she left the hotel, she had no idea what to do with the rest of her day. She walked aimlessly down the city streets, hoping to perhaps see a *Help Wanted* sign in some window. But no such signage appeared.

When she came upon a beautiful stone church, Isabelle stopped. Maybe this was exactly what she needed. To spend some time in prayer and listen for the Lord's direction. Nothing she was doing lately seemed to be working, but maybe that was because she was trying to solve all her problems by herself instead of relying on divine guidance.

Taking a deep breath, she entered the sanctuary and took a seat in one of the rear pews.

Immediately, a sense of peace flooded her system. Instead of pouring out all her woes in prayer, Isabelle sat still in the hushed silence and attempted simply to be. The Lord knew everything she was going through. She didn't need to list all her troubles.

She would just rest in God's peace for a little while and hope that an answer to her dilemma would come to her.

After half an hour, no real solution had appeared, but she left the church with a renewed sense of optimism. Even in the darkest of times, she had to believe God held her in the palm of His hand. She would find another job somehow and carry on from there.

The most important thing right now was that Marissa was safe at Bennington Place. Everything else would fall into place at the appropriate time.

The following day, Mark picked up Ruth at the maternity home and drove to the old deli, where he'd made arrangements for Mr. Remington to meet them. The realtor opened the store for them and left them to explore the interior alone, promising to return in twenty minutes. Clearly, he was hoping that a decision would be made today. Mark hoped that would be the case as well.

Ruth wandered around the main room. It was hard to determine from her expression exactly what she thought of the place, and Mark waited on tenterhooks to hear her verdict.

At last, she stopped in the middle of the kitchen area and nodded. "I see why you like this space. I think it would do quite well as a clinic. It's large enough to accommodate a good clientele but not too spacious." She turned to face him. "The only thing better would be a partner to share this enterprise with."

"Yes, well, it won't be Josh." That knowledge still stung somewhat.

"I was thinking of someone a little older." A hint of humor laced her voice.

He narrowed his eyes at her. "I know that look, Ruth Bennington. What do you have up your sleeve?"

An eager grin spread over her face, enhancing the wrinkles around her eyes. "I have been speaking with some members on a few hospital boards and asking if they knew of any doctors looking for a partner."

"And?" Mark's blood began to pump faster.

"They mentioned a couple of names, one that stood out as a potential match." She chuckled at the bewildered expression on his face. "Don't worry, I took the liberty of speaking with Dr. Axelrod before I got your hopes up." She shook her head slightly, as if in wonder. "God works in mysterious ways, my boy. This man shares the same passion for the underprivileged as you do and has been wanting to leave the practice he's in for a while now, but he just hasn't found the right fit."

"And he would consider a place like this, you think?"

"I believe he might." She laughed again. "Of course, it wouldn't hurt to do a few minor renovations before he sees it, like a coat of fresh paint, some furniture, a few pictures for the walls. . . ." She trailed off as she gazed around, clearly visualizing the new look.

"I can't do that until I sign a lease."

She snapped her fingers. "Exactly. Let's get this deal in motion."

Nerves somersaulted through his stomach. "Wait. What about the investors you were talking with? Don't we need their approval first?"

She waved her hand imperiously. "Oh, they'll agree. They've given me the go-ahead to do what I think is right. And I think that this will be a good investment."

Mark released an unsteady breath. "I guess that means we're doing this."

She tilted her head. "You're not backing out on me now, are you?"

He looked into her eyes, drawing strength from her conviction. If this was where God was leading him, then of course he would follow. "No, I'm not. I can't wait to get started."

"Excellent. Let's go give Mr. Remington the good news."

After spending the morning cleaning Aunt Rosie's kitchen and bathroom, Isabelle found herself at loose ends. In the early afternoon, Rosie had gone to deliver some sewing she'd done for a family a few blocks away, and Isabelle decided to drop by the maternity home to see Marissa. She didn't want her sister to worry about her, but she owed it to her to let her know that she'd lost her job.

Marissa had taken the news with the appropriate amount of sympathy. "I'm so sorry, Belle. What will you do now?"

"I'll find something else. In the meantime, I wanted to see how you were."

"You need to stop worrying. Laura and I are getting along fine. It helps to talk to someone who's going through the same thing as me."

They chatted some more until Isabelle could no longer find an excuse to stay, especially when it appeared Marissa sorely needed a nap. After bidding her sister good-bye, she headed down to the main level. As she did, Olivia came out of the parlor. "Isabelle. It's good to see you again. Is Marissa settling in all right?"

Isabelle nodded. "She seems to be."

"Oh good. I suspect she and Laura will get along famously."

"Thank you again for taking her in." Isabelle looked wistfully up the stairs one more time. If only she had her sister to go home to, maybe she would feel like going back there.

"You're not regretting your decision, are you?" Olivia's quiet concern caused a lump to form in Isabelle's throat.

"Not at all. In fact, I'm relieved Marissa is somewhere safe. I guess I'm just feeling a bit sorry for myself. You see, I . . . I lost my job yesterday." Somehow that sounded better than admitting she'd been fired.

"How unfortunate." Olivia gave her a sympathetic look. "Does Mark know?"

"No. I haven't seen him since it happened." And she had no idea how she was going to tell him after he'd used his connection with the hotel manager to get her the position. Now, with no source of income, it would be even harder to find somewhere else to live, no matter how much he wanted her out of Aunt Rosie's. But Olivia didn't need to know all that. "Well, I should be going." She edged toward the door.

"Isabelle, wait a minute." Olivia gestured for her to come into the parlor. "I just thought of something."

Isabelle considered acting like she hadn't heard her and dashing out the door, but that would be rude, so she followed her into the room and took a seat.

"I don't know what type of work you're looking for," Olivia began slowly, "but we have an opening here. One of our girls quit last week. Ruth and I were about to advertise for a replacement." She leaned forward, her expression becoming more animated. "The pay wouldn't be as much as the hotel, but we provide room and board, which might solve another problem concerning the polio outbreak in your area."

Isabelle's heart began to thud in her chest. This was almost too good to believe. "I-I don't quite know what to say."

"Your room would be on the third floor," Olivia continued. "It's not luxurious by any means, but it's clean and neat. You'd be out of harm's way and close to your sister too."

"What would the work entail?" She'd better make sure she could do this job before getting her hopes up.

"A bit of everything, really. The main duties would be cleaning the residents' rooms and bathrooms, and laundering the bedding and towels. It would also include cleaning the main floor areas as well as helping with the meals when Mrs. Neale needs it."

"I could manage all that." For the first time, Isabelle was grateful for everything she'd learned at the hotel. But she thought about Aunt Rosie and her promise to Fiona to look out for her. "Can I get back to you tomorrow with my answer?"

"Certainly. We'll hold off putting the ad in the paper until we hear back from you." Olivia rose with a smile.

This woman's simple kindness was hard to fathom, especially when Isabelle's former friends hadn't lifted a finger to help her in her time of greatest need. The fact that Olivia would offer her a job without as much as a reference was astounding. But then again, perhaps her friendship with Mark had a lot to do with it. "I appreciate the offer. Thank you."

"You're welcome. In the meantime, don't worry about Marissa. We'll take good care of her, I promise."

When Mark dropped Ruth off at Bennington Place, he was surprised to see Isabelle coming out of the gate. She seemed lost in thought and didn't even notice Ruth until she almost ran into her on the walkway.

Mark grinned, recalling the day in the hospital lobby when he'd collided with her. How indignant she'd been. How beautiful she'd looked. How much he'd wanted to kiss her even then.

He stepped out of the car and waited until she finished talking to Ruth.

When she noticed him, her eyes went wide, and a blush rose in her cheeks. "Mark. Hello."

"What good timing," he said. "Can I offer you a ride home?"

She bit her lip, then nodded. "I'd appreciate it. Thank you."

He held the passenger door open for her. Then he dashed around to the driver's side and climbed in. "Checking up on your sister?"

"Yes." One slim brow rose. "Am I pathetic for doing that so soon?"

He chuckled as he steered away from the curb. "Not at all. It just shows how much you care." He glanced over at her, noting the absence of her usual sparkle. "Is everything all right?"

She let out a sigh, gripping her fingers around her purse. "Not really."

"What's wrong? Are you still worried about Marissa?"

"It's not that." She paused, lines forming between her brows. "Yesterday, I lost my job at the hotel." Her voice quavered, and when she looked over at him, tears stood out in her eyes. "I feel terrible, Mark. After all the trouble you went through to get it for me."

He pulled the car over to the curb and put it into Park so he could give her his full attention. "I'll talk to Mr. Johnson again. I'm sure he can smooth this over with your supervisor."

"No. It was my fault. I'd been late twice before, and yesterday was the last straw."

"A couple of times being late is not enough reason to fire someone." He frowned. Couldn't they see that Isabelle was trying her best and give her the benefit of the doubt?

"It wasn't the only reason." She stared down at her lap. "Even if the bus hadn't broken down yesterday and I'd been on time, there have been complaints from the guests." She gave a dramatic sigh. "I guess I'm not very good at taking orders from snooty rich people."

"Oh, Isabelle." Despite the seriousness of the situation, Mark couldn't hold back his laughter. He almost doubled over, picturing her response to some entitled patron's demands.

"It's not funny, Mark Henshaw." She glared at him. "Why should I have to scoot under a bed to pick up something *they* dropped? And *I* certainly wasn't about to unclog their toilet."

He only laughed harder, and seconds later, he heard her giggle. Soon, she was laughing as hard as he was.

When the hilarity finally subsided, he wiped his eyes with his handkerchief and glanced over at her.

She was leaning back in her seat, a hand on her belly. "I haven't laughed like that in a long time."

"You know what they say. Laughter is the best medicine."

"I think that must be true. I do feel much better."

He reached over for her hand, suddenly wanting nothing more than to spend time with her. "Will you have dinner with me tonight, Isabelle? I have some good news I'd love to share with you." Suddenly realizing that might sound insensitive, he pulled back. "Oh, but you're probably not in the mood for a celebration."

She straightened on her seat with a soft smile. "As a matter of fact, I might have some news as well. And I could use your opinion about it."

His heart began to thump. "So you'll come?"

"I'd love to."

Warmth spread through his chest, and he couldn't stop the smile from creasing his face. "It's a date. I'll pick you up at seven."

29

As Mark ushered Isabelle into DiMarco's Restaurant, nerves twisted his stomach into knots. He'd made the reservation as soon as he got home, but now he was second-guessing his choice of eatery. Perhaps he'd been a bit too presumptuous for their first real date.

Just inside the entry, Isabelle came to an abrupt halt. "Mark, this is too fancy. We should go somewhere else."

He held his breath. He'd chosen the restaurant specifically for its romantic atmosphere, wanting to signal the start of a new direction in their relationship. "I've been meaning to try this place for a while," he said. "But I could never get Josh to come with me." He waited, hoping she'd think she was doing him a favor.

She bit her lip while she scanned the elegant décor. "Well, if you're sure."

"I am."

The maître d' seated them at a private table for two, draped in a burgundy cloth. Though it was still light outside, the moody interior was purposely set to create an intimate atmosphere, and the flickering candle in the middle of the table cast a romantic glow over the area.

Mark glanced at Isabelle as she picked up the menu. "I've heard the food here is fantastic. I hope it lives up to its reputation."

"Oh, it does," she said. "I've never been disappointed with any dish I've chosen."

His gaze flew to hers. "You've eaten here before?"

Slowly, she lowered the menu. "Yes, several times with my parents." A hint of sadness wisped over her features.

"Of course. I should have thought of that." No wonder she balked about coming in. She likely knew the price of every item on the menu. He'd hoped this would be a new experience for the both of them. Swallowing his disappointment, he managed a smile. "Well, I imagine you can make a good recommendation then."

She glanced back at the menu. "The steaks are excellent if you enjoy beef. Or if you prefer seafood, the baked salmon is equally good."

"I think I'll have the steak."

The waiter appeared and took their orders. Isabelle chose the veal cordon bleu with mashed potatoes and asparagus.

As they waited for their food, they enjoyed the fresh bread and creamy butter.

Mark chewed a bite slowly, trying to decide how to start the conversation. Tonight, he did want to tell her about the clinic, but he also hoped to get to know her better. Find out what her hopes and dreams were for the future and see if they aligned with his in any way.

"Have you heard anything from Josh, or is it too soon?" she asked before he could begin.

"He probably isn't settled yet. And those logging camps could be too remote to have telephone service. I might have to wait for a letter."

"You're right. I didn't think of that." She set down her piece of bread. "How are you doing with him gone?" Candlelight bounced off the waves of her golden hair and highlighted the sympathy shining in her eyes.

"I miss him," he admitted. "It's lonely in that big house without him."

"I can imagine. Even though I have Rosie, I still missed Marissa last night." Her expression brightened. "But that might not be the case for long."

His hand stilled as he broke off another piece of bread. "Why is that?" Surely Marissa wasn't thinking of leaving already.

"That's what I wanted to talk to you about. When Olivia heard I'd lost my job at the hotel, she offered me a position at Bennington Place."

He wasn't sure how to react. Part of him wanted to rush out and hug Olivia. The other part worried that the job might be another ill fit for Isabelle. "How do you feel about the idea?"

She scrunched up her nose in the adorable way she did when she was thinking. "I'm already used to changing beds and cleaning bathrooms, and I can learn to do laundry. I'm sure the residents couldn't be any more demanding than the people at the hotel." Her features became more animated. "The pay would be less, but it would include room and board. And I'd get to be near Marissa."

"That does sound perfect." In truth, he couldn't have orchestrated anything better himself. "So you're going to take it?"

"I think I will." Her smile dimmed. "The only hard part will be breaking the news to Rosie."

"She'll understand."

"But with Fiona up at the Templetons' summer estate, Rosie will be all alone. I can't seem to convince her to leave her apartment. How much danger do you think she's in?"

"Given her age, I'd say she's fairly safe. The virus is much more contagious for those who are younger, children especially." He leaned toward her. "It's you who'd be at greater risk if you stay."

She nodded. "I guess it's settled, then."

"Good." A huge weight seemed to lift from his shoulders, knowing she'd be safe. "I promise to keep an eye on Rosie and make sure she's taking care of herself."

"Thank you. Fiona and I would both feel better knowing you're looking out for her."

He admired the way her eyes brightened, the sincerity of her smile. "You have a big heart, Isabelle Wardrop. Always thinking of everyone else first."

A blush rose in her cheeks as she toyed with her napkin.

The waiter appeared at that moment with their meals. He'd no sooner set them down when a man appeared in the room, playing a haunting tune on a violin. He stopped at a table where another couple dined to serenade them.

"What big news are you celebrating tonight?" Isabelle asked as she cut into her meat.

"Ah, changing the topic, I see." He grinned at her. "My news also concerns my work. And like you, it started with something bad, which led to something pretty great. At least I hope it'll be great."

Her light laughter tinkled out. "Dr. Henshaw, I do believe that's the first time I've heard you rambling."

His cheeks heated. "I guess I am." He proceeded to relay the events of the past couple of weeks and how Ruth had been help-ing him with his new endeavor.

Her eyes widened with each detail. "That's wonderful, Mark. I'm so happy for you."

"I'm not going to lie. It's scary going out on my own. But if this Dr. Axelrod joins me, I'll feel much better. He's a little older and more experienced. He's been in a private practice for several years now."

"It sounds perfect." Her admiring smile loosened the knot of pressure in his chest. Part of him had worried that she might think less of him if he wasn't working at the hospital. But he should have known that she wouldn't judge him.

"How do you feel about painting walls?" he said suddenly. "I could use the help if you're free tomorrow."

A surprised laugh burst from her. "I've never done any paint-ing before, so I don't know."

"I'd be willing to teach you." He sobered. "The truth is, I enjoy spending time with you, Isabelle, and I'd like to get to know you better. If that's something you might want too."

Her lashes came down for a moment. Then she raised her gaze to his. "I'd like that very much."

A rush of relief filled his chest, and for the first time in a long while, he remembered what it was like to feel happy.

"Why don't we start the getting-to-know-you part right now?" he said as he sliced into his steak. "What was your life like growing up? Did you enjoy school?"

She patted a napkin to her mouth before responding. "I had a wonderful childhood. I attended a private school, the same one Marissa is at now." A wistful expression came over her. "And even though I wasn't the best student, I loved everything about school."

He quirked a brow up. "Your mother may have hinted that you found it hard to sit at a desk all day. And that your chattiness may have gotten you in trouble from time to time."

She laughed. "True. I did prove a challenge for my teachers."

"Did you ever consider attending college after graduation?"

She took a sip of water while she seemed to ponder her answer. "I think I would have if I'd felt passionate about a career. But nothing really captured my interest, and I didn't want to go on without a goal in mind."

"That seems sensible."

"I did enjoy assisting Mama with her charity work. Raising money to help others less fortunate was something my mother felt strongly about. And I did too." She shrugged. "Until I became one of the less fortunate ones."

"A temporary condition, I have no doubt."

"What about you?" She tilted her head. "What made you want to become a doctor?"

When her intense gaze met his, he found himself almost mesmerized by the reflection of the candle's glow flickering in their depths. He could stare into those amazing eyes all night.

He cleared his throat. "Well, my father was a doctor. Ever since

I was young, I looked up to him and wanted to follow in his footsteps."

She smiled. "Of course you did. I imagine your parents were happy with your decision."

"They were. Sadly, they didn't get to see me graduate."

Isabelle reached across the table and covered his hand with hers. "That must have been so hard."

He nodded, holding her gaze for several long seconds.

The waiter appeared again to fill their water glasses, breaking the intimacy of the moment. Probably for the best. Mark wanted to proceed with this relationship in a careful manner, and so he kept the conversation light for the rest of the meal.

"That was wonderful," she said as she patted a napkin to her lips. "Don't tell Aunt Rosie, but it was even better than her dishes."

Mark laughed. "Well, Rosie isn't exactly a trained chef."

"No. But her cooking comes pretty close. I'm especially fond of her Irish stew and soda bread."

"Much better than my meatloaf, I'm sure."

"Not at all. I enjoyed it just as much." She paused for a moment as though considering her next words. "I want to thank you, Mark, for everything you've done for me. I don't know where Marissa and I would be without you."

His chest expanded, and he couldn't resist lifting her hand to his lips. "I hope you know I'd do just about anything for you, Isabelle."

Her eyes flared with an untold emotion before her lashes fluttered down again. But she didn't remove her hand from his.

A throat cleared.

Mark looked up to see the waiter standing beside him. "Will there be anything else tonight, sir?"

"Isabelle, would you like dessert or coffee?"

"I'm afraid I can't eat another bite."

"Just the bill, then, please," he told the waiter.

Mark checked his watch. It was still early. Too early to let this magical evening end. "Would you care to go for a walk by the lake before it gets dark?"

Smiling, she nodded. "I'd love to."

Was there anything more romantic than watching the sun set over the water? Isabelle breathed in the warm evening air, pausing on the sidewalk beside Mark to appreciate the ribbons of gold and red that spread over the softly rippling water. As they stood together, his hand snuck over to entwine with hers. Her heart started an uneven rhythm in her chest as warmth seeped through her. Not just warmth from his hand, but an inner glow that spread through her system like the fiery streaks of sunlight over the water. At last, the sun sank below the line of the horizon, and dusk enveloped them.

He kept her hand in his as they continued down the sidewalk to a spot where the rocks jutted out into the lake. Soft waves broke over the craggy outcrops. Overhead, a handful of stars began to dot the dark sky.

"It's so beautiful here," Isabelle whispered, almost loath to break the silence. "I don't know why I don't come down here more often."

"Maybe you needed someone to share the experience with." Mark's husky voice sent shivers up her spine.

She turned to face him, surprised to see such passion glowing in his eyes. He looked so handsome, with his hair combed off his forehead and his beard neatly trimmed. When he reached over to brush a finger down her cheek, her breath seemed to tangle in her lungs.

"Isabelle, I think you're extraordinary. Not only because of your obvious beauty, but because of your inner fortitude and your generous heart. You've handled every situation that has come your way with strength and grace."

She blinked. No one had ever given her such meaningful

compliments, ones that weren't all about her physical appearance. "Thank you, Mark. That means a lot." She paused, grasping for the courage to be as bold. "I happen to think you're pretty amazing yourself."

His brows rose, and a smile broke over his features. "That's the best thing I've heard in a long time. Other than learning you weren't going to marry Elias Weatherby, that is."

Oh. He'd been worried about that? Tingles of delight spilled down her neck and arms.

Mark leaned closer. "Isabelle, if you're open to the idea, I'd like to keep seeing you. Now that things have settled down with Josh and Marissa, I don't want to wait any longer."

She remembered envying her sister and Josh in Rosie's backyard, and it seemed like a dream that Mark was asking to date her. Her pulse sped at an alarming rate, but she took it as a good sign. "I'd like that too," she said softly.

His face inched closer to hers, so close she could see a hint of gold in his beard. "I'd hate to let this romantic setting go to waste," he said in a low voice. "Would it be all right if I kissed you?"

She drew in a breath and slowly nodded. He reached up to cup her face, his gaze never leaving hers. Her lips trembled in anticipation, and her eyes drifted closed as his mouth found hers.

Immediately, sensation after sensation flooded her body. The warmth of his lips, the spicy scent of his aftershave, and the solid feel of his chest—all sent her heart rate soaring. He gathered her closer to him, intensifying the kiss until her head spun. Who would have guessed Dr. Henshaw could kiss like this?

At last, he drew back, soft joy radiating from his features.

Words failed her, and she simply stared into his eyes. How had it taken her so long to figure out what a wonderful man Mark was?

He took her by the hand, and they walked in blissful silence back toward the restaurant where he'd left his car. Isabelle's feet seemed to glide over the ground, weightless.

"Tell me, what is it you want out of life, Miss Wardrop?" Mark's soft voice broke through her haze of happiness. "Not for your sister, but for yourself."

She blinked. She hadn't spent much time focusing on herself lately, but now Mark was giving her permission to dream. "I guess I want what most people want. Love. A family." She swallowed. "A home." She never realized how much she missed having a home of her own. "I don't know if I'll ever be able to afford a place for Marissa and me, and now the baby."

He squeezed her hand. "One step at a time. Let's leave some of the details up to God."

She nodded. "I think I'll have to. I'm slowly realizing that I can't do it all on my own." She glanced up at him. "Thank goodness I have you."

"Hopefully you always will." He leaned down and kissed her again.

30

The next day, after Isabelle had discussed her job situation with Rosie and received her blessing, Isabelle finally called to accept Olivia's job offer. Olivia had been thrilled with the news, and since Isabelle had promised to help Mark paint his clinic, they decided she would move into the maternity home the following day. That would give her the weekend to settle in before beginning her duties at Bennington Place on Monday.

Mark arrived to pick her up shortly after nine o'clock. His clothing was already covered in paint splatters.

"I see you started without me," she teased.

Grinning, he shrugged. "I was up early so I thought I'd get a head start and figure out how the new paint roller works." He scanned her outfit. "Those are old clothes, I hope. They'll likely be ruined after today."

She held up a bag. "I've come prepared. Rosie lent me some work coveralls so my clothes will be fine."

He shook his head with a laugh. "You never fail to surprise me, Isabelle Wardrop."

Half an hour later, with her coveralls in place and a kerchief tied around her hair, Isabelle took a better look around the interior of the soon-to-be clinic. Mark explained his vision for turning the counter into a reception desk. The wall behind the counter housed several rows of shelving, which likely had held canned goods. Some old barrels that smelled of pickle brine had been pushed into one corner, and a large metal weigh scale sat on top.

"I'm going to get rid of those later," Mark said, coming up behind her.

"I don't see why. You could use that to weigh the babies." She tried her best to look serious until she couldn't hold in the laughter any longer.

He nudged her shoulder. "You had me going for a minute. I think I'll invest in something newer and cleaner." He pointed across the room. "I'd like to paint that wall today and maybe the adjoining one. The others will have to wait until I figure out what to do with all those shelves. Plus I want to sand down the counter and maybe refinish the floors."

"Sounds like a big job." She bent down to run a finger over the wooden floorboards. "These might only need a good cleaning."

"Maybe. I'll try that before I do anything else."

She squinted at the yellow streaks of paint on his plaid shirt. "Where did you start painting? None of these walls look touched."

"In the back, where the examination rooms will be." His hazel eyes lit up. "Come and see."

She followed him toward the rear of the building. One room had been an office for the store manager, the other likely a storage area. Both were a good size and would make perfect examination rooms. The first one had two walls of fresh yellow paint.

"Are we painting everything yellow?" she asked.

"For now. I thought I'd add a different color out front in the waiting area. Maybe pale green. Something more soothing."

"I like that idea." She walked over to a spot where he'd laid newspaper on the floor. A metal tray of some sort held the paint, and a tool sat on the edge. "Where's the paintbrush so I can get started?"

He picked up the tool. "I thought you might like to try this roller. It's a lot faster. I can do the more finicky areas with a brush."

"All right." She watched him roll the device into the paint and then he handed it to her.

Keeping his hand over hers, he placed the roller against the wall and started moving her hand up and down, demonstrating how it worked. The heat of his hand surrounding hers and the warmth radiating from his body so close behind her made it hard to concentrate on the actual technique.

"See how quick this is?" His breath fluttered a loose piece of hair by her ear.

"Very." She cleared her throat and stepped to the side. "I think I've got the hang of it now."

"All right. I'll start in the far corner. Holler if you need help." He gave her an admiring glance.

She turned back to the wall and blew out a breath. Who knew painting could be so . . . stimulating?

Three hours later, they had finished both back rooms and had moved into the front area of the building. Mark propped the door open to let in some fresh air. It had gotten a lot warmer over the course of the morning, causing Isabelle's clothes to stick to her skin. She stepped outside onto the sidewalk, hoping to catch a breeze, and sat down on a wooden bench that spanned the deli's large front window, not even caring that the people passing by on the sidewalk would see her coveralls splattered with paint.

Mark came out a minute later and handed her a cold bottle of soda.

"You're a life saver," she said, taking a long drink.

He sat down beside her with his own bottle in hand. "I've discovered that painting makes one very thirsty."

"And hungry. What should we do for lunch? I think I need fortification before I start working again."

He shifted to look at her. "Are you sure you want to stay? If you're tired, I can take you back to Rosie's."

She raised a brow. "And not see how it all turns out? No, sir. I'm committed to seeing this through. As long as you feed me, that is."

He laughed. "I'll be right back." He set his soda on the ground and dashed back inside.

A thrill of anticipation zinged through her system. What was he up to now?

He returned minutes later with a wicker basket, which he set on the bench between them. Opening the lid, he took out wrapped sandwiches. "We have ham and cheese or tomato and cucumber."

She laughed. "Looks like you thought of everything. I'll have the tomato, please."

He handed her a sandwich, and they ate in companionable silence, content to watch the pedestrians walking by on both sides of the street.

"Judging by how busy this area is," she said, "I think it will make a good location for the clinic."

"I thought so too. And it's not far from the tenements. Within walking distance or an easy bus ride."

"When is the other doctor coming to see the space?"

"Tomorrow afternoon. Once the painting is done, I want to clean out the kitchen and put the garbage in the alley. Maybe wash this front window."

She placed the cloth wrapper back in the basket. "I'd offer to help you tomorrow too, but I told Olivia I'd move in."

"That's okay. You've already done far more than I expected." His expression grew serious. "I really appreciate your help."

"After everything you've done for me, I'm happy to repay you in any way I can." She paused. "I'm proud of you, Mark, for having the courage to do this. I know your parents would be proud too."

His eyes darkened. "Thank you, Isabelle." He reached for her hand and lifted it to his lips. The intense look in his eyes brought instant heat to her cheeks.

A loud whistle startled her. Across the street, a young man

had stopped to stare at them. "Better hold on to that one, pal, or someone else will snap her up in a minute."

"Don't worry," Mark called back. "I intend to."

Isabelle waited for her pulse to settle back to normal. "Can I ask you something?"

"Sure. Anything."

She glanced over at him. "I've told you about Roger and Elias, but I don't know anything about your former girlfriends. I assume there had to be someone." Even though he'd said he didn't have time for relationships because of Josh, Isabelle couldn't believe that there hadn't been some girl in his past.

A shadow crossed his features as he looked away to stare across the street. "There was one, during my early days in university." He pressed his lips into a tight line.

Isabelle waited for him to continue, but he was silent for so long, she figured he was lost in his memories. "What happened?" she finally asked.

"I got so caught up with her that I almost failed my courses that semester. And she still complained I didn't pay her enough attention. I realized then that I had to choose between becoming a doctor or being her boyfriend." He shrugged. "You know what I decided."

"Do you regret it?" She held her breath. Was the reason he never dated because this woman still held his heart captive?

He turned to face her, his expression sober. "Not for a minute. It was the best thing that could have happened. She never would have stood for all the attention I had to give Josh once I became his guardian."

"She sounds rather selfish, if you ask me."

"You're right. She was." He reached up to cup her cheek. "I'm grateful for the experience, though, because it makes me appreciate someone as wonderful as you all the more."

He leaned in and kissed her, right out in plain view of the whole street.

SUSAN ANNE MASON

Another catcall had Isabelle pulling away, her cheeks flushed from the intensity of his embrace more than from embarrassment.

She jumped up from the bench and straightened her kerchief. "I think we'd better get back to work. Those walls won't paint themselves."

"Yes, ma'am." Mark's teasing smile tripped her pulse again.

She hurried inside, fearing her heart was becoming far too engaged by the handsome doctor. But even if she could, she wouldn't change a thing.

31

The next day, Isabelle finished packing her belongings, and after lugging her suitcase into the hallway and setting it beside her trunk, she turned to face Rosie. She never imagined how difficult it would be to say good-bye.

"I hate leaving you here alone," she said.

"I know, luv, but you can't turn down a job in the very place that Marissa's staying. It's nothing short of God's handiwork, I say."

"Maybe so." Fighting back tears, Isabelle gave her a watery smile. "I'll never be able to thank you for everything you've done for us."

"It was my pleasure having you here." Rosie came over to wrap Isabelle in a warm hug. "I expect you to keep in touch now. I want to know when Marissa has that baby."

"I will. And you have to promise to take care of yourself."

"I'll be fine. I've survived far worse than this virus."

A car rumbled up outside the front window.

"That will be Mark," Rosie said. "You don't want to keep him waiting."

Isabelle pulled her close for another tight hug. "You have my number at the maternity home. Call me anytime."

"I will. Now be off with you. And give that handsome doctor a hug for me." Rosie turned and marched briskly into her bedroom.

Seconds later, Isabelle thought she heard her blowing her nose. She swallowed hard, grabbed her purse, and hauled the suitcase out onto the front stoop.

"Let me get that." Mark ran up to take the heavy bag from her.

"Thank you. There's a trunk inside that has to go as well."

His eyes went wide. "You really are moving out, I see."

He set the case beside the car, then together they wrestled the trunk down the stairs and into Mark's back seat.

"I hope you don't mind if I drop you and go," he said as they pulled away.

"Of course not. I know you have a lot to do before Dr. Axelrod gets there." She glanced at his clothes, noting he wore the same paint-splattered shirt from the previous day. "You are going to change, I hope?"

He smirked at her. "You don't think I'd make a good impression dressed like this?"

She laughed and shook her head. "As a handyman, maybe, but not a professional physician."

"Don't worry. I'm off to shower and change before I meet him at the clinic. I'm sorry I couldn't pick you up earlier, but the last-minute touch-ups took longer than I expected."

"I could have taken a taxi, you know."

"And miss getting to see you today? No way." He winked at her.

When they reached Bennington Place, Mark got out and rounded the front of the car to open the door for her. Then he pulled out her bags and brought them up to the porch.

When he returned, he placed his hands on her shoulders and gave her a long look. "I wish I could stay longer."

"It's fine. I appreciate you driving me."

"I may have had an ulterior motive." He leaned toward her. "I wanted to do this again."

Her pulse rate kicked up in anticipation of his kiss. His lips were almost on hers when the front door opened.

They jerked apart, like marionettes under the control of a puppet master.

"Hello, Mark," Olivia said. "Welcome, Isabelle."

"Hi." Red patches bloomed in Mark's cheeks. "I'm sorry I can't stay, but I have a meeting to get ready for."

"Don't worry. We'll take good care of her." Olivia smiled.

"I know you will." He turned his focus back on Isabelle and reached for her hand. "I'll see you again soon. Remember, if you need anything—"

"I have your number." She laughed. It was becoming a running joke between them.

He smiled, and a pleasant warmth spread through her. Aware of Olivia watching, she couldn't stop the blush that spread into her cheeks. "Thank you, Mark."

"You're welcome." He squeezed her hand and winked.

Her heart stuttered in her chest, regretting that they hadn't managed to get in that kiss.

Isabelle watched him exit the iron gate and heard the car engine sputter to life. The reality hit her then that she was about to move in with a houseful of strangers.

An arm slipped around her shoulders. "It's all right, Isabelle. You're among friends, I promise." Olivia's soothing tone helped unwind Isabelle's tight nerves. "Come in and I'll show you your room."

Inside, Olivia insisted on carrying her bag up to the third story, which she managed without even breaking a sweat. They left the trunk on the porch for later.

At the top of the staircase, she turned to Isabelle. "Margaret, the other girl on staff, has a room up here as well, so you shouldn't feel too isolated."

Isabelle let out a relieved breath. "I'm glad to hear that. I was picturing living all alone in a spooky attic."

Olivia's laugh echoed through the hallway. She stopped at the first door. "This is it. Go on in."

Isabelle stepped over the threshold, not sure what to expect. It was a small room, but it had a decent-sized window that allowed light to stream in, brightening the area. There was a single bed covered in a blue floral quilt, a dresser, a small rug, and a nightstand with a lamp. Overall, it was a cheery space that would do quite nicely. "It's lovely."

"I'm glad you like it." Olivia set the suitcase on the floor. "I'll let you unpack and get settled. Dinner is at six o'clock in the dining room. Just come downstairs and follow the noise."

Isabelle laughed. "Thank you. I will."

As she set her case on the bed and looked around, she was thankful for some time to herself. She could unpack and rest a bit before meeting the other residents. The bright spot in all this was that she'd get to see Marissa every day now.

After putting away her things and taking a quick nap, Isabelle changed into a fresh blouse before heading downstairs. As Olivia had mentioned, it was easy to follow the low murmur of voices punctuated with the odd laugh. Some of the women lingered in the parlor, while a few were already seated in the dining room.

Isabelle entered somewhat hesitantly. Would Marissa be here yet?

A long wooden table stretched the length of the room, adorned with china dishes and cutlery. In the center, a vase of flowers gave off a lovely, sweet scent.

Several women looked up as she hovered in the doorway, but unfortunately, she didn't recognize a single person.

"Hello," she said awkwardly. "I'm Isabelle."

A few seconds of silence went by. Finally, one redheaded woman smiled. "You must be new. Please come in. I'm Mary Beth. These others are Helen, Georgia, and Annie."

"Nice to meet you." Isabelle nodded to the women. "Is there anywhere special I should sit?"

"No. Choose any seat you like." Helen, a heavier-set blond woman, gestured to the empty spots.

Conscious of their stares, Isabelle walked over and pulled out a chair near the end of the table but remained standing.

"Wow," said Georgia. "You aren't showing at all yet. How far along are you?"

Heat blasted up Isabelle's neck. "Oh, I-I'm not expecting."

"You're not?" Mary Beth's brows rose. "You do know this is a maternity home, don't you?" She grinned, and the other girls burst into giggles.

Isabelle gripped the back of the chair, unsure whether she should laugh too or if they were making fun of her naïveté.

"Isabelle. You're here." Marissa's voice was a welcome reprieve.

Relief seeped through her, and when her sister came over to hug her, Isabelle did her best not to cling. "How are you?" she asked.

"I'm well. So far, this place agrees with me."

It appeared she was telling the truth. Already Isabelle could see a difference in her sister. The lines of worry had lifted from her brow, and for the first time in months, she seemed relaxed.

Laura waddled into the room behind Marissa. "Hi, Isabelle. It's good to see you again." She plopped down on a chair.

Other women filed in, chatting away as they took their places around the table.

Then Olivia appeared in the doorway. "Oh good, Isabelle. It looks like you've met most of the residents." She smiled. "Everyone, this is Isabelle, Marissa's sister. For the next two days, she'll be one of us, and then on Monday, she starts work as Judy's replacement. I hope you'll make her feel welcome."

The women all murmured their greetings while Isabelle smiled at the array of faces. Some of the residents were young, barely out of their teens, whereas others seemed more mature. Apparently age didn't matter when it came to unexpected pregnancies.

Isabelle took a seat beside Marissa and Laura. Within minutes, a woman in an apron entered the room, carrying covered platters. An older plump woman followed with a soup tureen.

Soon the platters were uncovered and passed around the table. The aroma of beef and fresh bread wafted in the air, making Isabelle's stomach grumble. Suddenly, she realized she was ravenous but took only meager portions of each dish that came by her, not wanting to appear greedy.

The food was delicious, better than many restaurants she'd eaten in. Isabelle watched the women during the meal. Most talked easily with one another, seeming at ease. A few remained quiet, and Isabelle speculated they might be newcomers.

Because of Laura's friendship, Marissa seemed to have avoided that awkward stage. Having an ally who knew the lay of the land, so to speak, had helped her sister feel more at home.

After tea and cherry pie, the woman began drifting from the dining room.

"Isabelle, will you join us in the parlor?" Olivia asked as she pushed in her chair. "The residents usually listen to the radio after dinner and work on their knitting projects."

"I'd love to."

The parlor was as homey as Isabelle remembered, with enough seating to accommodate everyone. The clacking of knitting needles created a steady hum against the static of the radio.

Olivia motioned Isabelle over to a settee near the back of the room. "I thought we could chat a little."

"I'd like that." Isabelle smiled.

"Normally I leave before dinner so I can eat with my family, but since Ruth had a meeting tonight, I wanted to stay to make sure you felt at home."

"That was kind of you. I hope I didn't put you out."

"Not at all. My husband understands that situations sometimes come up that require my presence."

Isabelle's brows rose. "How modern of him." She found it hard to imagine a husband standing back for his wife's career.

"I agree. Darius is a rare man." Olivia's eyes lit with such love that Isabelle couldn't look away.

"You're a lucky woman."

"I am. But enough about me. I wanted to reassure you that Marissa seems to be settling in well."

"That's good to know. It's a great comfort to be close to her."

"I understand how important family is." Olivia's tone grew wistful. "Marissa is lucky to have your support."

Isabelle nodded.

"Speaking of support . . ." Olivia leaned forward and lowered her voice. "I couldn't help but notice that you and Mark seemed quite cozy together." Her brown eyes widened expectantly.

Isabelle hesitated, an uncomfortable heat spreading across her chest. Would Mark want her to say anything about the recent change in their relationship? "Mark's been very kind to Marissa and me since we lost our parents, and we've become . . . good friends."

"I see." Olivia's lips twitched at the corners. "Well, this is the first time I've seen Mark so . . . friendly with a woman. I was worried he might never find someone who interested him."

Isabelle's heart thumped as she squirmed on the hard settee. "He's a wonderful person, and I'm grateful for his friendship." There, a solid noncommittal response. "How did you and Mark become acquainted?" she asked. Better to go on the offensive rather than continue dodging such personal questions.

Olivia's expression grew serious. "He hasn't told you how we met?"

"No."

Tiny lines appeared between her brows. "The short version is that Mark and Ruth saved my life."

Isabelle's eyes widened with a start of surprise. She certainly hadn't expected that answer.

Olivia fiddled with a pleat on her skirt. "My family disowned me when they found out I was expecting. I ended up in the women's reformatory, and once I had my baby, he was . . . taken from me and put up for adoption." She paused for a moment. "When I was released from the reformatory, I had nowhere to go. My fiancé had been killed in the war. Ruth found me in her church, almost unconscious, and brought me here, to her home. I was very ill, but thankfully Mark nursed me back to health."

"I don't know what to say. I'm sorry for all you've been through."

She shook her head. "I was in a very dark place before Ruth took me in. She and Mark accepted me without judgment. They've become my dearest friends."

Without thinking, Isabelle reached over to grasp her hand.

Olivia squeezed her fingers and smiled. "We all have our hardships in this life—a reality I know you've experienced yourself. But I've found that God sends us angels to help us along the way."

Isabelle nodded. "Mark has certainly been that for me."

A squeal sounded from the hallway. Instantly, Olivia's face broke into a huge smile. "Speaking of angels, here come mine now."

A dashing dark-haired man entered the room, holding a little boy who looked like a miniature version of him.

"Mama! Mama!" The toddler kicked his legs and stretched his arms toward Olivia.

"There's my handsome boy." Olivia swept him up and covered his cheeks with kisses, while her husband wrapped his arms around them both.

Isabelle's throat tightened with an unexpected sting of tears. This is what she truly wanted from life. Not a career, not fame, not even wealth. Just a man who loved her and a family to cherish.

Olivia had overcome a tragic past and found love. God willing, Isabelle would be as fortunate herself one day.

32

"Come in, Dr. Axelrod. It's so good to meet you." Mark extended his hand to the tall silver-haired man standing at the door of the clinic. "I'm Mark Henshaw."

The man gripped his hand. "Good to meet you, son. I must say Ruth Bennington has been singing your praises, and I'm intrigued by what she's told me about your project here." He scanned the room with what appeared to be a discerning eye.

"I'm excited to show you around. I've started by making some small changes, mostly freshening the place up with new paint. But there are a few more renovations required." Mark gestured to the counter. "I'd like to turn this into a reception area. I'll put rows of seating for the patients on the other side, along with a few tables and magazines. Ruth suggested some plants would make the place more welcoming."

Dr. Axelrod nodded as he wandered around the large room. Then he pointed to the short hallway. "Are the exam rooms back there?"

"They are. Follow me." Mark led him to the newly painted areas. "You have to picture them with a desk and exam beds, but I think they'll work well."

"I agree. Looks like there's enough space for a consultation room as well."

"True. There's also another small area at the rear that could be a file room or be used for storage. And the kitchen is impressive. It could serve as a lab or a place to do minor surgical procedures."

They finished touring the whole space and ended up back in the main room. Mark pulled up two chairs in the otherwise empty area. "So, tell me, Dr. Axelrod, why are you considering leaving your current practice?"

"To be honest, I want more of a challenge. I've always dreamed of being able to help the underprivileged population of the city. Instead, I became entrenched in a comfortable rut in a wealthy part of town. But recently, I started to revisit that forgotten dream, and when Mrs. Bennington approached me, I felt it was a sign from the universe." He smiled, creating fine lines around his eyes. "From what she told me, it sounds like you've been treating the less fortunate in their homes."

"That's right."

"I respect that so much. And I would value your connection with these people to help them trust me as well."

"It may take some time, but I believe it's possible." Mark paused and crossed a leg over his knee. "I hope you don't mind that I've taken it upon myself to look into your background."

Dr. Axelrod squared his shoulders. "I expected as much, since I've done the same for you."

"Fair enough. I hope my record didn't disappoint you."

"On the contrary. I'm impressed with what you've accomplished in your short career. I can only imagine what lies in store for you going forward."

"Does this mean you've made a decision?" Mark couldn't hide the hopeful note in his voice. With his experience and good reputation in the community, this man would be a great asset to have as a partner.

Dr. Axelrod took a moment to look around the room again, then turned his focus back to Mark. "I'd like to discuss your vision for the clinic in greater detail, but unless we disagree on something fundamental, I can't see why I wouldn't jump at this chance."

Relief loosened Mark's tense muscles. "That's good to hear, sir. I think together we could make a real difference to the underprivileged people in this city."

"I agree. And please call me Allen." He studied Mark for a moment. "Are you a man of faith, son?"

"I am. I wouldn't be doing this unless I felt it was God's calling."

"Excellent. That's my view as well."

A sense of exhilaration rose in Mark's chest. What more of a sign did he need to know this was the right move? He rose and extended his hand. "Let's make a plan to meet again soon and iron out the details."

Allen nodded as he shook Mark's hand. "I'm looking forward to it."

On Monday morning, Isabelle rose right at six. She was determined to be a model employee and be on time every day. She met Margaret, the other maid, in the third-floor hallway promptly at six thirty.

"Good morning, Isabelle. We usually start by helping Mrs. Neale with breakfast preparations. By the time we finish there, the women will be coming down, and we'll have access to the beds and the bathrooms."

In the kitchen, Isabelle was put on toast detail while Mrs. Neale cooked the eggs and Margaret set the dining room table. Isabelle learned that the staff ate in the kitchen once the residents had been served, and although she would miss sharing meals with Marissa, she couldn't complain.

Once everyone was busy with their breakfast, and she and Margaret had eaten, Margaret took Isabelle upstairs and showed her the routine for cleaning the bedrooms and bathrooms.

"You catch on quick," Margaret said as they exited one of the rooms.

"It's similar to the work I was doing at the hotel. I'm grateful for the training I received there."

Margaret gave her a serious look. "Word has it that you and your sister grew up rich."

Isabelle flinched at the pejorative tone. "That's true. I'd never cleaned a toilet or changed a bed in my life. It took a bit of getting used to." She tugged the vacuum along the hallway. "But I've found there's a great deal of satisfaction in making a room sparkle."

Margaret smiled. "I know what you mean. I'll leave you to finish here while I tidy Mrs. Bennington's quarters."

"Thank you, Margaret. I appreciate your help."

"Just yell if you need anything."

Isabelle knocked on the next door before entering. When there was no answer, she entered the room, lugging the Hoover inside with her. She was scanning the room for an outlet when a muffled sound caught her attention. The quilt on the far bed shifted, and a blond head poked out.

"Oh, I'm sorry," Isabelle sputtered. "I didn't know anyone was in here."

"It-it's all right. You can come in." The girl swung her legs over the side of the bed, her extended belly making her lap disappear. She swiped a sleeve across her eyes.

Isabelle realized she'd been crying. A measure of alarm raced through her. "Are you feeling ill? Should I send for someone?" She had no idea what to do for a woman nearing her time to give birth.

"No. I'm fine. I just had some disappointing news yesterday that's weighing on me."

Isabelle took in her blotchy cheeks and disheveled hair, and her heart filled with compassion. She moved across the room. "Is there anything I can do?"

The girl shook her head.

"I'm a good listener if you'd like to talk about it."

"You don't want to hear my problems. As my father would say, I've brought this all on myself." She pressed her trembling fingers to her lips.

"I understand more than you might think. My sister is one of the residents here." She came to sit on the bed beside her. "I don't think I've officially met you yet. My name is Isabelle."

"I'm Eloise." The young woman glanced at her. "Your sister is the new girl? Laura's roommate?"

"That's right." Sensing that Eloise might open up if Isabelle shared some of her story, she took a breath. "Marissa got pregnant after our mother died. She hid it from me for a long time. I know she's scared and doesn't know what to do. But I hope the people here can help her make a wise decision."

Eloise rubbed a hand over her belly. "I don't have any options. I have to give my baby up." Fresh tears rose in her eyes.

"I'm sorry. That must be so difficult."

"It is." Eloise pulled a handkerchief from inside her sleeve and dabbed her eyes. "Yesterday, my baby's father confirmed that he's not willing to help me. And my family isn't prepared to raise another child."

Isabelle nodded, holding her tongue. No words could possibly comfort Eloise right now. Listening to her heartache might be the only thing she could do for her.

"I know it's the best thing for my baby. To have a happy home with two parents. But it will be the hardest thing I've ever done." A tear rolled down her cheek.

Isabelle patted her arm. "You're being very brave putting your child's welfare first. That's what a true parent does, no matter how hard it is."

Eloise nodded. "Thank you, Isabelle. I hope your sister has a happier outcome."

She squeezed the girl's arm and rose. "I'd better get back to work, or I'll be fired on my first day." She laughed. "If you ever want to talk, I'll be around."

"That's kind of you." Eloise pushed to her feet. "I'll get out of your way so you can clean in here." She gave Isabelle a genuine smile as she left the room.

As Isabelle plugged in the vacuum and pushed it across the floor, she reflected on something her mother had often told her.

"You were right, Mama," she whispered. "Giving is so much better than receiving."

33

Mark had never been so eager to visit Bennington Place. He wanted to find out how Isabelle had made out in her first week of work, and if he were lucky, he'd manage to find a moment to speak to her while he was there and perhaps invite her out on another date.

In addition, he'd finally received a letter from Josh, which had included an envelope for Marissa that he needed to deliver.

One of the residents opened the door when he knocked. "Hello, Dr. Henshaw."

Smiling, he stepped into the foyer of the maternity home. "Good afternoon, Georgia. How are you today?"

"I'm doing well, thank you."

He scanned the hallway and glanced into the parlor. He'd purposely timed his visit so that Isabelle might be on the main floor helping with dinner preparations.

"Are you looking for someone?" she asked.

Heat raced up his neck to the tips of his ears. "I was hoping Marissa or her sister might be around."

"Marissa's upstairs, and I think Isabelle is in the kitchen helping Mrs. Neale. Do you want me to get her?"

"That's all right. I'll go back myself."

The girl nodded and disappeared into the parlor.

Mark took a breath and headed to the kitchen. Slightly off-key singing drifted out from the open doorway. He poked his head inside and had to stifle a grin. Isabelle stood at the counter, holding a rolling pin over a lump of dough, singing in time with her movements. He stared in amazement. With all the servants she'd had growing up, he couldn't imagine she'd ever made dough before. Yet she seemed totally comfortable with the task. His lips twitched. It shouldn't really surprise him, given how well she'd taken to painting walls.

"Hello, Isabelle."

She jumped and whirled around. "Mark! You startled me."

He laughed as he came into the room. "Have you taken over the cooking duties already?"

"I'm not good enough for that." She smiled and set the rolling pin down. "But rolling out the dough is one thing I can do fairly well."

He moved closer and reached out to brush some white powder from her cheek. "You have a little flour there."

A blush gave her features an alluring color, reminding him of rose petals in summer.

She stepped back and lifted the edge of her apron to wipe the offending spot. "Are you here to check on the residents?"

"No, I haven't resumed my duties here just yet. But I do have some news. I've heard from Josh."

She moved to the sink to wash her hands. "That's good. How is he doing?"

"He says the work is hard, but he's getting used to it." He patted his pocket where an envelope sat. "He sent a letter for Marissa."

Isabelle dried her hands. "I'm sure she'll be happy to hear from him."

"How are you both settling in?" He prayed his suggestion hadn't turned out to be a bad one.

Isabelle's soft smile eased his worry. "Very well. Marissa's made friends with her roommate and seems much more accepting of her situation." Isabelle moved closer, her eyes glowing. "I can't thank you enough for suggesting she come here. It's exactly what she needed."

"I'm glad." His shoulders relaxed a notch. "You didn't say how *you're* doing though."

"At first I felt a little out of place. But the women have all made me feel welcome. Even though I work here, they don't treat me like a servant. One of the girls is even teaching me how to knit."

Mark couldn't help laughing. "Really?"

"Yes. Although I might need years of practice before I ever make a pair of socks." She chuckled. "Who would have thought I'd enjoy working in a maternity home?"

Mrs. Neale entered through the back door, carrying a basketful of cucumbers and tomatoes. "These should make a lovely sal—oh, hello, Doctor. How are you today?"

"Just fine, Mrs. Neale. I see you have a new recruit."

The plump woman nodded, her eyes twinkling. "Isabelle has been a godsend around here." She set her vegetables on the large kitchen table. "Take a break to talk with the doctor if you'd like, Isabelle. There's no hurry for the dough."

"Are you sure?"

"Absolutely. I'll cover it up until you get back."

"Thank you. I would like to go up and see my sister. If it's all right with you, Mark."

"By all means. I'd love the company."

As he went to follow Isabelle out, he turned back to see Mrs. Neale watching him with a knowing smile. Then she winked and turned back to her vegetables.

Mark gave himself a mental slap. Unless he wanted Isabelle to be the subject of the home's latest gossip, he'd better try to keep his feelings under wraps.

For the time being, anyway.

—— ❖ ——

That evening, Isabelle set down her knitting needles with a huff. "This doesn't resemble anything a person could ever wear. I think I'm hopeless."

Once she finished her work for the day, she and Mary Beth came into the parlor to chat and continue Isabelle's knitting lessons. But one glance at her new friend's beautiful baby blanket made Isabelle's feeble efforts seem even more pathetic.

"Nonsense." Mary Beth reached over and picked up Isabelle's latest attempt. She stretched the hapless shape into more of a rectangle. "Your stitches are becoming more even, and your edges have gotten straighter."

"You're just being polite." Isabelle shook her head. "This is the strangest-looking scarf I've ever seen."

Mary Beth's lips twitched, then she doubled over her lap, a burst of repressed laughter escaping.

"What's so funny?" Marissa came into the room, Laura behind her.

Isabelle held up the misshapen scarf. "My knitting project."

Marissa didn't even attempt to hide her snicker. "I hope that's not for anyone's baby."

Mary Beth started laughing all over again.

Isabelle twisted the wool into a clump and shoved it back in the wicker basket at her feet. "Don't worry. I'm nowhere near ready to make anything like that yet. Not even a scarf, it looks like."

"Practice makes perfect. Isn't that what Mama always said?" Marissa's wistful tone had Isabelle shooting her a concerned look. Ever since Mark had delivered Josh's letter to her sister, Marissa's demeanor had undergone a subtle change—and not the way Isabelle had imagined it would.

Instead of seeming pleased that Josh had found work and was saving for their future, Marissa appeared tense, troubled even. Had Josh said something in his letter to upset her?

"I do need a lot more practice, but not tonight." Isabelle rose and stretched her back muscles. "I think I'll go upstairs and read for a while. Good night, Mary Beth."

"Good night, Isabelle. Sweet dreams." Mary Beth focused back on her work as Isabelle exited into the hallway.

Marissa and Laura followed her out. "Belle, could we talk to you for a minute?"

"If you're not too tired," Laura added quickly.

Isabelle paused at the base of the staircase. "Is everything all right?"

"Laura wanted your opinion on something," Marissa said. "Could you come up to our room for a few minutes?"

"Sure." Isabelle was happy to have any excuse to spend more time with Marissa. The week had been filled with learning her new duties, and she'd barely had the chance to exchange two words with her sister. Now that she was on staff, Isabelle took her meals in the kitchen, so she was no longer privy to the conversations among the residents. It made her feel disconnected from Marissa, especially when her sister seemed joined at the hip to her new roommate. Still, Isabelle reminded herself how fortunate she was to be near her.

They made their way up to the second floor. Isabelle followed the girls into their room and waited while Laura took a seat on one of the chairs. Marissa sat near her on the bed, leaving Isabelle the other chair in the room.

"What's on your mind, Laura?"

The girl stared at her lap, her nose wrinkling in thought. "I need help deciding what to do about my baby."

Isabelle glanced at her sister. Why did they think she was the right person to ask? "Don't they have someone from the Children's Aid Society who counsels you on these matters?"

"Yes." Laura's features fell. "Mrs. Wilder. She's nice enough, but to be honest, she intimidates me."

"Well, I'm not sure how qualified I am to give advice on this subject, but I'll do my best." Isabelle recalled how talking with

Eloise seemed to help the girl and decided it couldn't hurt to hear Laura out. If there were any serious concerns, she'd tell Olivia or Ruth.

"Thank you." The ridges on Laura's forehead relaxed. She took out a handkerchief from a hidden pocket in her dress and twisted the piece of fabric between her fingers. For the first time, Laura's cheerful façade was nowhere evident, and true pain reflected in her eyes.

"I had pretty much decided to give my baby up for adoption. I even told Mrs. Wilder that I would. But now . . ." She rubbed one hand over the swell of her belly. "Now I think I want to keep him or her." Tears welled in her brown eyes.

Isabelle refrained from looking at her sister. Was this Marissa's way of getting Isabelle's opinion on the matter too?

"When is your baby due?" she asked Laura.

"Mid-August, if the midwife and Dr. Henshaw are right."

"Oh." Isabelle tried to mask her surprise. She'd figured the girl was due any day. "Well, you still have time to make your decision." She paused. "What about the baby's father? Will he be any help?"

The girl's gaze fell to her lap. "No."

Isabelle waited for her to offer any more information, but Laura only pressed her lips together and stared down at the floor.

As curious as Isabelle was about Laura's circumstances, it wasn't any of her business. "What about your parents? Or other family members?"

Laura shook her head. "They're the ones who sent me here. They told me to give the baby up or not to bother coming home."

Isabelle recoiled in disbelief. How could a parent be so cruel? She looked over at Marissa. Her features were tense, and moisture rimmed her eyes. Isabelle's parents would have been terribly upset to learn of her sister's condition, but she had to believe they would never have disowned her or given her such a harsh ultimatum.

"I'm so sorry." Isabelle reached over to put her hand on Laura's knee. "That must have been hard to hear."

Laura nodded. "I love my parents, and I want to respect their wishes. But I love this baby too."

Isabelle closed her eyes, sending up a silent prayer for guidance. Then she opened her eyes and met Laura's troubled gaze. "Though I'm not an expert on the subject, I'll tell you what I feel to be true." She hesitated, searching for the right words. "As much as you love and respect your parents, you can't make such an important decision solely to please them. If you give your baby up just to make them happy, you might regret it for the rest of your life."

Isabelle paused to let those words sink in for a moment before continuing. "On the other hand, if you believe it would be in your child's best interest to give him or her to a family that could provide a better life than you could, that would be a perfectly good reason to do so. One that might give you comfort over the years, knowing your loss meant your child would thrive."

Laura's lips trembled, but she remained silent.

"However, if you feel strongly about keeping your baby and you're prepared to make whatever sacrifices that might entail, I think you could find a way to make it work. There are a lot of factors to consider when making that decision, like how it will affect your relationship with your family. Only you can determine if it's worth the cost."

Tears now streamed down the girl's face. She wiped her cheeks with the handkerchief and gave a watery smile. "Thank you, Isabelle. That makes a lot of sense."

"I would talk to Olivia or Ruth as well and see what they think." Isabelle smiled. "I'll pray that the Lord gives you clarity and peace in whatever you decide." She squeezed her hand, hoping she'd said something that helped her. "Well, I'll let you two get some rest. Good night."

She left the room, feeling oddly deflated, wishing she was the one sharing the room with Marissa instead of Laura. Footsteps followed her down the hall.

"Belle, can I talk to you for a minute?" Marissa's tense voice halted her departure.

"Of course. What is it?"

"I've done a lot of thinking lately." Marissa drew in a breath, then released it. "And I wanted you to know that I've decided to give the baby up for adoption."

"What?" Isabelle's head swam from this unexpected declaration. "What made you decide this? I thought you and Josh had an agreement."

Marissa pressed her lips together.

"Did he say something in his letter that made you change your mind?"

"No."

"Then why the sudden turnabout?" Isabelle couldn't begin to fathom her sister's thought process.

"I think it would be in the baby's best interest to have a stable home. Something I don't think I can provide, even with Josh's help." Marissa tilted her chin. "It would be best for everyone. Josh would be free to live the life he wants, and my baby will have a good home."

Her reasoning didn't fool Isabelle for a second. Not when shadows of pain haunted her sister's eyes.

"Isn't this a decision that Josh deserves to be part of? He's the baby's father, after all, and he's taken on months of hard labor to provide for you two. You can't simply change the plan without telling him."

"I intend to tell him in my next letter. Then it will be up to him to decide what he wants to do next."

A mixture of emotions rolled through Isabelle as she attempted to corral her thoughts. As much as she wanted to rant at her sister for being so fickle, she needed to tread carefully. "Marissa, maybe you should take more time to—"

"I don't need any more time. I've made my decision and it's final. I need you to accept that, Belle." With that, she turned on her heel and headed back to her room, leaving Isabelle churning with disbelief.

Poor Josh. How would he feel once he received Marissa's letter telling him of her decision? Would he choose to stay in the lumber camps or return home and reconsider attending university in the fall?

Another thought caused her equal dismay. How would Marissa's decision affect Isabelle's relationship with Mark?

Seated at his desk in the living room, Mark poised his pen over the stationery, pondering the best way to begin his letter of resignation from the hospital. He wanted to sound positive and grateful for the training he'd received and not make it seem like they'd forced his decision with their ultimatum. He hoped to remain on good terms with the hospital superiors, since he would likely need access to the facility for seriously ill patients who came to the clinic.

A loud knock sounded on his front door.

Frowning, Mark looked at the clock on his desk. It was past nine. Rather late for someone to be calling. He went to open the door, his brows shooting up at the sight of the woman on his doorstep. "Isabelle. This is a surprise. What brings you by at this hour?"

"I need to talk to you, and I didn't want to have this conversation over the telephone."

As he looked closer, he noticed the tight lines around her mouth.

Mark glanced over his shoulder, debating the wisdom of inviting her in. Now that their relationship was progressing, it seemed unwise to tempt fate when they'd be alone. "It's a nice evening. Why don't we go for a short walk?"

Relief spilled across her features. "That sounds good."

He got his jacket and met her on the sidewalk under the glow of a streetlamp, and they headed down the street at a comfortable pace.

"I can tell something's troubling you. Did something happen with Marissa?"

"Yes. Tonight, she told me something upsetting." She glanced over at him nervously. "She said she's decided to give the baby up for adoption."

Mark came to an abrupt halt on the sidewalk. "What?"

"I know. I was shocked too. She's never given me any indication she was planning to do that. I . . . I don't know what's gotten into her." Isabelle rubbed her upper arms.

"Do you think it has something to do with Josh's letter?"

"She claims it didn't, but she did seem more withdrawn after she received it." Isabelle's voice trembled. "I've told her I'll help her with the baby in any way I can. I don't understand what made her change her mind."

Sudden raw anger rushed through Mark's veins. With all that Josh was sacrificing for Marissa, how could she turn around and give his child away? "Has she even thought about Josh? He deserves a say in this too."

Isabelle nodded. "That's exactly what I told her. She just said that it would be better for everyone, including the baby." She threw out her hands. "I don't understand anything about this. First, she turns down Josh's proposal. Now she wants to give away their child. Something seems wrong about this whole scenario."

"I agree. Unless . . ."

"Unless what?"

"Maybe your sister doesn't feel the same way about Josh. Maybe she thinks their relationship was a mistake and wants out of it."

A pretty heartless way to achieve it, in Mark's opinion.

Isabelle kept walking for several seconds, as though pondering his words. Then she stopped and looked up at him. "Somehow that doesn't ring true for me. I believe she cares for Josh a great deal. She keeps talking about not wanting to ruin his life. In fact, giving the baby away will be better for everyone *except* Marissa."

"I don't think Josh would agree with that. When he finds out what Marissa is planning, it will devastate him."

"I know." Isabelle shook her head. "What can we do?"

Mark fought back his own resentment and tried to focus on Isabelle's distress. She was equally upset by this sudden development with her sister and was looking to him to help her come up with a solution. "I'm not sure it will do any good, but I could try talking to her. Maybe I can get her to explain her reasoning."

"It's worth a try. As long as you can stay calm and don't put her on the defensive. You know how stubborn she can be."

Mark's lips quirked up. "I have some idea, seeing that she takes after her big sister."

Isabelle made a face. "Very funny."

He looked down at her, his heart thudding in his chest. He'd missed seeing her this past week, missed kissing her. The desire to pull her closer became almost an ache.

A car rumbled past them on the road, leaving a cloud of dust in its wake, reminding him how very inappropriate such a public display would be.

Mark cleared his throat. "When do you think would be a good time to come by?"

"How about first thing tomorrow morning?"

"I'll be there."

She gave him a look that communicated her gratitude. "I don't know if it will make a difference, but I appreciate your willingness to try."

As they headed back to the house, Mark vowed to do whatever he could to convince Marissa not to give away his niece or nephew. Josh had already endured so many setbacks in life. He didn't deserve to lose his child as well.

34

The next morning, Isabelle lingered over her cleaning in the dining room, waiting for Mark to arrive. She wanted to catch him for a quick conversation before he went up to speak with her sister. Their talk last night had gone better than she'd hoped. Granted, he'd been upset about Marissa's decision, but not to the degree Isabelle had expected.

When a loud knock sounded on the front door, she shot out of the room, relief spilling through her. "I'll get it," she called to no one in particular.

As she headed down the hall, a more insistent pounding sent her pulse skittering. That couldn't be Mark. He'd never act in such a rude manner.

She took a breath and opened the door. A large man stood on the other side, his face contorted in a scowl. Right away, Ruth and Olivia's warnings about unwanted male guests came to mind. Apparently, it wasn't unheard of for the partners of some of the women to try to coerce them into leaving with them.

"Can I help you?"

"I'm here to see Marissa Wardrop. And I'm not taking no for an answer."

Isabelle's brows winged up. There was something familiar

about him, but she couldn't place where she knew him from. A teacher, perhaps? "Who may I say is calling?"

"Justin Henchley."

Her breath caught at the familiar name. "You're the church choir director."

His eyes narrowed. "That's right. Do I know you?"

Obviously, he didn't recognize her, but then again, they'd never been formally introduced. Isabelle had always stayed at the back of the church hall when she attended Marissa's choir practices. She crossed her arms and held her ground. "I'm Marissa's sister. What do you want with her?"

For a second, he appeared taken aback, but then he jutted out his jaw. "That's between her and me." He stepped into the foyer. His sheer size forced Isabelle to move out of the way.

Her palms grew damp. What should she do now?

"How did you know Marissa was here?" she demanded. "The names of the residents are confidential."

He tensed, and it looked like he was about to tell her to mind her own business. Instead, he shrugged. "One of her friends told me."

Dismay bit through her. It had to be Gloria. She was the only other person Marissa had confided in about her situation. "Why would her friend tell you? It's no concern of yours. Marissa quit the choir weeks ago."

Mr. Henchley frowned. "She thought I had a right to know that Marissa is carrying my child."

Isabelle's limbs began to shake as a multitude of emotions swept through her—disbelief, confusion, and finally anger. "That's ridiculous. I know who the father is. Marissa told me herself."

He folded his arms over his chest. "Really? And who would that be?"

She bit her lip against the instinct to blurt out Josh's name. "I'm not at liberty to say, but it definitely isn't you."

Mr. Henchley gave a harsh laugh. "I don't know what stories she's been telling you, but I intend to find out the truth."

Doubts crept through Isabelle, swiftly eroding her confidence. Suddenly Marissa's inexplicable actions—her refusal of Josh's marriage proposal, her decision to give the baby up for adoption—all started to make sense. And if this man even considered it a possibility that he could be the father, it meant he and her sister had . . .

A wave of nausea crashed in her stomach. She raised her head to glare at the man. "How dare you take advantage of such a young girl." Her voice shook with the outrage that coursed through her. "You were in a position of authority. How could you violate her trust like that?"

"Hey, I wasn't the one who started things." He held up his hands. "I'm not a saint. I could only resist her advances for so long."

"Marissa would never do that. You're the one lying now." Heat scorched Isabelle's neck as helpless anger boiled up within her, and her fingers itched to slap him.

"What's going on here?" Olivia's sharp question sounded from the hallway behind her. "Isabelle? Is this man bothering you?"

Isabelle's throat seized. The walls seemed to be closing in around her. "Excuse me. I need some air." She rushed down the corridor, through the kitchen, and out the back door. Sinking onto the top wooden step, she inhaled deeply, struggling to get a grip on the kaleidoscope of thoughts and feelings surging through her.

"I could only resist her advances for so long."

It couldn't be true. Her sister would never act in such a brazen manner. He had to be lying to cover up his own guilt.

She focused on breathing in and out, staring blindly out at the garden. She'd believed that Marissa and Josh had gotten swept up in their love and that an error in judgment had resulted in this pregnancy. Now, the idea that her sister might have been involved in a more sordid relationship made Isabelle physically ill. Mr. Henchley was at least thirty years old. He could even be married for all she knew.

She dropped her head into her hands. Surely Marissa hadn't seduced him. And even if she had made some sort of overture toward the choir director, shouldn't it have been his responsibility to set his student straight?

The door squeaked open behind her, and the weight of advancing footsteps caused the wood to creak beneath her. Isabelle ran a hasty hand over her damp cheeks. "I'm sorry I ran out on you, Olivia. Is he gone?"

"It's not Olivia." Mark's quiet voice sent shivers down her spine. He sat down beside her on the step, his leg brushing her skirt. "She told me you were pretty upset. Would you like to talk about it?"

Isabelle couldn't meet his eyes. How could she ever tell Mark what that man claimed to be true? That all this time, Marissa had allowed Josh to believe he was the father? That he might have given up his future for nothing?

"Is it something to do with Mr. Henchley? He's in the parlor with Marissa right now."

She closed her eyes. "Oh, Mark. I don't even know where to begin." Her lips trembled, and fresh tears burned behind her lids.

His arm slid around her, bringing with it an immediate sense of comfort. She turned her face into his shoulder and breathed in the clean scent of him. All she wanted to do was stay in the shelter of his embrace forever.

"You can tell me anything," he said gruffly. "I hope you know that."

Several minutes went by before she could speak again. She lifted her head to look into his concerned face. "Mr. Henchley claims to be the father of Marissa's baby." The words came out as barely more than a whisper.

"He what?" Mark's eyes widened in horror.

"When I told him we knew who the father was, he just laughed." She bit her lip. "The fact that he thinks it could be true means . . ." She trailed off, unable to voice the terrible truth aloud.

"It means that someone should teach that lout a lesson." Mark stood and whirled around toward the door.

"Mark, no. Wait." She scrambled to her feet, but he'd already stormed into the house.

By the time she caught him, he was barging into the parlor.

"Excuse me, Marissa," he said tersely. "I need to speak to Mr. Henchley. Alone."

Her sister's face was totally devoid of color. She stood, clutching her hands together over her belly.

Isabelle froze in the doorway, torn between rescuing her sister and keeping Mark from inflicting violence on the choir director.

"It's all right, Mark," Marissa said. "I'm handling it."

"No, it most certainly is not all right." Mark walked up to Mr. Henchley until his nose almost touched the other man's. "You should be arrested for defiling a minor."

"Whoa." Mr. Henchley backed away, his hands up. "There's no need to get so worked up. Now that I know about Marissa's condition, I'm here to do the right thing."

Stunned silence shrouded the room. The scowl on the man's face proved he wasn't exactly thrilled about the situation.

Isabelle crossed to her sister's side. "Marissa?" She couldn't quite bring herself to ask if Mr. Henchley's claim was true. "What do you have to say about all this?"

Her sister's face was wreathed in misery, and her legs trembled. "I-I think I need to lie down."

Then, without warning, she crumpled to the ground. Instantly, Mark was at her side, taking her pulse.

Isabelle turned to face Mr. Henchley. "Look what you've done. You need to leave now."

"I'm not leaving until we hash this out."

Mark rose and stood beside Isabelle. "Marissa is in no shape to hash out anything at the moment. Don't make me call the authorities."

The two men stared at each other, an undercurrent of anger

pulsing between them. Even though Mr. Henchley outweighed Mark by at least twenty pounds, she had no doubt Mark could best him in a physical altercation but prayed he wouldn't try.

"I'll go for now," he said, glancing at Marissa's still form on the ground. "But I'll be back."

Isabelle paced the corridor outside Marissa and Laura's room, trying to determine what course of action to take. Once Marissa had come around, Mark had carried her upstairs to her room, where he examined her to make sure everything was all right. He determined she and the baby were fine, and that the shock had simply been too much for her. Still, before he left, he advised caution and bed rest for the remainder of the day.

Isabelle had been somewhat relieved that Mark had to leave for an appointment at the hospital, presumably to hand in his resignation. Before she talked with him again, she needed to have a frank conversation with her sister to determine the true paternity of her child.

She opened the bedroom door a few inches and peeked inside. Marissa lay on her side, facing the wall. Her back rose and fell in soft waves. A little of the tension eased from Isabelle's shoulders. Sleep was probably the best thing for Marissa right now. She'd wait until tomorrow to see how her sister was doing. And then she would ask to hear the truth.

The next morning, Olivia reported that Marissa had come down to the dining room for breakfast and, other than seeming more subdued than usual, appeared none the worse for wear from her episode the previous day. Thankful for that, Isabelle waited until after lunch before approaching her.

She poked her head into the dining room, where her sister sat with two of the other residents who had lingered after their meal. "Marissa, could you help me in the garden for a few minutes, please?"

"I was just about to head upstairs for a nap."

"This won't take long."

Marissa gave her a wary look but nodded.

Isabelle led the way to the kitchen, where she picked up a wicker basket and headed for the back door. "Mrs. Neale wants beets for supper. I told her we'd pick them for her."

"Do I look like I should be picking beets?" Marissa grumbled, rubbing a hand over her belly.

"You don't have to do the bending. Just hold the basket for me."

Isabelle made her way around the perimeter of the rectangular garden to the spot that Mrs. Neale had shown her. She crouched down, grasped the green leaves, and pulled out a clump of beets. After shaking off the dirt clinging to the roots, she deposited it into the basket Marissa was holding.

"I can't believe you know how to pick vegetables." Marissa's lips twitched into a half smile.

"I know." Isabelle pulled out another two beets. "There's something quite satisfying about selecting the food you're going to eat." She picked a few more beets, put them in the basket, and dusted the excess dirt from her fingers. "I'm sure you know the real reason why I asked you out here."

Her sister's gaze swung away as she busied herself arranging the vegetables in the basket.

"I need you to be honest, Marissa. No matter how bad it might be."

The girl released a breath, then nodded miserably.

"Is Mr. Henchley telling the truth?" Isabelle studied her sister for any hint of deception.

Marissa closed her eyes and nodded again. "I'm sorry, Belle," she whispered. "I never wanted you to find out."

Isabelle remained silent. She'd half-expected that answer, so it didn't come as the total shock it once would have been.

"I didn't mean to deceive you, but . . ." Marissa pressed her lips together and shook her head. "I was just so ashamed."

Part of her wanted to comfort her sister, but the other part knew she couldn't pass off Marissa's transgression as unimportant. Isabelle stiffened her spine and did her best to control her conflicting emotions. "How did it happen? Did he force his attentions on you?"

"No, I was the one who had a crush on him," she admitted. "I made my interest pretty obvious. Josh tried to warn me, but I wouldn't listen."

A tidal wave of disappointment engulfed Isabelle. So the man was telling the truth. Marissa had been the one to initiate the affair. Still, she was a seventeen-year-old girl. He should have been mature enough to realize how inappropriate her advances were and have the decency to resist.

She and Marissa moved over to a wooden bench by the fence and sat down. A cool breeze played with the ivy growing over the fence posts.

Isabelle attempted to organize her thoughts. "Why didn't you tell Mr. Henchley you were pregnant? Why did you let everyone believe Josh was the father?"

"I intended to tell him, but when the time came, I . . . I couldn't do it." Marissa fiddled with the basket handle. "Then you and Mark assumed Josh was the father, and Josh insisted we go along with it, for my sake. He didn't want me to have anything more to do with Justin . . . Mr. Henchley." Tears welled in her sister's eyes. "I didn't know what to do, and it was easier to let Josh take charge. He said he wanted us to raise the baby together."

"That's a big sacrifice on his part, raising another man's child."

"I know." Marissa stared down at the grass. "That's why, after a lot of soul-searching, I decided to give the baby up for adoption. I never dreamed Justin would find out and come here."

Isabelle clenched her back teeth together. The way her sister called the man by his first name only highlighted the inappropriateness of their relationship. He was a teacher, a mentor. A mature man with years of experience who should never have taken advantage of a schoolgirl crush.

"Whether we like it or not," Isabelle said slowly, "Mr. Henchley had a right to know he fathered a child."

Marissa nodded. "Yesterday, I was furious at Gloria for telling him, but I suppose it was only right."

Isabelle rubbed a hand over her apron. "He said he wanted to do right by you and the baby. Would you consider marrying him?" The words tasted like ash on her tongue. She couldn't imagine her sister married to him.

"No." Marissa lifted her chin, a gleam of defiance glowing in her eyes. "I've learned the hard way that he's not a man I would ever want as a husband."

Every protective instinct in Isabelle's body reignited. "Why? Did he do something to hurt you?"

"Not the way you mean." Marissa paused for a few seconds. "The day I went to tell him about the baby, I saw him kissing another woman. I realized then that he'd never been serious about me."

Isabelle shoved herself up from the bench, her shoes sinking into the soft grass. "What kind of man would take advantage of your affections when he's involved with someone else?"

"A person with flaws, just like me," Marissa said in a quiet voice.

"His flaws are far worse, trust me." Isabelle crossed her arms over her chest, as though she could contain the outrage coursing through her. "He's a lot older than you. He should have known better."

Marissa didn't reply but continued to caress her abdomen.

Isabelle's anger melted at the look on her sister's face. It was obvious that Marissa already loved her child. It had to be killing her to think of giving the baby away. She went back to sit beside her and took one of her hands in hers, purposely gentling her voice. "Are you sure about your decision, honey? If Josh is willing to help you raise the baby, why wouldn't you consider it?"

Marissa shook her head. "I won't saddle him with a responsibility that's not his. And I don't want him to resent me or my child one day when he realizes we've ruined his life." She gave a sad smile. "I think adoption is the best answer for everyone."

Isabelle studied her sister's flushed cheeks. "You care about Josh a great deal, don't you?"

She nodded. "He's one of the best people I know." A tear slid down her cheek. "If only I hadn't ruined things."

"Oh, honey." Isabelle put her arms around her and let out a sigh. "How did we end up in this sorry state?"

Marissa buried her face in Isabelle's shoulder and hung on. "I wish I knew."

Isabelle sat with her sister on the bench for several minutes, holding her close. Despite the horrible circumstances, Isabelle relished their connection. With this secret out in the open, perhaps Marissa could trust her more and lean on her for support.

"No matter what happens, you're going to be okay." She stroked a hand down her sister's silky hair. "I still believe God has a plan for us. That He'll see us through these hard times and bring us to happier days ahead."

"I hope you're right." Marissa pulled back to wipe her eyes. "I'm more than ready for some happiness to come our way."

Isabelle couldn't help but agree. However, faced with the daunting task of telling Mark the truth, she doubted happiness would come anytime soon.

35

Mark left Dr. Shriver's office, unable to shake a sense of trepidation. Had he done the right thing by resigning his position at Toronto General? Certainly Dr. Shriver hadn't expected that his demand for Mark to stop working at the maternity home would result in this outcome. Who could blame the man for thinking Mark wouldn't want to give up a secure job at the hospital?

But then again, Dr. Shriver didn't really know Mark's heart—the one that beat for the unfortunate and the downtrodden, and not just the upper crust of society. Yet even though his superior didn't understand Mark's choice, Dr. Shriver had had the grace to wish him well in his new endeavor.

Mark would work out his two weeks' notice while he continued to oversee the renovations at the clinic, with the intent of opening by the beginning of September, which was only a few weeks away. With Ruth's investors' help, he would have the necessary funds to purchase any equipment they would need and to furnish the other areas. He'd also already decided what to do about his staffing requirements, thanks to a suggestion from Isabelle. Most of the details had fallen into place, and pending another meeting with Dr. Axelrod, they would open their new clinic on schedule.

If only Mark could dispel his unease over the whole situation and rest in the confidence that he was following God's calling for his life. Surely, a healthy dose of fear was normal for anyone starting such a new direction in their career. He hoped that as time went on his apprehension would fade.

His misgivings over Marissa and her baby, however, would not be set aside so easily.

Although he'd called Ruth the next day to make sure Marissa was feeling better after her fainting episode, he hadn't been back to Bennington Place in a while. He told himself he was giving Isabelle time to get to the bottom of the situation, but he feared he already knew what the answer would be and didn't know how he would handle it if he learned that Marissa had been lying to Josh all this time, making him believe the baby was his.

Josh was already so invested in Marissa and this baby. If he learned that the baby wasn't his and that Marissa had betrayed him with Henchley, he didn't know how Josh would react.

The fact that Isabelle hadn't tried to contact him told him she was likely dreading their next conversation as much as he was. He blew out a breath as he headed into the emergency department. Isabelle and he were just beginning what could be a wonderful relationship.

If only their siblings wouldn't keep getting in the way.

Isabelle hadn't seen Mark in almost a week, which was both a relief and a disappointment. She learned from Ruth that he had been busy ordering the equipment required for his clinic and working out the details of a partnership with the other physician.

Secretly, she felt he must be avoiding her, and she hated that she might have to bring more stress into his already-busy life. But sooner or later, he would have to know that Josh wasn't the father of Marissa's baby.

Maybe Isabelle was a coward for not seeking him out to tell

him. But she justified her lack of action with the fact that a few more days wouldn't change anything.

As they edged toward September, the weather had turned gloomy, punctuated with heavy rains and high winds. Being cooped up indoors had left the pregnant residents on edge and somewhat cranky. After a busy day, Isabelle was more than happy to retire to her room once she'd finished helping Mrs. Neale tidy the kitchen.

As she prepared for bed, the sound of rain against her windowpane brought back feelings of nostalgia. She'd always loved thunderstorms as a child, protected by her father's arm around her shoulder as they watched from the back porch. Marissa, however, hated them and nearly always crawled into Isabelle's bed in the middle of the night if the thunder woke her.

Almost as though echoing her thoughts, a booming clap of thunder erupted, making the floorboards groan in protest. Then, seconds later, a flash of light illuminated her room briefly before another boom sounded, this one closer than the last.

Isabelle got up and went to the window. The tops of the trees swayed in the wind, casting wild shadows over the lawn and the neighboring buildings. There was something so primitive and raw about the weather that it made Isabelle feel more alive than she had in months. For a moment, she could almost feel her father's presence beside her as she watched the rain.

A knock on her door startled her. "Who is it?"

"It's me." Marissa poked her head inside the door.

Warmth spread through Isabelle's chest. Maybe her sister still needed her after all.

"Can you come downstairs? Laura's having pains, and I'm afraid she might be going into labor."

Isabelle's heart rate kicked up a notch. She opened her mouth to say that she knew nothing about labor, but recognizing the fear in her sister's eyes, thought better of it. If it made Marissa feel better to have her there, then of course she'd go. She'd assess the situation and, if warranted, she'd awaken Ruth. "Let me get my robe."

She shoved her arms into the cozy garment and secured the belt around her waist, then followed Marissa down to the second floor. Another flash of lightning illuminated the hallway. This time, though, the thunder had dulled to a growl.

Marissa opened the door to their room and beckoned Isabelle inside.

A lamp on the night table gave off a soothing glow. Laura was sitting up in bed against the pillows, her eyes wide.

Isabelle crossed to her side. "How are you doing, Laura?"

"I-I'm scared." She laid a hand over the blankets covering her belly.

"I know you are." Isabelle pulled a chair over beside the bed. "Are the pains close together?"

"About every ten minutes."

Marissa stepped up behind Isabelle's chair. "That's good, I think."

Laura's face crumpled as she let out a groan.

"It's happening again," Marissa whispered. "A lot sooner this time."

Isabelle held the girl's hand until the tension eased from her face and she could breathe easily.

"I-I think I need to use the bathroom. Could you help me up?"

"Of course." Isabelle waited while Laura swung her legs over the side of the bed. Then she and Marissa each took an arm and helped her to stand. They took a couple of small steps across the floor when suddenly Laura came to an abrupt stop. She bent over as a cry escaped her.

"What is it? Another pain?" Marissa asked.

Laura shook her head. "I think my water broke."

Isabelle looked down at the floor, where a puddle of liquid had begun to pool beneath Laura's feet. Grimacing, the girl freed one of her hands to clutch her stomach.

Nerves somersaulted through Isabelle. There was no doubt about it now. This baby was coming sooner rather than later.

She gave Marissa a worried look. "Can you help Laura to the bathroom? I'll wake Ruth and ask her to call the midwife."

Half an hour later, Isabelle and Marissa sat with Laura, attempting to help her manage the pain. Ruth had come in a few minutes ago to say that Mrs. Dinglemire was out attending another birth and wasn't available, so she'd called Dr. Henshaw instead.

"You'll be in good hands with him," Isabelle had said, praying it would be true and that Mark would be able to guide Laura to a safe delivery.

Now, as they waited, the pains were coming quicker and harder. After a particularly intense contraction, Laura's chin trembled.

"Hang on, honey," Isabelle said. "The doctor will be here soon."

Laura gripped Isabelle's hand. "Please don't leave when he comes." Two fat tears rolled down her cheeks.

"I'll stay as long as the doctor will allow." Isabelle took a damp cloth and wiped her face. "You're going to be fine."

A knock on the door sounded. "It's Dr. Henshaw. May I come in?"

Marissa, who had been pacing nervously, crossed the room to open the door.

"Hello, Marissa. I've come about—" Mark stopped abruptly when he spied Isabelle. "Isabelle? I didn't expect to see you."

She rose from her seat, relief spilling through her. "We've been trying to help Laura through the contractions. She's been doing a wonderful job so far."

Mark gave her a long look. "Thank you." His gaze swung from Isabelle to Marissa. "But if you ladies will give us some privacy, I can take it from here." He set his bag on the dresser and began to unbutton his jacket.

"Please, Doctor," Laura said. "I'd like Isabelle to stay."

Grasping her hand, Isabelle glanced down at the scared girl, then up at Mark. If he allowed it, she would do her best to encourage Laura through the birthing process.

Mark's brows drew together as he seemed to debate his reply. "It's not common for an unmarried woman to take part in a birth. Do you think you'll be able to handle it, Isabelle?"

She lifted her chin. "I might as well get an idea what I'll be in store for when it's Marissa's turn." She turned to smile at her sister, but Marissa's face had drained of color, as if just realizing that in about four weeks' time, she would be facing the same situation.

"Very well." Mark opened his bag and took out his stethoscope and some other instruments and set them on the top of the dresser. "I suggest it might be better for Marissa to wait elsewhere. There's no need to give her undue anxiety before her time arrives."

Marissa twisted her hands together and glanced over at her friend.

"It's all right, Marissa. I'll be here with her." Isabelle placed a hand on her sister's shoulder. "You can use my room to lie down if you'd like."

At last, Marissa nodded. "I'll be praying for you, Laura."

Laura managed a weak smile in return before another pain hit.

Mark pulled a chair over to the bed, then looked at Isabelle. "I'll ask you to step out while I examine Laura. Once I determine where things stand, you can come back in."

She squeezed the girl's hand. "I'll be right outside the door. You're going to be fine."

Hours later, Mark wiped the sweat from his brow, a wave of relief and gratitude loosening his tense muscles.

Thank you, Lord, for another safe birth.

He took a minute to watch the new mother enjoying the first moments with her son. These happy occasions were ones that made his work worthwhile. Bringing new life into the world was truly a gift. One he never took for granted.

His gaze strayed to Isabelle. Her braid draped over one shoulder, and several loose strands of hair had escaped to frame her face. Tears streamed down her cheeks as she reached over to touch the infant's cheek. "He's beautiful, Laura. A true miracle."

Isabelle had been amazing throughout the delivery, never faltering for a second. She kept Laura calm and gave her encouragement when her energy was fading. Her assistance had made his job a lot easier.

"Isabelle, perhaps you could go and let Marissa know the good news?"

She looked over at him and nodded. "Is it all right for her to come back now, if she's still awake?"

"Certainly. Just give me about twenty minutes to finish up here."

Isabelle bent to kiss Laura's forehead. "You did a fine job, Laura. Congratulations."

Mark couldn't let Isabelle go without thanking her, since he wasn't sure if he'd see her again tonight. "Excuse me one moment, Laura." He stepped out into the hall. "Isabelle? A word?"

She turned around, her brows raised.

He came close enough to smell the floral scent that always surrounded her. "I want to thank you. You were wonderful with Laura. And a big help to me."

A smile bloomed on her face, brightening her eyes. "I'm glad. It was truly miraculous to witness a new life come into the world."

Warmth spread through his chest. She understood the sacredness of what they'd just experienced. Not everyone did, especially when the mother was unmarried.

"You were amazing as well," she said. "So calm and reassuring. I hope you'll be the one to deliver Marissa's baby."

He didn't usually encroach on Mrs. Dinglemire's territory unless absolutely necessary, but if it meant that much to Isabelle, he'd be willing to risk annoying the midwife. "We'll see when the time comes." He didn't want to promise anything, now that the paternity of the child was in question. But tonight wasn't the right time for that discussion. He needed his full attention on the new mother and infant.

"Good night, Mark. I hope we can talk soon." She gave him a meaningful look, one that told him she was equally aware of the issue lingering between them.

"Count on it." Before he could reason with himself, he cupped her cheek and dropped a light kiss on her lips.

Then he returned to his patient wearing a smile, imagining what an asset it would be to have Isabelle as his wife.

36

The next day, when Laura asked for Isabelle to come to her room, Isabelle was more than happy for an opportunity to see the baby again. Maybe she'd even get to hold him this time.

Laura was sitting up in bed, cradling the infant, when she entered.

"Good morning. Or is it afternoon? I've lost track of time after getting up so late today." Isabelle laughed. She'd finally fallen asleep just as the sun was beginning to rise, and Ruth had kindly suggested she take the morning off. "How are you feeling today, Laura?"

"Sore, of course. But very happy." Laura smiled down at her son. Then she raised her head, her gaze serious. "I've decided to keep him, Isabelle. I can't bear to give him up."

"That's very brave of you," Isabelle said slowly. As she looked down at the innocent face, she couldn't imagine ever having to make such a decision.

"Will you stay with me while I break the news to Mrs. Wilder? She'll be here any minute now."

"If you want me to, I will."

"Yes, please."

As they waited, Laura told her she had decided to call the baby

John after her father and hoped it would help soften his attitude toward her. It was a lovely gesture on Laura's part. Isabelle would pray even harder that Laura's family would find it in their hearts to welcome her and her son back home.

Isabelle was holding the baby when Mrs. Wilder arrived. The social worker entered the room, looking very professional in a navy blue suit and carrying a briefcase. She seemed somewhat surprised to see Isabelle in the room. "Good morning. I'm Mrs. Wilder. Are you a relative of Laura's?"

"No. Just a friend." Isabelle placed the baby back in Laura's arms, hoping the meaning wasn't lost on the woman.

"I asked Isabelle to stay for our meeting," Laura said.

"Very well." Mrs. Wilder set her case down, opened the flap, and took out some papers. "I assume you're prepared to surrender the child."

"Actually, I've changed my mind." Though Laura's chin trembled, her gaze remained steady. "I've decided to keep my son."

"I see." Mrs. Wilder set the papers on the dresser. "Have your circumstances changed, then?"

Laura clutched the baby a little tighter. "Not really. Except that the people at Bennington Place have offered to help me. I can stay here until I find employment and somewhere to live."

"That could be a lot harder than it sounds," Mrs. Wilder said in a gentle tone.

"Hard, but not impossible." Isabelle stepped forward, the need to defend Laura's choice burning in her system.

Mrs. Wilder turned to Isabelle. "I like to give my clients a fair idea of the reality facing them before they make such a life-altering decision. It's my job to determine whether or not the infant will be in danger of neglect." She held up her hand. "Not neglected on purpose. Simply by virtue of the hardships a mother might end up experiencing."

When Laura remained silent, Isabelle held her tongue as well, waiting to see what Mrs. Wilder would say next.

"What I usually propose to the mothers in this position," the woman finally said, "is that I touch base with you in about two or three weeks, and we can reevaluate the situation then. If at any time before that you wish to discuss the matter, you can ask Mrs. Bennington to contact me."

"That sounds fair," Laura replied in a quiet voice.

A sympathetic expression softened Mrs. Wilder's features. "Please understand, Laura, I'm not trying to be difficult. It's my job to look out for the welfare of all children. If they can feasibly remain with their mother, then of course I support it." She moved closer and gazed down at the sleeping infant. "I hope you find a way to make it work."

"Thank you," Laura whispered.

Mrs. Wilder picked up her papers and placed them back in her satchel. "Now, where might I find Marissa Wardrop? She's my next appointment."

Isabelle's shoulder muscles seized. Had her sister contacted the Children's Aid, or was this a routine visit? "I believe she's downstairs in the parlor."

"Thank you. Good day, ladies."

Isabelle followed the woman into the corridor.

Mrs. Wilder stopped and looked back at her. "Oh, you don't need to show me the way. I'm very familiar with the layout of the house."

Isabelle met the woman's gaze. Marissa might have decided what to do about the baby, but Isabelle wouldn't let anyone put undue pressure on her. She intended to determine for herself if Marissa was truly prepared to give up her child. "It looks like I'll be sitting in on your next appointment as well, Mrs. Wilder. Marissa Wardrop is my sister."

Mark pocketed the checks from two new investors and rose from his seat in Ruth Bennington's office. "Please thank your friends again for their generous contribution to our clinic. I'll write a personal note of thanks as soon as I get the chance and invite them to the opening."

"They'd be thrilled to attend. In the meantime, I'll be sure to pass on your appreciation." Ruth smiled.

Mark grew serious. "I want to thank you too, Ruth. Without your efforts, this clinic would not be happening."

"I was more than happy to help. It does my heart good to see a young man achieve his dreams." She patted his arm, tiny laugh lines forming around her eyes.

"Well, I'd best let you get on with your day." Mark squared his shoulders as he walked out of the office. His next order of business would not be as pleasant.

Although he longed to spend time with Isabelle, he wasn't looking forward to the conversation they needed to have. The summer was rapidly coming to an end, and he still had much more to do before the opening of his clinic. For the last couple of weeks, he'd been kept busy dealing with more cases of polio in the tenements and setting up his office at the new clinic, and he hadn't had time to deal with the issue of the paternity of Marissa's baby. But soon his brother would be returning from up north. If Josh wasn't the father of Marissa's baby, Mark needed to know. It could change everything for Josh's future.

"If you're looking for Isabelle, I believe you might find her in the back garden." Ruth's somewhat amused voice came from behind him. "She often takes her lunch outside when the weather's nice."

"Thank you." Mark managed a smile.

With a sense of dread rolling through him, he went in search of Isabelle. Just as Ruth predicted, he found her in the backyard, seated on the bench among the flowering shrubs. Her head came up as he approached.

"Mark. It's good to see you." Her usually open gaze seemed somewhat guarded today. Perhaps she was dreading this conversation as much as he was. "You look tired. Is everything going well with the clinic?"

"The opening is on schedule. But this polio outbreak has been running me ragged. The virus seems to be spreading faster now."

"That's too bad. It makes me even more grateful to be here."

He came to sit on the bench beside her. "I think it's time we talk."

"You're right." She set the plate with her half-eaten sandwich on the ground. "I'm sorry if it seems like I've been avoiding you. The truth is I wasn't sure how to tell you what I found out."

His gut clenched. "Josh isn't the father of the baby, is he? It's Henchley."

She nodded. "I can't believe it myself."

Mark inhaled and blew out a slow breath to delay the stirrings of temper. He should be relieved since that meant his brother was off the hook. But he couldn't help but feel betrayed on Josh's behalf. "Does this mean Marissa has been deceiving Josh all this time?"

Isabelle's eyes widened. "No, of course not. He's known about Mr. Henchley all along."

"I don't understand." Mark got up to pace the lawn. "Why would Josh go along with Marissa's scheme? He's given up his whole summer—would have given up his whole future—for this ruse."

Isabelle rose slowly from the bench. "It wasn't Marissa's idea, Mark," she said with quiet firmness. "Josh was the one who came up with it, although it's true she did nothing to dissuade him."

He clamped his jaw together. He didn't buy that for a minute. No doubt Marissa had batted her eyelashes at him, maybe cried a few tears, and Josh had been willing to do anything to help her.

Isabelle reached over to pluck a blossom from the bush beside her. "I guess they both had their reasons for leading us to believe Josh was the father. Reasons that don't really matter anymore." She twirled the flower's stem between her fingers. When she lifted her gaze to Mark's, her expression was troubled. "You should know that Mr. Henchley came by several days ago to speak to Marissa again, and she turned down his offer of marriage. She said it was evident that he really didn't want to marry her and only asked out of a sense of obligation. Clearly, her infatuation with the man is over, which is for the best." She paused. "Mr. Henchley also agreed that giving the child up for adoption was for the best. In fact, he appeared greatly relieved that she'd decided to go this route."

Mark pushed his fingers through his hair, doing his best to hold back the dangerous swirl of emotion snaking through his system. "That's all well and good, but where does that leave Josh?"

She gave him a sad smile. "I guess it leaves him free." Isabelle came closer and laid a hand on his arm. "Marissa says she'll write to him and tell him what's going on." Her earnest blue eyes searched his. "Is there a chance he could still start at the university in the fall?"

How he wanted to pretend he could simply ignore everything that had happened, sweep it all under the rug, and assure Isabelle there were no hard feelings. But the anger churning in his gut wouldn't allow him to utter such falsehoods. "I'm pretty sure Josh gave up his spot before he left. The best he could do is enroll for the winter semester, if there's room."

"I'm so sorry, Mark. I feel terrible about this whole situation."

"I know you do." He stared off in the distance, unable to meet her eyes.

"I'm sure it will all work out once Josh gets home."

"We'll see." His terse response sounded harsh even to him, so it didn't surprise him when Isabelle flinched. He drew in a breath, raking his fingers through his hair. "Look, Isabelle, I know this isn't your fault. But I can't deny how angry I am at your sister."

Her brows drew together. "I don't believe Marissa had evil intentions. She was scared and turned to Josh for help. She truly cares for him."

"She has a funny way of showing it."

Isabelle's mouth fell open, then she quickly closed it. "I think we need to let Josh and Marissa work out their issues without our interference." She gave him a stern look. "Or our judgment."

Mark paced over to a tree, doing his best to control his emotions before he said something he couldn't take back. "I need time to process all this. I also need to hear Josh's side of the story."

After a beat of silence, she said, "You do that." Irritation snapped in her blue eyes. "If you'll excuse me, I need to get back to work." Without another glance in his direction, she marched across the lawn toward the back door.

His chest squeezed with regret. If only he could separate his anger at Marissa from his feelings for Isabelle. But right now, they were all tangled up together in one toxic ball. Glancing down, he noted the forgotten sandwich lying upside down on the grass.

Upended, like all four of their lives.

37

On Isabelle's day off at the end of August, she took the bus to Rosie's apartment. She needed to see for herself that the dear woman was doing all right on her own, and no phone call could take the place of an in-person visit.

Likely Mark wouldn't be thrilled about her coming back to the neighborhood. However, from her conversations with Rosie, Isabelle knew she had been taking precautions about who she saw and had taken Mark's advice about boiling all her water before using it, even to wash with.

Rosie welcomed her with a warm embrace. "Isabelle. How wonderful to see you. Please come in. I've just made a fresh pot of tea."

A lump swelled in Isabelle's throat. How she missed this simple pleasure. She looked around the kitchen, drinking in the familiar sights and smells—the pot of soup simmering on the stove, the aroma of fresh-baked scones, the chipped brown teapot.

She took a seat at the cozy table.

"How is Marissa doing?" Rosie asked as she poured two cups.

"Physically, she's doing well. Emotionally, however, I worry about her." Isabelle stirred milk into her tea. She'd already decided she wouldn't reveal Marissa's secret to Rosie. It wasn't anyone else's business who the father of her baby was.

"Has she finally agreed to marry the Henshaw boy?"

"No. She's still insisting she doesn't want to ruin his life." Isabelle took a quick sip, then looked over at Rosie. "She's decided to give the baby up for adoption."

"Oh." Rosie's hand stopped with her cup halfway to her mouth. "I can't say I'm sorry to hear that. I think it's probably what's best for the babe and for Marissa."

Was it, though? The sorrow on Marissa's face told a different story. What if her sister never got over the loss? What if it affected her for the rest of her life?

"You don't agree?" Rosie's brows winged upward.

"I'm not sure. I think deep down Marissa wants to keep the baby, but she can't seem to find a way to do that. It's a shame because I believe Josh really loves her, and she might love him too. If she'd only accept his offer, they could be a happy family."

Rosie opened her mouth, as though about to jump in with further thoughts, but the front door opened, and Fiona breezed in, bringing a gust of air with her.

Isabelle jumped up. "Fiona! I didn't know you were back in town." She rushed over to embrace her friend.

Rosie beamed at her niece. "Fiona, luv. It's wonderful to see you. Come and join us."

Fiona's face was flushed, and the familiar twinkle shone in her green eyes. "I'm so happy you're here. I have so much to tell you both."

"I'm dying to hear all about your adventures." Rosie stood up to get another cup and saucer from the cupboard while Fiona pulled up a chair.

"I had the best summer. It's beautiful country up north. Reminds me a wee bit of home with all its greenery. I even learned how to sail."

"That sounds wonderful." Isabelle studied her friend. Fiona's level of happiness seemed a little extreme. "Are you back for good now?"

"Only for a few weeks. Adam has to take care of some business. We'll probably go back and stay until Thanksgiving. I can't wait to see the magnificent fall colors he's told me so much about."

"Adam, is it?" Rosie asked as she poured the tea. "That seems a mite personal."

Fiona's cheeks flushed even brighter red. "Everything was more informal up north." She fiddled with the handle of her teacup. "But there is something else I want to tell you."

"Well, what is it, child? Don't leave us in suspense."

Fiona bit her lip and leaned over the tabletop. "I'm getting married."

Aunt Rosie's mouth fell open, and she set the teapot down with a thud.

Isabelle blinked. "Who are you marrying?"

"Adam, of course."

"Adam Templeton?" Isabelle's brows flew upward.

Fiona snorted. "Are there any other Adams in my life?"

Isabelle's mind spun with questions. She couldn't imagine Adam marrying one of his maids. Or his mother ever condoning such a union. "How did all this come about?"

Fiona gave a slight shrug. "It happened gradually over the summer. Adam seemed freer in the country. More relaxed. He took me out on his boat and taught me to play tennis. We went hiking and fishing. . . ." She trailed off with a happy sigh. "Then, last week on my birthday, Adam had flowers for me and . . . he gave me this." She held out her left hand, which sported a large emerald stone in a gold setting. A dreamy smile drifted over her face.

"Oh my." Aunt Rosie moved closer for a better look. "It's lovely." She lifted her gaze to her niece. "Is his family . . . pleased with the news?"

Isabelle doubted it. She couldn't imagine the Templetons being happy about his choosing to marry someone out of their class.

"Not at first." Fiona sobered. "Not until we'd spent more time together. Adam's sister and I got friendly, then his mother gradually came around. Turns out she has relatives in Ireland near our village. I do think they're happy he's found someone to love and who loves him in return. And they've expressed their gratitude to me for helping him to stop working so hard."

Isabelle leaned forward. "But won't it be strange to suddenly become the mistress of the house? How will the other servants feel about taking orders from you?"

"Adam's already thought of that." Fiona smiled. "To avoid potential problems, he wants to leave his mother to manage the main estate and find us a smaller home. He'll hire new help who won't know any different and will accept me as their mistress."

"How . . . thoughtful of him." Isabelle shook her head. For Adam to be willing to move out of his family estate, he must really love Fiona.

"Congratulations, luv," Rosie said. "If anyone deserves such good fortune, it's you."

"Thank you, Auntie." Fiona reached over to hug Rosie. "It all feels a bit like a dream." She laughed out loud, her joy infusing the room.

"Adam always struck me as a good man," Isabelle said at last. "I know he'll treat you well."

"Speaking of good men, Dr. Henshaw is another fine one." Rosie pulled a piece of paper from her pocket and unfolded it. "I've been handing out these flyers he gave me to advertise his new clinic."

Isabelle scanned the ad, regret pulling at her. She hadn't been back since the day they had painted the rooms. And after their argument, she wasn't certain she'd be welcome. "It will be a great success, I'm sure, with Mark at the helm."

"I think so too." Rosie pinned Isabelle with a direct look. "If I'm not mistaken, the handsome doctor is somewhat smitten with you."

Heat flooded her cheeks, but she didn't answer.

"Oh, really?" Fiona clapped her hands together. "Will there be another announcement soon?"

"Heavens no. There are too many obstacles right now. Especially regarding Josh and Marissa's situation." They didn't need to know about her argument with Mark. It was still too hard to talk about. "Besides, getting the clinic up and running is Mark's top priority at the moment." She lifted the cup to her lips, wishing she could stay wrapped in the bubble of Fiona's happiness for a while longer. Then maybe she could believe all her problems would be resolved, and she and Mark might be able to resume their short-lived romance.

But somewhere deep inside, she worried that if Mark were forced to choose between her and his brother, she had a good idea who would win.

On the first Saturday in September, Mark walked over to the reception counter and scanned the platters of sandwiches and tarts arranged along its polished wooden length. Dr. Axelrod—or Allen, as he kept urging Mark to call him—had employed his favorite caterer to prepare the simple food trays for their open house.

Mark looked at the clock on the wall. Only half an hour until the guests would begin to arrive. A knot of tension still occupied the space between his shoulder blades. What if, despite their flyers and the ad in the newspaper, no one showed up? What if the clinic was a colossal failure? The thought of all the money Ruth's colleagues had invested, not to mention the amounts he and Allen had put in, made him queasy.

Sending up a quick prayer, he had to trust that God had things under control.

Mark cast an appreciative glance over the main room. Painted in a pale green, the area exuded peacefulness. Simple furnishings, a few potted plants, and some cheery artwork, courtesy of Ruth, gave it a welcoming atmosphere, exactly as he'd envisioned.

The consulting and examination rooms looked very professional with the new walnut desks, white enamel exam tables, sterilizers on the counters, and new scale beside the sink. Mark smiled, recalling the rusted deli scale that Isabelle had joked about him keeping, and a pang of regret seized him. How he wished things were back to the way they were the day they'd painted the clinic instead of this awkward tension that now existed between them.

A hand clamped down on his shoulder. "Don't look so worried, my boy. Everything is going according to plan." Allen's gray eyes twinkled.

"How can you be so confident?"

"Years of experience." He chuckled. "Trust me. It takes a while to get a practice off the ground and for word of mouth to spread, but it will happen. The one guarantee is that people will always need doctors."

"True."

"And you've already said you'll continue doing house calls until the residents start coming to see us here. Their trust in you is what will make this a success."

"I hope you're right." If only he could calm the nerves wreaking havoc with his system, perhaps he could enjoy the culmination of their hard work.

A bell sounded, indicating that someone had entered the building.

"Showtime." Allen thumped his back again as they headed to greet their first guests.

An hour later, Mark finally let himself relax a little. As Allen predicted, the open house was going well. At least a dozen residents from the tenements had shown up, wrinkled flyers clutched in their hands, as well as several businessmen, who Mark figured had come at Ruth's request.

The fleeting thought crossed his mind that Ruth hadn't shown up yet. The last time he'd spoken with her, she told him she would be there. Perhaps something had come up at the maternity home.

He turned his attention back to an elderly gentleman he recognized from the neighborhood. The man wore an outdated suit that was clearly too big for him and gripped a cap between gnarled fingers. "Thank you for coming," Mark said. "What do you think of the place so far?"

"It's all right, I guess." His thick white brows drew together. "I came as a favor to Rosie O'Grady. She about badgered me to death to make sure I came."

Mark laughed. "That sounds like Rosie."

The man squinted at him. "You sure you're old enough to be a real doctor?"

"I assure you, I am. My diploma is hanging in one of the back rooms in case you need proof." He held out his hand with a smile. "Dr. Mark Henshaw."

"Henry Thatcher."

"Nice to meet you, Henry. And don't worry, you can always see Dr. Axelrod over there if his age suits you better."

The man looked a little chagrined, but he shook his head and smiled, revealing two missing bottom teeth.

The door opened again, and Ruth Bennington entered in a flurry of feathers. Dressed in a purple suit, white boa, and a matching hat, she commanded the room's attention. She scanned the area in a regal manner, her eyes lighting up at the sight of all the people milling about.

"Excuse me, Henry. There's someone I need to greet." Mark made his way over to where she stood. "Ruth. Thank goodness." He kissed her cheek. "I was worried something had held you up."

"Yes, well, we had a new girl arrive at the home. I had to get her settled before I could get away. But we're here now, so that's all that matters."

"We?"

Someone stepped up beside Ruth. "Hello, Mark. Congratulations on your clinic. Everything looks wonderful."

He froze as his gaze fell on Isabelle. After their argument, he hadn't dared hope she'd show up. But here she was, looking more stunning than ever in a stylish blue belted dress and a pert hat set at an angle over one eye. For a moment, Mark was taken back to the days when her parents were still alive and she lived the life of a pampered heiress. "Isabelle. I'm glad you could come." He hesitated, not knowing whether to hug her or shake her hand. In the end, he did neither.

"And who are these charming ladies?" Allen's voice boomed as he joined the group.

"Dr. Axelrod, this is Ruth Bennington. I believe you've spoken on the phone."

"Ah, this is the infamous Mrs. Bennington. The woman responsible for bringing me here. It's a pleasure, ma'am."

Ruth inclined her head. "Likewise, Dr. Axelrod."

"And this is my friend Isabelle Wardrop," Mark said. "She works at Bennington Place with Ruth."

"Enchanted." He bent over Isabelle's hand, as if he were a knight saluting a maiden.

Isabelle gave him a wide smile. "I'm happy to meet Mark's new partner. I wish you both every success with this endeavor."

"Thank you, my dear. I'm very much looking forward to opening our doors on Monday."

Isabelle turned to Mark. "I'd love to see how the back rooms turned out. Will you show me?"

"Of course."

"Since I've already had the tour, I'll wait out here," Ruth said. "Perhaps, Dr. Axelrod, you'd be good enough to escort me to the refreshments."

"At your service."

The two moved away, and Mark led Isabelle down the hall to the consultation rooms. He showed her his office first.

The large oak desk took up a big portion of the space, with two wooden chairs for patients. In the corner stood a metal file cabinet, where he would keep his medical records.

Isabelle stopped beneath his framed degrees and attempted to read the inscription. "It's in Latin. Fitting for a doctor." She trailed a finger over the surface of his desk and looked up with admiration shining in her eyes. "It's perfect."

"Thank you. I'm pretty pleased with how it turned out." He left the room to head to one of the exam rooms. "These two rooms we'll use for examining the patients since they're a little more private." He stepped through the first door, a rush of pride swelling his chest. Every time he walked in to see the pristine exam table and the enamel medicine cabinet against the soothing yellow walls, he still couldn't quite believe this was his own practice.

"It's very professional, yet at the same time it gives a cozy feel. Patients will feel right at home here, I'm sure." She smiled, sending waves of butterflies through his stomach.

How he'd missed seeing her, the way her eyes lit up her entire face, the way she always made him feel he could conquer anything. Regret pulsed in his veins. "Isabelle, I need to say I'm sorry—"

She shook her head. "This day is not about apologies or regrets. This is a celebration of all your hard work. Of accomplishing your dream. We can talk about personal issues another time."

The relief that crashed through him was overwhelming. "Thank you for being so understanding." He took a step toward her. "I'm very glad you're here to share this with me."

"I wouldn't have missed it for anything." Her gaze locked with his.

The air between them fairly crackled with energy. Surely, she must be able to hear his heart beating loudly in his chest.

"Can we get together tomorrow afternoon?" he asked.

She nodded.

"Good. I'll come over after lunch."

"I'll look forward to it." She squeezed his hand, then stepped away. "Now, I'd like to see what you've done with the kitchen."

38

Isabelle hung a sheet on the clothesline and set a wooden peg at each end to hold it in place. She was grateful for the physical work keeping her occupied until Mark arrived for their talk. She prayed they could resolve the tension between them, because his absence in her life had left a gaping hole in her heart.

The large bedsheets flapped in the breeze. For September, the day was unusually warm. Perfect for drying laundry in no time. She moved the wicker basket of wet laundry farther down the grass.

A movement from the side yard captured her attention. Mark stopped for a moment and stared before he started walking toward her. "Hi."

"Hi." The awkwardness between them caused a pang of regret. Would they ever get back to the way they once were?

"Here. Let me help you with that."

Before she could protest, he picked up a sheet. She grabbed the other end and together they pinned it in place. Within five minutes, they had the rest of the basket emptied.

"Thank you. That went much faster with your help."

"No trouble at all." He picked up the empty basket. "Should we sit on the stoop or on the bench in the garden?"

Nerves rioted through her system. Keeping busy might be the preferred way to have this conversation. "Maybe we could talk while I pick vegetables from the garden."

"All right." He set the laundry basket down by the back steps while she retrieved the bushel basket Mrs. Neale used to collect the produce.

"Were you pleased with the turnout to the open house yesterday?" she asked as they crossed the lawn.

"Very. Thanks to Rosie spreading the word, we had more people than I anticipated."

"That's good." She set the container on the grass near the leeks and bent to pull a few from the earth. "Dr. Axelrod seems nice. His experience will be an asset to the practice." She dropped the vegetables into the basket.

"Yes. I believe we'll be a good team." Mark frowned, his eyes clouding with remorse. "Look, Isabelle, I owe you an apology for the way I acted the last time I was here. I should never have taken out my frustrations on you."

She wiped her hands on her apron and took a breath. "I'm to blame as well. It was childish to walk off in a huff. I understand how it must seem from your viewpoint, and you have every right to be upset with Marissa. I just hope we can keep our personal lives separate from our siblings' drama."

Mark nodded. "I promise to try my best." He reached for her hand. "I hope you'll have patience with me and remind me when I'm slipping into old habits."

She smiled. "I can do that."

The immense relief that spread over his features would have been comical if she hadn't felt the exact same loosening of tension throughout her body. She turned back to her task of picking vegetables. "Have you heard from Josh?"

"I got a letter a few days ago. He said they've asked him to stay on for a few more weeks and he agreed. He still hopes to get here in time for the baby's arrival."

She looked beneath some of the large leaves for the ripe squash. "That's only a few weeks away."

"I know." Mark paused. "He did address the paternity issue, though. You were right. He was the one who came up with the idea of letting us believe he was the father. And he doesn't apologize for that, claiming that he still wants to marry Marissa when he returns."

Isabelle plucked a butternut squash and set it in the basket. "Does he know she intends to give the baby up?"

"He didn't mention it, so it seems unlikely."

She rose slowly and looked at Mark. "I feel he has a right to know, especially if he's basing life-changing decisions on Marissa keeping the baby."

"I agree."

They moved farther down the garden to where the brussels sprouts were growing.

"Do you think it would be all right for me to tell him?" Mark's tone was hesitant. "I don't want to overstep."

Isabelle dropped a handful of vegetables into the basket, then straightened. "Marissa has had ample time to let him know what she's decided. And she never said it was a secret, so I don't see how she could have an issue with it."

"Good. I'll tell him in my next letter." He stepped forward and put his hands on her shoulders, his gaze capturing hers. "I've missed you, Isabelle."

Her heart sputtered to life, fluttering like a hummingbird's wings. "I've missed you too." She held her breath, willing him to come closer.

He took another step, and the next thing she knew, his lips were on hers, gently at first but then with increasing intensity. Everything around her faded into the background. The only thing that existed was the warmth of his mouth and the electricity racing through her body.

She barely registered the back door opening.

A throat cleared. "Excuse me, Isabelle. Dr. Henshaw?"

Isabelle jerked back and smoothed her hair. "Yes, Georgia?"

"Marissa's not feeling well. She asked me to come and get you."

Alarm snaked through her veins. "I'll be right there."

Mark picked up the basket of vegetables. "Would you like me to come too, in case I can be of help?"

"Yes, please." She took off at a quick pace across the lawn. *Please, Lord, don't let it be the baby yet.*

Mark's pulse thrummed as he retrieved his medical bag from the car and followed Isabelle upstairs to Marissa's room. He prayed this was nothing more than discomfort due to the late stages of Marissa's pregnancy.

"Let me talk to her first," Isabelle said before she entered the room. "I'll let you know if she needs you."

"I'll wait right here." Mark gave her a look he hoped inspired confidence that everything would be all right.

She slipped inside and closed the door. He heard some whispering and a few moans before Isabelle appeared again. "I think she might be having contractions. Could you come and take a look?"

He walked in and right away noted that Marissa was curled into a fetal position on her bed, her eyes closed. Dragging a chair over to the bed, Mark sat down. "Are you having pains, Marissa?"

She nodded. "And my back is hurting."

"How long has this been going on?"

"Since this morning. I thought they would go away if I lay down, but they're getting worse instead of better."

Mark took out his stethoscope and listened to Marissa's heart rate and then the baby's. Other than Marissa's being slightly elevated due to her distress, everything appeared normal.

Then she stiffened and clutched her belly. Mark laid a hand on her abdomen, felt the tightness, and bit back a sigh. These were not false labor pains. "Breathe through the contraction, Marissa," he said in a soothing tone, "and try to relax your muscles."

She opened one eye to glare at him.

Isabelle came closer to the bed. "Is she in labor?"

"I'm afraid so." He frowned. "We'll time the next contraction and depending on the result, I might suggest we take her to the hospital. If the doctors can't stop her labor, the baby will need special care."

Isabelle bit her lip as tears formed.

He reached out to squeeze her hand. "Try not to worry. We'll take it one step at a time, but I promise she'll be in good hands."

Marissa let out a huge breath, signaling the end of the contraction. Mark checked his watch to make a note of the time before the next one began. Then, in a soothing voice, he repeated what he'd just told Isabelle to her sister.

Marissa's eyes widened in fear. "But it's too soon."

"The hospital is well equipped to handle premature babies. It's the best place to be so that the infant can get instant care once it's born. And it's the best place for you as well so you can be monitored constantly."

Marissa's lip quivered.

"By my calculations, you're about three weeks from your due date—not ideal, but not the worst case by any means." He smiled to reassure her. "Try to relax while we wait."

Isabelle moved closer to her sister and held out her hand. Marissa clutched her fingers like a lifeline.

They sat in relative silence for several minutes, each second passing with agonizing slowness, until Marissa sucked in a deep breath. "It's starting again."

Mark checked his watch. Eight minutes. He'd help Marissa through this contraction and then he'd get her to the hospital. The sooner the better.

Isabelle paced the hospital hallway for the hundredth time. How long had it been since the nurse had ousted her from Marissa's room? It seemed like hours now.

She paused outside the room and pressed her ear to the door. Was Marissa scared? Was she in unbearable pain? If only they'd let her stay in the room, but Mark and the nurses had insisted she wait outside. Thank goodness Mark still had privileges at the hospital and was able to be with Marissa. It was the only thing keeping Isabelle sane.

A hand came down on her shoulder, and she let out a small cry of surprise.

Olivia stood behind her, wearing a sympathetic smile. "Sorry. Didn't mean to startle you. I thought you might like some company while you wait."

"How did you know we were here?" Since it was Sunday, Olivia would have been home with her family.

"Ruth called me. Darius offered to watch the kids while I came down. He knows what it's like to wait on a baby being born—and how beneficial it is to have someone to pass the time with."

A lump formed in Isabelle's throat. "Thank you, Olivia. It is scary waiting alone, imagining all the terrible things that could be going wrong."

Olivia gave her arm a sympathetic squeeze. "How long has it been since you've had an update?"

"A few hours."

"Ah. Well, from experience, I know it can take a long time before the baby arrives." She looked down the hall. "Why don't we go and sit in the waiting room for a while? We can say some prayers for Mark and Marissa while we wait."

Isabelle smiled. "That sounds more productive than pacing."

She followed Olivia into the room, gratitude filling her soul for the dedicated doctor in the delivery room with her sister and for the friend who'd come to share the excruciating wait.

Eight hours after they'd arrived at the hospital, Mark wrapped a blanket around the squalling infant and handed the bundle to Marissa.

"Congratulations. You have a beautiful little girl."

He made sure she had a proper hold on the infant, then stepped back to let her experience the wonder of her child. Too often doctors whisked away the baby the moment it was born, especially in the case where the woman was considering adoption. But Mark believed the mother deserved a moment to see the miracle of the child she'd just labored to bring into the world.

Relief allowed him to expand his lungs and take his first easy breath in hours.

Thank you, Lord, for a safe delivery.

Two nurses scurried around the delivery room, readying the weigh scale and tape measure they would need to assess the newborn. He would give Marissa a few more moments before he allowed them to swoop in.

Marissa gazed down at the infant. Tears mixed with the perspiration dripping down the new mother's face. The baby's cries calmed right away, and the tiny girl opened her eyes to stare at her mother.

"She's the most precious thing I've ever seen." Marissa stroked a finger down the infant's cheek.

Mark glanced over at the nurse who had assisted him during the last stages of labor. "Give them another moment together, please."

"Yes, Doctor."

As soon as the senior nurse removed the baby from Marissa's arms, Mark resumed his seat on the stool at the end of the bed, preparing to deliver the afterbirth. Thankfully, no complications arose, and despite the early arrival, the baby seemed in good health.

"What's the weight, Nurse?"

"Just a hair under five pounds. All her vitals seem within normal range."

"Excellent."

"What does that mean?" Marissa asked.

"It means your baby is healthy and I don't think she'll need an incubator. I would like her to stay in the special-care nursery for the first twenty-four hours, just to be extra cautious."

"Whatever you think is best."

He went to the sink and washed his hands. "I'll go and let Isabelle know the news."

"Can she come in and see the baby?" Marissa looked from him to the nurses.

He nodded. "Just for a few minutes. I'll be back soon."

As he walked down the hallway, exhaustion started to set in. For a first baby, the little girl had come in a relatively short twelve hours from the time Marissa had first felt contractions, yet Mark felt as tired as if it had been twenty-four. He removed the white cotton mask and the cap covering his hair as he walked.

When he entered the waiting room, Isabelle shot up from her chair. "How is she?"

Olivia, who was seated beside her, stood as well.

"Marissa is fine. She has a beautiful little girl."

"Oh, thank you, Lord." Isabelle's eyes filled with tears, and she pressed a hand to her mouth.

"How is the baby?" Olivia asked.

"She's on the small side. But overall, she looks quite healthy."

Tears spilled from Isabelle's eyes. Mark wished he could take her in his arms to comfort her. But he had to remain professional since he still had a patient who needed tending.

"When can I see them?" Isabelle managed to ask.

"Give us another fifteen minutes or so and she should be ready. You can stay for a short time, then we'll move Marissa into the maternity ward."

"Thank you, Mark, for taking such good care of her."

The immense gratitude shining in her eyes created a knot of emotion in his chest. He gave a brisk nod. "I'm just glad that they're both doing well." As he headed back to the delivery room, he couldn't help but think of Josh and how he'd feel when he learned he'd missed the baby's birth.

39

Isabelle stepped into the hospital room and simply stared at the sight in front of her. Marissa was sitting up in the bed, holding a swaddled bundle in her arms. The expression of sheer bliss on her face brought another sting of tears to Isabelle's eyes. Her baby sister was a mother. How had this happened?

"Isabelle! Come and meet your niece." Marissa's eyes shone brighter than the glow of the overhead lights. "She's beautiful."

Isabelle walked over and gazed down at the most precious little face she'd ever seen. "She's beyond beautiful, Rissa. She's a miracle."

"Yes, she is." Marissa looked up. "Would you like to hold her?"

"I'd love to." Isabelle pulled a chair over, took the baby in her arms, and sat down. The girl's tiny nose scrunched as though she was about to sneeze, but then she let out a soft sigh and snuggled into the blanket. If the rush of love in Isabelle's heart was this strong, she could only imagine how Marissa must feel. How could she ever think of giving away something so precious? "She's perfect."

Smiling, Marissa nodded, tears sliding down her cheeks. "I never thought I could feel such love for . . . anyone. But the moment Mark put her in my arms, my heart seemed to double in size."

As Isabelle gazed at the sleeping infant, every instinct in her body told her this girl was meant to be part of their family. "You can't give her up, Rissa," she whispered. "She belongs with us."

Marissa stared at her, and a sob broke free. "I was hoping you'd say that. Because I don't think I can bear to give her to someone else. I already love her so much."

Isabelle blinked back tears herself. For the first time in what seemed like a year, the band of tension around her chest loosened. "It's settled, then. Welcome to the Wardrop family, little one." She dropped a kiss on the downy cheek, then rose and placed her in Marissa's arms.

There would still be hurdles ahead, but for now, Isabelle reveled in the love and joy that filled her soul. And she thanked God for bringing this most wonderful little girl into their lives.

She leaned her forehead against Marissa's. Together she and her sister would do whatever was necessary to give this child a happy, healthy life.

No matter the cost.

A week after Mark delivered Marissa's baby, he arrived at the station to meet Josh's train. Since the temperature was still mild enough, he opted to wait outside on the platform and enjoy the night air. Unable to stand still, he paced the length of the platform, the anticipation of seeing his brother after three months making him antsy. As soon as Josh had learned that Marissa had had her baby, he'd bought a train ticket home and sent Mark a telegram to let him know.

Mark couldn't help but worry about what his brother would face when he returned. It appeared that Marissa had changed her mind again and was now determined to keep her baby. What that meant for Josh, Mark didn't know. All he could do was be there to support him, no matter what happened between the young couple.

A cloud of gnats swarmed the outdoor lights as the train finally pulled into the station and the passengers began to disembark. Mark eagerly scanned the faces, but when Josh stepped off the train, he almost didn't recognize him.

His brother had always been on the thin side, leaning toward lanky. But now he appeared almost gaunt. Had he caught some type of illness while he was away?

Mark hurried over and pulled him into a close hug, then clapped him on the shoulder. "It's good to see you. How are you feeling?"

"Tired. But otherwise I'm fine."

Mark picked up the suitcase and guided Josh through the train station to the exit. "The car isn't far away. Are you hungry?"

"Starving." Josh laughed. "The food was good at the camp, but there was never much to go around."

Mark quirked a brow. "I imagine seconds and thirds weren't an option."

"Definitely not. And the bigger guys got the larger portions. No one argued with them."

Ah, maybe that's why he looked thinner. That and all the physical labor.

"Good thing I saved some roast beef for you. I thought you might want to eat when you got here." He slung his free arm around Josh's shoulders. "It's good to have you home. I've missed you."

"I missed you too."

Mark opened the trunk and placed Josh's suitcase inside, then they both got in the car.

Josh chatted the whole car ride home, regaling Mark with stories of the logging camps. Once they arrived home, Josh went to wash up while Mark made a roast beef and cheese sandwich and poured him a tall glass of milk.

It was nice to have someone to fuss over again.

A few minutes later, Josh appeared in the kitchen and sank onto his chair with a sigh. "It's good to be home. I can't wait to sleep in my own bed." He took a huge bite of his sandwich.

"The house has been far too quiet without you." Mark set his cup of tea on the table and joined his brother while he ate. "It will be nice to have someone else around again."

"How have things been going with your patients?"

Mark held back a jolt of surprise. For the first time, Josh sounded genuinely interested in Mark's work. "This polio outbreak is keeping me busy. Especially in the tenement housing where it's been spreading like wildfire."

"Can't you do anything to prevent it?"

Mark shook his head. "The problem is the sewage system and the tainted water in those areas. I've tried to get some of the residents to move, but that's easier said than done. It's hard enough for them to afford the housing there." He set his cup down. "All I can do is remove an ill person as soon as I find them. Get them into the hospital away from the others and hope for the best."

"I'm glad you got Marissa and Isabelle out of that neighborhood." Josh wiped a smear of mustard from his lip with a napkin. "How is the new clinic going?"

"It's been a slow start, though that's not uncommon, according to Dr. Axelrod. I'm still seeing my patients in their homes and hope to gradually coax them into the clinic." Mark drained the rest of his tea. "What are your plans for tomorrow?"

Josh pushed his now-empty plate aside. "Other than sleeping for twelve hours straight, I plan to see Marissa if I can." His mouth turned down. "I still can't believe I missed being here for the birth."

"Well, it did happen three weeks early. No one could have predicted that." Mark hesitated to say anything more. "I still don't really understand why you let everyone believe you were the baby's father."

Josh squared his shoulders. "I told you in my letter—to keep

Henchley out of her life. I love Marissa, and I'll do anything I can to protect her . . . and her child." He pushed up from the table and headed down the hall.

Mark followed him. "I'd like to hear the whole story from your perspective, if you don't mind." He gestured to the living room.

Josh searched his face, then nodded and headed into the front room. Instead of sitting down, he walked to the window and stared out at the dark street.

Mark remained standing and waited for him to begin.

At last, his brother let out a shuddering sigh. "I knew about Marissa's crush on the choir director for a while. It seemed harmless enough until around the time her mother died. That's when she started becoming more intentional about gaining Mr. Henchley's attention." Josh ran a hand through his hair. "I tried to warn her against getting involved with him, but she wouldn't listen. It was as if she couldn't see or hear anything that went against her romantic fantasy of the man."

"That must have been difficult for you if you had feelings for her," Mark said carefully.

"It was, especially once I learned how far things had gone between them." Josh's jaw twitched.

Mark nodded, not sure what to say to that.

"When Marissa found out she was expecting, she was scared but excited. In her mind, Henchley would be thrilled with the news, declare his undying love, and ask her to marry him."

"But that obviously didn't happen."

"No. When she went to tell him, she found him kissing another woman in the choir room. She was so upset, she left without ever telling him about the baby." Josh moved away from the window and shoved his hands in his pockets. "The night you found us at her old house, I was trying to console her. When you and Isabelle jumped to the wrong conclusion, I didn't correct you because I'd already come up with the idea that I could be the baby's father. Marissa didn't want anything more to do with Henchley once she realized how he'd betrayed her. And she was desperate, not knowing what she was going to do about the pregnancy. That was when I offered to marry her. I think you know the rest of the story from there."

Mark nodded, sifting through the events with this new filter. He paced the carpet for a minute then stopped to face his brother. "I don't know what to say, except that I'm incredibly proud of you. Not many young men would have done something so noble."

Josh's eyes went wide. "Really? I thought you were going to lecture me about being too naïve."

"A year ago, I might have. But I've done a lot of growing myself lately." He went to sit on the sofa, and Josh followed his lead. "I've come to realize that my main goal in raising you was to help you become a morally responsible person. Now I know I've achieved my goal. You're a caring, compassionate, and honorable young man." A lump rose in Mark's throat. "I hope I haven't been too hard on you along the way."

Josh shook his head. "Only as hard as you needed to be." His voice was gruff. "Thank you, Mark, for everything you've sacrificed for my sake. It took me going away to truly appreciate all you've done for me. And I'll always be grateful."

Mark's throat was too tight to force any words out. Instead, he reached over and clasped Josh in a hug. When the boy pulled away, Mark cleared his throat. "You should brace yourself for seeing Marissa. I have no idea where her head is these days."

A determined expression came over Josh's features. "Can you get me in to see her?"

Mark smiled. "I think I can manage that. She's due to be released from the hospital tomorrow. If so, we'll go over to the maternity home instead."

Isabelle placed the baby in the bassinet beside Marissa's bed and placed a kiss on the tiny girl's soft forehead.

Thank you, Lord, for this blessing.

The hospital had released them both that morning, and Isabelle had gone to help bring them home. She'd taken a bus to the hospital and ordered a taxi to bring them back to Bennington Place. The residents were all waiting in the parlor when they arrived, eager to see the baby. But it soon became apparent that Marissa's energy was waning, and Isabelle insisted she lie down for a rest.

Marissa had snuggled under the quilt right away. "It's so good to be back in my own bed again."

"Sleep as long as you like. I'll keep an eye on little Lisette." Isabelle adored the name her sister had chosen for the baby in honor of their maternal grandmother.

Marissa smiled. "I love hearing her name. Mama told me once that Lisette means 'God's promise.'"

"It's beautiful. Though I'm rather partial to her middle name." Isabelle laughed. Marissa had chosen Monique and Isabelle as the baby's other names.

"You're her aunt and you're going to be her godmother too. I couldn't think of anyone more fitting to name her after."

A knock sounded, and Olivia peeked in the door. "I'm sorry to disturb you. Joshua Henshaw is here, asking to speak with Marissa." She glanced between the two women. "I didn't know what to tell him."

"She was just about to take a nap," Isabelle said.

"No, it's all right. I need to talk to him." Marissa swung her legs over the side of the bed and slid her slippers on. "Is there somewhere we can speak in private?"

Olivia hesitated. "Ruth is in the office. I'll check the sunroom and make sure no one is there."

"Thanks." Marissa looked at Isabelle. "Will you watch Lisette for me?"

"Of course." Isabelle bit back a thousand words of advice. But in the end, it wasn't really her place to tell Marissa what to do. The look of sadness on her sister's face did not bode well for this re-union. If she really loved Josh, shouldn't she be happy to see him?

Unable to sit still, Isabelle paced the bedroom, pausing every few minutes to check on the baby. After twenty minutes, she opened the bedroom door and peered down the hall, straining her ears for any type of conversation. Silly, really, because she'd never hear them if they were still in the sunroom.

Finally, Marissa returned. She closed the door and headed straight for the bed. "I think I'll take that nap now." Her nose was red, and her hands trembled.

"Are you all right? Can I get you anything?"

Marissa shook her head. "No, thanks. You can go. I'll wake up if the baby cries."

"Are you sure?"

"Yes." She faced away from Isabelle and pulled the covers up to her chin.

Isabelle fought the urge to bombard her with questions. There would be time enough for that later. "I'll check on you in a while. Sleep well."

But even as Isabelle closed the door behind her, she could hear soft sobs coming from inside. She laid her palm against the door, her heart aching for her sister. Apparently, the talk with Josh had not gone well, and nothing Isabelle said would make things any better.

Only time and God's grace could accomplish that.

40

Mark stared at Josh's closed bedroom door, wishing he knew what had transpired between his brother and Marissa yesterday after he dropped him off at the maternity home. Whatever it was, Josh had come home completely defeated. Yet no matter how tactfully Mark had tried to question him, Josh remained tight-lipped. The only thing he'd revealed was that Marissa had turned down his marriage proposal for the second time.

Now, Mark's protective instincts warred with his compassionate nature. He tried to remind himself that the girl had just given birth and was likely in no position to be making huge life decisions. She had enough on her plate simply trying to adjust to motherhood. Deep down, however, raw anger churned in Mark's gut at the cavalier way she'd treated his brother's feelings—not once, but twice. If she had no intention of marrying him, then why had she let him take that summer job to earn money for them? None of her actions made any sense to him.

Mark's heart ached at the pain his brother was suffering. He only hoped that once Marissa adjusted to her new role, she might change her mind and allow Josh back into her life. Either that or cut ties with him completely and let him move on with his own life.

Mark opened the icebox and pulled out the orange juice. As he poured himself a glass, he glanced at the clock. He needed to get to the clinic. If time allowed, he'd come home on his lunch break and see how Josh was doing. Maybe then he'd be ready to discuss the situation and make a plan for the future.

The morning passed quickly enough. Mark was pleased that two new patients had come in today. Laura, one of the residents from Bennington Place, was turning out to be a natural at the receptionist position, even with her baby sleeping in a cradle beside her. Mark marveled again at Isabelle's timely suggestion that he hire some of the women from the maternity home to work here. An idea that was beneficial to all involved.

Shortly after noon, Mark approached the reception desk. "I'm going home for half an hour in case anyone asks."

"Okay, Dr. Henshaw." Laura scanned the appointment book. "You have Mrs. Carberry at two o'clock."

"Thanks. I should be back long before that."

Mark arrived at the house ten minutes later. He let himself in, looked in the living room, which was empty, and headed back to the kitchen. The room was exactly as he'd left it. No extra dishes or cups. Was Josh still in bed at this hour?

A niggling sense of unease spurred Mark upstairs. He knocked loudly on his brother's door in case he was still asleep. "Josh? You okay?"

No response.

He knocked again, then, too impatient to wait, opened the door. The room was empty. Josh's bed was neatly made, and for once his clothes weren't scattered all over the floor. Maybe he'd gone out to look for a job. Or maybe he'd gone to see Marissa again. Mark wouldn't put it past him. His brother was nothing if not persistent.

His gaze swept the room. Another wave of unease attacked him. Josh's guitar was gone. With a thumping heart, he opened the closet. Only a couple of shirts remained, along with a dozen wire hangers. Even his duffel bag was missing.

The blood seemed to chug to a halt in Mark's veins.

Josh is gone.

In a daze, he walked over to his brother's desk. An envelope bearing his name sat on the blotter. Slowly, he picked it up, staring at the hastily scratched word. His stomach muscles tightened as he opened the flap.

Dear Mark,

I'm sorry but I can't stay here right now. I have to face the fact that Marissa isn't going to change her mind, no matter how many times I ask.

I've been thinking about this for a while. You won't like it, but I've decided to join the army. I'm not sure how much longer this war will last, but maybe fighting for my country will help me forget about her. In any case, I need some time and space away. I hope you understand. I'll send word when I can.

Thanks for everything,

Josh

P.S. Please give the enclosed letter to Marissa. And try not to worry about me.

The air whooshed from Mark's lungs, his legs suddenly going weak. He sat down heavily on the desk chair and stared at the wall. He understood why Josh might feel the need to get away, but running off to join the war? That was plain reckless. Was he trying to get himself killed?

Mark's pulse raced, spurring him to his feet. He had to try to stop him. But where to begin?

With new purpose, he ran down to the phone in the kitchen, dialed the operator, and asked where the nearest recruitment offices were located. Next, he called the clinic and told Laura to reschedule his appointment with Mrs. Carberry. Then, armed with three addresses, he raced out to his car. If he was lucky, Josh might still be at one of these places, especially since he'd likely have to go through some type of test or a medical exam. If Mark found him, he would pray for the right words to change his brother's mind.

He had no luck at the first location, but the second try proved fruitful.

"Yes, I believe there was a young man by the name of Joshua Henshaw who signed up earlier. Let me see if I can find him on the list." A stocky woman with a pair of glasses sitting on the end of her nose scanned the paperwork in front of her. "Here it is." She indicated the name with a flick of her pen.

"Can you tell me if he's still here?" Mark licked his dry lips, hoping he didn't sound as desperate as he felt.

Suspicion darkened her gaze. "Why?"

"I'm Dr. Henshaw, his brother, and I need to speak with him. It's urgent."

The woman regarded him for a minute. "I guess that would be all right. He's probably having his medical exam right now. The office is down the hall to the right. Third door."

Mark could have kissed the woman. "Thank you very much, ma'am." Before she changed her mind, he bolted down the hallway, counting doors as he went. When he got to the third one, he hesitated. Should he knock or wait for someone to come out?

The door was slightly ajar, so Mark nudged it open and attempted to peer into the room.

A man in a white coat, presumably the army doctor, sat at a desk, writing on a piece of paper.

Josh came into view, buttoning his shirt. "What's the verdict, Doctor? Did I pass?"

"You're a tad underweight, but other than that, you're in peak condition." The man inked a stamp and then pressed it into the paper. "You're approved."

"Thank you, sir."

"Report to Room 103, where you'll receive your uniform and your instructions where to report for training. Good luck, son."

Josh accepted his approved paperwork, picked up his jacket and his bag, and headed toward the door.

Mark's mouth went dry. *Lord, give me the right words to get through to him.*

Josh exited the room and passed right by without even noticing him.

"Josh." Mark's throat tightened on a rush of emotion.

His brother whirled around, an incredulous look on his face. "What are you doing here?"

"I couldn't let you leave without trying to get you to see reason."

Josh's brows crashed together. "You're wasting your time. I'm not changing my mind." He started down the corridor.

"Wait." Mark rushed after him. "What if you get injured, or worse yet, killed? You're my only family."

"I'm not going to get killed."

"You don't know that."

Josh stopped and turned to face him. "Look, this is something I need to do for my own sanity. I'm sorry you're not happy about it, but I'm going. With or without your blessing."

Mark's stomach sank as he took in his brother's resolute stance, his unwavering stare. Mark had been prepared for irrational anger and immature behavior, but in no way was he prepared for the quiet determination that masked Josh's underlying pain.

People hustled down the corridor around them, creating a buzz of energy.

"Isn't there something else you could do instead? Something less dangerous?" Mark swallowed hard. "I can't lose you too, Josh."

His brother frowned. "I pray you won't have to lose me. But I can't base my decisions on whether or not you approve. This feels like the right choice for me now." He hiked the strap of his duffel bag higher up on his shoulder.

Josh had a point. He couldn't live his life based on what his big brother wanted. Still, shouldn't he give Mark's opinion some consideration?

He blew out a breath. "Can you at least promise to be careful? Don't go off half-cocked, trying to be a hero."

Josh just stared at him. "You really don't have much faith in me, do you?"

"That's not what I . . ." Mark raked his fingers through his hair while pressure seemed to build in his chest. "Please." The single word came out as a croak. "I'm asking you not to do this. Find some other way to deal with Marissa's rejection."

Josh sucked in a breath and grimaced.

"You could go back up north and work for the lumber camps again. Or go out west and get a job. See a bit of the country. Didn't you say you wanted to see the Rocky Mountains?" It was a desperate plea, but anything would be better than going to war.

Josh pulled his shoulders back. "It's too late. I've already signed the paperwork, and it's been approved. I've made my decision." His steady gaze met Mark's. "I don't want to leave on bad terms. Can't you accept that this is what I need to do and wish me well?"

The fight seeped out of Mark's system as the truth sank in. Nothing he said was going to sway him. He'd lost any control he used to have over his brother, and there wasn't a thing he could do to change that. He rubbed at the tension in his chest. "I guess I don't have much of a choice."

As much as he hated Josh going off to fight in this never-ending war, he couldn't let him go with any bad feelings between them. He'd never forgive himself if the last words he said to his brother were ones of anger or criticism. "I'm going to miss you, brother."

Josh's features softened. "I'll miss you too. But when this war is over, and I come home, I promise things will be better." He started moving away. "I'd better go. They're expecting me down the hall."

"I guess this is good-bye, then." The ache in Mark's chest spread outward. The uncertainty of not knowing when—or if—he'd see his brother again was the hardest part of all. Mark pulled Josh into a tight hug. "Stay safe and watch your back out there."

"I will." Josh's eyes were damp as he pulled away.

Mark's gut clenched, but he forced his mouth into a semblance of a smile. "I'll be praying for you. Don't forget to write when you can and let me know how you're doing."

"I will. I promise."

"And if you need anything . . ."

"I know. Thanks." Josh hoisted his bag over his shoulder. "Did you find my letter for Marissa?"

Mark patted his breast pocket. "It's right here. I'll give it to her today."

Josh nodded, a film of moisture glistening in his eyes. "Thanks. I appreciate it. And hey, watch out for her, will you?"

Mark clenched his teeth, pushing back the tidal wave of emotion threatening to erupt, and nodded. "I'll do my best."

41

nstead of heading straight to his car after he left the recruitment office, Mark set off down the sidewalk at a brisk pace in a vain attempt to rid himself of the toxic emotions swirling through him. He hated feeling so helpless, so out of control. Thinking back to the spring, when his only concern had been Josh skipping his science lab, he almost laughed out loud at how absurd life had gotten since then. Worse than anything he'd ever even imagined.

And all because of Marissa Wardrop. The name left a sour taste in his mouth.

Just as he'd feared, a girl had turned Josh's head, derailing his studies, and now, potentially costing him his life. Because of her rejection, Josh didn't seem to care whether he lived or died.

Breathing hard, Mark stopped beside a fence and leaned over his knees, waiting for his lungs to catch up. When he straightened, he kicked hard at an empty can lying in the gutter, sending it spiraling across the street. A pedestrian nearing him on the sidewalk paused and then crossed the street to avoid him. He must look like a lunatic. With a snort of disgust at himself, he headed back toward his car.

When he got there, he climbed in and sat staring at his medical bag on the seat beside him. How was he supposed to set aside his inner turmoil and retain his professional objectivity with so much resentment churning in his gut? Especially when he was expected to treat the very object of said resentment?

With a prayer in his heart, he started the engine and pulled away from the curb.

Lord, I need your help to get through this. Give me the grace to act with compassion and not let my personal feelings get in the way.

Before heading back to the clinic, Mark decided to get his visit to the maternity home out of the way first. He'd planned on going over later to do a final postpartum check on Marissa. Might as well do it now and deliver Josh's letter.

When he arrived at Bennington Place, he found Marissa feeding her baby easily, like she'd been doing it for months. He'd seen countless new mothers breastfeeding before, but for some reason today he felt out of place. Perhaps it was because his connection to Marissa was a bit too personal. The contentment on her face, however, sent a fresh jolt of resentment coiling through him. What right did she have to be so happy when she'd caused Josh such pain?

She looked up and spied him hovering in the doorway. "Good afternoon, Mark. Please come in." She pulled a blanket more discreetly over the baby's face.

He did so reluctantly and set his bag on the dresser. "How was your first night home with the baby?" Did his voice sound as unnatural as it felt?

"Not bad. Isabelle stayed with me and got up with Lisette a few times so I could rest."

Mark's hand stilled on the handle of his bag. "Lisette?"

"Yes. I'm naming her Lisette Monique Isabelle."

"It sounds like you've decided to keep her."

She sobered. "I have. Once I held her, I knew I couldn't bear to give her up."

He opened the flap of his bag with a hard snap. "How do you plan to support yourself now that you've turned down Josh again?" He couldn't keep the bitterness from creeping into his voice.

She lifted the baby to her shoulder and patted the tiny back. "I know you must think I'm awful, but I'm doing this for Josh's sake. He deserves a decent life. Not to be stuck with me."

"Well, your plan backfired." He took out his stethoscope and walked over to the bed.

"What do you mean?"

He bit back the accusation that hovered on his tongue. Instead, he pulled the envelope from his pocket. "Josh asked me to give you this letter. It should explain everything. I'll examine the baby while you read it."

Wordlessly, she handed him the infant.

He crossed to the other bed and laid the baby down so he could examine her. After he finished, he looped the stethoscope around his neck. Everything about the child seemed healthy and normal. "She's doing great so far." He wrapped the baby in her blanket and picked her up. When he turned around, he froze.

Marissa held a hand over her mouth, tears dripping down her cheeks. "This is what you meant about my plan backfiring?"

He gave a curt nod, then took a moment to place the baby in the bassinet.

Marissa dashed a hand across her face and raised anguished eyes to him. "This is all my fault."

The memory of parting with his brother hit Mark anew. "I guess a person can only take so much rejection before he gives up."

She clutched the letter to her chest. More tears welled in her amber eyes. "I wish things were different. . . ."

Mark took in her blotchy cheeks and trembling fingers. He knew it wasn't fair to heap all the blame on Marissa. She was doing what she thought was right. But somehow he couldn't bring himself to offer her any comfort or attempt to relieve her guilt.

Marissa folded the letter and tucked it under her pillow. "I'm sorry, Mark. I feel terrible." She straightened her shoulders. "But right now, my priority has to be my daughter. She's the most important thing to me."

Mark gave her a long look. "I take it Isabelle has offered to help you raise her." A new burst of resentment ripped through him. It sounded like the two women had joined forces about their future.

A future that didn't seem to include him or his brother.

"Yes. Once she has enough saved, we'll get a place of our own."

He stiffened, fighting a wave of hurt. He cleared his throat and pulled his stethoscope out in an attempt to get back to business. "I'd better examine you before the baby wakes up again."

"Mark?"

He stilled.

"Please don't take this out on Isabelle. She cares for you. I know she does." Her expression was earnest. "Don't punish her for my mistakes."

He had to remind himself that despite becoming a mother, Marissa had just turned eighteen. "You worry about yourself and the baby," he said brusquely. "Everything else will work itself out in time."

It was as close as he could get to offering her grace. Maybe once he'd regained his sense of equilibrium, he could forgive her for driving his brother away.

And for driving a huge wedge between him and Isabelle.

Isabelle was nearing the end of her break in the dining room when she heard Mark's voice as he came down the stairs. The knowledge that he was here sent a thrill rushing through her system. She jumped up and headed into the hallway as he and Georgia appeared.

"Good-bye, Doctor. See you next time." Georgia threw Isabelle a wink as she moved past her toward the kitchen.

The moment Mark saw her, he paused, his medical bag in hand. "Hello, Isabelle."

"Hi, Mark." Her lips curved upward.

"I'm glad I ran into you." He stared at a point near her chin, not seeming glad at all. The twinkle in his eyes was missing, as was his welcoming look. Instead, his features appeared grim. "If you can spare a few minutes, could we go somewhere and talk?"

Her smile faded. Had he received bad news of some sort? Or maybe he had more insight about what had transpired between Josh and her sister. "I have a little time," she said. "Where shall we go?"

"There's a park about a block from here. I thought that might do." Mark's flat tone unnerved her.

She nodded. "I know the one." She retrieved her light jacket from the coatrack, and Mark helped her into it.

They left the house and walked in silence. The total change from his usual demeanor had nerves roiling in her stomach. She clasped her hands together as she walked, too unsettled to even make small talk.

They took the main path into the park, and at the first bench, Mark indicated for them to sit.

"Tell me what's wrong," she said without preamble. "Is this about Josh?"

He nodded, but his mouth remained set in a tight line.

She longed to reach out and smooth the tension from his jaw, yet something held her back.

At last, he released a weary breath. "Josh has left to join the army."

"What?" She stared in disbelief. "When did this happen?"

"This morning. He left me a note telling me where he'd gone." The terse answer didn't disguise the pain in Mark's voice.

"That must have been a terrible shock."

"It was. I couldn't let him leave like that, not without talking to him first. So I tracked him down at the recruitment office."

"How did it go when you saw him?"

"Not the way I'd hoped. He refused to listen to reason." A nerve at Mark's temple pulsed. "For the first time, I realized how much pain my brother is in. I think Marissa's rejection this time was the last straw."

Isabelle stiffened. His tone sounded harsh, condescending even. Not like Mark at all.

"I'm sorry," she said slowly. "I know this is hard." She hated that Josh was hurting and that, in turn, Mark was suffering too. He had to be terribly worried about what might happen to his brother and whether he'd make it home alive. How she wished they could go back in time before this whole mess had started. "Will he be sent overseas right away?"

Mark's knuckles were white against the bench. "He'll have several weeks of training first. But after that, yes."

They sat in silence for several moments as Isabelle pondered the gravity of the situation. After everything Mark had done for his brother, all his dreams for Josh's future had turned to ashes. He must be devastated.

Mark straightened against the bench, his body rigid beside hers. "This whole situation has led me to make a difficult decision." He exhaled a long breath.

Chills of apprehension rippled through her as he turned to face her.

"Despite my feelings for you, Isabelle, I think we should take a step back." Deep lines formed grooves across his forehead as he met her gaze.

Her lungs seized. "I don't understand."

"I think we could both use a little space to reevaluate our priorities."

The hard inflection in his tone made her bristle. "What does that mean?"

"It means that I have the new clinic to focus on, while you . . ." He took a breath. "You seem to have made your sister and the baby your priority." Resentment oozed from his tone. "And to be honest, I'm finding it very difficult to be around Marissa right now. In fact, I'm turning her care over to Mrs. Dinglemire."

Isabelle's jaw went slack. She stared at him, unable to reconcile this bitter person with the Mark she knew. "Surely you're not laying all the blame on Marissa?"

His head whipped up. "How can I not blame her? She's treated my brother like a pawn in her game for months now. Then, after everything he was willing to sacrifice for her, she rejected him again." Mark pushed off the bench. "Now he's running off to risk his life in order to forget the pain she's caused him."

Hot fury raced through Isabelle's veins. She sprang to her feet and stalked over to face him. "You act like my sister's some sort of calculating siren, luring Josh over a cliff. She made some bad choices, but your brother isn't exactly blameless either. He's the one who initiated the lie in the first place."

"He was trying to protect her. Much to his own detriment." Mark's eyes sparked with disdain.

She took a step back. "I can't believe this. I thought you were so level-headed. So compassionate and kind. I guess that's only true for people who manage to live up to your high standards." Her legs shook with the force of her outrage. "You said you wanted space. Well, consider your request granted. I'm only glad I discovered your true nature before we went any further."

Isabelle whirled around and strode away before her tears could betray her. The autumn wind picked up, making the dead leaves dance on the path ahead of her, cutting through her thin coat.

She'd never felt colder in her life.

42

Later, after Isabelle was all cried out, she went to see Marissa. She found her sister pacing the floor of her bedroom, rocking the baby as she walked.

"How is our princess today?" Isabelle forced her lips into a semblance of a smile as she crossed the room.

Marissa looked up. The dark circles under her eyes bore testimony to her lack of sleep. "A little fussy for some reason."

"Would you like me to take her for a while?"

"I'd love it. Thank you." She walked over and transferred the baby to Isabelle's waiting arms. "She's been fed and changed, so I'm not sure why she won't sleep."

"Don't worry. I'll take her downstairs for a change of scenery and let you nap. You'll feel better after that."

The tears that formed in Marissa's eyes halted Isabelle's departure. "Is there something else upsetting you?"

Marissa bit her bottom lip and nodded.

"It's Josh, isn't it?" Isabelle swayed with the baby, whose whimpers finally subsided.

Marissa's chin trembled. "He's going to get himself killed, and it's all my fault." Her features crumpled as a cascade of tears broke free.

"Oh, honey." Isabelle wrapped her one free arm around her

sister's shoulder. There was really nothing she could say to help the situation, so she let Marissa cry. It seemed it was a day for them both to weep out their sorrows.

After a few minutes, Marissa pulled back and wiped her face. "If only there was some way to stop him. To tell him . . ."

"Tell him what? That you've changed your mind?"

Marissa pulled her bathrobe tighter around her. "What if I have?"

Isabelle studied her sister. "It's likely a reaction to the shock of his leaving. You're feeling guilty, and it's making you think—"

"That's not it." Marissa shook her head, causing wisps of her honey-colored hair to cling to her damp cheeks. "I love him, Belle. I have all along. I really believed that sending him away was for his own good. I thought he'd go back to school or get a job. I never dreamed he would join the army."

Isabelle went to lay the baby down in the bassinet as she considered her sister's words. Then she led her over to sit on the side of the bed, the mattress sagging under their weight. "Maybe this is something Josh needs to do for himself. You're both so young. You have your whole lives ahead of you. Maybe when he returns, you'll both be ready to begin a more mature relationship."

"I have a bad feeling that if Josh goes overseas, he'll never come back." Fresh tears magnified the amber in her eyes.

Isabelle's heart squeezed with compassion. How would she feel if Mark decided to enlist? Despite how angry she was, she couldn't imagine the constant worry. "From what Mark said, Josh was adamant about doing this. Nothing is going to change his mind. We might not like it, but we have to respect his decision. Just as he's respecting yours."

Marissa hung her head. "I guess so."

Isabelle laid a hand on her arm. "Can I make a suggestion? Take some time to pray hard and listen for God's guidance. And ask for the strength to accept whatever the future might have in store for you and for Josh. In the meantime, focus all your attention on that beautiful little girl."

Marissa sighed, then leaned over to hug her. "I guess you're right, Belle. I have to believe that God knows what's best. For all of us."

The next two weeks flew by as Marissa adjusted to being a mother and Isabelle tried to formulate a plan for their future. She needed time to save money to be able to afford a place for them to stay. And she needed to know how long Marissa and Lisette could stay at Bennington Place without becoming a burden.

After lunch, when the other residents had drifted away from the dining room, Isabelle joined Olivia and Ruth at the table. "Can I speak to you both for a minute?"

"Of course. We were just about to have coffee." Olivia handed Isabelle a mug, then turned to the silver urn on the sideboard to pour herself some.

"Thank you." Isabelle took a seat at the table.

"What's on your mind?" Olivia asked. She sat down and poured cream into her cup.

"I was wondering how long a new mother can remain here."

"Nothing is set in stone." Ruth raised her gaze from the letter she'd been reading. "Generally, six months is about the time it takes for a resident to come up with a workable plan and find a job. Although women who are able to find one are in the minority. Most of the residents eventually decide to give their child up for adoption."

Isabelle sighed. "If only there were some sort of affordable childcare for these women. Some way that they could work and keep their babies."

"Don't we know it." Olivia nodded thoughtfully. "We've often discussed ways we could expand and offer such a service to the mothers here. Clearly there's no extra room in this house, so it would mean finding space somewhere else, possibly getting a license, and staffing it with qualified people. There's a lot to consider before starting such an endeavor."

Isabelle frowned. "I wish I could do more for them." Her thoughts turned to Eloise, Helen, and Annie, who had had their babies and surrendered them to the Children's Aid Society. Mary Beth had been one of the rare lucky ones who was able to take her child home to her parents.

"You've done a lot already by getting Laura and Georgia part-time jobs at Mark's clinic." Olivia smiled. "That was a brilliant idea."

"All I did was make the suggestion. It was Mark who agreed to it."

Ruth studied her thoughtfully. "Isabelle, you seem to have a real heart for people in need."

She smiled. "It's true. I used to love helping my mother raise money for her charities, but I've found it so much more rewarding to reach out to real people in need." She paused. "I want to be able to help others the way Fiona and Rosie O'Grady helped us when we were homeless."

Ruth pursed her lips, staring at Isabelle with an intent look. "As much as we love you and appreciate your hard work around here, my dear, is this the type of work you have in mind for your future?"

Isabelle's gaze swung to the older woman. Her question sounded a lot like criticism. "What do you mean?" She loved her life at the maternity home. Ruth had become like a surrogate grandmother and Olivia like another sister. Why would she question that?

Ruth took a slow sip from her cup before responding. "Have you ever considered going back to school and furthering your education?"

"I have thought about it," she confessed, "and I think one day I will." With a resigned sigh, she set her mug down. "But that will have to wait, I'm afraid."

"What if you didn't have to wait?" Ruth regarded her with an expectant expression.

Isabelle shot a glance at Olivia, who only shrugged.

"There's no use wishing for things that aren't possible," Isabelle said firmly. They were the same words she'd told herself over and over again with regards to Mark. "I have no money for tuition. Nor do I have the luxury of time since I have to earn a living right now."

Ruth removed her reading glasses and set them on the table, a sure sign that a lecture was about to follow. "As Olivia will attest, I also enjoy helping people. Which of course is why we opened Bennington Place to begin with. When I see someone with great potential, as I did when I met Olivia, and as I did with Mark's clinic, I feel an obligation to share my good fortune." She leaned forward on her chair. "Lately I've been sensing a gentle nudging from the Lord to help you, Isabelle."

"Me?" Nerves began to swirl in Isabelle's stomach. "But you've already done so much."

"It's not as if you've been a burden," Olivia soothed. "You go above and beyond your job requirements. Mrs. Neale in particular has said how grateful she is for your support."

Ruth nodded. "And more than one of our girls have mentioned how kind you've been to them. Being able to accept people as they are and offer unconditional support and encouragement—not only to your own sister, but also to complete strangers—is a rare gift. A gift that shouldn't go to waste."

"I appreciate that, but I don't see how—"

Ruth waved her hand, like a queen dismissing a peasant. "I'd like to pay for you to attend university. If it's something you'd want to do."

Isabelle stared, certain she must have heard wrong. "Oh, no. I couldn't allow you to do that."

"Why not?" Ruth folded her arms in front of her, her gaze boring into Isabelle.

Scattered thoughts raced through her mind with dizzying swiftness. How could she refuse without offending the dear woman? "That's very generous, but I could never accept such . . . charity."

"Charity?" Ruth's eyebrows rose. "Is that your pride talking, perchance?"

Heat infused Isabelle's cheeks. The woman seemed genuinely miffed, which was the last thing Isabelle wanted. "Maybe it is prideful," she admitted. "But ever since we lost our family home, I promised myself I would take care of my sister and find a way to support us on my own."

Ruth's eyes narrowed. "Forgive me for being blunt, but it seems to me you've been relying on the kindness of others from the very beginning. First your former maid and her aunt took you in, then Dr. Henshaw helped you get the hotel position, and later we provided you with a job and a place to stay."

Isabelle bit her lip as the sting of truth hit hard. Ruth was right. She'd really accomplished nothing on her own. She'd even considered marrying Elias Weatherby in order to secure a future for her sister. Tears sprang to her eyes. *Pride goeth before a fall*, her mother used to say.

Ruth patted Isabelle's arm. "It's not a failing to accept help, my dear. It actually takes great strength of character to do so."

Isabelle's throat seized, making speech impossible.

Olivia came around the table and placed a hand on her shoulder. "It's true. No one felt more undeserving of help than I did. I was humbled by Ruth's generosity, and once I grew stronger, I was able to take her kindness and turn it outward to benefit others. Maybe you could do the same."

Isabelle managed a shaky smile. "Thank you. Both of you. If you don't mind, I'll need some time to think about it and pray about it."

"Certainly," Ruth said. "I imagine the next semester doesn't begin until January, so there's plenty of time. In the meantime, Marissa and the baby are welcome to stay as long as they need."

Isabelle's heart swelled with gratitude for these women who had shown her and her sister such kindness. She would heed Olivia's advice, and no matter what happened in the future, she would strive to be an example of the generosity she had received from others in her darkest times.

After Ruth had left the room, Olivia lingered at the table. "Isabelle, before you go, may I ask you something?"

"Of course. What is it?" She hoped Olivia didn't resent Ruth's offer to her.

"I'm concerned about Mark. Have you talked to him lately?"

Isabelle's muscles tightened. "Not since Josh enlisted in the army." She hesitated, not wanting to divulge the personal issues between them. But Olivia had always been candid with her, and she deserved an honest answer. "The truth is that Mark blames Marissa for driving Josh away. He said he needed space to come to terms with everything that's happened." Her gaze fell. "I haven't heard from him since."

"Oh, Isabelle. I'm sorry." Olivia's features softened. "This is such a complicated situation. But it's not like Mark to stay angry for so long." She patted Isabelle's arm. "Not to worry. I'm sure he'll come around given enough time."

"Maybe so." Isabelle didn't hold out a lot of hope. Especially with Josh's fate so uncertain.

Still, she prayed that God would bring peace to Mark and help him adjust to whatever was to come.

And that somehow in the meantime her bruised heart would heal.

43

Mark stepped out of the mayor's office, a feeling of satisfaction warming his insides. Mayor Conboy had met with him and listened to his concerns over the health issues in the impoverished areas of the city. It wasn't the first time the dire conditions had been brought to the mayor's attention. He assured Mark that the city was taking steps to dismantle that part of town, encouraging the residents to relocate elsewhere. Within the next five to ten years, the city planned to have the tenement housing completely demolished and new commercial buildings, as well as a new city hall, erected in their place.

Nevertheless, after listening to Mark's concerns that this did little to help the current situation, Mayor Conboy promised to send the health inspector out to see what could be done to improve the present sanitation system. Even though the polio outbreak had been mostly contained, the method of handling sewage in the neighborhood still needed a major overhaul. Since most polio outbreaks occurred in the summer, Mark hoped that if the government managed to improve the sanitary conditions, there wouldn't be a repeat of the epidemic next year.

Mark left downtown with a renewed sense of accomplishment. As he steered his car toward home, he found his thoughts turning once again to Isabelle, wishing he could share his good news with her. But the memory of their last heated encounter caused another surge of regret to rise in his chest. Once again, he'd let his anger toward Marissa create a rift with Isabelle. He should have known she would defend her sister against any criticism. He'd have done the same thing if anyone maligned Josh.

Over the past few days, Mark had felt his resolve weakening and toyed with the idea of reaching out to her. Yet a clutch of fear held him in an iron grip. What if he resumed their romantic connection and things didn't work out? It would be even harder to part ways with Isabelle then. Besides, from what Marissa had told him, Isabelle seemed to have her future all mapped out with her sister and the baby, leaving him to wonder just how important he was to her after all.

No, it would be far wiser to leave the situation as it was for the present. God willing, this war wouldn't last much longer, and once Josh returned, they could see how things played out. For now, he would leave the matter in God's hands.

Mark turned onto his street, parked the car, and stared at his house for several long seconds before getting out and approaching the empty residence. Instead of beckoning him inside, the cold, lifeless exterior was as unwelcoming as a morgue. His mood took an even greater nosedive when he entered the house and the suffocating silence within almost propelled him back outside. He set his bag down in the hall, attempting to push back the crush of loneliness. Maybe he should get a dog. At least then there'd be someone to greet him when he got home.

He turned on the lights and made his way to the kitchen, where he searched half-heartedly in the sparce icebox for something to eat. Only half a pound of butter, a bottle of milk, and a couple of shriveled apples graced the inside. He huffed out a disgusted breath and shut the door. He should have gone to the market yesterday. Now he'd be lucky to find a scrap of bread for his supper.

What he wouldn't give for one of Mrs. Neale's platters of fried chicken. The cook often sent him home with a plate for his dinner if he was leaving Bennington Place around that time. The way he'd been avoiding the maternity home lately, it would be a while before that happened again.

The doorbell rang, jarring Mark in the house's utter silence. Who could that be?

Picturing Isabelle on the other side of the door, his heart gave a leap of anticipation. It hit him anew just how much he'd missed her. All his resolve to keep her at arm's length vanished in an instant. If she was here, he'd do everything in his power to get her to forgive him.

He swung the door open, and disappointment crashed over him. "Olivia."

"Hi, Mark. May I come in?" She wore a bright cherry-colored jacket and white gloves.

The brisk evening air seeped inside, making him glad he still wore his tweed sports coat.

"Um, sure." He stepped back to let her pass, then helped her with her coat. "What brings you by?" he asked as he led her into the living room.

"Nothing much." She tugged off her gloves and took a seat on the sofa. "I'm just here to check up on you."

He narrowed his eyes as suspicion curled in his chest. "Why is that?"

"Do I need a reason?" She tilted her head with an innocent smile.

"I have a feeling you're on a fishing expedition."

She laughed out loud. "You know I don't like to fish."

Mark sat on the arm of his wingback chair and folded his arms, prepared to wait until she revealed her real reason for dropping by.

Her expression changed, becoming more serious. "I've been worried about you. I know it must be hard with Josh gone. And you've been avoiding the maternity home lately. I wanted to make sure you're all right."

The image of his empty icebox flew to mind. He shrugged one shoulder. "I've been better, I guess. This house seems far too big with only me here." He rose and crossed to the fireplace, eyeing a framed photo of Josh. "I was thinking I should get a dog to keep me company."

"You could. Or how about a wife instead?"

Mark slowly turned around. "Ah, now the real reason for your visit."

"Don't look so grumpy." She got up and came to stand beside him. "From personal experience, I can tell you how much marriage has enriched my life. It could do the same for you."

Irritation warred with amusement, and his lips twitched. "I suppose you have the perfect candidate in mind?"

She tapped a finger to her lips. "I do know someone who would suit you perfectly. There's only one problem."

"Do tell."

"The two of you seem to be at odds with each other. I was wondering what we might do to rectify the situation."

All humor disappeared. "I'm not discussing Isabelle with you." He pinned her with a hard stare until she let out a sigh.

"All right. I won't interfere. But as your friend, let me say one thing." She laid a comforting hand on his arm. "You deserve to be happy, Mark. You have so much love inside you to share if you'd only allow yourself." Her gaze held his. "I imagine at one time this house was filled with love. Don't let pride or stubbornness rob you of that type of happiness. All you have to do is reach out and ask for it."

The muscles in Mark's chest curled into a knot of tension. He clenched his teeth together to contain the emotion welling inside him. She was right. This house *had* been filled with laughter and happy memories. But ever since his parents died, it had become simply a dwelling place, a roof over his head, and nothing more.

Had Josh felt that way too? If so, was it any wonder he was so eager to leave?

Mark looked into Olivia's warm brown eyes. "You're right. This place hasn't felt like a home in a long time."

She gave him a sad smile. "You have the power to change that if you want to. I'll be praying for you and for Josh. I hope by the time he comes back you'll have figured out what you truly want out of life." She rose on her tiptoes to kiss his cheek. "If you ever need to talk, I'm only a phone call away."

"Thank you, Olivia, for your concern and for the pep talk."

Her eyes grew misty. "You were a good friend to me a few years ago when I was struggling. I only want to return the favor."

As he watched her walk down the sidewalk, it occurred to him that she'd never tried to force her opinion on him. She'd merely reminded him of a few simple truths and made him see that he needed to take a good hard look at his life and where he was headed from here.

After finishing two pieces of toast and a cup of black coffee that served as his dinner, Mark wandered around the house, too restless to sit and read or to listen to the radio. He scanned the living room with a critical eye. The faded wallpaper, the tired-looking sofa, and the frayed area rug had all seen better days. Everything in this room needed refurbishing, not to mention a good cleaning.

Just like the state of Mark's soul. *Blemished. Flawed. In need of an overhaul.*

Instead of taking responsibility for his mistakes with Josh, he'd blamed Marissa for leading his brother astray, when the truth was Mark had given Josh a mighty shove out of the nest with his overbearing attitude.

Shame washed over him like an avalanche. He owed both the Wardrop sisters a sincere apology for his callous behavior, something he would rectify the next time he saw them.

Mark climbed the stairs to the upper level and flipped on the light in Josh's bedroom to survey the space. Nothing much had changed in here since Josh was a kid. The same blue paint, the same striped bedspread. It was time for an overhaul of more than just the downstairs. Everything in this house seemed to exist in a state frozen in time.

Before his parents' accident.

He headed down the hall to the room he hadn't entered in almost five years. The scent of his mother's favorite perfume hit him first, almost sending him to his knees. He closed his eyes and breathed deeply until he found the courage to turn on the light. His parents' bed, their dresser, and the night tables all remained the same, as though the couple would be back any minute. His dad's reading glasses still sat on top of the book he'd been halfway through.

Mark ran his fingers through the dust on his mother's vanity table, and his throat thickened. What a coward he'd been to neglect this room for so long. It was long overdue for him to sort through everything, donate his parents' clothing, and give the walls a new coat of paint.

He realized that avoiding the dreaded task for so long had only kept him trapped in a perpetual state of limbo. Instead of dealing with his grief, he'd poured all his energy into his career, using it to mask the pain. Then he'd fixated on his brother's life at the expense of his own. How could he have been so blind?

It seemed clear to him now that in order to truly be happy, he needed to let go of the past, once and for all.

Fresh energy filled him as he opened the door to the guest room, which had doubled as his mother's sewing area. This room was larger than Mark's bedroom, much better suited for a couple. His mind spun with what he could do with it, if given the right circumstances.

He closed his eyes on a smile, picturing the house once again filled with a loving family and the laughter of children. It was exactly what his parents would have wanted.

What had Olivia said? *"Don't let pride or stubbornness rob you of that type of happiness. All you have to do is reach out and ask for it."*

Only one question remained. Did he have the courage to do so?

44

Ruth scanned the sign on the impressive stone building and smiled. "This appears to be the right place. Let's go in, shall we?"

Isabelle couldn't seem to force her legs to move toward the cement steps. "I really don't see the urgency to do this now. As you said, the next semester won't start until January."

For some reason, Ruth had insisted that Isabelle accompany her to the university campus today to see what programs were available in social work, her desired field, and the criteria necessary for admission. Isabelle had barely had time to wrap her mind around the concept of becoming a student again, yet here they were.

"No time like the present," Ruth said. "Besides, we're only collecting information. We don't have to register right now if you still need time to think about it."

Register? That idea hadn't even crossed her mind.

At the top of the stairs, Ruth held the door open with a look that brooked no arguments. The woman could certainly be formidable when she chose.

Isabelle made her way into the dim interior of the building. The smell of old books and cleaning supplies wrapped around her.

"The office is over here." Ruth pointed to a frosted glass door with gold lettering.

Isabelle almost tiptoed over to the door, not wanting her heels to make a loud noise in the hushed space. She patted her hair in place, making sure no strands had escaped the roll she'd spent so much time perfecting, then entered behind Ruth.

Inside, a long counter separated them from the people working at their desks. Immediately, a woman rose and came to greet them. "Good morning, ladies. What can I do for you?"

"Hello. I'm Ruth Bennington, and this is Isabelle Wardrop."

The woman's eyes widened. "Mrs. Bennington! It's lovely to meet one of our benefactors," she gushed. "I'm Beth Ingleman."

Isabelle almost laughed. It shouldn't surprise her that Ruth supported the university.

"Thank you, dear." Ruth beamed at the other woman. "We're looking for information on your courses. I believe you have a two-year social work program."

"We do indeed. A highly acclaimed program if I might boast a tiny bit." Beth gave a somewhat nervous laugh.

"That's good to know. Miss Wardrop may wish to enroll in your next semester. Would you have any brochures on the courses required and perhaps an application she could fill out when she's ready?"

"Certainly. I can put together a package for you in a jiffy." Beth turned to Isabelle. "I presume you've obtained your high school diploma?"

"Yes. But I graduated several years ago. Will that be a problem?"

"Not at all. You'll be enrolled as a mature student. If you'll wait here a moment, I'll get that information for you."

"Thank you." Ruth gave the girl a warm smile, then turned to Isabelle. "Why don't you have a seat? I need to find the ladies' room. I'll be back in a few minutes."

"All right," Isabelle said weakly as she sank onto a wooden chair.

This was all happening too fast for her to process. She closed her eyes. The truth was she didn't feel confident that she was university material. What if she failed her courses and wasted Ruth's money?

"Here we are." Beth's bright voice bounced off the walls. "Oh, where did Mrs. Bennington go?"

Isabelle went over to the counter. "To the ladies' room. She should be back any minute."

"Well, since this information is intended for you, I'll show you what's in the folder." She pointed out the brochures and the application form and told Isabelle what to do if she decided to enroll.

"Thank you, ma'am. I appreciate your help." Isabelle gathered the materials into the file.

"Don't forget that the deadline to apply for the winter term is November fifteenth."

"I won't. Thank you again." Isabelle glanced out the door, but there was still no sign of Ruth. "I'd better go and find out where Mrs. Bennington has gotten to."

"Tell her if she needs anything else, we'd be happy to help."

"I will." Isabelle stepped into the hallway and blew out the breath she'd been holding. What could be taking Ruth so long?

She peered down the corridor, feeling like an intruder who didn't belong here. Only a handful of people were visible, none of whom were Ruth.

A throat cleared behind her.

Isabelle turned around and simply stared, not quite believing her eyes.

Mark stood there, holding a bouquet of pink and white roses in his arms. He wore a dark suit and a light blue shirt with a striped tie. His beard was neatly trimmed, and his hair was combed off his forehead, highlighting his handsome features. "Hello, Isabelle," he said hesitantly.

She reined in her instant delight, forcing herself to recall their last unpleasant conversation. Had he forgiven her sister for her

supposed mistreatment of Josh? And if so, would it change anything between them?

"What are you doing here, Mark?"

He gave a small shrug. "A mutual friend told me you'd be here
today." Smiling, he came toward her and held out the bouquet.
"These are for you. I hope you'll accept them as a token of my
sincerest regret."

Reluctantly, she took the flowers from him. "Regret for what
exactly?"

"For the way I reacted when Josh left." His easy manner slipped
away, and his hazel eyes shone with remorse. "I didn't handle his
enlisting very well. I blamed Marissa for everything that had happened, and I realize now that wasn't fair. It certainly wasn't fair
to end our relationship because I had issues with our siblings. I
acted out of resentment and anger, and I'm sorry."

"I see." She took a moment to inhale the bouquet's heady floral
scent and formulate her response. "What brought about this sudden revelation?" Maybe she sounded cold, but she couldn't simply
ignore the rejection and disillusionment he'd put her through.
Why should she trust him again?

"It was a combination of things." He gave a tentative smile.
"Olivia came to see me one night when I was feeling particularly
sorry for myself. She seemed to sense that I might need a friend."

Sympathy battled with a flare of jealousy. *She* should have been
the one to offer him comfort or a shoulder to lean on. Instead,
it had been Olivia.

"She reminded me that I deserved to be happy. A simple concept, but it made me realize that I haven't been happy in quite
a while. Almost as though I'd been punishing myself for failing
Josh and failing my parents."

Her walls of resentment began to crumble. She understood
all too well how easy it was to feel responsible. "Oh, Mark. You
didn't fail anyone."

"I think I did," he said in a quiet voice. "I was so busy organizing

Josh's life that I didn't let him simply live it." He stuffed his hand in his pocket. "That's all beside the point now. He's made his decision, and I have to accept it."

She hesitated. "What about Marissa? Have you forgiven her?"

He held her gaze. "Yes, I have. I shouldn't have taken my anger out on her when the person I was really mad at was myself."

The sincerity in his eyes told her that he wasn't just saying it to please her. She nodded. "I'm glad. Marissa may have made mistakes, but she's trying her best to do the right thing for everyone involved."

"I know that now. I've had a letter from Josh, and he said that he's heard from Marissa. I don't know what she said exactly, but it's given him new hope. I'll be forever grateful, because I think he now feels he has a real incentive to make it home alive."

"I hope he does. For your sake and for Marissa's. She really loves him, you know."

"I do. But that's not the reason I'm here." He moved closer, and the masculine scent of his soap filled her senses. "I was a fool to push you away, Isabelle." His voice was husky. "Do you think you can ever forgive me and give us another chance?"

A rush of warmth filled her chest. Either the scent of the roses was making her dizzy or the man before her was the culprit. Either way, her mind felt muddled. Could she lower her guard and let him fully into her heart? "What happens if Marissa ends up hurting Josh again? What guarantee do I have that you won't react the same way?"

"Only my word." He pulled himself up taller. "I've promised myself that when Josh comes home, I'll let him live his life as he chooses. Whatever happens between Josh and Marissa will be their business."

Isabelle wavered. She wanted to forgive him, more than anything. Her mouth went dry as she tried to sort through her jumbled emotions.

"If you need time to think about it, that's fair. I realize you have no real reason to trust me right now." His gaze was shrouded in disappointment. "I'll let you go, then." He started walking slowly backward.

Her heart gave a painful lurch. Did she really want him to disappear from her life again?

"No, wait. I . . ." She gulped in a lungful of air. "I know our argument was out of character. You're normally compassionate and levelheaded. Traits I admire very much." She exhaled slowly. "I-I forgive you, Mark."

The tension drained from his features. "Thank you, Isabelle. That means the world to me." He came forward and took one of her hands in his. "I'm so sorry for hurting you."

Her heart was beating fast against her ribs as heat from his fingers spread across her palm. "I'm sorry too for the things I said that day."

Relief spread across his face. "Does this mean you might be willing to have dinner with me?"

"Right now?"

"If you're free."

"Well, actually, I'm waiting for Ruth." She frowned, looking back over her shoulder. "She brought me here, but she went to the restroom and never came back. I'm getting worried about her."

Mark chuckled. "No need. She's gone home."

"How do you know that?"

"It was all part of my plan. If you'd refused my apology, I was going to call you a cab to take you home." He held out his hand to her. "Will you come with me, Isabelle?"

He stared at her with so much hope in his eyes that she couldn't have refused even if she'd wanted to.

With a tremulous smile, she reached out and took his hand. "I'd like that very much."

Mark shot a quick look at Isabelle in the car beside him, holding the bouquet of flowers on her lap. He still couldn't believe she'd agreed to come with him.

"Ruth mentioned you were thinking about going back to school. Did you enroll in one of the programs?"

"Not yet." She exhaled softly. "I haven't totally made up my mind what to do."

"What would you want to study?"

"I think social work. I like helping people with their problems."

"That's great. I think you'd make a terrific social worker."

"You do?"

"Definitely. You have a wonderful way with the residents. Laura can't stop raving about you."

Isabelle laughed, a blush infusing her cheeks. "She's my biggest fan, apparently, though I didn't really do much."

"You did a lot. You gave her the confidence to keep her son. You suggested her for the receptionist job. You changed her life, Isabelle, and that little boy's too."

She paused, as though digesting what he'd said. "I've discovered that helping people is very rewarding. But I guess I don't need to tell you that."

"Indeed. It's what keeps me going on the hard days."

Mark pulled up in front of the Royal York Hotel and turned off the engine. Nervous energy rioted through his system, making his heart pound and his hands perspire. Would the rest of the evening go as he'd hoped? No matter what, he didn't want to rush her or scare her off. After all, she'd only forgiven him five minutes ago. He told himself to follow her cues and simply be happy to be with her again. "I hope you don't mind coming here," he said.

Her brows rose. "I thought we were going somewhere to eat."

"We are, don't worry."

"At the hotel?"

"That's right." He got out and rounded the front of the car to open her door for her.

A frown creased her forehead as she slowly got out, still clutching the bouquet of flowers.

"Do you trust me, Isabelle?"

"I do."

"Good. Then let me spoil you just a little." He grasped her hand, and they headed inside.

But as they neared the bank of elevators, she pulled to a stop. "I don't know if I'm allowed to use these." She looked back over her shoulder as if expecting a police officer to come and arrest her for not taking the staff elevator.

He took her gently by the shoulders. "It's okay. You're not a staff member any longer. Tonight, you are a VIP. My VIP to be exact."

The elevator doors slid open, and they rode the car to the fourteenth floor, then made their way to the room Mark had reserved.

Once again, she hesitated. "The Garden Penthouse?" Indignation flashed in her eyes. "I think you'd better explain yourself, Dr. Henshaw."

Laughing, he fit the key in the lock and pushed open the door. "You said you trusted me, remember? Go on in and see for yourself."

She threw him a wary look as she cautiously entered the room.

Not wanting her to feel uncomfortable, Mark left the door open and followed her in.

Isabelle stood in the middle of the living room, staring around the elegant space. High ceilings showcased a marble fireplace, two velvet sofas, mahogany side tables, and a pair of crystal lamps.

On the far side of the room, a small table had been set up in front of the window, just as he'd requested. Two covered silver dishes awaited them. That would be the French onion soup to begin the meal.

Isabelle set the flowers down on a side table before walking toward the wall of windows that overlooked the lake. "This view is breathtaking." She turned to him with a troubled look. "How can you afford all this, Mark? It must have cost a fortune."

"Not really. Don't forget, I know the manager. Mr. Johnson gave me a good discount." He took her hand in his, relishing its softness. "I wanted you to feel on top of the world tonight, just like I feel when I'm with you."

"Oh, Mark." Moisture glistened in her eyes.

He was about to pull her closer when two quick knocks sounded on the open door.

Seconds later, a waiter appeared, pushing a service cart containing several bottles. "Good evening, sir. Would you and the young lady care for some wine or sparkling cider?"

"Isabelle, what would you prefer?"

"The cider, please."

"Make that two," he told the waiter.

The man bowed. "Very good, sir." He quickly poured two glasses, then lit the candles on the table. "The main course will be ready in about thirty minutes."

"Thank you."

The waiter bowed again, then discreetly left the room.

Mark picked up his glass. "I'd like to make a toast. To a very promising future."

She smiled and raised her glass. "To the future. May it be filled with good things."

He took a sip, and the tart flavor burst on his tongue.

He set his glass down and took her hand in his, his heart thudding heavily in his chest. Though he'd planned to wait until the perfect moment as the sun set over the water to tell her what was on his heart, now seemed the appropriate time. "I know we've talked about the future in general terms," he began. "But not in a very romantic way."

"Well, you're making up for it now," she teased. "You brought me roses. And this"—she waved a hand toward the dinner table—"is definitely romantic."

He pursed his lips. "Maybe . . . but I think I can do better." He paused to choose his words carefully, and then looked deep into her beautiful eyes. "I've missed you, Isabelle. More than I ever thought possible. And this time apart has made me reevaluate what's important to me." He rubbed his thumb over the soft skin of her hand. "Without you, the color has gone out of my world. As though everything around me is nothing but muted shades of gray." He inhaled and slowly let out a breath. "I love you, Isabelle. And I want us to build a life together, if that's what you want too."

Her chin quivered as she nodded. "I love you too, Mark. I have for a while now."

Joy spilled through him, spiking his pulse. He reached into his jacket pocket and withdrew the box he'd put there. "I want to share every moment with you. The good and the bad and all the in-between. I want us to create a family together and make memories to carry us through to old age." Without taking his eyes off her face, he opened the lid. "Will you marry me?"

Moisture welled in her luminous blue eyes. She brought a hand to her mouth as she stared at the ring. Suddenly he realized how unimpressive it must seem to her, a girl who was used to the best that money could buy.

"If you don't like it, we can get another one. It's just that this was my mother's and I thought—"

"It's perfect." She smiled through her tears. "I love it."

He held his breath as he searched her face. "Does this mean you're saying yes?"

Isabelle's lips trembled. Was this really happening? Was she brave enough to take this leap of faith?

She looked deep into his eyes. Eyes that shone with love for her, and the answer welled up inside of her. "Yes, Mark, I'll marry you."

A grin broke over his face as he gathered her into his arms and slowly brought his mouth to hers. Her heart sprang to life, beating wildly in her chest. She wrapped her arms around him and returned his kiss with an intensity that shocked her.

At last, he drew away, and they grinned at each other like besotted fools.

Isabelle held out her hand while Mark slipped the ring on her finger. She turned her hand to make the diamond shimmer in the light. The fact that it had belonged to his mother made it all the more special. "I'm honored to wear your mother's ring, Mark. I'll cherish it always."

"Isabelle." He breathed her name like a prayer, then kissed her again, almost reverently. This time as he moved back, however, his expression grew pensive.

"What is it?" she asked softly.

"I think it's only fair to warn you what you'd be getting into by marrying a doctor. I work long hours. I can get calls anytime, day or night, for any sort of emergency. It can be a challenging life."

She laid her palm against his face, relishing the softness of his beard beneath her fingers. "Being a doctor is who you are, Mark. Your dedication to your patients, your empathy, and your kindness are the reasons I love you. I'd never change that."

He kissed her again. "Well, now that we've settled that," he teased, "what do you say we have our dinner?"

"Yes, please."

"Good." He pulled out a chair for her at the round table, then took his seat. "And after we finish, you can fill out that application of yours." Calmly, he lifted the lids from their soup plates, releasing a wonderful aroma into the air.

Food, however, was the last thing on her mind at the moment. Not with the hard ball of fear curling in her belly. "I-I'm not sure I'm ready to do that yet."

"What's holding you back?"

She bit her lip. "Well, I have Marissa and the baby to consider, and I'll have to see if I can fit in my studies around my job."

"What if you didn't have to?" Taking her hand again, he fixed her with an intense stare. "We could get married before Christmas and you could start school full-time in January."

Her mouth dropped open. "Christmas is only two months away. We couldn't plan a wedding that fast."

"I don't want to waste any more time apart. You and Marissa and the baby could move in, and you wouldn't need a job. You could devote all your energy to your studies." One brow raised. "Well, not all your energy. I hope you'd save a little for me."

She ignored his attempt at humor and fought to stay serious. "What about when Josh gets back? What if things are awkward between him and Marissa?"

"Then we'll figure it out together." His hazel eyes flashed. "I've come to realize that I can't put my life on hold for what may or may not happen with Josh. I've already done that for far too long. It's time to focus on my happiness for a change."

She nodded, pausing to sift through everything that he'd said about her starting school. "You wouldn't mind having a wife with a career?"

"Not at all."

"What if we have children?"

He studied her. "If and when we have children, we'll make a decision that best suits our family."

Tears of happiness threatened again. He never once questioned the idea of her going to school or having a career. Not many men were as progressive.

"What do you say, Isabelle?" he asked softly. "Will you be my Christmas bride?"

Slowly, she shook her head. "I don't think so."

Disappointment crashed over his features. "All right. I can wait until you're ready."

She pursed her lips. "I think early December might be more practical. Then our wedding wouldn't interfere with anyone's Christmas celebrations. And it will give me time to move into your house before . . ." She swallowed. "Before I start my classes."

Mark's brows shot up. "Are you serious?"

She inhaled and let out a long breath. "I do believe I am."

A huge grin crept over his face. "I'm beginning to appreciate your practical side. Very much."

She laughed, a wonderful release of the joy spilling through her as she leaned forward to receive his kiss, one that promised a wonderful future ahead.

At last, he drew away and sat back in his chair. "I suppose we'd better eat before everything gets cold. The main course will be here any minute."

She placed a napkin on her lap with a happy sigh. "I want to enjoy every second of tonight. Because after this, I'm going to be very busy planning our wedding."

He pointed a finger at her. "And enrolling at the university."

"That too." She laughed again, hardly able to believe that after all the trials she'd endured, her life was finally turning around. She and Marissa had come through the worst period of their lives and had survived. Now, Isabelle had a bright future to look forward to with a man who loved her.

Her heart swelled with gratitude to God for remaining faithful during her darkest days and for bringing her back into the light once more.

Epilogue

May 1946

The squeal of a little girl's laughter drifted upstairs to where Isabelle sat at the desk with her textbooks spread out in front of her. She could picture Marissa pushing Lisette on the swing that Mark had installed in the backyard and wished she could join them.

There should be a law against having to study when the weather had turned so beautiful, especially when her husband was home on a rare day off from the clinic. However, time for leisure would come soon enough. Final exams were in a few weeks, and if Isabelle passed, she'd receive her certificate and officially begin her career. She'd already been volunteering at the Children's Aid offices under Jane Wilder's tutelage and was enjoying every minute. She loved the fact that Jane had taken her suggestion about starting a babysitting service seriously and was looking into how they might make that a reality.

Isabelle looked around Mark's old bedroom that he'd converted into an office for her after they married. Having a private space to study, with a door to close off any disruptions, had helped tremendously. She'd even managed to squeeze in extra courses so that she could graduate with the rest of the students who'd started a semester before her.

But the most amazing thing about the room was the addition of her mother's French provincial desk, which Mark had given to her as a wedding present. She ran her palm over its beloved surface, remembering her joy on the day he'd surprised her with it. Apparently, he'd gone back to her old house, and after talking to the new owner, learned that the desk was still there. He wouldn't tell her what he did to get the people to sell it to him, but she was immensely grateful that they did. Every time she sat here, she could picture her mother smiling at her in approval.

Isabelle stood and stretched her back muscles. The material she'd been reading over and over wasn't sticking in her mind. Time for a snack and a change of scenery. Maybe a few minutes outside with her family would do her some good after all. She walked into the kitchen just as her sister came in through the back door with Lisette on her hip.

"Somebody's hungry, I think." Marissa smoothed the wisps of fair hair off the girl's forehead. "Mark's weeding the garden. He'll be in shortly."

"Hey, sweetheart," Isabelle crooned. "Want a snack with Auntie Belle?"

"Snack," the girl repeated, her face lighting up.

Isabelle opened the new refrigerator Mark had purchased, replacing the outdated icebox. "How about some sliced apple?" She grabbed a piece of fruit and set it on the counter while Marissa put the toddler in her wooden high chair.

"Rosie called earlier," Marissa said. "She wants to know when your graduation ceremony will be so she and Fiona can plan to attend."

"Really? I thought they'd be gone to Adam's summer home by then." Soon after Fiona and Adam had wed, they'd found a smaller home for the two of them, and Aunt Rosie had moved in too. She'd agreed only on the condition that she would do the cooking for the household and help with the other chores so as not to be a burden. Isabelle was thrilled the kind woman was now living in such improved conditions.

"Apparently they're going to wait until after the graduation." Marissa tweaked her daughter's nose, which sent the girl into a fit of giggles.

Isabelle was immensely grateful for such wonderful friends. As soon as her studies were over, she would invite them all over for a celebratory dinner.

From the front of the house, the door opened and slammed shut. Isabelle frowned. Had Mark gone around and come in the front? She glanced at Marissa, who wore a worried expression.

Heavy footsteps came down the hall toward them.

"Who's there?" Isabelle called in a firm voice. She picked up the paring knife from the counter.

A man in uniform appeared in the kitchen doorway and grinned. "Is this the type of welcome a soldier gets around here?"

Time seemed to freeze. Then Marissa let out a cry and launched herself at Josh.

He wrapped his arms around her, lifting her feet off the floor. Marissa's frame shook with silent sobs.

Isabelle pressed a hand to her mouth, her own eyes welling with tears.

Josh set Marissa down, took her face in his hands, and kissed her deeply.

Isabelle tried to avert her gaze to give them some privacy but found she couldn't tear her eyes away.

"Mama, Mama." Lisette banged her tiny fists on the tray, breaking the couple's embrace.

"I'm here, sweetie." Marissa beamed, swiping the dampness from her cheeks.

"Welcome home, Josh." Isabelle gave him a hug. "Mark will be so happy to see you." Her throat constricted even more, picturing her husband's joy at having his brother home safe at last.

"Not as happy as I am." Josh's gaze found Marissa again. He looked taller, more muscular, and there was a new maturity around his eyes.

The back door opened, and Mark stepped inside. "I think a rabbit got to the lettuce again." He froze as he registered the man standing in the kitchen.

"Hey, big brother." Josh grinned. "What gives? I expected a parade to mark my homecoming."

Without a word, Mark walked over and pulled him into a bear hug. The two men clung together for several long seconds, and when they parted, both had tears in their eyes.

Isabelle wiped her wet cheeks. At last Mark would be able to relax now that Josh had returned in one piece.

Mark cleared his throat. "How are you? When did you get in? Are you hungry?"

Josh laughed. "I'm fine. I got here a few minutes ago. And I could eat, but . . ." His gaze strayed to Marissa again and lingered.

"Why don't Mark and I give Lissie her snack," Isabelle suggested, "so you two can catch up in private?"

Marissa smiled at Isabelle through her tears. "That's a great idea." She held out her hand to Josh, who immediately clasped it, then led him out the back door.

Isabelle walked over to her husband and wrapped her arms around him. "You'll have plenty of opportunity to talk later. They need this time first."

Mark let out a breath. "You're right. If it were me, I'd want to get you alone and make up for lost time." He dropped a sweet kiss on her lips. "He looks good though, doesn't he?"

"Yes, he does."

Lissie kicked the high chair and gave a loud squawk.

Isabelle laughed. "Okay, sweetie. Your snack is coming."

As she sliced the apple, her heart filled with quiet gratitude. *Thank you, Lord, for keeping Josh safe and bringing him back to his family.*

———— ❖ ————

Two months later

"Hurry up! She'll be here any minute." Olivia rushed into the maternity home parlor and waved at everyone to take their place.

Isabelle moved away from the doorway, marveling how thirty guests somehow managed to duck down, squeeze behind furniture, and attempt to generally make themselves invisible. As if that were even possible.

Mark's warm hand came down on her shoulder. "You may think you're hiding, but I bet that belly is sticking out like a sore thumb."

She looked up and stifled a laugh. "Stop it," she whispered. "I'm hardly even showing yet." She knew he was teasing her since she was barely four months along and had only recently stopped fitting into her regular clothes.

Her husband's eyes warmed as they always did before he kissed her. His lips lingered on hers for a few seconds longer than a mere peck, evoking a soft sigh of pleasure. After a year and a half of marriage, life just seemed to be getting better and better.

Behind them, someone cleared their throat. "Can you lovebirds try to control yourselves for a few hours? Bad enough I have to put up with this at home."

Isabelle pulled away from Mark to shoot a glare at her sister. Seeing Marissa's happy smirk, and Josh standing beside her, beaming, caused Isabelle's sarcastic remark to die on her lips. Instead, fresh gratitude filled her heart. Josh's reunion with Marissa had been wonderful to witness, and they'd set their wedding date for the end of the summer.

The sound of the front door opening pulled her attention back to the present.

"Honestly, Darius. This really wasn't necessary." Ruth's mildly annoyed voice echoed in the unusually silent hallway. "I could have easily waited until—"

"Surprise!" The guests jumped out from their hiding spots as Ruth appeared in the doorway.

The always unflappable woman froze, her mouth falling open. She clutched her throat with a nervous laugh. "Good grief. Don't do that to an old woman."

"Happy birthday, dearest Ruth." Olivia came forward to embrace her.

Ruth scanned the faces around the room, then focused back on Olivia. "You did all this?" Her voice quavered with a hint of tears.

"With a lot of help, I assure you." Olivia waved a hand toward the other residents of the home.

Ruth turned to Olivia's husband and wagged her finger. "Now I know why you insisted we swing by here, Darius Reed, you scoundrel."

"Happy birthday." He chuckled as he kissed her cheek.

The woman visibly melted. "It's fortunate you're so cute or I might have to stay mad at you."

The handsome man, who reminded Isabelle a lot of the movie star Clark Gable, laughed out loud. "Come on in and greet your guests. They've been patiently waiting for you."

Olivia ushered Ruth over to the armchair that had been decorated for the guest of honor. A pile of gifts was stacked on the coffee table. For once Ruth seemed totally flummoxed, staring from the wrapped parcels to the faces of the people surrounding her. She took out a handkerchief and blew her nose. "I can't believe you're all here."

"It's not every day a person turns seventy-five." Jane Wilder stepped forward and handed Ruth an envelope. "This is a small token of appreciation from . . . well, from the whole Children's Aid office, really."

As the newest employee of the organization, Isabelle's chest swelled with pride. She'd helped Jane collect money for Bennington Place to present to Ruth on her birthday. Mark squeezed Isabelle's hand as they watched Ruth open the envelope.

Ruth scanned the card inside, signed by all the employees of the Children's Aid office as well as the children's shelter. Tears welled in the older woman's eyes as she fingered the card. Then she pulled out the check and her eyes went wide. "Oh my. This is so generous of you. Thank you, Jane and Garrett."

Garrett put an arm around his wife. "We figured you'd rather have a donation for the maternity home instead of something more personal," he told her. "We wanted to show you how much we admire what you've done here and how much we value your partnership in caring for your residents and their children."

"You're giving me too much credit." Ruth wiped her cheeks.

"No, they're not." Olivia came forward. "Without you, none of this would have been possible. Thank you for believing in my vision and for making it a reality. I love you, Ruth."

"Oh, dear girl. I love you too, with all my heart. You're the daughter I always dreamed of having." Ruth stood and clasped Olivia in a tight hug.

Isabelle wiped her cheeks. When Mark cleared his throat, she guessed her husband was battling his own emotions.

"What's with all the tears in here?" Mrs. Neale bustled into the room, pushing a cart topped with a multilayered birthday cake. "This is supposed to be a celebration." The plump cook set her hands on her hips and gave the room a mock scowl.

Olivia broke away, dashing a hand to her eyes. "Thank you, Mrs. Neale. I hope you'll stay and join us."

The cook's cheeks reddened. "I'd be honored."

"Good. Now, Ruth, you need to cut the first slice and make a wish."

Ruth moved over to the cake with a smile. "I have nothing to wish for. I have everything I could possibly want right here."

Isabelle hummed a happy tune as she stacked the dirty plates on a tray. Most of the guests had left, and only a few people remained to help clean up. Marissa and Josh had gone home to relieve the neighbor who was watching Lisette. Mark and Darius had stepped outside for some fresh air, and Ruth was in the foyer, seeing the last few guests off.

Olivia and Jane had stayed back to help. Isabelle had expected it of Olivia, but she wasn't entirely sure why Jane hadn't gone with Garrett to drive a few of the women home. Instead, she'd asked her husband to come back for her later.

Jane came over to stand beside Olivia as she dusted cake crumbs from the sofa. "Olivia . . ." she began hesitantly. "I have something for you." She held a plain white envelope in her hand.

Isabelle had gotten to know Jane fairly well since she'd started working with her, and she could sense the woman's nerves. What was this all about?

Jane shot a glance at Isabelle, the only other person in the room. "Would you like to go somewhere more private to open this?"

Olivia straightened slowly. Eying the envelope, she shook her head. "I have no secrets from Isabelle."

Warmth spread through Isabelle's chest at the gift of friendship she'd received from Olivia. She stepped forward to offer her support, praying this wasn't some sort of bad news.

Without a word, Jane gave Olivia the envelope. Olivia's hands trembled as she opened it. On a deep inhale, she pulled out a black-and-white photo.

Isabelle stared over her shoulder at the picture of a young boy with dark hair and large dark eyes, not quite understanding the sob that escaped her friend. Olivia's hand came to her mouth as she sank onto the sofa.

Isabelle sat down beside her. "Are you all right, Liv?"

She nodded, despite the tears streaming down her face.

"There's a letter too," Jane said quietly.

Ruth had entered the room, and a frown creased her brow as she took in the scene. Wisely, she didn't interrupt but watched as Olivia took out a piece of paper filled with a neat script. She scanned the short note quickly, then bent over her knees, weeping.

Isabelle wrapped an arm around her and glanced up at Jane, stunned to see that the usually stoic woman had tears on her own cheeks. Suddenly, the significance of the photo and letter dawned on Isabelle, and her throat closed up.

"Matteo," Olivia whispered. "They kept his name."

"I know," Jane said, wiping her face. "I'm sorry I could never tell you anything, Olivia. Not until his adoptive mother came to see me and asked me to give Matteo's birth mother this envelope."

Ruth moved closer. "Oh, Olivia, my dear. I'm so happy for you."

Olivia picked up the photo again and ran her fingers lovingly over the little face. "He's so beautiful."

"He looks just like you," Isabelle whispered. Indeed, the boy had Olivia's dark hair and large eyes, clearly favoring her Italian heritage.

"His mother says he's going into the first grade and that he likes playing ball and riding his bike." Olivia stopped, seemingly unable to go on.

Isabelle swallowed hard. Pregnancy was certainly making her more emotional than usual.

Olivia picked up the note again. "She also said, 'Thank you for being brave enough to give up your son. You have given us the greatest gift of our lives, and no words can ever repay you for your sacrifice.'" Fresh tears spilled down her cheeks.

Isabelle squeezed her shoulder. "That's a lovely thing to say."

"I didn't get the impression Matteo's parents would be open to a visit yet," Jane said, "but this is still a wonderful first step."

Olivia sniffed. "It's more than I ever expected."

Just then, footsteps entered the room. A frowning Darius rushed forward. "Olivia, what's wrong?" His tone was accusatory as he flashed a glare at Jane.

Olivia stood, clutching the letter and photo, and flew into her husband's arms. "Oh, Darius. It's Matteo. His mother wrote to me." She collapsed against his chest.

He enfolded her in his arms and closed his eyes. When he opened them again, they glistened with moisture.

"Look." Olivia held out the photo to him. "Isn't he beautiful?"

Darius stared at the picture, not bothering to hide his emotion. "He is. He looks just like his mother." Then he pressed a kiss to Olivia's temple. "Thank you, Lord, for answering our prayers. For giving Olivia the closure she needed concerning Matteo. And please bless Matteo's adoptive parents. Give them patience, love, and wisdom as they raise him to be a member of your kingdom."

"Amen," Olivia whispered. She turned back to Jane. "Thank you, dear friend. This is the greatest gift I could have received."

"I'm so glad." Jane enveloped Olivia in a hug.

Mark and Garrett entered the room as the two women pulled apart.

"I hate to break up this party," Garrett said to Jane, "but I think we should get going. We still have to pick up the kids."

Isabelle laid a hand on Olivia's shoulder. "You and Darius should go too. It's late. I'll finish cleaning up here."

"Are you sure?"

"Definitely."

Mark crossed the room to take Isabelle's hand. "I'll even dry the dishes for you."

After a flurry of good-byes at the door, Ruth turned to Isabelle. "Thank you for everything, you two. It has been a most memorable evening."

"We're glad you enjoyed it." Mark bent to kiss her cheek.

"I did indeed, but if you don't mind, I think I'll head up to bed."

"You go ahead. We'll finish in the kitchen and use the spare key to lock up," Mark assured her.

"Thank you both." Ruth smiled. "This was the best birthday I can remember." With a last wave, she started up the stairs.

While Mark watched Ruth, Isabelle headed back to the kitchen. She'd sent Mrs. Neale off to bed, right after the gifts had been opened. The dear woman got up at five a.m. and was normally asleep by nine.

The quiet of the kitchen enveloped Isabelle like a warm hug as she moved to the sink. Being back in this room with its yeasty aroma brought back the peaceful times of helping Mrs. Neale when she and Marissa had lived at Bennington Place. This home would always hold a special place in Isabelle's heart. It was here she'd learned the true meaning of acceptance, of friendship, and of love, and where she'd found her calling to help others.

Mark slid up behind her at the counter and wrapped his arms around her. "Well, my love. What are you so deep in thought about?"

She leaned her head back against his shoulder. "Just counting my many blessings," she said. "The greatest one of those being you."

When he gently turned her around to face him, the intensity of emotion shining in his eyes created another lump in her throat. "I'm the lucky one," he said. "To have found such an amazing woman and to somehow have earned her love. I went from having only a brother to having a house full of family. Josh and Marissa and little Lisette. A beautiful wife"—he moved his palm to her abdomen—"and now this blessing too. God has been so good to us."

She smiled up at him through misty eyes. "You know, when the bank repossessed my parents' house, I feared I'd never have a real home again. But God has given me the dearest desire of my heart."

Mark's brows rose. "I wouldn't have thought my house was the dearest desire of your heart. Not after seeing where you grew up."

"Not the house, silly. You." She brought her hand to his cheek. "You are my home, Mark. And you always will be, no matter where we live. I love you with every part of me, and I'm so grateful God brought us together."

"I love you too, Mrs. Henshaw. More than words can say." He brought his lips to hers and once again her soul sighed in contentment.

She'd been through so much hardship, yet she'd persevered, and by the grace of God was all the stronger for enduring it. Without a doubt, she knew that she could weather any challenge that might come her way, because God was always with her.

"As much as I'd love to stay here and kiss you all night," Mark said finally, "we'd better get these dishes done and get home."

"Home." Isabelle couldn't stop her smile from spreading. "I couldn't agree more."

A Note from the Author

Dear Friends,

I had a great time showcasing the different parts of Toronto in this story. For a long time, St. John's Ward (or the Ward as it came to be known) was a very impoverished area of the city, made up mainly of immigrants. The conditions they lived in are hard to fathom. I thought it would make an interesting setting for Isabelle to find herself in after coming from such opulence. A true picture of the dichotomy of the city.

I also enjoyed finding out more about the famous Royal York Hotel. Believe it or not, I attended my high school prom in the ballroom there. Yet I don't remember a great deal about it, except that I tripped over my long dress going up the curved staircase!

I found a wonderful article online from a *Maclean's* magazine circa 1944 that gave me amazing insight into the inner workings of the hotel at that time. I learned how the keys for the rooms were made onsite and about the intricate training involved in working on the hotel's switchboard. Today, the hotel still remains one of the most prestigious in the city.

I hope you enjoyed Mark and Isabelle's journey to happiness. It has been a great privilege sharing my stories with you.

Until next time . . .

Susan

Susan Anne Mason describes her writing style as "romance sprinkled with faith." She loves incorporating inspirational messages of God's unconditional love and forgiveness into her stories. *Irish Meadows*, her first historical romance, won the Fiction from the Heartland contest sponsored by the Mid-American Romance Authors chapter of RWA. Susan lives outside Toronto, Ontario, with her husband and two adult children. She loves red wine and chocolate, and is not partial to snow, even though she's Canadian. Learn more about Susan and her books at susanannemason.net.

Sign Up for Susan's Newsletter

Keep up to date with Susan's news on book releases and events by signing up for her email list at susanannemason.net.

More from Susan Anne Mason

In the midst of WWII, Jane Linder pours all of her dreams for a family into her career at the Toronto Children's Aid Society. Garrett Wilder has been hired to overhaul operations at the society and hopes to earn the vacant director's position. But when feelings begin to blossom and they come to a crossroads, can they discern the path to true happiness?

To Find Her Place
REDEMPTION'S LIGHT #2

You May Also Like . . .

Haunted by painful memories, Olivia Rosetti is singularly focused on running her maternity home for troubled women. Darius Reed is determined to protect his daughter from the prejudice that killed his wife by marrying a society darling. But when he's suddenly drawn to Olivia, they will learn if love can prove stronger than the secrets and hurts of the past.

A Haven for Her Heart by Susan Anne Mason
REDEMPTION'S LIGHT #1
susanannemason.net

Determined to keep his family together, Quinten travels to Canada to find his siblings and track down his employer's niece, who ran off with a Canadian soldier. When Quinten rescues her from a bad situation, Julia is compelled to repay him by helping him find his sister—but soon after, she receives devastating news that changes everything.

The Brightest of Dreams by Susan Anne Mason
CANADIAN CROSSINGS #3
susanannemason.net

Libby has been given a powerful gift: to live one life in 1774 Colonial Williamsburg and the other in 1914 Gilded Age New York City. When she falls asleep in one life, she wakes up in the other without any time passing. On her twenty-first birthday, Libby must choose one path and forfeit the other—but how can she possibly decide when she has so much to lose?

When the Day Comes by Gabrielle Meyer
TIMELESS #1
gabriellemeyer.com

◊ BETHANYHOUSE

More from Bethany House

Natalia Blackstone relies on Count Dimitri Sokolov to oversee the construction of the Trans-Siberian Railway. Dimitri loses everything after witnessing a deadly tragedy and its cover-up, but he has an asset the czar knows nothing about: Natalia. Together they fight to save the railroad while exposing the truth, but can their love survive the ordeal?

Written on the Wind by Elizabeth Camden
THE BLACKSTONE LEGACY #2
elizabethcamden.com

Michelle Stiles has stayed one step ahead of her stepfather and his devious plans by hiding out at Zane Hart's ranch. Zane has his own problems, having discovered a gold mine on his property that would risk a gold rush if he were to harvest it. But soon danger finds both of them, and they realize their troubles have only just begun.

Inventions of the Heart by Mary Connealy
THE LUMBER BARON'S DAUGHTERS #2
maryconnealy.com

While Brody McQuaid's body survived the war, his soul did not. He finds his purpose saving wild horses from ranchers intent on killing them. Veterinarian Savannah Marshall joins Brody in rescuing the wild creatures, but when her family and the ranchers catch up with them both, they will have to tame their fears if they have any hope of letting love run free.

To Tame a Cowboy by Jody Hedlund
COLORADO COWBOYS #3
jodyhedlund.com

◈ BETHANYHOUSE